The Linotype Operator

by

Michael Robert Wolf

FLP Editions
a division of Finishing Line Press
Georgetown, Kentucky

The Linotype Operator

To Rachel, who encourages the best in me creatively

ACKNOWLEDGMENTS

Editor: Leah Maines

Front and back cover design: David Kasdan www.davidkasdan.com
Additional cover work: Elizabeth Maines

Cover photograph:

New York City Sunset Panoramic 2014
Modified Image, Original Image by Anthony Quintano
Licensed under Creative Commons 2.0 Attribution

Inside photograph:

Linotype machine
Modified Image, Original Image by Emma Jane Hogbin Westby
Licensed under Creative Commons 2.0 Attribution

Printed in the USA on acid-free paper.
Order online: www.finishinglinepress.com
also available on amazon.com
Author inquiries and mail orders:
Finishing Line Press
P. O. Box 1626
Georgetown, Kentucky 40324
U. S. A.

TABLE OF CONTENTS

WINTER

CHAPTER ONE

On a frigid flat-gray New York mid-February day almost two months after Chanukah and Christmas, a man in a tight black leather jacket, dark glasses, and jeans, stalked a bearded Chassidic Jew, wearing a traditional long black coat.

The stalker lurked behind a door just west of the elegant first floor Jangmi Jewelry Store on West 47th Street. Then he followed the young Chassidic Jew for about two blocks, through the Diamond District, until he got his chance. When he did, the bullet that discharged from the silencer caused a bright red stain in the center of the Chassid's shirt that, at first glance, could have passed for a red tie against the clean white of the shirt and pitch black of the coat. He instantly fell to the ground, mortally wounded.

It wasn't long before personnel from the New York Police Department arrived to cordon off the scene and identify the victim. The jewelry store owners and shoppers were cleared from the area by several policemen. After forensic evidence was placed in a plastic bag by one of them, he showed the driver's license to Inspector Ralph Lewis, who was standing over the corpse. He shook his head and spoke in a hushed tone to a fellow officer.

"Oh well. That's a damn shame. A *damn* shame. He's younger than he looks with that beard. They always are. Let's see what his name is. Mandy. Mandy Mendel. That's an interesting name. It's got a nice ring to it. I hope his mother's not alive to hear it today. Of course his wife will be, and all those kids. They always have a lot of kids, these ones. Damn shame."

All of the shop owners were standing outside their shops discussing the possibility that this was the work of Muslim radicals, when Inspector Lewis got back in the cruiser. He wasn't sure of that opinion, but it didn't really matter what anyone's opinion was. There was one thing he *was* sure of. Where this ended up division-wise would depend on the direction the investigation took. And that direction had barely begun, just as the red blood on the shirt was barely dry.

CHAPTER TWO

David Kaplan, holding an instantly recognizable Santa cap in one hand and an old gray cloth pillow case with the protruding outline of small boxes in the other, walked slowly in the flush light of the Brooklyn Maimonides Medical Center corridor. He was clad in a black wool coat, black scarf, and black cloth yarmulke—or *kippah*—the traditional Jewish head covering. He approached the youthful red-headed nurse at the station and pointed his finger at her.

"Still here on Christmas Day, Anna? You should be home having Christmas dinner with your family. Who's next?"

She looked up at him with her deep green eyes and smiled warmly, her face cocked to one side.

"*You're* the hard worker, Mr. Kaplan. Thank you so much for coming in and helping us today. You'll never know what it means to the children."

To him, it was a just a *mitzvah,* a good work done from the heart. And he did it with compassion and joy befitting the season.

"Well, it means a lot to me. It's a mit…it's a…it's a…how should I say…it's a privilege, a privilege to help."

"I love the Santa hat. I don't think you'll fool them without a beard, though."

"Well…it's the thought. They're not stupid. A beard wouldn't convince them anyway. It's the spirit of the thing, isn't it?"

"Of course it is, Mr. Kaplan. The children love it. His name is Sammy. He's one of the sweetest children you can imagine."

"Aren't they all?"

"You're so right, Mr. Kaplan. His mother left a few hours ago. He's four, African American, with quite a head of hair and the brightest smile." She lowered her voice as she handed him a card…"and not doing well."

"*Shmuel*" he responded, using the Hebrew pronunciation. "Okay. Room 451, bed 2. This way?"

"Right. That way. He'll be so excited to see you."

"I can't wait. I'm on my way."

As he walked down the hall, he pulled the cap over his head with his right hand, adjusting it on one side and then the other. He had just finished adjusting it by the time he walked through the hospital room door. Redheaded Anna watched him disappear into the room.

CHAPTER THREE

The freshly polished brass Chanukah menorah with the two-lion design first sat on a table in Kiev in 1882.

It illuminated the excited eyes of small children who grew up and left this world sometime in the Twentieth Century. Now it sat on the dining room table of the Kaplan home in Brooklyn, New York.

Naomi Kaplan—single, in her late forties, and almost as excited as those toddlers—scraped the remains of the first four nights' candles with a sharp kitchen knife. The remnants fell like dirty snow on the clean white table cloth. She leaned in and hovered over the menorah, instead of pulling it close to her. The pre-dusk stillness was broken only by the sound, through the window panes, of tire treads on snow—and the indistinct sound of high heels clicking on the second floor.

Naomi could hardly see the menorah in the darkened room. She tenderly felt the raised bumps of smooth wax with her fingertips. She too was barely visible in the light of the setting sun. In broad daylight, she looked all of her forty-eight years, with dark brown Eastern European eyes, and dark curly hair that reminded her of Gertrude Berg's from the ancient black and white TV show *The Goldbergs*. To her, ancient was the perfect description.

A raised voice came from the second story.

"When does Dad get home from his Christmas Day hospital thing? Marc and I already got a sitter in Englewood and we're going out with friends after we light the candles. "

Naomi whispered for her own ears.

"How should I know?"

The voice got louder, as Naomi continued to scrape.

"Where did you hide the gifts you bought for Dad?"

Naomi shouted back.

"I TOLD YOU FIVE TIMES. THE TOP OF MY CLOSET."

The voice and high heels belonging to Naomi's sister Lisa came down the stairs, with a few wrapped packages in tow. She clicked on the chandelier lights.

"Okay. Okay. I heard you…what are you doing in the dark, Naomi? Making a mess?"

"I'm cleaning our menorah, like I always do."

Naomi dropped the knife onto the table, got up, and walked out of the room.

"Happy Chanukah and Merry Christmas," came the sarcastic reply.

Naomi stuck her head back in the living room. She didn't want to respond in kind. She wanted to be stoic in the face of disrespect coming from someone five years younger, twenty years prettier, and on a different planet.

"I don't know when he'll be home, Lisa. How should I know? Every year it's different. So why are you asking? And by the way, if I didn't scrape the menorah, the candles would fall out and burn up this whole room, complete with the Artscroll rabbinic commentaries and Potok novels…in short, everything Dad loves."

"It wouldn't kill you to scrape it over the sink."

"I like scraping it on the table. That's where it belongs…on the table cloth, on the table."

Lisa started sweeping the wax shavings onto one hand with the other hand.

"And I just love cleaning up your mess."

Just down the street from the Kaplan house, Marc Silver's stylish black rubber boots navigated the iron-grey slush. He walked quickly from his parked black Mercedes through the middle class Brooklyn neighborhood. He wore a tan cashmere coat, brown scarf, and black dress slacks. He arrived at the row home his wife's grandfather had purchased in 1946, after the war.

Lisa saw him from the porch window.

"He's here."

She opened the front door while Marc was still on the sidewalk. Naomi looked up from the menorah.

"Dad?"

"No Naomi. It's Marc. Who knows when Dad'll get here? We should just light the candles without him."

"We're not doing that." She was carefully twisting the candles into the sockets one at a time. "You're wasting heat with that door open."

"Is your boyfriend Marvin coming? Because if he is, he needs to get here soon or you can forget him for the fifth day of Chanukah just like we forgot him for the first four."

"He's not my boyfriend."

"That isn't what *he* says."

"He's not coming. He's with his mother tonight."

"Good. That's where he belongs."

Marc Silver walked through the door and quickly shut it behind him.

"It's damn cold out there. Where's Mr. Christmas mitzvah? We have maybe twenty minutes tops."

"He'll be here soon. Naomi's just finishing with the candles."

"Let's just do it now. We're not waiting for the nerd, are we?"

Naomi rolled her eyes.

"We're waiting. Marvin isn't coming. We're waiting for Dad."

"We hit the first two nights, didn't we? Let's just light them if he doesn't get here soon."

Lisa jumped in, restraining her husband.

"No...no. He...he wants us to wait. He always wants us to wait."

"Why can't he get a cell phone. It's selfish." Marc held his tan cashmere coat as if he was about to don it again. Naomi stopped squeezing the fourth candle into it's holder.

"Selfish?"

She paused her labor of love and left the room again. Marc flopped onto the faded grey sofa.

"Merry *Chanukamas*."

Chapter Four

David Kaplan's eyes were still wet from his visit with four-year-old Sammy in room 451. The more excited Sammy had become over his cobalt-blue Hot Wheel eighteen wheeler, the more David had struggled to keep his eyes dry. He had managed a few "Ho Ho Ho's" that sounded more like "Oy-Oy-Oy's," to which little Sammy had responded, "He doesn't sound like that. You're funny."

Now, as David wished Anna the red-headed nurse a merry Christmas, silent tears began to form. As he left, she shouted after him, "Bye Mr. Kaplan. Happy holidays." He proceeded directly to the elevator where he faced the rear, waited until it arrived on the first floor, and then quickly walked out of the hospital. The tears began to freeze at the start of his walk to the bus stop.

A strange look by the first black hatted Chassidic Jewish acquaintance in his path reminded him that the Santa hat was still pulled over his head. But he didn't care. He was deeply focused on something closer, on the flakes of snow that rendered the stare a distant blur. The falling flakes transported him back almost forty years, past his wandering and frustrating odd-job years after his untimely retirement back in 1978 at a mere forty years old. They took him all the way back to the unmistakable clicks, grunts, and whirs that no sound on Earth could ever approximate. He could try to imagine that the sound of crunching snow under his feet came close, but he knew it didn't. Nothing could.

No, actually it wasn't the sound. It was the falling snow that took him back to the distribution mechanism—or magazine—that released the letter matrices, falling like snow flakes into their appropriate channels, or pouring down more like a blizzard when he worked quickly. He would preside like Moses over the peculiar Linotype keyboard whose letter and number pattern he remembered even after all these years. And like the miracle of the Ten Commandments on Sinai, the words and sentences would find their place, cascading from above as from the finger of God. They would descend through their channels and into the assembler, where they would be used to cast hot lead slugs before returning automatically back up to the magazine.

He had been good at what he did—actually, *very* good. In fact, he was one of the best at the *New York Times*. And although it had been many years, falling snow like this always took him back. He had only seen one working Linotype machine over the last forty years, and that in a typesetting establishment that was more like a museum. But the odor of the hot lead and oil was imprinted in his mind like the print in the newspapers he composed. Still, it was the sound and the sight of the falling matrices that he remembered most.

David walked through the increasingly blinding precipitation. For this reason, he was glad he was wearing the Santa hat, which was becoming whiter with each step he took—as if it was being purged, cleansed. He could still hear the echo of the click and grind of the Linotype's Victorian machinery as he approached the house. Through the porch window he saw none of the five candles—or the higher servant *shammas* candle that was used to light the others—flickering on the dining room table. The door swung open. There were Lisa and Marc.

Naomi was at the table, leaning over and adjusting the menorah like an antique music box. Lisa's frustration gave way to relief.

"Finally, you're here. Marc and I have to go soon. Light the candles, Naomi."

Naomi ran over to her father and threw her arms around him.

"Happy Chanukah, Abba. Did you have a good day?"

He hugged her back, dropping his sack of small toys on the floor.

"Well, for one thing I think maybe I sort of made it a good day for a dying child, or contributed to it anyway. That's better than having one, as the sages tell us…not in those exact words, of course."

Marc eyed the soaked bright red again hat.

"It looks like you really got into your Christmas mitzvah spirit this time. I guess your kippah is under there somewhere. I forgot mine."

David pulled the Santa hat off and gave it to Marc.

"If you don't mind, I think I'll pass."

Naomi lit the shammas candle. Just before they started chanting the blessing, David said, "I love this menorah, I guess because it's old, like me."

CHAPTER FIVE

December 26th is the day of many disappointed returns, which makes up for the happy returns of the day before. Every department at Macy's in Manhattan—*the* Macy's—was Black-Friday crowded. Naomi Kaplan had skipped her usual cup of coffee on purpose. The housewares department—located temporarily in the basement level during a time of rearranging and renovation—was at least as crowded as the other departments, partly because customers could take returns back to any department.

Naomi knew she wouldn't see the inside of the women's restroom until way beyond the usual early break time, so she had forgone her morning coffee. She was a soldier in Macy's army, and this was a major skirmish, if not an all out war. Her hands were filling out forms, stapling receipts, inspecting toasters, knife sets, and crock pots, re-folding sweaters with snow flakes, shirts with tags still on as well as off, and ties with subtle and not so subtle patterns. She placed them and dozens of other things half back in their torn boxes and Macy's bags. She was taking credit cards that didn't typically give back their namesake—credit—and keying them into the computer for just that purpose. And all the while, she made every effort to serve with a smile.

But that wasn't easy. The lines were long, forming in front of her and one or two other employees in barely organized jagged patterns, and moving very slowly. And tempers were often short. Sentence fragments floated around the counter like word balloons in a cartoon strip.

"This doesn't fit."

"It broke."

"It's missing a part."

"No, I don't want credit. I want cash."

"I don't have the receipt, but I bought this here last week…at this very store."

"Could you please hurry? I'm on my lunch break."

"Something's wrong with it. Okay, I just don't like it."

Naomi's feet hurt, her hand was cramped, and she increasingly had to go to the bathroom in spite of her coffee fast. As time progressed and things got louder, she found herself shouting over the din. As soon as she got finished with one demanding mother of three broken toys, another would squeeze her way in with four wine glasses—all with no abatement. She knew she had to take a break soon. It was becoming an unmanageable emergency. Normally, taking a quick break wouldn't be a problem. Macy's was very good about breaks. But this morning she was caught in a crossfire and pinned down in the trenches.

Suddenly, like a Gentile angel from a distant planet, the most strikingly handsome forty-something man anyone could imagine was standing in front of her, holding several medium and large boxes. Her co-workers noticed him first, and couldn't stop staring. Naomi was in too much discomfort to even look at his face. He had a porcelain straight nose, soft baby blue eyes, and plenty of straight straw-blonde hair—not to mention perfect professionally whitened teeth, the kind you can't help but noticing. She eyed him for a millisecond and then spoke up.

"Um…yes…next…you…"

"I'm sorry. I know this is a lot…but…I've got a few tasteless distant relatives, and they were all there yesterday."

"Receipts?"

"Sure. What's the matter? Are you okay? You look like you're in some sort of discomfort."

Apparently, the pain was radiating from her facial expression, try as hard as she could to suppress it with a smile. Then, in an unusual unguarded split second, she leaned toward and over him like she had the menorah the night before, her mouth almost touching his perfectly formed ear. She whispered impulsively.

"I've been here all morning. I have to go to the bathroom, and I can't get free."

Immediately, her face reddened. She thought, *What did I just say to this strange man?*

He grabbed her writing hand, stared into her eyes, and said, "As a certain person whose birthday is celebrated around now said, 'It's better to give than receive.' I'll wait. Go!"

As her eyes met his, she noticed for the first time how extraordinarily handsome he was. His last comments were still registering in her mind.

"Wh…What?"

"You know. Yesterday? December 25th?"

She flinched, which he noticed.

"Listen. This is your sixth night Chanukah present from me. Go… go…I'll wait. Now! I'll stay here and tell the others you'll be right back."

"I can't…"

"Go, go, go. Before it's too late."

Before she could think another second, she dropped her pen and quickly disappeared back behind the other workers. She was gone for less than three minutes, and when she returned he was still there.

"I've calmed the natives. Take your time."

"How can I thank you? You've made my day, sir."

"Like I said, it's better to give than receive. Making your day is better than making mine."

Head down, she mechanically started writing up his returns—mostly sweaters and shirts, and one tie. She knew where she'd heard the phrase he used before, from the wisest man she knew, her personal sage—her father.

CHAPTER SIX

Naomi finally got a lunch break at 2:15 p.m. That was almost two hours after the latest time she usually took it. That morning, she had decided to treat herself to Ben's Kosher Deli on 38th Street. So she hadn't packed the usual egg or peanut butter sandwich for a quick lunch in the employee lounge.

She had told Marvin she would get ahold of him when she was on her way, and they could have a short lunch at *the usual place.* He was unemployed from his low end janitorial job, a casualty of economic times and his lack of trained skills, among other things. His *buy-minutes-up-front* phone could make and receive calls, and text with a limit. So she texted him, and left Macy's in the bitter cold and wind of a post-snowstorm New York December winter.

I'll be there in a minute. I know you have a short time. I'm almost there, was his response. He never used text short-hand, even though he knew his phone had very limited texting. Somehow all those "u"s and "r"s didn't seem kosher to him. But even if he *was* lavish with his texting, he was still broke. So she generally covered the lunch bill during these occasions. After all, Macy's salespeople made more than unemployed janitors. And today she was glad to do it. It was the holiday season and time for a treat. She didn't have the rest of the week off, especially since she always got Shabbat off in what was practically a deal breaker when she was first hired. So this lunch would have to be holiday treat enough.

When Naomi arrived at the window of the deli, there was Marvin—sitting inside in one of the green booths, with his dirty tan coat, pea green scarf, orange sock hat, and black ear muffs. The Yiddish word for nerd, *schlemiel,* was too weak a word to describe him. But she had long ceased to think of that word when she saw him. The word that came to mind was just *Marvin.* She walked in and over to where he was sitting.

"How have you been?"

"Huh?"

"I said how've you been?"

She often repeated things. And he often responded without answering.

"You getting the pastrami with the slaw? I got the roast beef."

There it was, quarter eaten in front of him.

"I don't know, Marvin. I haven't thought about it. Probably. You could have ordered it for me. You know I always get it. How's your mother?"

"I'm cold."

"I can see that. But I think you could take your earmuffs off. It's not *that* cold in here. How's your mother?"

The second attempt at a question usually worked.

"Fine."

She didn't want to compare him to the Gentile man she'd just met at Macy's. But it happened without her permission. His nose was what one might call silly-putty swollen, kind of like one of the Disney dwarfs—although she couldn't say which—while *returns-man's* was porcelain straight. And Marvin's orange sock hat covered an undecidedly graying and partially bald patchwork, instead of abundant straight blonde hair. Marvin's face was almost two dimensionally flat, other than his nose. He was short and squat. And his eyes were difficult to see behind the thick lenses. In fact, she never could tell if he was looking straight at her. She had been standing. Now she sat down across from him.

"Marvin, do you think you'll come over for the sixth candle tonight?"

"Huh?"

"Do you think you'll come over for the sixth candle…tonight?"

"Well…I don't feel too good. Sciatica. And I didn't sleep too good either. I walked all over Brooklyn…so cold…but no bites…nothing…

and I'm broke, as you know."

"I'm so sorry to hear that. Something'll break through soon. So you're not coming?"

He answered her flatly.

"I'm not coming."

"What are you doing?"

He answered directly again.

"I'll probably watch something with Mom. She likes the Hallmark movies. The holiday ones. Something I could do without. When Mashiach comes they'll make good Jewish ones. What can you do? She likes them. They make her cry. Good for the eyes, I guess."

He laughed one of those inhaling laughs that sounds almost like drowning. She waited for him to finish.

"I see. Dad was hoping maybe he would see you."

"Pretty funny, heh? They'll make Jewish ones. Pretty funny."

"I said, Dad was hoping maybe he would see you."

"How did the mitzvah go?"

"He visited a little boy who is dying of cancer."

"Oh well. I guess the goyim suffer too."

He inhale-laughed again.

"Of course Gentiles do. That's not funny. We're talking about a little child."

The waitress came up and took the pastrami order. It took seven minutes to arrive and another ten minutes to eat. She tried to make the most of the rest of their time together.

"I like those Hallmark movies. They're romantic. You like romantic, Marvin. I know you do. You took me to that movie with that Brad Pitt and…I think Sandra Bullock or somebody. Remember? You like romantic."

"Yeah, I like romantic, Naomi…but not Hallmark, and not with my mother."

Time was up and she had to go back to the battle of the returns.

"Thank you for lunch, Naomi. You're very kind to me, and when I get work I'll make it up to you."

He always said that, and she always answered, "That's okay, Marvin. I know that."

CHAPTER SEVEN

Never was the bond between Naomi and her father stronger than on the Jewish Sabbath—or *Shabbas* in the dialect of Hebrew they spoke—when she sat in the balcony above and behind him in the traditional Orthodox synagogue. This was especially the case when Lisa wasn't there, which she usually wasn't. Naomi so treasured those special times. Everything in the synagogue sanctuary was ancient polished wood with a patina worthy of the most expensive antique. It even smelled like an antique, with the perfect musty quality she had known all her life. *Surely,* she thought, *God must love that smell, like the incense in the Beis Hamigdash, the great Temple in Jerusalem.*

The streaming sunlight shone through the red, blue, and clear window panes, creating shafts of silvery and tinted dust particles that were like cords connecting her and her father. There was no need, or ability, to sit next to him. The men sat separate from the women in their synagogue, as in all Orthodox synagogues in Brooklyn. But she could feel the warmth of her father's love right where she was. Sometimes, as he stood up for the standing *Amida* prayer, he would look back at her and smile. Among the rows of black yarmulkes, or kippahs, as well as black hats, only her father's face turned back and up. When that occurred, it was as if they were the only two people in the sanctuary.

She loved to watch him chant the blessings that are recited before and after sections of the weekly Torah portion. He was no great singer, but to her he had the perfect voice for it. Sometimes when she would hear Cantor Feld chant in Hebrew, "*Ya-amode Dah-veed Ben Schlomo La-Torah*, come up David son of Solomon, to the Torah scroll," tears would fill her eyes. This wasn't because the cantor had a great voice, although he did, but because he was introducing the greatest Jew in the world, indeed the greatest man in the world as far as she was concerned—her father David Kaplan.

As special as the times in the synagogue were, they were only a prelude to the next chapter in the story that unfolded every Saturday. Naomi knew that the stroll home, the quiet *kiddush* blessing over the wine in their living room, and the simple dairy meal with the long anticipated discussion, were yet to come. That discussion was the pinnacle of the Shabbat, a time of immediacy and intimacy, Naomi's definition of true rest.

On this zero-cold winter Shabbat and seventh day of Chanukah, Naomi and her father sat across from each other at the dining room table, the wax drenched menorah between them.

They sipped green tea from cups warmed in the pot that had been on very low heat since a timer went on that was set before sundown Friday. And they nibbled on swiss-cheese sandwiches. The room radiated an uncanny warmth that contrasted with the cold outside. Naomi longed for these times all week. David patted his hand on the Artscroll book before him.

"A light is on this table, and I don't mean the menorah."

"Yes, Abba, the *sefer*."

She was referring to the ornamented book in front of him.

He gingerly opened it. These were times Naomi could ask whatever she wanted, and could talk about anything that concerned or bothered her—not that something always bothered her. But David could sense on this day that something did. He took a small bite, befitting a truly restful Shabbat after-service meal.

"Yes Naomi? What is it? A study is not a study until your mind is prepared and free of trouble."

"I'm okay, Abba. Please just read the Artscroll book. I love it when you talk about the *parshe* and read from the sages. I love the *Aggada*, I love the *Halacha*. That's all I need."

The Parshe was the Torah portion for that week, taken from the first five books of the Bible. The Aggada were the stories the rabbis told about the portion, and the Halacha were the instructions, guidelines, and rules based on it.

"I can always hear what's on your sister Lisa's tongue, but I can see what's on your face."

A silence commenced that Naomi didn't want to break. And her father was in no rush either. He had three-quarters of a sandwich left, most of a cup of lukewarm tea, and all afternoon.

The silence, made only more dramatic by the Doppler effect created by the car engines passing by, was almost too holy to interrupt. But Naomi knew that there would be no pearls from the treasury of Jewish wisdom until she interrupted it.

"Abba, there is something. Marc, and Lisa…and, well…and Marvin too…they all say things…about you."

"What things?"

He stopped himself with a wave of his hand.

"No, you shouldn't speak those things to me. *No Lashan Hara,* no evil tongue of gossip."

Then he changed his mind again.

"But on the other hand, you are distressed. So maybe you should tell me what's distressing you."

"Well Abba, I can say it in just a few words. You always say that many words are not so good. So if I transgress, maybe it's a little transgression. I'll say it fast."

She took a deep breath and then spoke quickly.

"They don't like the mitzvah, the Christmas mitzvah. The Santa hat… the whole thing."

She nervously took another bite from the cheese sandwich. He shook his head slowly. Then he carefully opened the book, leafing through it and stopping at a particular page.

"*Perkei Avot* 4:1. The sayings of the fathers. Ben Zoma…a very famous quote."

"Yes, Rav Ben Zoma. I'm ready, Abba."

"Well, just Ben Zoma…okay. They didn't happen to refer to him as Rabbi. We just say Ben Zoma…son of Zoma."

"Okay Abba. Ben Zoma."

"'Who is wise? The one who learns from all people.

Who is mighty? The one who subdues the evil inclination.

Who is rich? The one who rejoices in his portion.

Who is honored? The one who honors other human beings.'"

He paused.

"What do you think of that?"

"I like it, Abba."

"Yes, but *why* do you like it?"

"Well...."

These were the times Naomi loved best—the house all to themselves, the peace of the Shabbat, even the cheese sandwich, and questions like these.

"I guess...."

She paused. He spoke again.

"Just the last line. 'Who is honored? The one who honors other human beings.'"

"I guess, it's honorable to honor others."

"Just Jews?"

"No. I guess not. But...I think it's the hat. They...."

"My darling daughter, what does the sage say?"

"Well...you are honored if you honor other human beings. I mean, that's exactly what it says. Right?"

"Yes, that is exactly what it says. I honored Sammy."

"Who?"

"The little boy...the little dying boy, who wanted a visit from Santa...I mean, someone with Santa's hat whom he could receive a little love from. So what would Ben Zoma think?"

"I don't know. I guess he'd like it."

"He would. I honored little Sammy. And God honors me. I don't expect everyone else to."

Naomi leaned way over the table, past the Menorah, and kissed him on the forehead before taking another sip of almost cold tea.

Chapter Eight

The Monday morning train commute from Brooklyn to Manhattan was Shabbat's direct opposite. It was a loud kind of silent, a crowded kind of isolated, a cold kind of heated.

The subway traveled a route somewhat older than the brass menorah on the dining room table.

Launched as a steam locomotive under the Brooklyn-Manahattan Transit (BMT) on October 9th, 1863, the name *transit* had oddly stuck. It must have been a very modern word then. Now, as a part of the New York City Transit Authority, it was an old word, an archaic word, a Victorian word.

Naomi sat amidst standing riders, one of three commuters on one of those sideways benches that movies always depict lonely people on. A pink scarf covering much of her tight curly hair, her green wool coat was bundled around her. She locked eyes for a swift instant with a forty-something Jewish businessman who reminded her of a slightly older Marc Silver with a black cashmere coat instead of a tan one. Her eyes shifted to his wedding ring as he moved toward the doors, and then glanced through the window to the dark blackness in the tunnel enveloping the train. This was punctuated by the red and white lights, and the Doppler effect, of a train flying by in the opposite direction.

She could never bring herself to read a book or newspaper during the forty-five or so minute ride, let alone a prayer book. The accumulated early morning and late afternoon minutes were spent in enforced observation—*wasted minutes in a wasted life,* she sometimes thought. But then her father would never countenance that thought, let alone someone like the Eleventh century sage Rashi, whose complex writings he loved to study.

She was entertaining these thoughts in slow motion for the thousandth time, when she noticed something in her extreme peripheral vision—a familiar face, a recognizable presence. It was the man with the straw hair and porcelain nose. When had he gotten on? Had he seen her? No, probably not. He would have acknowledged her, and he seemed to be focused elsewhere, in another direction half-opposite her. But it was definitely him. She could almost see his eyes. She could never forget those eyes. She blushed as she remembered the emergency bathroom incident. She quickly glanced at his hand. No ring. Not that it was her business. He wasn't Jewish.

As the 34th Street station approached, she realized he wasn't planning to get off. Something in her couldn't bear to miss thanking him one last time. As the train pulled into the station, her feet momentarily froze in place. She knew she should get off immediately or she'd be late for work—but she hesitated just long enough for the doors to open and close. Now she would *definitely* be late for work. When would he notice her? And how many stops would pass before he got off?

They were pulling into Times Square Station when he moved toward the doors. She watched him, knowing that once he left the train she would probably never see him again. So what? Why would that even matter? He was a nice goy, a Gentile. And she was—well, she was who she was. But a slight grin formed on her face as she realized the odds of seeing him at all in this throbbing sea of eight and a half million people. The train slowed as the station came into view.

"Goodbye, beautiful wonderful man," she whispered to herself, as she prepared to get off.

"*Besheirt!*," she suddenly mouthed to no one, and pushed through to get as close to him as possible. She wasn't sure if she believed in the Yiddish word's meaning, *meant to be,* but today she decided that maybe she did. So what if she'd be slightly late to work. This wouldn't be the first time that happened. She could catch the next train back to 34th Street, or the train after that. But for now, she would get the attention of the straw-haired man. The doors flew open, and she followed the crowd a few passengers behind him. Her feet seemed to operate on their own. She could see the top of his head and that straight blonde hair, leading the way like a yellow beacon in the dull green light of the station. She pushed her way through the turnstiles, and eventually up the stairs and onto the street. She wouldn't even let herself think how crazy her behavior was. All she vaguely acknowledged is that she was being carried along, perhaps by the evil inclination the rabbis talked about. She ended up on 8th Avenue right in front of the *New York Times* building. The friendly goy entered through the revolving door. Naomi stood on the street and watched him walk toward the elevator. For the first time, she noticed his cashmere black coat and his slim-cut figure.

He must be a journalist, she thought. He looked like a journalist, like a blonde Dana Andrews in State Fair, telling Jeanne Crain he was a columnist, careful to pronounce both the "m" and the "n." No, he looked more like a blonde Clark Gable in *It Happened One Night.* What was his name in the movie? Peter Warren. That was it. Maybe his name was Peter. That was a good Christian name, wasn't it?

Naomi stood there on the sidewalk—already a minute or two late for work—and talked to Peter while staring at him through the big glass window of the *New York Times* Building, as he waited for the elevator.

I want you to meet my father. He worked as a Linotype operator for the very newspaper you work for...oh, you are fascinated by Linotype machines? You know about them? Well, he was the very best Linotype operator in the whole world, no, in the whole universe. You both have so much in common. I'm sure you must both love old things with old words on them, like lead slugs forming whole sentences in the Linotype machine... and the Torah. I know you'd love the Torah...you don't know what the Torah is? Well, wait till Abba shows you. You and my father could talk for hours about that...and the sages. Oh my goodness! He'll tell you all about the sages. You already talk like a sage. Remember? You said, "making your day is better than making mine"...just like Daddy...just like Rashi. He'll tell you all about Rashi.

Peter was still waiting for the elevator in the Times building when she chose to take him to meet her father in the warm glow of their living room. They had both just kissed the mezuzah on the way into the house. She had taught Peter how to do that correctly. Someday, she might kiss *him,* God forbid.

Father, this is Peter. Peter, this is father. Abba, Peter wants to convert. He'll be very observant, very observant...an observant Jewish journalist. And he'll be the kindest Jew there is to me, much kinder than Marc is to Lisa...much kinder. And he knows all about the mechitzah curtain separating the men from the women in the synagogue, because he put one up with Claudette Colbert before they were married and called it the walls of Jericho. Only I'm not spoiled like she was...or like Lisa is. He's very romantic, Abba...and very old fashioned, like the Linotype machine, and the menorah. He'll love our Chanukah menorah.

Naomi was just getting to the good part—where her father is reciting the Numbers six *May The Lord bless you and keep you* Aaronic Benediction over both of them and blessing their impending engagement—when she realized that the elevator doors hadn't opened yet. Besheirt again! She ran across the street and into the building. Now she was operating completely out of something in the base of her brain, or maybe somewhere below her neck, which was completely unlike her. She pushed her way up near *Peter,* eliciting an angry stare or two, until she stood right next to him. As she pretended to wait for the elevator, the doors finally opened. There were people in front of them, and as everyone was squeezing toward the doors, *Peter* seemed to look straight at her. She cringed, then smiled slightly, and he smiled back slightly before looking somewhere beyond her. She'd come this far. She had to say *something.* The crush was at the doors. Surely if she spoke he would remember everything—the gift return, her bathroom emergency, his act of kindness—everything. She looked right at him and spoke as clearly and as loudly as she could. He was now focused on the elevator in front of him.

"Hi."

The noise surrounding her drowned out the word. *Peter* moved into the elevator and beyond her reach. She wasn't able to get on. She knew there was no way she could do that anyway. It would be at least fifteen minutes before she ascended floor by floor and then came all the way back down. And she was late for work already. She backed away and out of the building into the chill grey winter air. It was the first time she noticed how cold it was and how slippery with patches of old snow and ice the sidewalk was.

"What's the matter with me? What *is* the matter with me!," she mouthed through clenched teeth.

It was no use going into the subway station and waiting for the next train going the opposite direction. That would take way too long. She walked quickly all the way from 42nd Street to 34th Street, weaving in and out of people going to work. By the time she arrived at Macy's, she was at least twenty-five minutes late for work. Finally, she was in her right mind and very angry at herself.

CHAPTER NINE

David Kaplan rode the subway into Manhattan twice a week, on Tuesdays and Thursdays—as if he were not retired, as if he were going to work. He always left the house at 10:00 a.m. and came back at 4:00 p.m. And he always carried a bag with a kosher salami on rye, an egg salad on rye, or a tuna fish on rye. The predictable schedule was important to him. Retirement schedules tend to be rare and therefore special.

At approximately 10:45 a.m. he would get off at Times Square subway station and walk to the New York Public Library, which was founded in 1895, about twelve years after the Linotype machine was invented.

It was also thirteen years after the menorah first sat in the home of David's great grandparents in Kiev.

The imposing structure of the main Manhattan branch served as a sort of third home, after his actual home and his synagogue. The final destination was always the DeWitt Wallace Periodical Room, down the hall on the left from the main entrance.

It was named after the founder of the Reader's Digest, born in 1898, just a few years after the New York library and sixteen years after the menorah first sat on David's ancestors' table.

With its glowing wooden panels, paintings of New York publishing monuments hung like ancestral royal portraits throughout the room, and labyrinth of long polished wooden tables with warm bronze lamps, the fairly small room was almost a Victorian invention in its own right— except for the wireless signal, which was of no interest to David.

By 11:00 a.m., David Kaplan's two fellow "workers" always arrived, one after the other. First there was Stanley, who had retired from his several Manhattan delicatessen counter jobs a few years back. He was tall and hulking, with the ancient remnants of acne like lyricist Oscar Hammerstein, thick black framed glasses, and full of exotic New York Jewish *Shtetl* neighborhood tales. He had long ago left his brothers' Orthodox kippahs and prayer shawl fringes behind for a more liberal lifestyle. But he never left their Yiddish sensibilities. They were disappointed with him, but he loved them for that, with the affection of his deepest childhood memories.

Then there was Mahmoud, a retired cab driver. He was as New York as he was Arab, and as wrinkled as he had been smooth-talking on the job. And he was bald, like Gaza Strip sand. He started frequenting Room 108 to read the Arabic newspapers years before he knew what the Internet was. The truth was, none of the three cared to read their news like that anyway. Stanley's only use for anything related to a mouse had been to set a trap to kill the un-kosher little beasts before they could shut places like the 2nd Avenue Deli down. Mahmoud didn't trust the Internet. He felt there were too many prying eyes, and his reading habits were no one else's business. And as for David—well, he liked reading real newspapers on principle. At one time his philosophy was, if it didn't start with a lead slug, it wasn't worth reading. Of course, the words on the pages he read in Room 108 wouldn't recognize lead slugs as their parents, let alone their grandparents. They were born of the same computer fonts that Steve Jobs had borrowed from the dying Linotype machine in the seventies—or stolen, if you asked David. But newspapers were the lesser of all evils. And at least the *New York Times* still *looked* somewhat like the *New York Times*, even if it wasn't created the *real* way.

Their part-time retirement "jobs" brought these three disparate old men together. If they met anywhere else in the company of anyone else, they wouldn't know what to say to each other and might even feel awkward acknowledging each other. But like secret paramours meeting for regular trysts, they anticipated their weekly rendezvous.

Stanley arrived first, toting his lunch bag. He didn't so much limp with one leg as he did with both of them, just as he had double-limped from one side of the counter to the other to cut lox—but perhaps even more so in his retirement years. After all, his legs had grown stiff with age and lack of exercise. He dropped the bag, complete with apple inside, on the table. This was one of the many things he did that mildly irritated David.

"Shhh."

"What are you shushing me for?"

The ritual of the dropped lunch and official shush was now ended. But the battle of the volume level had just begun.

"Our Arab prince is yet to arrive, as per usual. I'm sure you had a good Shabbas with the *mishpacha?*"

He was referring to David Kaplan's family, using the standard Hebrew word, but spoken in the colloquial Yiddishized way, sort of squeezed together and with the accent on the second syllable.

"So how's your spinster daughter? And the other one and her husband...I never quite got his name."

David didn't answer, so Stanley dropped that subject.

"So what's the news today?"

David breathed an unsettled response.

"Keep it down a little, would you Stanley? And please don't call Naomi a spinster."

"Sorry. Your oldest daughter...unmarried."

"And I don't know the news. I haven't read it yet. Here, I got your Daily News."

"Very good...very good. Thanks."

He leaned over and grabbed it off the table.

"I already read in the Subway someone else's paper, but it wasn't news. It was gossip."

"You must still have pretty good eyes to snoop on other peoples' newspapers."

"Like a hawk. I could also see a picture in the obituary. A Broadway big shot, you know...a *Macher* named Gold-something...he died. He came in...he came in many times...many many times. Always a half pound of nova lox and I don't know what else. My guess is it was Aids."

"May he rest in peace."

"I'm just saying. I'm just saying. A very nice man. He was a very nice man."

"Okay. Quieter."

"Quieter," Stanley whispered loudly, his index finger up to his mouth, and sat down.

Mahmoud walked through the door. He knew how to whisper even from across the room, a skill learned in his father's household.

"Aaaay, my old friends," he projected with his mouth.

He put his bag down, but there was no apple inside…just the gentle sound of pita and hummus. He walked away to get his Arab newspaper.

"I like Mahmoud," David observed. "He's a nice man."

"You like everyone…even me, God forbid. You're the Jewish Will Rogers. You never met a man you didn't like."

"A man that has friends must show himself friendly, Stanley."

Stanley slapped the table loud enough to startle the closest readers.

"Which dead rabbi this time?"

"Schlomo."

"Never heard of him, but I'll take your word for it."

"Not a rabbi. Solomon…Proverbs."

Mahmoud returned and opened the newspaper, surrounding himself 180 degrees with it. Stanley spread the Daily News out on the table like a map and leaned close, taking out a magnifying glass and hovering over the words like an explorer. David smiled.

"You always talk about your hawk eyes and you always use that magnifying glass."

"You know it helps me with the small print."

David folded the front page of his *New York Times* into quarters and began reading the top article. Mahmoud sat down with his paper as well.

"My family in Bethlehem are well…my old mother, my sister," Mahmoud declared from behind his paper.

Stanley looked up from his exploration.

"Does it say that there?"

"No. It's about the mayor. However, as I'm reading it I'm reminded I would like to be with them now."

David couldn't help himself.

"I would like to be there also, so I could be buried on *Har HaZaytim*, the Mount of Olives, when I die."

"I think my family will precede you, David. The Mount of Olives is ours, I believe…or will be…not to argue. I never argued in the cab…or with you."

David responded in kind.

"May we all be buried there, Mahmoud, and may we all be with our families."

Stanley chimed in.

"To tell you the truth, I'm the only Jew who doesn't want to go to Israel. I don't like the water there. It's not like New York."

Mahmoud ignored him and turned to David.

"That's what I like about you, David. You get along with everyone. I would have charged you a low fare. Terrible news in North Korea. Did you see it?"

CHAPTER TEN

Marc Silver drove his black Mercedes into Manhattan every day to service delis. And at appointed times, he entered a modern office building to meet with a man named Prima. He always waited for him in his office on the twentieth floor. He sat in a comfortable tall black leather chair placed around a huge oval glass table, along with twenty-five identical empty chairs. His tan cashmere coat and scarf lay over the chair next to him. On this day, the table reflected an almost stationary cloud in the sky outside the lightly grey tinted glass ceiling-to-floor window twenty stories up. He had once been told by some low level gopher that the table's see-through feature allowed Prima to see what was going on under it. Everyone who ever sat around the table suspected that. When Marc was new, an underling couldn't wait to let him in on the "secret."

He sat there alone, waiting for Prima to enter, staring at his tiny reflection in the large black flat screen TV angled in one ceiling corner like a vast rectangular eye. He considered an infrequent meeting with Prima to be a necessary formality. The gopher had told him that Prima wasn't his real name, but that he liked an old band leader named Louie Prima, whoever that was. So everyone knew him as Prima—just Prima.

Marc was a very savvy businessman. He had grown his business from a small concern serving a few restaurants with fruit brought in through the docks, into a much larger and very successful business. He had graduated with nothing but knowledge and knack from Wharton School of Business at the University of Pennsylvania twenty years earlier. Now he arranged with dock workers for fresh fruit to be delivered to mostly *mom and pop* restaurant operations all over New York City. In addition to this, he did rounds himself, taking orders and keeping all of the store owners satisfied. Everything was *coming up apples,* as he sometimes joked. But this being New York, he had to play the game. That's why he was in Prima's office.

He swiveled nervously as he waited. Prima was always late. That, along with a small cut, was a small price to pay for the protection that helped him run a smooth operation. He would usually be in and out in a few minutes, and back on the street overseeing operations.

Prima entered, dressed like the late Steve Jobs at an Apple expo, in a black long sleeve shirt and jeans. Maybe fifty-five, he was pencil thin with a full head of wavy black and silver hair. He carried a folder in his left hand, which he opened with his right hand and glanced at quickly.

"Please, stay seated, Marc. How's the family?"

His Italian-New York accent was subdued but still evident.

"Fine."

"Good. Your accounts seem to be in order. I love that coat, by the way. Did I ever tell you that?"

"Yes."

Prima smiled ever so slightly.

"Last winter probably. As I always say, you're my most reliable account, which I appreciate. And you know you're like a son to me. Any troubles out on the street?"

"No. Everything's fine."

"Good. We aim to please. You know, one time I saw in one of your clients' men's bathroom a sign saying, 'We aim to please. You aim *too,* please.' Pretty funny."

Marc let out a half breathed snicker as he rose and put a tight stack of bills in Prima's left hand. Without looking, Prima held it next to the folder with his thumb.

All of a sudden, a Brooklyn Chassid in a full black coat and hat broke into the room. He seemed totally out of place, as if he was walking off stage and into the wings in some old Yiddish theater production. Marc winced slightly, feeling an irritating wave of embarrassment wash over him. He always felt at least some of that when Chassidic *Lubavitchers* passed him by, walking on the streets of Brooklyn and Manhattan like Groucho Marx, with their ears glued to their cell phones, rattling rapid Yiddish to whomever it was they were doing business with. But he felt greater shame here. Yet, he couldn't help but notice that this Chassid seemed to have a particularly frightened look. Prima's face snapped quickly around to face the man.

"Mandy, you shouldn't be here. I told you, it's not my department. Please leave right away."

Mandy glanced at Marc and froze. Marc had finished his business and somehow knew he should also leave. He grabbed his tan coat and scarf and practically backed out of the room, as if he was leaving the presence of a high potentate.

CHAPTER ELEVEN

Naomi was standing at the register in the housewares department at Macy's. She'd been twenty-five minutes late, due to her foolish and impulsive behavior, and she knew that she could have her pay docked later when the time clock was read. But Mrs. Lazar hadn't said anything that morning. Sometimes she herself didn't show up for an hour or so after the store opened, and this was apparently one of those days. Fortunately, no one had approached the counter since the store opened. Usually, there was a flurry of sales every morning, followed by a relatively quiet time that usually ended by about 10:30 a.m. Even one customer would definitely have been a problem, because Naomi opened alone that day. But these were the dead post-Christmas days of January, and she was pretty sure no one had appeared or she would have heard about it. She checked in at the register and took a deep breath.

She finally had a few minutes to ruminate about what she had done during her subway ride in. The daydreaming incident in front of the *New York Times* building had triggered her old obsession about a kind-hearted gorgeous and observant husband, lovingly approved by her greatest hero—her father. He would be ten times the man Lisa had found. The obsession had begun when she was about eighteen and Lisa was a hugely popular and prematurely attractive thirteen-year-old, getting calls from at least one hormone-saturated boy a day. Somehow Naomi knew even then that Lisa would be married with at least two children by the time she was in her thirties, while she—Naomi—would be a matronly and unmarried "Aunt Naomi" in her forties. She had begun her daydreaming with Jewish sort of Zac Efron types (although he was probably in diapers then), but it had since spilled over to "Brad Pitt" Gentiles who were anxious to convert. She had, six months or so before, used virtually all her will-power to come to a firm "reality-check" conclusion that she would never marry. That put a halt to the daydreaming—until now. But it was accompanied by a kind of flattened spirit that she suspected was depression.

However, now the obsession was back like an aggressive cancer that had come out of remission and spread to every organ in her body. And presently, it was all focused on the kind man with the straw blonde hair and perfect porcelain nose. She knew she'd never even find out what his name was, let alone ever see him again. But that didn't stop her from imagining every detail about him, including everything from his meeting with her father to his willing conversion. This was usually entered into with a zeal that matched her father's *Davidic* compassion and Solomonic *seychel*, or wisdom.

As she stood before her computer terminal, Naomi felt suffocating sadness rise in her throat and come out through her eyes in small tightly controlled tears. She tried valiantly to turn them off, realizing that someone could approach the counter at any moment. After all, she represented Macy's, the finest department store in Manhattan—indeed in the world. She breathed deeply and attempted a small professional smile, even though no one was anywhere near to observe all of this.

It was then that Naomi had a brilliant, almost miraculous thought. What about the computer? It hadn't been that long, less than a month. She could check the computer records. And if anyone approached, she could say she was just checking something for a customer. That was sort of true anyway. After all, this was all a part of customer relations. The man had been kind, and he deserved a thank you from a loyal Macy's employee.

Remembering the date was the easiest part. It was the day after her beloved father visited the Maimonides Medical Center, the 26th of December to be exact. She efficiently clicked the mouse over the appropriate links in various areas on various screens, like a barber clipping various parts of a cute little boy's hair with the accomplished clicking snip of his scissors. As she expected, hundreds of returns came up in a long list. But only so many had her ID attached to them. She looked up, her heart beating softly but rapidly in anticipation of learning the name—and even the address—of her secret "lover." But instead of seeing a vision of him, his eyes longingly egging her on in her pursuit, she looked up to see a sour-mouthed Asian woman of a considerable age standing before her. The woman practically threw a broken teapot on the table.

"You replace? This broke."

Naomi involuntarily thought, *If you treated it this way, no wonder it broke.*

"Um…do you have the receipt?"

"No receipt. But it was bought here…Christmas gift. You replace? Something not right. These not supposed to break like this. See?"

She pointed to a cracked and chipped spout in the small porcelain pot.

"Okay? You change? Please customer?"

The woman cracked a small smile in place of the sour mouth. Her round face nodded up and down as if to direct Naomi's actions.

"Okay."

Actually, Naomi had some latitude with things like this, even though it seemed obvious the woman had mistreated the pot. The man of her dreams wouldn't do such a thing. That's why he would be open to conversion to Judaism. He was a righteous Gentile. But that was beside the point. She just wanted to get finished with this transaction before someone could come along and further interrupt her search. She asked the woman to find the same pot and bring it to her.

"Thank you, Ma'am. I thank you very much. I will return."

"Right. You just come to the front of the line."

"There is no line."

"Right. Well, if there is one."

"Okay. I be back."

"I'll be right here."

The woman left. It would be at least a few minutes until she returned. Naomi had to work quickly. She scanned the long list, undeniably the longest one of the whole year. Her transactions were dotted in different locations on the list. What was she looking for? Her mouse hand was beginning to shake and her forehead was breaking out in a light sweat. There were several shirts in a row, more sweaters, and a number of ties. Next she saw a number of toys, and then one shirt, a crock pot, and a set of bowls. And then—one, two, three shirts and a sweater…and another one…and…the tie. There it was! Okay. This was her day. He had a Macy's card and the credit went on there. If he had wanted exchanges, she would have his "tasteless" relatives' exchanges to deal with. But thank God, he asked for credit. She remembered that. So his name *had* to be there.

Both of her hands were beginning to shake uncontrollably. She wanted to finish before the woman came back and she'd have to use the computer to input information. She looked up, and there was Mrs. Lazar, not fifteen feet from her. How could she stop her from hearing the beating heart that was causing her neck to pulse like a time bomb?

"Please, don't look this way," she half mouthed.

Then, suddenly there it was. *Brock!* That could be easily changed to Brockman. Darrin, Darrin Brock. What a name! A movie star name! Much better than Peter. And the address was Teaneck, New Jersey. West Forest Avenue. She had heard there was a good Jewish neighborhood in Teaneck, with at least one Orthodox synagogue in which to take conversion classes. She grabbed a pen and a scrap of paper with her still shaking hands. Sometimes they were easier to handle than a mouse, at least for a really stressed person. She quickly jotted the valuable information down and unthinkingly stuffed it in her bra close to her wildly beating heart, just as the Asian woman approached with a box.

"You okay? I put important stuff there too. This pot not same…a little more…you give me same price?"

CHAPTER TWELVE

David Kaplan was cold. Actually, chilled is a more accurate word. As usual, he had gone outside the library with Stanley and Mahmoud to eat his bag lunch on a cement bench, with a layer of snow and ice under his worn black oxfords. Food was not permitted in the DeWitt Wallace Periodical Room. Although the three returned after lunch for another few hours—usually pointless hours, he often thought—the warm wooden panels, glowing polished tables, and golden brass lamps didn't solve his chill problem that day. And the subway ride home didn't help either.

I don't think this is the best way to spend my winter days, he thought as he swayed to the rhythmic click of the wheels. *On the other hand, what else would an old Linotype operator have to do but read the latest* New York Times *with two other old men, a retired* Daily News-*reading deli man and an old Arab taxi driver, out of all the other citizens in New York City?*

"Plenty," he whispered to himself after a pause, "like for instance my infrequent volunteer job at Maimonides. Maybe it should be from Monday to Thursday every week. Who ever heard of a once in a blue moon mitzvah anyway?"

The forty-five minute ride home seemed to last for forty-five eternities. The fact that he had the luxury of sitting on the bench seat in the half-empty pre-rush hour train was of little comfort.

The sharp-edged winter wind cut into him as he walked the few blocks to the house. When he finally entered, he was shivering uncontrollably. He collapsed on the sofa with his coat and hat still on. He knew he had a temperature, and that it was climbing. But he was too weak and exhausted to go the bathroom, dip the thermometer in alcohol, and rinse it in water. He lay on the sofa for more than an hour, trying to warm himself in his winter coat. He dozed momentarily once or twice. In between he recited the ancient Jewish healing prayer, the *Mi-shebeirach*, from memory.

Mi-Shebeirach Avo-say-nu...may He who blessed our ancestors... rescue from any distress and from any illness, minor or serious...*im kol Yisrael, V'nomar,* for all Israel, and let us say, Amen.

When darkness had finally fallen like the final moments of a child's winter afternoon Hebrew school class, Naomi turned the lock and opened the door.

"Abba?"

He was awakening from one of his short dozes and preparing for another Mi-shebeirach prayer.

"Abba? What are you doing lying there with your coat still on?"

He mumbled something unintelligible.

"What?"

He barely opened his eyes and just made out her face in the dusk light.

"Nothing. I'm a little sick I think. That's all."

"What!"

Naomi immediately sprung into action. She felt his forehead, ran to the bathroom, and dipped and shook the thermometer. She quickly returned, and he involuntarily opened his mouth as she inserted it. She ran to the refrigerator and brought out the pot of leftover Shabbat chicken soup, throwing it on the gas stove.

Meanwhile, David struggled to a sitting position. Naomi returned and removed his coat and hat as he twisted and turned to accommodate her. Then she pulled out the thermometer and read it.

"One hundred and one."

"Oy vey," he responded

"You're burning up. I told you not to eat lunch outside in the winter with those two...two friends of yours."

"They're like honored *ushpizin* guests on *Sukkus,* visitors from another world who visit our little shelter during the fall Holy Day...and yes, I admit they're a little *meshugana.* Who isn't?"

"They're from another planet."

He grunted and shivered.

"Okay, another planet. What would I do without you?"

Naomi paused and betrayed a thin smile.

"Maybe you won't always have me."

David looked up at her.

"And that means?"

"I don't know. Just maybe you won't."

"You're planning to go somewhere?"

"Well...that depends on who I go somewhere with."

"Marvin. Did you finally say yes? He should be so lucky."

"You need to take some Tylenol and get under blankets. Come on."

Naomi took his arm as he rose and stumbled toward the bathroom. He tugged gently on her arm.

"You remind me of your mother, you know...more than Lisa, although there's a part of her...I'm not sure what part...that reminds me of her too."

"The pretty part."

"Don't say that. Yes, your mother Lillian *was* beautiful...*Bei Mir Bist du Schon,* as the song goes...*to me she was beautiful*...may she rest in peace. And I miss her dearly. We all do. But her beauty shines through you in a very special way. I know what I'm talking about. She was my wife and you are my daughter."

Naomi didn't want to talk about her "beauty" any longer.

"Go to the bathroom and then put your pajamas on."

He stopped her short as she pushed him forward.

"That can wait a minute. So what do you mean I won't always have you? Is it Marvin?"

"It's not Marvin, believe me Abba."

"I didn't think so. When your mother said there was a good Jewish man out there for you, I don't think she meant Marvin."

"That was many years ago."

"And many years left for the right man to come along...a good Jewish man...a provider...a *neshama,* a real soul, a *mensch.*"

"Like my father."

"Younger of course…but not so young…he's at the door almost, if you open it and look for him."

"Like Elijah, right?"

"Younger."

Naomi betrayed another thin teasing smile.

"Maybe, just maybe I've found him, this neshama, this soul, this mensch you speak of."

"Okay. Tell me, who is this "messiah" for my daughter?"

She laughed playfully.

"And maybe I haven't. Get to bed. I'll get the Tylenol."

She lovingly shoved him into the bathroom and went to get his pajamas out of his bureau drawer. She knew some of her mother's things were still on her side of the bureau, and she made a habit of purposely never opening the drawers. She had taken her mother's place watching over him right after the breast cancer took it's toll five years earlier. And she decided then and there that she didn't have to open her mother's bureau drawers if she didn't want to.

After David was tucked in bed and wrapped in two warm blankets, Naomi suddenly remembered the chicken soup. She rushed into the kitchen just in time to keep the pot from boiling over. She felt guilty, like a nurse who had neglected to administer the evening dosage of meds to an ailing hospital patient. But there was another patient who could use the medicine just now. That patient was her. She poured the steaming soup into a bowl and sat down at the table with a spoon. She needed the elixir herself for her aching heart.

As Naomi sipped the chicken soup, her father dreamed a fever dream. In it, the familiar letter matrices were flying down the Linotype channels. They kept going faster and faster as he observed his own fingers type furiously on the 90 character keyboard, trying to keep up. The unmistakable sound of cogs, levers, pulleys, and chains was deafening, louder than he could ever remember. A painful ringing was building in David's ears. Sweat was breaking out all over his body as the resulting hot lead slugs started pouring uncontrollably all over the floor and his lap. In the middle of all this, he could sense a foreman's eyes burning the back of his head like a heat ray. He knew it was someone he didn't know. "Blasphemy against God, that's what this is. Blasphemy against *HaShem*," he heard the voice say. HaShem, meaning *The Name*, was a reference to God. "Put the words back in the book. Put the ancient words back in order! Blasphemy!" The floor was piling high with hot slugs.

He let out a desperate cry that was so deep and long that it seemed to reach all the way back to Linotype inventor Mergenthaler in 1884, two years after the menorah on the table was built.

"Help me gather the words," he cried out in the dream. "Please help me. Please!"

David's eyes popped open. His body was drenched in sweat from head to toe.

CHAPTER THIRTEEN

Marc and Lisa Silver owned a truly beautiful home in Englewood, New Jersey. Not long before he died, Lisa's grandfather—David's father—had compared it to the Kremlin his father had described to him from tinted Russian photographs.

The whole town of Englewood had burned down in 1907 during the time Upton Sinclair lived there and was experimenting with a socialist utopia.

That was about twenty-five years after the Kiev menorah was built.

Since those days, Englewood had risen from the ashes to become one of the finer northern New Jersey suburbs—fine enough for the first seven digit direct dial phone call to be made from there in 1951. And Marc and Lisa Silver's house was one of the finer homes in Englewood. They purchased it fifteen years ago, during the housing bubble. Standing on two and half acres, the house was built in the late 1950's and was constructed of brick and stone. It stood on a quiet cul-de-sac, which was perfect for ten-year-old Lindsey and seven-year-old Noah.

If it were summer, Lisa might be sitting on the backyard patio deck, looking somewhat like the suburban Holocaust survivor's daughter in the Pawnbroker, a book she had never read and a movie she had never seen. However, it was February, and she was sitting at the round glass breakfast table in the spacious kitchen, bathed in blue winter light emanating from the large floor-to ceiling patio doors, and dressed in her beige terrycloth bathrobe which concealed her sheer negligee. She was on her iPhone.

"I don't know, Sharon. I'm just glad the kids are back in school after the break. It's all over now…the crazy holidays, schlepping through traffic or on the subway all the way to Brooklyn to see Dad during Chanukah… he's fine…just got over something. God knows what. I don't know. Naomi was there, *of course*…Daddy's favorite *alta moid*…old maid…no, he doesn't call her that. I call her that, and sometimes she calls herself that. Anyway, Marc's never here of course, so I get some time to catch up on things. What are you and Steven up to?"

She got up and walked over to the refrigerator to grab a banana while she listened with the phone pressed to her shoulder.

"Uh-huh."

She peeled the banana while she went back, sat down, and glanced at the Daily News. There on an inside page was a picture of a young Chassid named Mandy Mandel. The caption below the picture said, *Orthodox Jew Killed in Diamond District in Broad Daylight.*

"Oh God," she breathed out. "Nothing. I just saw something in the paper…a murder I guess of some sort…no, a Chassid in the Diamond District, of all places. I hope Dad is safe in Brooklyn, with all those black kids beating on old Jews, and Marc in Manhattan with all those Muslim radicals, and I don't know what…oh well, forget it. How are the kids?"

Lisa walked over to the bathroom, the phone still on her shoulder, and entered it with the door open just a crack.

"Uh-huh."

The toilet flushed, the sink ran, and the door opened.

"Uh-huh."

"We're not in that place yet, thank God. But someday, they'll cost us a fortune…or go to City College, God forbid. But Marc must have learned something at Wharton, because we're doing pretty well, knock on wood. I don't know how he does it or where it comes from…I'm not bragging, Sharon. I'm just saying, he's amazing…even with this economy and this crazy cost of living."

Light snow began to fall outside the patio window at the same exact time that snow was falling in Manhattan, where David Kaplan sat in the DeWitt Wallace Periodical Room with Stanley and Mahmoud on one of his Tuesday mornings. There was no bag lunch next to him. He had already decided to head home at lunchtime instead of staying for the afternoon. He had told his friends that he was still recovering from a twenty-four hour virus. But in his heart, he had already made up his mind to come only Tuesday mornings at most—a distinct change from the last few years. And he was considering not coming at all if he found voluntary work to do on Tuesdays and Thursdays, perhaps at the hospital. But he hadn't shared any of that with them yet.

Stanley looked over the stretched out Daily News with his magnifying glass.

"They found some *Chabadnik* dead not far from here…killed."

A flash of unexpected emotional pain stung David like a bee bite. But when it left as quickly as it came, he paid no further attention to it.

"May he rest in peace."

"Maybe you recognize him? Of course, they all look alike in those *meshugana* crazy hot black sweat suits…those *schvitz* outfits."

David leaned over and looked at the picture.

"Mandy Mendel. I've never heard of him. I think I would remember a name like that."

Mahmoud glanced at it out of the corner of his eye.

"Too bad. Maybe I drove him somewhere. Maybe not."

Light snow was also falling outside Marc's black Mercedes as he inched past the lower Manhattan restaurants and stores. The newspaper lay next to him face up, with the picture of the Chassid visible on the soft leather passenger seat. His breathing was stressed and his lips were pursed. He opened them to breathe more easily.

"Come on. Move!"

He irrationally honked the horn twice, only to have three others respond instantly like barking dogs.

"Shut up," he whispered.

He glanced at the paper again.

"Oh God. I hope it's not the one I saw in the office. It *is* him…maybe not. I hope not."

He looked up to see the car in front of him close in on his quickly. He jammed on the brakes and his car slid into the other car's bumper with the jolt of a three-mile-an-hour collision.

"Shi…oh, crap. Stupid driver."

He got out of the car to a chorus of horns.

"Shut up!," he shouted out loud.

He walked up to the car he hit, a recent model Honda Accord. The electric window came down and an impeccably dressed middle aged African-American man opened the door, which knocked Marc in the stomach in the process. Marc responded angrily.

"What the hell you think you're doing?"

The man, taller than Marc by two inches, got out of the car as the chorus of horns increased.

"What am *I* doing? You hit *ME!*"

A man in the car behind Marc rolled down his window.

"Take it somewhere else. You're blocking traffic. It's snowing. Call the police, report it, but get the hell out of here."

Marc exploded.

"Shut the F up."

He turned back to the man in the car.

"And you, you braked. You owe me if you did anything to my car."

"*ME?* Are you crazy? I'm calling the police. Get out of my face and get back in your car before I beat your ass. Now!"

Marc didn't need this…not with that picture of the Chassid in the front seat. The man looked at the back of his Accord and the front of Marc's Mercedes.

"It's nothing," he spoke to himself. "Stupid ass."

He got back into his car and drove down the now clear lane in front of Marc who, after examining the front of his own car, got back in and drove off.

He breathed the racial slur *Shvartze* to himself. Then he put on the windshield wipers and focused on more pressing matters.

"If that's him…I didn't see who it was. Not really. So what am I worried about? One dead Chassid? Who cares?"

His car's blue tooth rang. He looked at his phone. The name *Prima* shown clearly on it in white letters.

Chapter Fourteen

Naomi had absent-mindedly left the note with Darrin Brock's information in her bra when she took it off the evening of the day she found it. Normally, she would have thought about where she put it the next time she daydreamed about Darrin—probably the next day, which was a Tuesday. But she'd been so pre-occupied with her father's short illness that she'd forgotten about it. In fact, it was the next Sunday morning as she lay in bed before she wondered where she had put the note. Was it in her purse? Had she put it in her bureau drawer when she got home? She knew he lived in Teaneck, but there was no way she could recall the exact street. Did she jot down his phone number? She thought she had, but the whole thing was so vague now, swirling around in her mind along with the returned teapot, the Asian lady who banged it down on the table, and the more expensive replacement. One thing was certain. There was no way she wanted to "hack" into the Macy computer again. She was just glad she didn't get caught the first time.

Where did I put that note? I can't believe I lost it. I must have put the stupid thing somewhere. What in the world is the matter with me? Am I really that old and forgetful?

In the midst of all this turmoil came a more pleasant sense of accomplishment. She had actually gone six days without thinking about the man with the straight blonde hair and the porcelain nose! She sat up in her bed, in the upstairs back room of her father's Brooklyn dwelling, and felt almost normal, almost like the thankful, grateful, and modest Jewish daughter she knew she should be. However, dwelling on her great victory opened the gushing floodgates of her obsession, and Darrin Brock washed up once again on the shores of her longing heart in all of his kind and gentle glory. She *had* to find that note, and his contact information.

After not being able to find the note that morning, Naomi went on with her Sunday, cleaning the Kaplan house and cooking dinner for her father. Before she knew it, Monday came, and with it, work. Then Tuesday came, and then Wednesday. In fact, three whole weeks went by and still she hadn't found the note. There was a good reason for that. She had thrown her bra in the wash the evening of the day she had placed it there, and water and detergent had taken their toll. The note with the address was gone, but the daydreams had returned with a vengeance.

She was lying in bed on a late February Sunday much like the one six days after the note was written, when she suddenly threw off the covers and got out of bed, her flannel pajamas draped above her cold feet on the bare wooden floor next to the small worn light green throw rug. Notwithstanding the pajamas, she was cold. So was her memory about the note. What in the world did she do with it? Try as hard as she might, Naomi still couldn't remember where she'd put it. But she *did* remember Darrin Brock's name and the city he lived in. Finally, her mind was clear enough to at least consider an alternative method to retrieve the information she desperately wanted.

Over a cup of tea and her three-year-old PC laptop, she typed out the *white* pages URL. Maybe his address would pop up. The internet pause seemed to go on for minutes. But it was actually only perhaps thirty seconds before she was given a choice of Darrin Brocks. And within less than a minute more she found what she was looking for. There he was—at least it seemed so. He was listed as the son of a husband and wife who lived on West Forest Avenue in Teaneck. And the age, forty-eight, seemed to be right. This *had* to be him. So he wasn't married. Or maybe he was divorced and had moved back home to his parents' house. But he couldn't be a Mama's boy *nebbish* like Marvin. He was way too sophisticated for that. Maybe he was just a very good son, just like she was a very good daughter. At any rate there they were, Lester and Velma, not exactly Jewish names. But then again, she already knew that they weren't Jewish, and at any rate they weren't the objects of her search.

Naomi was awake enough now to be in the early stages of a plan that could realistically be put into action in a matter of an hour or two. It was a quiet cloudy winter Sunday, The streets were now clear, and there was a very high probability that there would be access to a car—a Lexus no less—and Aunt Ida to drive it. Not *her* aunt Ida. God forbid. She didn't have an Aunt Ida, or an aunt remotely like Ida. Aunt Ida was just about the last person Naomi would want as an aunt, with her Gentile Goyisha nose job, her short opaque black hair like Elvira the vampire lady, her stoplight-red lipstick, and her obnoxious Long Island Reform Jewish ways.

Aunt Ida drove Naomi crazy. She was always talking about as fast as Naomi's father prayed, as he swayed back and forth in what's called *davinning*. Only in Aunt Ida's case her talk was about non-sensical things. She definitely wasn't *her* aunt Ida. She was *Marvin's* aunt Ida, and an aunt so obsessed with talking about men, even as a seventy-five-year-old widow, that she couldn't imagine Naomi without one. And the most convenient man for Naomi was her nephew Marvin.

Yet with all these challenges, Aunt Ida could at times come in very handy. And on this particular Sunday morning a plan was taking real shape, as Naomi began to type her own Brooklyn address and Darrin Brock's Teaneck address into MapQuest. Again she waited impatiently, this time for the route to pop up. Naomi just *knew* that Aunt Ida would be thrilled to drive her and Marvin out of New York and into Northern New Jersey. And the Sunday traffic would be light enough to make the trip somewhat pleasant, if not short.

As Naomi waited for the MapQuest information to pop up, she tried to imagine the house where Darrin lived. She didn't realize that Google Maps provided an option that would show her an image of the house. Her computer skills were too elementary. And even if they weren't, they still couldn't give her one more peak at the mensch who was not only one in a million, but also one of a haystack of millions. Yet today she might be just inches away from him in the *bedroom* community of Teaneck, New Jersey—wonderful suburban Teaneck, New Jersey!

It wasn't long before Naomi had called both Marvin and his aunt, and only about an hour after that, about 12:00 p.m., when the "fully loaded" late model silver Lexus was on its way to pick her up. She got dressed quickly and threw her coat on. She hadn't thought about what she would say to her father, and when he finally asked where she was going she could only say, "Abba, I'm…I'm going on a picnic with Marvin and his Aunt Ida. You know, his Aunt Ida?" A picnic would throw him off the trail if by some chance he was on one.

"In winter?"

"Well…not exactly a picnic…a late lunch at a kosher deli in Teaneck New Jersey…a really good one…totally kosher."

"You have to go to Teaneck? The delis around here aren't good enough for you?"

"Well…it's a special one…Marvin saw it advertised. It's like an outing. That's what makes it like a picnic…sort of."

Her father looked straight at her, exposing the ridiculousness of her end of the conversation.

"I see. Are you sure you're all right, Naomi?"

He reached out and put his hand on her forehead.

"You didn't catch what I had?"

"No Daddy, I didn't. I'm fine."

"Okay. So who in their right mind says a word like picnic in winter?"

"I'm just…just thinking of…of the bagels…you know, like we take on picnics."

"Oh. I see. I suppose that's reasonable if you say it is."

He shrugged.

"Well…have a nice time. Say hi to his aunt for me. I thought she got on your nerves, by the way."

"She's better," Naomi lied. "Anyway, she can drive. We can't."

"Just barely, the way she throws her hands around like she's conducting Stravinsky."

A peck on the cheek and hand kiss on the doorpost mezuzah cut things short, and Naomi left, shutting the door behind her. She breathed a long expiating sigh. Just then the gun metal Lexus pulled up, and there was Aunt Ida sitting in the driver's seat, with her short dyed black hair and fire engine red lipstick, stylishly ready for the trip to Northern New Jersey. The front passenger-side door opened to reveal Marvin, looking like he always did in winter, with his orange sock hat and black earmuffs. Aunt Ida directed him with her right hand.

"Get in the back, Marvin. You too, Naomi. Come on. We don't have all day…maybe half a day. And it's cold."

Marvin got out and slammed the door shut, as if to give his aunt a quick slap. He stopped to look at Naomi.

"What?," she asked with rolled eyes.

"Hi."

"Aren't you going to open the door for me, Marvin?"

"My mother says hi."

"Open the door, Marvin."

He opened the door and got in, sliding over to make room for her.

"This is why Darrin is a mensch, a real gentleman," she whispered to herself. Marvin stared at her again.

"What?"

"Nothing, Marvin."

She got in. Aunt Ida adjusted the rear view mirror so she could eye them both.

"So just where are we going, darling?"

"A house?"

"What house?."

"A house in Teaneck. I have it here."

She pulled a folded sheet of MapQuest directions out of her small purse. She felt technically sophisticated in the presence of such a worldly Reform Jewish woman. Marvin just sat there, oblivious in his orange cap and black earmuffs, like a baby in an infant seat. Aunt Ida grabbed the sheet and tossed it back at Naomi.

"What the hell is this? Just give me the address so I can put it into the GPS."

"Um…please Aunt Ida…don't talk like that. It's the *yeitzah rah,* the evil impulse."

"*Yeitzah what?* You sound like my mother, may she rest in peace. Please speak English. If you mean 'hell', it's a perfectly good word. I think it's in the Torah."

"I don't think so, Aunt Ida."

Naomi then decided to drop the war over words, concluding that she could never win with Aunt Ida, who wasn't even her aunt anyway. It was useless to argue any further.

"The directions are on this sheet here, Aunt Ida."

Naomi handed the open sheet back to Aunt Ida.

"Okay, okay. What's it say here in your ancient document?"

She began typing the address into her GPS with one hand while she steered the wheel and began to pull out into the street with the other. After a short pause, the lady in the device began to pleasantly dispense directions.

"Make a left in one hundred feet..."

"Just where in Teaneck are we going...and *why?*

"A customer...he took something back...um, I need to see him to... to give him a special...a special receipt...hand delivered. He asked for it."

Naomi was totally unprepared, making things up as she went along.

"So what is he, the President, that they had to send you on a special trip?"

"Well, sort of. He's a very important person...a big buyer. So that's why."

She hoped that ended the conversation.

"Jewish?"

"I don't know...no...I don't think so. Maybe. Well no, he's not. He's just a very nice man."

"Why would he be anything else? Where did you meet him...this *customer?*"

"In housewares. He was returning something."

Naomi was getting in too deep. She looked up and caught Aunt Ida's piercing gaze out of the corner of her eye.

"I see. And you have to take something that he brought back...back to him?"

"Sort of."

"Is he good looking?"

"I guess so. I don't know. Okay, yes, he's good looking, Aunt Ida. He happens to be *very* good looking. And very nice. Could we change the subject?"

Why did she say all of that? Was she actually curious about garish Aunt Ida's opinion of him? She silently prayed that Aunt Ida would stop interrogating her.

"Where's the receipt?"

"What receipt?"

"The receipt you're bringing him."

"Well, I don't exactly have it with me. It's a courtesy call. Then I'll email it to him...after that."

"A courtesy call."

Aunt Ida wasn't buying the story.

"You know Naomi, a Jewish girl could even marry a goy if he was the right goy. Isn't that right Marvin?"

Aunt Ida threw her hands up, as Naomi's father had warned, and then shrugged. Naturally, she took them off the steering wheel in the process. Naomi gasped. Marvin sat there stoic, frozen.

"Turn right in point one mile onto West Street NY 9-A."

"I mean if it was the right goy. It's better than nothing...better than not marrying at all...isn't that right, Marvin?"

Marvin finally spoke. He never liked to disagree with his aunt. The closest he would come would be to *not quite* disagree. However, in this case he knew he had to summon up all the courage he could and make a valiant effort to disagree with her.

"I think...I think...um..."

"What do you think, Marvin? What? Spit it out!"

"I think...I mean, not to disagree, Aunt Ida. But...I think that Jews should marry Jews. *That's* what the rabbis say...isn't it?"

Aunt Ida's eyes shifted to Naomi.

"Well, Naomi? What do you think?"

"He would have to convert. That's what the rabbis say."

Why was she even bothering to disagree with Marvin? Still, she knew Aunt Ida would have the last word. She always did.

"Naomi, you will marry a good Jew, some good old Jew, *if* you ever get around to marriage at all. See Naomi, I'm a modern woman...a twenty first century Jew. I live in the *real* world. Look at you two, sitting there in the back seat together like two Chabanik with a *mechitzah* dividing curtain between you."

Then she slapped the steering wheel.

"What the hell are you two waiting for? You might as well just move in together."

She took both hands off the steering wheel and let out a blast of a laugh. Naomi blushed redder than her winter red cheeks.

"Please, Aunt Ida! That's not Torah."

Naomi continued trying to avoid Aunt Ida's piercing glance in the rear view mirror. She began pounding one hand on the steering wheel while she let the other hand fly around.

"Torah? I'll tell you what Torah is! Doesn't it say be fruitful and multiply somewhere in there? It's not just for the Catholics, you know. Look at the *Haredi* Orthodox Jews in Israel. They have more children than rabbits have rabbits. Well, you two haven't even put two and two together, let alone multiplied. And doesn't it talk about one flesh somewhere in there?"

Marvin released a short grunt. He shifted his weight uncomfortably while still staring out the window.

"Take I-95 George Washington Bridge Exit 14."

"You two don't look like much by yourselves. But together it kind of works. What are you waiting for? I mean, you've been together since the Middle Ages."

Marvin finally spoke up.

"That's what I've been telling her."

Naomi lost her patience.

"Stop it, Aunt Ida!"

"I'm sorry Naomi. But I'm only telling you what your father would tell you if he had the guts. But he's too nice. Marvin, you're right. She's the perfect Jewish match for you and visa versa. For one thing, you're both as observant as fried matzoh. Okay, so talk among yourselves now. I'll shut up."

"Merge onto I-95 South toward GW Bridge/New Jersey."

After several minutes of silence, Marvin finally got the courage to rouse himself and speak directly and to the point.

"She won't say yes, Aunt Ida. She won't say yes." He finally turned to Naomi. "You won't say yes. Isn't that right, Naomi?"

Naomi wanted to get out of the car right there on the bridge, but she wasn't sure she would live through the experience. All she could think of was that if she hadn't planned this whole trip out herself, she would swear it was a conspiracy between Marvin and his aunt to corner her into marriage. She had to say something, *anything* to stop this inquisition.

"My father wouldn't tell me that. I happen to know he doesn't think we're a perfect match. He *did* have the guts to tell me. And neither did my mother, may she rest in peace. Are we almost there?"

Naomi felt like an eight-year-old who had just shouted "so there!" and stuck out her tongue to another little eight-year-old girl. How could she have gotten herself into such a humiliating situation? Marvin, on the other hand, was just the hurt little boy.

"He never said that. My mother told me he...."

He paused. Naomi stared back, daggers in her eyes.

"Told you what, Marvin?"

"She told me...told me...."

Aunt Ida looked at the GPS.

"Okay. Let's stop this childish quarreling, you two love birds. We're almost there...just a minute or so. We're in Teaneck now."

There was silence the rest of the way, save for the pleasant voice of Ms. GPS.

"In three hundred feet, turn left onto West Forest Avenue...the destination is one tenth of a mile on the right."

The car pulled up to a charming three story brick and frame house, with neatly trimmed snow capped shrubs on either side of a neatly painted off-red door. The walk leading from the door had been carefully and thoroughly shoveled. There were no cars in sight, and no windows on the garage door. Aunt Ida turned around and faced Naomi directly for the first time.

"Well...here we are at the house of Prince Charming, or whatever his name is."

Naomi was beginning to feel the combination of guilt and shame that often accompanies mindless impulsive foolishness—along with a sprinkle of sheer panic.

"His name is Darrin Brock, Aunt Ida, and he's obviously not home. I think we should leave and go to a little deli that...that I think must be around here. I think it's kosher."

"What! Are you *crazy*. I'm not leaving here until you go up and knock on that door. I believe you owe it to Macy's, if not me and Marvin. Right Marvin?"

Marvin had fallen asleep, his mouth wide open like a child waiting for a spoonful of oatmeal.

"Marvin! Right?"

He snapped out of his stupor.

"Right, Aunt Ida."

Naomi was frozen with fear. What would she say to Darrin now that she was actually here in front of his house, so close to him? He hadn't recognized her at the *New York Times* building. Would he recognize her here? Even if he did, what would she say to him? What *could* she say? For the first time since that late walk to work from the Times building weeks earlier, she wanted to slap herself hard so she could wake up from this obsessive dream. Only this time she wasn't ten blocks out of her way. She was a state out of her way, with Marvin and his aunt yet.

"Well, Naomi?"

Aunt Ida would not be put off. Slowly, Naomi opened the door and encountered the sharp wind of a below-freezing February Sunday. The Lexus had excellent heat, so she had almost forgotten about the outside temperature. She tried to gather her thoughts as she began to walk the shoveled path to what felt like her execution. She had to think creatively, and think fast. What would she say? *Mr. Brock, I happened to be in the neighborhood, and I just want to thank you for your faithful commitment to Macy's over the years.* Over the years? Maybe he was a new customer. *Mr. Brock, I'm here to represent Macy's. We have a new customer satisfaction policy. I just have a few short questions, and we like to sometimes ask in person and not in an Internet survey.* That would work. And she could just fake her way through the oral survey with questions like, *How did you feel about the service you were given?*

With great fear and trembling, Naomi approached the front door. She looked back to see an impatient Aunt Ida staring at her as she had in the rear view mirror. Slowly, she picked up the knocker and knocked once. There was no response. She waited a minute or so and looked back at Aunt Ida again. Now both she and Marvin were staring at her, and Aunt Ida pantomimed three knocks. Naomi turned back and followed her lead, knocking three times. She waited another minute or so. When it became obvious no one was home, she breathed a sigh of relief and headed back to the car. Once back in the warm back seat, she stated the obvious.

"He's not home."

"I can see that. You should have given him a courtesy phone call, or whatever they do at Macy's. Now what do we do?"

Naomi felt like a total idiot. Just like the time in front of the Times building, she had followed that place somewhere in the base of her brain. Only this time, she had involved two other people, and wasted their whole day. She could only think of one thing to do.

"Um…I wonder if that deli's right around here…the kosher one, I mean. it's lunch time, and I'm hungry."

"Well, there's lots of those in Brooklyn, for God's sake. But…I guess it's as good an idea as any, considering."

Aunt Ida pressed the *Yelp* app on her iPhone, and dictated "kosher deli" into it. Naomi had never seen anyone do that, although she had often watched people use their iPhones at work and on the subway. She had a small flip phone that could only call and take calls and texts. Aunt Ida typed an address into the GPS as she spoke it, at the same time wheeling the car out of the parking place.

"Noah's Ark Deli. Looks pretty good. 493 Cedar Lane."

It took just a few minutes by the friendly voice of the GPS for the car to pull into the restaurant parking lot, and another few minutes in the crowded lot to find a parking space. They were all really hungry by this time. Marvin in particular wanted to get out of the warm Lexus, through the freezing cold lot, and into the warm deli.

Just then, like a miracle from a benevolent Heaven, either Darrin Brock or someone who looked just like him walked past the Lexus, pushing an older woman in a wheel chair and accompanied by an old man. He stopped beside a late model white Chevy Impala that was parked just three spaces from Aunt Ida's car. Naomi turned and watched as he opened the passenger side door. She had been so used to dreaming about him that she wondered whether she was dreaming now. She quickly got out of the car, like the victim of a tractor beam. Then Darrin, in his familiar black cashmere coat, looked her way and actually seemed to stare straight at her for a split second, as he had inside the *New York Times* building. *It's him!*, she thought to herself. She instinctively walked toward him as he began to help the woman—whom Naomi guessed was his mother Velma—into the car. The man, whom she guessed was Lester, stood next to Darrin, waiting for him to finish his task. Naomi drew closer to Darrin, waiting for him to settle his mother into the passenger seat. Aunt Ida stared from the heated comfort of her Lexus.

"What in the world is she doing? Come on, Marvin. Get out of the car. We might as well get in there. There's probably a half hour wait."

Darrin opened the rear door for his father to get in. Then, suddenly and without warning, he walked the few feet over to Naomi.

"Well...this is the third time. I absolutely never forget a face. That's a sometimes useful gift of mine. And anyway, yours is unforgettable... distinctive. I recognized you a little late the last time. Sorry."

He *did* see her at the *New York Times* Building! She couldn't help noticing that he had the same kindness in his electric blue eyes as the first time she met him in the housewares department. He glanced over at the Lexus.

"Are you and your family coming or going?"

"Oh no. They're not my family. But...we just got here."

"Oh. I see...."

She suddenly realized he was saying with a glance that he wanted to know her name.

"It's...it's Naomi. Naomi...Naomi Kaplan."

"Naomi. That is such a beautiful name. It's one of my favorites, from the Book of Ruth. It means pleasant, doesn't it?. Yet I seem to remember that Naomi said 'Call me Mara,' meaning *bitter*, when she became bitter over her life. Perhaps it's bittersweet in your case...and more sweet than bitter, I'm sure. I'm Darrin...Darrin Brock."

She was melting inside, though freezing outside.

"That's a nice name too, although I don't know what it means. Um... we just happened to be in the area, so we thought we'd grab something. Is it good?"

"It's very good. I think they're known for their Philly steak sandwich."

"Thank you. We'll try it."

Aunt Ida was becoming more curious by the second. Just who was this gorgeous man, and how did Naomi know him? Naomi, on the other hand, was transfixed, hopelessly staring at Darrin. She felt like the female lead in a romantic movie. This was more than surreal. And yet it was real enough for her to be getting in deeper than she knew was wise, or safe, for David Kaplan's daughter. But miracle of miracles, he seemed to know where her name was in the Bible, and what it actually meant. Maybe he was secretly Jewish somewhere, or at least would love to be.

Aunt Ida continued to watch with interest. She detected that something was going on, although she didn't know just what. Marvin, on the other hand, was clueless about Naomi's reverie, and just wanted to be warm and fed. He headed straight for the restaurant without another word.

Meanwhile, Darrin smiled a very warm smile and put his gloved hand on Naomi's winter coat-covered arm. A jolt went through the fabric and all throughout her body, melting her heart and emptying her brain of all her recently coined creative strategies. She blushed beyond her red cheeks.

"It's very nice to see you again, Naomi. So I guess we need to be going, while you're coming."

Naomi let out a nervous giggle.

"Of course."

She noticed that Darrin's father was looking up at her from the rear seat, and smiling with the same gracious smile as his son. Darrin recognized his oversight and opened the rear door.

"Dad, this is Naomi. I met her in the housewares department at Macy's. She's a very nice and kind person. Naomi, this is my father...and my mother."

"Nice to meet you," Lester Brock nodded.

"Nice to meet you," Naomi responded, still in somewhat of a dreamy fog.

Darrin then got into the driver's seat, and they pulled out—but not before he waved to Naomi. Naomi waved back. Aunt Ida walked up to her as she began to walk toward the deli.

"Wait a minute...before we go in. Who is that man? How do you know him?"

Naomi couldn't lie in response to a direct question like that from someone as sharp as Aunt Ida."

"That's him. That's Darrin Brock"

"Well, he *is* gorgeous. So did you *know* he'd be here at this...this kosher deli?"

"No...no, I didn't, Aunt Ida. I guess it was luck...*Bisheart* really."

"I see. So did you tell him you were here on Macy's business, like you were going to at his house?"

Naomi looked down. She couldn't face Aunt Ida directly and admit the truth.

"No, because I wasn't."

"I don't understand what the hell this is all about. Do you know him outside of work? I mean, have you ever talked to him outside of Macy's?"

"No...no I haven't...only at housewares, when he came with some returns on December 26th."

There was a long pause as Aunt Ida struggled to take it all in. Naomi kept her head bowed. Aunt Ida wasn't sure if she should ask anything else, but she couldn't help asking at least one more thing.

"Did you get his address from Macy's?"

Naomi stood motionless. In the mid-afternoon light, Aunt Ida could just see one tear-drop fall from Naomi's eye onto her cheek. She grabbed ahold of Naomi's arm.

"We need to get you some matzah ball soup. What do you think about that?"

She pulled a crumpled tissue out of her coat pocket and transferred it from her gloved hand to Naomi's. They walked together, arm in arm, into the Deli.

Chapter Fifteen

A few times a year, David Kaplan awoke with the fading hangover of what he termed a *Linotype overdose* dream. All the sights, sounds, and smells of the Rube Goldberg-like device invaded his unconscious and remained for a conscious instant like the fading impression of the sun after a blinking second of staring at it. When the dream occurred the night before a third Thursday, he considered it a possible sign from God. It was on such days that a small retro-printing company by the name of Midwood Press, located conveniently in the Midwood section of Brooklyn, gave tours for schools throughout New York City and beyond. David wasn't totally convinced these dreams were a sign from God. After all, he sometimes had them on other nights as well. But on the rare occasions when they took place before the third Thursdays, he usually chose to take that as a sign.

On the aforementioned occasions, David would rise early and prepare to take a trip by train to the small company. He had decided never to mention his years of professional experience with the machines, nor to inquire about using the working Linotype machine onsite. He simply hoped to watch the vast machine at work for just a few minutes—

and remember. Not all of his Linotype memories were pleasant. Some of his dreams were more like nightmares. But then again, so were some of the four thousand year long memories of *Klal Yisra-el*, the community of Israel. Still, hadn't Israel's God commanded remembrance?

He dressed in his black jacket and pants, and put on his overcoat, hat, scarf, and gloves. The snow had stopped. The sidewalk was predictably icy, and made even icier through the sealing effect of a below-freezing winter sun. He knew he was in his brittle bone, hip-breaking season of life, so he walked gingerly and prayed the prayer for protection as he headed toward the bus stop. He had fully recovered from the effects of whatever kind of virus had overtaken him the month before, and it was good to get out. But he couldn't help wondering why he felt such a gnawing need to be in the presence of a Linotype Machine even just a few times a year. What was it about these machines of his young adulthood that attracted him so strongly?

When he arrived at the Midwood section of Brooklyn, he walked up to the building which housed Midwood Press. It looked, with its red brick exterior, almost as oddly Victorian as the Linotype machine itself. By the time he climbed the stairs to Suite 208, a small classroom of elementary school students had already arrived, and he was glad to see them there. He could quietly observe, perceived as harmless because he was clearly a religious old Orthodox Jew who could be a benign presence in his own peculiar way—a holy man of sorts in a sort of holy place.

Of course, no one there knew he was a one-time top Linotype operator at the *New York Times*. He quietly chose his usual corner of the room, as he watched and listened to the explanation about the pizza oven-hot 500 degree plate, the innovative-for-its-time matrix letters that dropped down the channels, and the silver colored snow-like shavings on the floor. And then he closed his eyes as he listened to the clicks, whirs, and turning cam shifts. And he remembered.

He always thought he would remember Lillian at these times, and perhaps Naomi when she was a little girl. But he never did. The mind doesn't work that way. It responds to sounds, sights, and smells, and transports one back to similar exact pinpoint moments, in words, pictures, emotions, and stories. Any number of Linotype memories may have risen from the dead in past visits to Midwood Press. But this time, a long-buried string of typeset words came to life—and along with them the disturbing pain of grief and fear.

The man's name was Steinberg, and he was not much younger than

David—a young father of three. He was a good-looking Jewish boy who owned a truck to carry goods in New York. He didn't want the mob to own his truck, so he asked the police to help him. One morning at dawn, as he started his Queens route, they shot him in the back and left him to bleed and die in the cab. The door was half open, and the red blood trickled down the well and the aqua-blue enamel side of the truck, like Abel's blood in bright primary colors. That's how he was discovered—by a young Puerto Rican boy on his way to school. Years later an old mobster finally talked, and revealed that one of the corrupt cops had gone back and told a mob boss.

Even before all of that was revealed, David wanted to investigate the crime further. As a Linotype operator he was honored and treated like a mensch, a real gentleman, by the *New York Times*. He was given opportunities to edit and sometimes even make minor content decisions. What a job! Perhaps he should have honored the life of the young man, just as he was honored, by inquiring further into his death. As a respected Linotype operator at the most respected newspaper in the world, perhaps he could have made a difference in some way. But not only did the reporter-journalist get a life-threatening call. He got one too, and just after Shabbas yet. It was as if they knew he was observant just like they knew he was a Linotype operator. So maybe he saved a few lives—including his own—by saying nothing. But maybe not.

How he hated the mob! It reminded him of the Nazis. He could never comprehend the taking of innocent life. How could anyone ever do anything but try to protect life, the greatest gift the Holy One ever gave? Back then he used to think, *what would the sages have done if they were in his position?* But over the passing years, he had more or less allowed himself to forget the story, or forced himself to forget…that is, until now at Midwood Press.

How many other stories had he forgotten? There were so many other exciting and sometimes troubling ones. And there could have been more, if he had stayed with the Times and learned the computer process. Instead, he quit, just walked out on the "Grey Lady," and at forty years old yet. He had been the best Linotype operator in the room. He was proud of the difference he made. Sure, Lillian and he had discussed the change to computers, and she was completely against his leaving. But he just couldn't see himself sitting at a cold desk amidst electronic machines that stared at him stupidly like one-eyed freaks. That would have been unbearable.

Still, maybe Lillian was right, what with all the dead end jobs he held since he quit the Times. Just how many were there? The cheap un-kosher *kosher style* Brooklyn restaurant waiter, the shoe salesman at Macy's (that's when he referred Naomi to be interviewed for a position as a sales person), the guard at one of the indistinguishable Manhattan office buildings, the others—all of them so horribly forgettable.

The class left, bag lunches in hand. It was time to leave also, and to bury all those memories again. He walked through the cold and clamoring street to the bus stop. At least he'd be home way before rush hour.

CHAPTER SIXTEEN

Marc Silver drove his black Mercedes down Manhattan's Avenue of Americas like the royalty he knew he was. The vehicle might as well have been slowly floating ten feet off the ground. After all, he never had to look for an impossible-to-find parking space—a situation that convinced many inhabitants of the crowded island to not even bother purchasing a car. The special numbers and letters on his license plate permitted him to pretty much park anywhere he wanted, courtesy of the City of New York—with a little help from Prima. He was headed from uptown Manhattan to a small Greek restaurant on the Lower East Side, and he had one stop to make before then. Even there, the powerful parking space privilege applied.

He pulled directly across from the public library, in front of the Orvis Store. He hadn't been inside the library since sometime during his University of Pennsylvania Wharton School years, and he had no great interest in visiting the place again. However, he needed to make a quick stop on this Thursday. He had promised Lisa he would drop off a warm thick black microfiber scarf she had received in the mail from L.L. Bean. He had argued with her about it because his day was busy and he didn't want to end up in meaningless conversation with his slow-speaking sage-quoting father-in-law.

"Can't Naomi find something to keep his neck warm? That's the kind of thing she's good for anyway, isn't she?," he had asked.

But Lisa had pointed out that number one, that the scarf was warmer than anything else her father owned or Naomi would buy for him. Number two, it had been at the Silver house for four cold days already. And number three, the choice came down to getting it to him that day or sending it back.

"Send it back then!" he had shouted at her. But of course the fact that he was now parked across the street from the library told the rest of the story.

Marc pulled the scarf out of the black Mercedes, crossed the street, and navigated the salt-covered concrete steps. He walked through the large front doors, turned left, and then quickly found the Dewitt Wallace Periodical Room. He had no time to reminisce about the massive portraits, or the paintings of New York landmarks he hadn't seen since his college years—let alone the labyrinth of long polished wooden tables with warm bronze lamps. He rapidly scanned the room for David Kaplan. Suddenly, he saw a familiar face, someone from some aspect of his work on the streets of Manhattan. *Who is that?*, he thought. He approached the man, who just might by some remote chance have seen his father-in-law.

"Um…"

Stanley and Mahmoud were sitting in their usual places, with their newspapers stretched out before them just the way each of them liked. Stanley looked up to see Marc Silver. He rose from his chair, his large bulky frame forcing the chair back. A very faint hint of startled panic came and then went.

"Marc Silver. What are you doing here?"

Marc finally remembered the inconsequential deli counter man.

"Stanley. Isn't that right?"

"Yes, it's me. I'm retired and this is my new counter, so to speak…and my friend Mahmoud."

"Pleased to meet you, sir," Mahmoud stood and gestured, hand out.

Marc stood awkwardly and shook the Arab's hand, withdrawing his almost immediately. He wanted to get all of this over with as soon as possible.

"Salaam," he said hesitantly.

"I can understand hello, sir. That's what the cab fares said to me for… twenty-five years."

"Of course. Sorry."

He turned his back on Mahmoud and then turned to Stanley.

"Well, how are you since those deli days."

"Living, thank God. And you? Are you still…"

"Still what?"

"Well…the car is parked in a no-parking zone as usual, I would suppose?"

Stanley turned toward Mahmoud.

"You know, Mahmoud, he has a deal with the city.…"

Marc interrupted.

"Look…Stanley…I can't stay long."

"What? They meter your parking now?," Stanley winked.

"I…I'm looking for an old man who comes in here Tuesdays and Thursdays, I believe. He wears a yarmulke, you know, a head covering… black usually. No offense Mahmoud. He…he…"

"You mean Kaplan…David Kaplan?," Mahmoud asked.

"You know him?"

Mahmoud was now a little more than irritated, which is the kind of behavior Marc expected from him.

"Of course I know him. He's my friend…my good friend…my *very* good Orthodox Jewish friend. And just who are *you*, sir?"

"Me?"

Their voices were now becoming elevated, which prompted a "shush" from someone nearby. Marc whispered his response.

"I'm…I'm his son-in-law. He's my wife's father."

Stanley, who had taken his seat again by this time, stood up again and pushed back his seat even further.

"What!," he whispered.

"Yes, I happen to be his daughter Lisa's husband, for what it's worth."

"I didn't know that. He never told me. I knew Lisa had a husband… and children too…but I didn't realize it was…it was *you*."

"Yes, well it's me. And I have to leave now…but, I thought he would be here."

"No, no he isn't. He comes here sometimes, but then again sometimes not these days. We don't know where he is. But…if we see him, we'll tell him you were here."

"Don't bother," Marc responded with a stiff edge to his voice. "Yes, well I remember all the free halvah you gave me…and the corned beef as well. I appreciate it. Look, please do me one last favor, and don't mention that you met me, or I was here…please. Well…I've got to go."

With that, Marc Silver left through the Dewitt Wallace Periodical Room doors. Stanley pulled his seat up and sat back down once again.

"He's *Meshugena*," Stanley whispered, using the Yiddish word for crazy.

"I can see that," Mahmoud was glad to agree.

"I can't believe he's Lisa's husband."

"And why can't you believe it? I have a son-in-law who is the exact Palestinian equivalent."

"But he's not tied up with the mob. They *own* Marc Silver."

"No, you're right about that. My son-in-law is not in the mob," Mahmoud considered. "Maybe in some group you wouldn't approve of, but not that one."

Stanley still couldn't believe the connection he had just discovered.

"Should I tell him?"

"I think he told you in so many words not to. At any rate, why tell him? Will David then save him from that life? What would be the purpose? Why should David worry? This man makes a living, I suppose. Would telling David make things better for him?"

"I guess you're right."

Having finished with the matter, they went back to reading their English and Arabic papers.

CHAPTER SEVENTEEN

One day later, the same black microfiber L.L. Bean scarf sat on the passenger seat of Lisa Silver's black Cadillac Escalade. Lindsey and Noah sat in the back seat, strapped into their seat belts and each in their theater-going outfits. Lindsey wore a pink frilly dress which peaked out from her winter coat, a dress almost worthy of the Cinderella musical they were looking forward to seeing at the Broadway Theater. Noah sported a little midnight blue coat and tie under his winter coat, likewise almost worthy of the prince. Lisa was checking her hair and lipstick in the rear-view mirror as they travelled north on I-95 into Manhattan.

"Make sure your seat belts are on. We're almost there."

A car honked as she almost cut in. She, like Marc, owned the road.

"We'll grab some lunch and then…that matinee at two. Is everyone excited?"

They answered together in the affirmative. Lindsay was particularly excited.

"Marissa is the *only* one in my class who's seen it. I'll be the next one."

Noah had another reason to be excited.

"I just like that we don't have to go to school today. Mommy, can we go to McDonald's?"

"*No no no,* Noah. We're not going there. And we're not telling Aunt Naomi that we *ever* go there. Do you understand?"

"Aunt Naomi?," Lindsay interjected.

"She knows," seven-year-old Noah interrupted. "Milk and meat cheeseburgers and everything."

His hands followed his words with something that looked like an umpire's safe sign, just to emphasize the point. He knew all about Orthodox Jews separating milk from meat, and not going to places like McDonald's.

"I don't care. We don't mention it. We don't *ever* mention it. Do you understand? Answer me."

"Aunt Naomi?," Lindsey asked again. "Where are we going now?"

"We're dropping something off with your Aunt Naomi at Macy's... something for Grand Pop."

"*Some* great day," Lindsay changed her tone to disappointment.

"It'll only take a minute."

"You always fight with her, and it takes a long time."

"Noah. Answer my question about McDonald's."

She glanced in the rear view mirror like Aunt Ida.

"Okay. We're probably not going to McDonald's anyway."

"No, we're not. We're going somewhere better."

Like Marc's license plate, Lisa's had special numbers and letters. The immense vehicle pulled up to the no parking zone outside of Macy's.

"Let's go. You can both say hi to your aunt. You haven't seen her for a month."

Lisa exited the Escalade with the scarf, and then retrieved the children from the Macy's side. It was approaching the noon hour, and the Manhattan street was packed with hungry winter-steam breathing pedestrians. Lisa and the children walked through the store doors and down to the basement level. Sure enough, there was Naomi, just finishing up with a customer. They waited for a moment or two, and then stepped forward. Naomi looked down to see Lindsay and Noah. She was a great lover of little children, and her niece and nephew were no exception. For her, children were the closest thing to the image of God, and her faith in mankind was always renewed when she was around them. It always amazed her how, no matter how often that image faded in a prior generation—her sister being a prime example—it always shown bright in the tiny examples of the next one.

"What a treat! My niece and nephew! Are you in New York for an adventure?"

"Yes," Noah looked up over the counter at his aunt. "Cinderella."

"Oh, in your own little corner in your own little room," Naomi quoted the Rodgers and Hammerstein tune.

"No. In a big theater, in the front row."

Naomi chuckled.

"Are you looking forward to it, Lindsay?"

"Yes, Aunt Naomi. My friend Marissa said it was good."

"I understand it is."

Lisa got down to business.

"This is for Dad so he doesn't get one of those colds again, when he walks to services on Shabbas."

"I could've gotten something here at a discount. Besides, he has scarves at home."

"Not like this one. This is a special L.L. Bean microfiber scarf."

"But I'm sure you didn't have to come all this way…"

That was about all Lisa could take of her sister's nicey-nicey nastiness.

"Just *give* it to him! If he has to walk in sub-zero temperatures to synagogue on Saturdays, he should wear this."

"Of *course* he's has to walk on Shabbas. What do you expect him to do?"

Their voices rose with every sentence. Lindsay knew this would happen. She tried to hide her face in her mother's coat, as Lisa's anger increased.

"Fine! That's why I got him the scarf, stupid! I love him just as much as you do, you know."

"I'm sure you do, and that you're *shomer Shabbas,* keeping it meticulously over there in Englewood, not driving, not turning on lights, especially where the synagogue is across the whole stupid town from your house! So I hope you got one each for you and Marc, too, for your Shabbas walk!"

Naomi knew she was being purposely mean to her only sister, her little sister, and she knew she was wrong. She felt horrible inside about it. On top of that, she was so worked up that she failed to notice a very special customer that had gotten in line behind Lisa and the children. Noah got the last word in just as she saw Darrin Brock, return box in hand.

"We go to McDonald's on Saturdays, but sometimes we walk."

Before Lisa could respond with a jab, Naomi interrupted.

"Darrin Brock. I'm so sorry to keep you waiting. You're such…such a loyal customer. This…this is my younger…my younger sister Lisa. We're just about finished with our transaction, aren't we, Lisa?"

Lisa turned to Darrin, her blood pressure still elevated.

"Yes, I suppose we are."

She eyed him up and down. Then she turned back to see that Naomi was clearly blushing. She turned back to him again and then back to Naomi again, then back to him once again."

"Nice to meet you. Okay. Well, we're out of here. We're going to the theater…after we hit the kosher deli."

"How lovely," Darrin said. "And these are your children?"

This was going on too long for Naomi, who was in no mood to have her dream world violently collide with the stark reality of her plain-and-princess relationship with Lisa.

"Yes, these are her adorable children Lindsay and Noah. I don't have any. Well…bye Lisa."

"Don't forget to give it to him," Lisa emphasized, staring Naomi down. Then Lisa and the children headed down the aisle and toward the escalator on the way to the waiting Escalade. Naomi turned to Darrin.

"Well…I hope you didn't hear that. Can I help you?"

"Yes, I think I did…and that's okay. This is from me…a genuine return to the housewares department from a not so close relative."

Naomi tried to be as professionally businesslike as she could be. After all, Darrin had no idea what her dream life was like. Maybe Aunt Ida had more than a hint, but not Darrin Brock. And somehow, Naomi knew that Aunt Ida wouldn't say anything to anyone, especially her father. So most likely things were safe. In front of Darrin, she could still choose to be the upright Jewish daughter of David Kaplan that she, in reality, was.

She removed a red and green Christmas coffee mug from its box, scanned the tag, and typed information into the word processor. All was going well. She was well hidden behind the Macy's computer, where she had originally met this Gentile prince who knew what the Hebrew word *Naomi* meant. She could rewind reality back in time and pretend she had never done anything crazy, like going all the way to Teaneck just to catch a glimpse of him. The Christmas mug helped.

But then she remembered that he knew her name meant *pleasant*, and also that the Naomi in the Bible ended up calling herself *Mara*, or bitter. How could he know those things? And furthermore, how could he know how well they both applied to her? Here she was, so cruel to Lisa just moments earlier, and right in front of *him!* He had told her she was more pleasant than bitter, but today she had been more bitter than pleasant, God forbid.

Just then, the oddest sensation overcame her, as if she was being scanned like the tag, revealed by someone with x-ray vision. Her guard dropped ever so slightly, and she peered out from behind the flat-screen. In that unguarded split second, she asked a question worthy of Lois Lane.

"Who *are* you?"

"What do you mean?"

She couldn't afford to fully open up her heart. So she tried to shut it down again and choose a professional demeanor.

"I mean…I was just curious as a Macy's customer, what is it you do… for a living? I'm just asking…as your friendly Macy's employee, that is."

He thought for a second or two, and then lowered his voice.

"Well…I'm a sort of policeman without a uniform, a detective, if you want to know the truth. I started years ago with the Giuliani administration. But I have to admit it's gotten pretty boring."

She realized now why he probably went into the *New York Times* building, perhaps to do some kind of investigating.

"I see. Actually, it sounds like very important work. Very interesting."

Against his better judgment, he let down his own guard to betray a little "bitterness" of his own.

"Believe me, it's not. It was different in the nineties, ten years after the Mafia's "five families" went to jail. There was still some cleaning up to do in the police department. But these days. I guess I'm just not too crazy about chasing has-been small time hoods. I'd rather help troubled kids than catch fading mobsters."

He was referring to the five mob bosses arrested in 1986, and dealing with the likes of Prima. But she didn't understand any of it. Still, she wanted to keep the conversation going.

"Well…I like this job here. You meet people, very nice people… like you, for instance. And my sister also sometimes, my sister whom I love…I *do* love her. We just…we're typical sisters. But we do love each other. Of course she's married to a good husband and provider…Marc Silver…and I'm not…not married. I myself never married. I never did. Oh well."

Why did she say that? She bit her lip in frustration and embarrassment. But he wasn't taking notice. His mind was elsewhere.

"With a "C" or with a "K"?

"I don't understand. What do you mean?"

"Nothing. I just wondered if it was Marc with a "C" or Mark with a "K.""

Oh. Marc Silver? With a "C." Why? I mean, almost no one spells it that way...but some Jews do, for some reason I never understood. He's Jewish. But you knew that."

"Yes, I understand. Do you know what he does for a living?"

This conversation was taking a strange turn, which was making her uncomfortable.

"Why do you ask?"

"Nothing. It's just that I know someone with that name..."

"Do you know him? It would certainly be a small world if you knew Marc, wouldn't it?"

"No...no, I probably don't know him. I'm sorry I asked. I'm sure it's just a coincidence."

"Well, Marc makes a good living...nothing to be ashamed of. He sells food to restaurants around here. They live sort of near you...in Englewood. I live with my father in Brooklyn. We live together in a...in a house...me and my father. We live together...the two of us, that is."

She was fidgeting nervously with her hands, folding the receipt over and over. He could sense that a customer had stepped in line behind him.

"Well, it turns out we both live with our parents. Interesting. Um... do I get a voucher or something?

"Oh...sorry. You get cash if you want it."

"Sure. That'll work."

"Whoopee. That's Macy's for you. It's really a great store. Just sign here."

She was trying to keep things intentionally light, although she was sure her heartbeat shown in her neck. She gave him the sheet that had arisen from the printer as she opened the drawer, taking the cash out and counting it. He signed the sheet.

"Well, I hope we meet again sometime. You're a very nice Macy's employee."

Things had returned to a businesslike status, which is where Naomi knew they should be. She extended her hand and shook his firmly.

"Goodbye."

"Goodbye."

As he left, he turned one last time and said with a smile, "I may visit you here again sometime soon…during a break in my day…just for some nice conversation."

"Sure. Anytime."

His last comment surprised and excited her. Perhaps she *would* see him again. She watched him for several seconds as he left, finally turning to the next customer.

SPRING

Chapter Eighteen

There are certain places in Manhattan where the only way to know for sure that spring has recently arrived is by the comfortably gentle five-to-ten mile an hour breeze on the faces, and sometimes bare arms, of the pedestrians. Those places are the ones with long concrete and stainless steel caverns, created by cloud-high buildings that admit very little direct sunlight and allow for very few trees. It was in one such place that Marc Silver parked his spotless black Mercedes, as usual, in the no parking zone.

Marc liked spring in New York much better than winter. It allowed him to work more quickly, like a car engine with thin warm motor oil flowing through its crankcase. He could, as they say, operate on all cylinders. And operate he did, maneuvering his car as he changed lanes and then changed again—loosely spinning the steering wheel with his index finger, flying from one mom-and-pop restaurant to another. Finally, he made his regular stop to see Prima.

Prima kept Marc waiting longer than usual. Consequently, he began to nervously swivel in the black leather chair he always chose, as he looked at his black suit-slacks and polished black shoes through the glass table. He wished he could look through Prima the same way.

After several minutes had gone by, an attractive young twenty-something woman came in to tell him Prima would be there soon. She reminded him of a nurse coming into the waiting room in a doctor's office. Indeed, Prima was a doctor of sorts, at least by way of examinations. While it was true that he sometimes treated Marc like a son, at other times he treated him like a patient being probed.

At last, Prima arrived with a big smile on his face and two large glum-looking bodyguards, one on each side. His grey spring silk suit was steak-knife thin and just as sharp. He walked over to a now standing Marc and extended his left hand. A small folder was in his right.

"You're looking good today, Marc. Nice suit."

"Your's too."

"Thank you. I love the spring, don't you? We can wear our suits outside without those ridiculously heavy overcoats. Sit down, please. Take a load off your feet, eh? You work too hard. Sit…please."

Prima sat in the adjacent chair and beckoned Marc to sit back down in his usual place. They ended up sitting knee-to-knee, which was disconcerting to Marc. Prima looked straight into his eyes.

"So Lisa's doing well?"

"Yes. She's fine."

"Spoiled, I suppose. They're all spoiled, when it comes down to it. I know my wife is, and I'm sure Lisa's no exception. And I bet Lindsay and Noah are growing like weeds, and cuter than ever."

"Yes…yes, they are…when I get the chance to see them."

"Well, we'll have to send you on a nice vacation sometime soon…the whole family. Would you like that? I have some contacts in Italy."

Right after that friendly comment, his smile morphed into a straight line.

"Well, we might as well do a little business while you're here…I mean besides the financial transaction. You can take care of that on the way out."

He placed the folder on the glass table and flipped it open with his right hand. A light grey shadow seemed to wash over his face. The top item in the folder lay exposed. It revealed a close-up picture of Darrin Brock which was taken at the Macy's returns counter. Naomi was in the background, out of focus and barely recognizable. Prima pointed at Darrin.

"You know who this is, I'm sure. You've seen this guy. I know you have."

"No...no, I don't...I don't know him."

The body guards leaned in. They weren't used to anyone disagreeing with Prima. He, however, leaned back and spoke deliberately slowly, one word at a time.

"Okay. I did *not* expect that answer."

He tossed the picture aside, revealing another one of Darrin Brock walking in what looked like the atrium of a Manhattan building. Marc drew near and glanced at it. He could clearly see that it was the same man. He looked up at Prima and shook his head. Prima sighed.

"Okay. This one will jog your memory."

He flipped the picture onto the floor. The bodyguard on his left picked it up and carefully placed it on top of the first one. The third picture was now exposed. We were back at the Macy's counter, and now not only Darrin Brock was clearly visible, but also Naomi and Lisa, who was standing just in front of him.

"My wife...and sister-in-law. But...I still don't know him."

Prima slammed his hand down on the glass table, his palm leaving an imprint on the surface. Marc flinched. His heart jumped and began to race. The bodyguards were unmoved. Prima moved to within a hair's breadth of Marc's face.

"You know what I think?"

Marc tried not to shake. That would make him look guilty when he didn't even know what this was all about. Prima repeated himself.

"Do you know what I think, my friend?"

Marc shook his head minimally, holding his breath. Prima paused and looked in Marc's eyes again. Then he suddenly stood up.

"I think you've never seen this guy. That's what I think. I think you've never been introduced. What do you think about that?"

The bodyguards pulled back and relaxed their bodies. Prima slapped his hands on his sides and let out a sharp laugh, releasing some of Marc's tension like air escaping from a rapidly shrinking balloon.

"Okay, you guys can leave now."

The bodyguards left the room like robots who had been given an audio cue.

"You know what else I think?"

He repeated himself again.

"Do you know what else I think, my friend?"

This time Marc sat motionless. Prima repeatedly pressed his finger

78

on the images of Naomi and Darrin.

"I think that ugly *sister-in-law* of yours is telling this *man* things about you…this man, Darrin Brock…you don't know him? You've never heard of him?"

"I told you…no."

"Everything could blow up…in our faces. In our *faces!*" He then slowly repeated those last three words.

"In…our…faces!"

Marc was really confused now. Was Naomi even capable of telling anybody anything about him, or anyone else for that matter? All she seemed capable of doing was chanting prayers with that miserable grating voice, walking back and forth to synagogue, and selling housewares in that stupid department—and oh yes, seeing that schlemiel Marvin. As he continued, Prima pointed a finger several times at Marc.

"And I'll tell you what else I think. I think she's working with that wife…that cute sexy little wife of yours. And I'm rarely wrong, Marc. I'm very rarely wrong. Rarely meaning *never.*"

The thought instantly popped into Marc's mind that Prima had been wrong as recently as a minute before when he was sure he, Marc, knew the man in the picture. But then again, Prima seemed so confident about this. It begged the question, who was this mysterious man, and why was he meeting with Naomi and Lisa? Prima sat down next to Marc again. He spoke more thoughtfully now.

"We have to stop this, and we will. You know Marc, it's fortunate that I'm a gentlemen. My father was a gentleman. One of the old school. And I'm a gentleman too. Of course not everyone is."

Prima hesitated, not sure if he should say the next thing that was on his mind. But he proceeded, which he found himself doing more and more lately—unlike in years past. And he was pretty confident that no one else was listening to this particular conversation.

"Unfortunately, we don't run the whole show anymore. Circumstances force us to do business with some others…for instance, the Russians. They have their *own* way of doing business…not quite like gentlemen. But they *do* bring in some very good fruit from South America, don't they?"

Marc didn't know about Russians, any more than he knew about Darrin Brock. But he nodded nervously anyway. Prima, however, wasn't watching. He had shut his eyes after his last remark. Then he opened them even wider than before.

"But what does that matter? Let's get back to your friend Darrin Brock. Oh, that's right. You don't know him...do you?"

"No, I don't. I swear, Prima. I've never even seen him, except in those pictures you just showed me."

Prima paused again, his eyes examining Marc's like a scanner.

"Well, we can't have him talking to your wife and her sister, or more likely them talking to him...and wrecking your job...and mine...and more...much more...can we? After all, he's kind of like the competition. We can't let him win."

Prima put his arm on Marc's shoulder and pressed down lightly.

"You know, I've always observed that your wife Lisa had a big mouth and was just way too curious. Just an observation. But of course, I've always told you not to talk business with her, haven't I?"

Marc shot up, protesting.

"And I never have, Prima. Never. I swear. She doesn't know *anything* about anything. I know she doesn't! Not from me. I promise you. Look, I don't know what this is about. I really don't. But she doesn't...and I never..."

"She's a smart girl...got it up here."

Prima pointed to his cranium.

"Up here, and just everywhere else in that cute little body of hers... *capiche?* All right. Well...we'll see. Go back to work. Have a beautiful rest of this spring day."

With that, Prima shook Marc's hand hard and walked out of the room. Marc's hand fell limp to his side. He was drained. But he was also relieved to get through another meeting with Prima. Now he could go back out and be king of the road and ruler of the restaurants on this gentle Manhattan spring day. He gave the receptionist in an adjacent room the envelope full of cash and headed down the hall to the elevator.

CHAPTER NINETEEN

If there is a direct opposite to a bustling Manhattan spring day, it's a lush Prospect Park spring day. Designed by Central Park architect Fredrick Olmsted, it was opened to the public a few years after that famous park, in 1872.

That was about ten years before the menorah first sat on the table of David Kaplan's ancestor in Kiev.

Prospect Park was and is the crown jewel of Brooklyn. And one of the finest rubies in the Prospect Park crown is the Cherry Esplanade. Located in the Brooklyn Botanic Gardens section of the park, cherry trees line the charming Victorian walking trail that runs through that part of the Gardens. The cherry trees fully blossom in early spring and create a blushing pink celestial ceiling. The sun shines through the branches, leaving shadow patterns on the little road-path. You would think you were in a pastoral English countryside scene painted by Thomas Gainsborough or Joshua Reynolds. But you would actually be in Brooklyn on a gentle early spring day. And it was on one such day—as usual, on a Sunday—that David Kaplan and his daughter Naomi strolled arm in arm under the cherry trees.

Their *cherry blossom walk,* as they referred to it, occurred for two successive weeks a year at most. There usually wasn't room for a third week because the cherry blossoms died as quickly as they had blossomed, like the *flesh that withers as grass* in the Isaiah 40 passage David knew by heart.

This particular Sunday was the first of their two such walks, the one they looked forward to most. After David quoted the Isaiah passage in Hebrew while gazing up at the all-too-alive blossoms, he took his daughter's arm and proceeded to open his heart.

"I love both of my daughters equally. You are both special to me, each in your own way."

Naomi waited for his next words.

"But I'm not fooled. You are the one who will carry on the legacy of traditional Judaism in this family, a legacy that goes back to the Kiev shtetl, the small village we came from, and then all the way back to the giving of the Torah...to Moshe Rabbeynu himself."

He paused again as they walked at a leisurely pace between the cherry trees.

"Don't misunderstand me. I'm very thankful that your sister has a Jewish husband, two gorgeous children...a Jewish home with a mezuzah hanging at the front door. But...I know that Marc doesn't *daven* the traditional morning prayer, or don the *teffilin* leather straps on his arm or forehead...or even go to synagogue more than a few times a year. These things I know. And Lisa doesn't even follow the monthly ritual bath *niddah* laws. That I know too. We didn't raise her to neglect her Jewish responsibilities. But children have their own minds. They do things their *own* way. You, however..."

He turned toward her for a moment and affectionately pulled her arm closer to him as they walked.

"You have chosen a different path. You carry on the tradition."

Naomi knew he was waiting for her response. She too paused for quite a while before expressing what was in her heart. She didn't want to dishonor her father's words. But she had been raised to share openly with him. After they were three-quarters through the pink canopy above them, she finally spoke.

"In a few years, the laws of niddah and the monthly visit to the *mikveh* pool won't matter for me any more. And you'll have an old dried up barren childless woman as a daughter...like an old prune from a left over *tsimis* carrot dish from someone *else's* wedding...a Sarah with no

Isaac. Better you should have had a son."

Momentarily disconcerted, he paused again before speaking. They were almost at the end of the trees—just about finished their immersion in their own unique pink blossom *mikveh* pool, their long awaited yearly spring celebration. Yet this was turning out to be no celebration.

"Naomi..."

He slowed their walk down with his arm.

"You are better than ten sons to me, and you know that very well. As Moshe Rabbeynu said, *'Bitzelem Adonai bara oh-to, zachar oo-nikeyva...* in the image of God He made them, man and woman.' You are my heir, and much more."

Naomi knew what was coming next. It was at times like this that David Kaplan would mention one of his favorite rabbi-heroes, and tell Naomi a story she had heard since she was a very little girl, usually at bed time. Though she knew what he was about to say, she always loved hearing him say it. David was about to refer to Rabbi Yisrael Meir Kagen, using his more popular name *The Chofetz Chaim,* which appropriately meant *desire for life.*

Kagen was born in Belarus in 1838, and lived in a city called Radun during 1882, when the brass menorah first graced the dining room table in the Kiev Kaplan household.

"The Chofetz Chaim knew the Jewish legacy that a woman such as yourself could carry. Even the ancient rabbis, may their memory be blessed, did not encourage women to study Torah."

He sometimes added "may their memory be blessed" to honor the memory of the sages and rabbis. However, at times he added it when saying something not so positive about them, as if to remind the hearer that there were also overwhelmingly positive things to say on their behalf. This was one of those occasions. And Kagen would be pleased with such a gracious caveat, since he himself wrote much on the subject of the evil tongue, or gossip.

"Yes, as I was saying...and I know you've heard this before...but to remind you, the Chofetz Chaim, giant of a rabbi that he was, did not agree with the sages on this subject. When he was expected to rail against the news of the *Beit Ya-akov* schools, which educated women in *Talmud-Torah,* he instead marched through the streets and rejoiced."

He squeezed Naomi's arm as he looked at her.

"You learn quickly for a reason, Naomi...because HaShem, the Holy One of Israel, wants you to learn and carry on the tradition. You will impart it to others, your nephew and niece perhaps…your future observant Jewish husband…God knows. But you *will* carry it."

There was nothing else for Naomi to say. When she was with her father, she always loved listening more than speaking. But she also knew when it was time to speak. This was not one of those times, especially because she was harboring secret hidden dream/desires which she herself was fearful of and which she knew he would disapprove of.

"I love to hear you tell that story," was all she could say as they reached the end of the cherry trees. And she reached over and kissed her father on the cheek.

CHAPTER TWENTY

By the time Marc slipped into bed that Monday evening, he was more exhausted than usual. He had spent a full day on the street. Mondays tended to be the busiest days for him. The restaurants ordered more after the weekend in preparation for the coming week. But there was an added reason for the greater exhaustion. He couldn't shake off the oppressive anxiety that had haunted him every second of every minute since his last encounter with Prima toward the end of the previous week.

Lisa lay on her side, her back to him. He lay on his back, sheets thrown aside, and looked up at the reflection of moonlight on the high ceiling. Then he turned toward her and quickly back again. His thoughts seemed almost loud enough for her to hear.

How appropriate. She's turned her back on me. Who is this I'm living with? When will the knife enter my back?

Suddenly, Lisa turned.

"You're home. What time is it?"

"Late…that is, after midnight."

"I'm up…and the children are asleep."

"So?"

She reached over to kiss him on the mouth. Instantly, he sprung out of bed, landing on his feet like an olympic gymnast. Lisa sat up.

"What's wrong with you? You usually have to beg me. Are you a crazy man?"

"I'm…I'm not in the mood. I have a splitting headache."

"Isn't that supposed to be my line?"

"I have to get something in my stomach. I need something to eat."

"With a bad headache? You'll throw up."

"I mean, some Advil…or something…and maybe some hot tea. I'll fix it for myself. You get some sleep."

He walked out of the room. Lisa looked at the clock and lay back down. Marc knew he couldn't sleep now even if he wanted to. He went downstairs and walked into the den. Lisa's phone lay on the kitchen counter, and he could see it through the dark silver grey space between the two rooms. He walked over to it and, looking back toward the hall, picked it up. He had to power it up, which took more time than he had the patience for.

"Come on, come on. Hurry up!," he whispered to himself.

It seemed too dangerous to look through her phone while he was standing right there. He went into the hall powder room and locked the door, flipping on the light and sitting on the top-quality aluminum toilet seat. He closed the bathroom door with his foot. Finally, the phone powered up. Fortunately, he knew her iPhone passcode. Within a few seconds he was spinning through her phone history, one day, two days, three days, four. Nothing suspicious. *What was his name? Brock, something Brock…Darrin.* He always did have a good memory for names he had heard just once, and even more so when they came from the lips of Prima. But the name wasn't listed. Then he looked for suspicious phone numbers. He recognized the numbers that had no names attached. None of them seemed suspicious.

He left the bathroom, powered the phone off, and placed it back on the table in the exact position he'd found it. Then he headed back to the den and sat down at the computer. That too took more time to boot up than he had patience for.

"Come on…come on!," he whispered to himself. He looked back at the front hall and then back again. The screen came to life. He knew Lisa's Gmail password. He had just gotten into her email when he thought he heard her at the top of the stairs. He had to make sure she wasn't coming down to check on him. With what he knew now, it was imperative that he not allow her to see what he was up to. Not that he hardly knew anything. *There must be something to this,* he thought, *or Prima wouldn't be so concerned.* He walked as quietly as a cat, the balls of his feet leaving small impressions in the rug. Creeping upstairs, he went over to the bedroom and peered in. She seemed to have gone back to sleep, just as he suggested. He walked past the half-open doors of the children's' rooms. They too were sound asleep. He quietly crept back downstairs.

Back at the computer, he quickly ran through Lisa's emails. Nothing again. He went to Facebook and typed in *Darin* Brock, *Daren* Brock, *Darren* Brock. There it was under *Darrin.* He recognized the picture. There was no profession listed—in fact, no personal information. He scanned the posts. Some seemed to have Bible verses and links to some ministers, and others were about Alzheimer's Disease. There were even one or two posts about Israel, and a few about Russia. Was there some kind of an underworld connection there? Was he connected to the people Prima mentioned?

All of a sudden, he heard Lisa coming downstairs. He couldn't turn the computer off in time, but he could leave the Facebook site.

"What are you doing on the computer so late? You have work tomorrow. I thought you said you had a headache. That screen will make it worse."

"It's better. I was just checking my email, and I didn't see anything worth looking at, so I shut it down."

"Guilty conscience?," she teased.

He turned and stared her down.

"What? Why are you saying that?"

She was startled by his response.

"I…I don't know. What's the matter with you? Hey, I hope you weren't watching pornography, especially when I was right here ready for you. That would be disgusting."

"Of course not," he barked. "I don't watch that stuff. And my conscience is perfectly clear. What about yours?"

"It's just fine. Why are you acting so strange?"

"Maybe there's a good reason."

"I don't know what in the world you're talking about. Come on. Let's not argue."

As she took him by the hand and led him to their marriage bed, he realized that Prima must indeed have been onto something. Otherwise, why would she ask about his conscience? Apparently, she was capable of anything. She might even be part of a competitive organization—or worse. He felt like he was being led upstairs by Mata Hari, the spy under his own roof. It hadn't dawned on him how her life and limb could possibly be endangered by Prima's people. He was too busy thinking about his own neck. When it came to her, all he could think of was, *how could it be that I didn't really know the woman I've lived with all these years? And how could I ever trust her again?* He realized it would be too risky to bring up Darrin Brock's name with her, at least for now. But somehow, he had to figure out a way to find out more about this guy, and what if anything Lisa knew about the restaurant supply work. But how? As soon as that thought came to him, Naomi's name and homely face followed on it's heels. What did she have to do with all of this?

CHAPTER TWENTY-ONE

From behind the Housewares register, Naomi could tell it was spring by the colorful blouses and dresses lining the Macy's aisles. They were full of primary colors, and royal purple. She could pretend she was walking through the Art Deco-influenced Channel Gardens at the Rockefeller Plaza, a place she enjoyed almost as much as the Cherry Esplanade—except that her father wasn't by her side when she took a spring walk there. She always tried to get there for at least one lunch break each year during Passover, when all the flowers were in full bloom. And here it was already the middle of the week of *Pesach*—Hebrew for Passover—and she hadn't made the trip yet.

On this particular day she planned to eat her matzah, complete with a side of leftover traditional *charoses*—the apple mixture representing pyramid-building mortar—on a quiet little bench at Herald Square, adjacent to Macy's. Her female Chabad acquaintances, with their *sheitel* wigs of various shapes and sizes, would never even think of darkening the door of a department store during the eight days of Passover, lest they inadvertently come into contact with even a small morsel of leaven. They stayed home, even away from the subway. They could afford to stay home. They didn't have to work. But Naomi adhered to her father's view, and simply avoided restaurants during Passover week. She trusted her father's wise decisions about issues like this. She was thankful for his quiet steady guidance, and his encyclopedic knowledge of all things Jewish.

As Naomi waited for the next customer to show up at the counter, the angle of her view from behind the counter triggered the memory of her sister Lisa standing in front of Darrin, with Lindsay and Noah in tow. An unexpected shot of bitter gall rose in her, accompanied by a few choice thoughts.

How dare she interfere with the only pleasure this washed up alteh moid has...stealing my one and only dream. She had no business being here when Darrin Brock showed up. She had no business flirting with him! I would treat him so much better than she treats Marc. She didn't even deserve to lay eyes on him with those filthy adulterous eyes of hers.

She was shocked that she was capable of such cruel thoughts about her sister. It was truly the *yetzer hara,* the evil inclination! If she were to examine the origin of the thoughts more deeply (which she wasn't in the mood for), she would have to admit that she was basically jealous that the *Yetzer Tov,* the good inclination for marriage fulfillment with a devoted husband, was fulfilled for Lisa but *not* for her. Try as hard as she could to stop it, the envy ended up seeping out in another thought or two.

This is like that movie Amadeus. She has something she doesn't deserve, and I don't have something I do deserve. I hate her!

Naomi was more shocked now than before. What would her father think of such evil? And what would he suggest as a remedy? He might tell her to entreat the Almighty for her own husband. He had suggested prayers for other things, like a Mi-shebeirach prayer when she was sick. But he never shared a prayer for this with her. She had once met a group of women who recited five specific psalms a day for forty days as an act of prayer for husbands. However, she didn't have time for that now, behind the housewares register. Still, it wouldn't hurt to pray *something.* She quickly bowed her head and began to pray the introductory words every Jew from Reform to Orthodox knows.

"*Baruch Ata Adonai...*Blessed art thou oh Lord..."

"Are you okay?"

Naomi knew the familiar voice. She slowly raised her head and opened her eyes.

"Do you need to go to the bathroom again? I'll man the register."

"No...I was...I'm fine. I was just...taking a moment to...pray a prayer...sort of."

Darrin smiled broadly.

"Prayer is a good thing. I'm sorry I interrupted you."

She pulled herself together.

"No. It's my fault. I'm supposed to be working. Can I help you today... Mr...Mr. Brock...that's it, isn't it?," she pretended.

"Yes. With all the customers you see, it's amazing that you remember my name. And you're Naomi, right? Pleasant Naomi. I could never forget that...from the book of Ruth."

Her blushing continued as her heart rate rose, a condition she felt at a loss to conceal. Her only recourse was instant professional behavior.

"Yes...that's right, Mr. Brock. How can I help you today?"

Naomi continued to fight every screaming vital sign in her body to be as business-like as possible. And while she was fulfilling her professional responsibilities, Darrin Brock was doing the same thing, pursuing information about her brother-in-law's connections. Normally he would have gotten down to business already. After all, he was a skilled investigator. But he couldn't bring himself to approach this particular situation the usual way. He decided on the spot that, because they had met under such unusual circumstances, he would use an unorthodox approach to ease into things. And that approach involved a subject he had a true passion for since he was a young man. It happened to be the Jewish people, and all things Jewish. At some point in the near future, he would change the subject and interview her about Marc Silver.

"Yes, you can help me. I just have some questions about you and your family...um...some things about your Jewish upbringing that I'm curious about. Jewish history and culture have always fascinated me, since I was a boy. My parents had that same interest and passed it on to me."

Naomi was beginning to melt, so she tried to freeze instead by sounding suspicious.

"That's ridiculous. Why would you do that?"

That didn't come out right. She knew she was sounding too harsh. He, on the other hand, realized he had to explain himself better.

"I know it sounds unusual. But it's not unheard of for people like myself to have a heart for these things."

"People like you?"

"Well, you know, committed Christians like myself."

That wasn't what Naomi wanted to hear. She iced over.

"Well...I don't know what to say, Mr. Brock. I mean, isn't religion a personal thing? It doesn't seem like my religious life should be any of your business, to tell you the truth."

Too harsh again! What if he was dallying with the possibility of eventual conversion? And here she was, foolishly shutting a miraculous door in his face. He, on the other hand, had to think fast on his feet to keep the conversation going.

"I'm so sorry. I don't mean to pry. But...look, it must almost be lunch time. You know Ben's Deli on West 38th Street? Can we talk over lunch? There are just some things I think you can help me with. That's all. Believe me, my intentions are totally honorable."

Naomi's heart was trembling in her neck. She tried to turn to the side farthest from the pounding vessel.

"Well, I don't know. I've never been asked anything like this before. I'm somewhat uncomfortable."

"I understand."

Her heart screamed in her chest, "Don't let him get away! Don't let him get away!"

"Well...I do get off for lunch soon, but I can't go *there* today. For one thing, it's closed."

"Oh. I never noticed that. I just passed it last week, and it looked very much open. I'm sorry to hear that."

Once again, Naomi's voice got involuntarily colder. He certainly didn't know the first thing about Passover.

"No, they didn't close like *that*. It's Passover. They close for eight days...and anyway, I don't go to *any* restaurants during that time, even open ones."

She whispered the next sentence, though she knew there was nothing to be ashamed of.

"See, I brought my lunch...matzah. I'm sure you must have seen that before."

She pulled a brown paper bag out from under the counter and held it up for him to see. Now *he* blushed slightly. How could he have missed the fact that the kosher delis were closed on Passover?

"Of course. I should have remembered that. Oh well...let's just take a walk then. You can take your lunch with you. I've got just the place in mind. It's a magnificent spring day and we can sit outside."

Naomi felt fear rise to further fuel her already racing heart. Could this be a dangerous Gentile stranger, ready to take advantage of her when no one was looking, to grab her and drag her into a back alley or den of sin somewhere? Her father had warned her about such men, and about occasions just like this.

No, that didn't seem right. This was a *nice* man. He had helped her, and he cared for his parents. He seemed like a real mensch in his own Gentile way. And yet, she knew she should not be with a Gentile man at *all*, not even a nice one—maybe *especially* not a nice one. She shouldn't even be *seen* with a Gentile man, especially on Passover. It was wrong, just plain wrong!

In the middle of these thoughts, she once again impulsively responded from somewhere at the base of her brainstem, involuntarily grasping at the hope that he would end up converting and becoming a better Jew than Marc.

"Yes. I'll just be a minute."

She disappeared into a back room down the hall, and within a few minutes came out, bag lunch in hand. She handed off the register to another sales person, and Naomi and Darrin proceeded to walk down the aisle full of colorful dresses and out of the store, without exchanging a word.

As they traveled from one short block to the next, through the avalanche of Manhattan lunch-time crowds, Naomi wondered if the sweet warm exhaust fumes mixed with gentle spring air had caused her to hallucinate. Could it be that she was actually walking beside the man whose hand she had been yearning to hold since December 26th? What would it feel like to hold it now? She momentarily challenged herself to just abandon all decorum—if not sanity—and grab and squeeze it tightly as they pressed on toward wherever it was they were going. So what if breakfast's leavened buttered toast and sausage grease dripped from each well manicured fingertip? Such was the wild fantasy that possessed her. But of course, she restrained herself.

Within another five minutes, Rockefeller Plaza came into view, and with it the explosive color of the Channel Gardens. Just then Naomi, in an involuntary flash of praise to HaShem, began to count up the miracles that only He Himself could have arranged.

Number one, *Darrin showed up just as she was praying for a husband.*

Number two, *she was just thinking about the Channel Gardens while she eyed the aisles of flowered spring dresses.*

Number three, *Darrin asked her out to lunch.*

Just as her reverie reached it's climax, the gaudy topiary Easter Bunny, his forest-green arms stretched out before the Christian gods and a huge pink flower-filled Easter egg balanced on his nose, appeared before her like Aaron's Golden Calf. In one split second, her interpretation of the day's events was transformed from heavenly to hellish. Darrin pointed to a bench near the bunny.

"Come on. Let's sit over there at that bench."

Naomi yielded like a Passover lamb led to the slaughter. She knew in her rational mind that the Easter display was just a powerless American flower statue created for the delight of little children—like her father's Santa hat—and all she had to do was to ignore it. But that wouldn't be easy. After all, she wouldn't have minded being close enough to smell the flowers that made up the *egg,* if she wasn't about to sit down with a Christian man who undoubtedly celebrated Easter. If the topiary bunny had any power at all, it was the power of association—her association with Darrin Brock.

They sat down on the bench. Naomi knew she needed to be back at work within a half hour or less, so she had to start her lunch soon. She took the piece of matzah and small red Tupperware container of traditional apple charoses out of the bag, and then suddenly realized that she could fulfill the mitzvah of sharing the matzah with this *stranger* in her midst, just as the *Ha Lachma*—a hymn dedicated to sharing the *bread of affliction*—encourages. *Let all who are hungry come and share the Passover,* it intones. *Darrin must be hungry,* she thought. A horrendous sin was morphing into a glorious mitzvah, one her father would approve of, just like he approved of visiting sick children on Christmas—and with his Santa hat yet. She broke the matzah, which was coated with kosher for Passover margarine, and gingerly handed a piece to Darrin.

"Are you sure? That doesn't leave much a of a lunch for you. I can grab a burger later."

She tried not to betray any discomfort with his plans, which were totally within bounds for him, at least at this point in his life. He turned to her, buttered matzah in hand.

"So...you have a sister...the one I met...and she's married to Marc Silver...and has two children."

The last person on the entire planet Naomi wanted to talk about was Lisa. Her mouth twisted involuntarily. Darrin took that to mean he should go back to his original plan. He waved his free hand and spoke through a small mouthful of buttered matzah.

"I'm sorry. I don't know why I brought that up. I was just curious, I guess. What I *really* meant to ask you about was your upbringing. I'm so fascinated by Judaism and Israel, and all of that. So were you always Orthodox?"

Naomi was at once both uncomfortable and immediately delighted with the question. She wondered why he was so curious about Jewish people, and yet she was more than ready to give him an answer. Perhaps this was the open door she had been dreaming about for weeks. She took a quick breath and started.

"Of course. Everyone in my neighborhood is Orthodox. Everyone I know is...well, almost everyone."

She didn't want to lie, but she also didn't want to bring up Lisa and Marc...or Aunt Ida.

"*Basically* everyone, actually. And we all love the way we were raised. I mean, you probably like the way you were raised...but, how can I explain it? Let me put it this way. If you knew my father, you'd know why I love being an Orthodox Jew."

She came dangerously close and looked deep into his baby blue eyes, eyes like those she'd seen in movies. He could detect a glowing spark of joyous excitement in hers.

"And you would *adore* him. You would fall in love with him right away, and to fall in love with him is to fall in love with Judaism. See, if you took all the wisdom of all the sages...do you know about the sages?"

"I think so...Maimonides, um...Rashi...Akiba...those sages?"

The spark in her eyes turned into a fire. He knew about the sages! He was halfway there.

"Yes! You know them! Are you sure you're not secretly Jewish?"

"No, I don't think so."

"Have you read them?"

"In college I have. I took some religion classes. And I still study them sometimes."

"Really? But have you *really* read them?"

He grinned ever so slightly.

"Maybe not...not like you have, I'm sure."

Naomi glowed with anticipation. She drew even closer, much too close, especially for Passover week. Her heart skipped a beat.

"I wish you could study with my father sometime. Well, like I was saying, if you took all the wisdom of the sages, and put them all together in a big…a big…scroll, or something like that…that would be my father…the wisest man in New York…no, in the whole world."

"He sounds like a wonderful man."

"He *is*. You'll have to meet him. He's retired. But he used to be the best Linotype operator at the *New York Times*. You'd want to convert in a second if you spent time with him."

The last comment was way out of line, maybe even insulting. She knew that Jews shouldn't try to proselytize people like some Christians do. And she'd already crossed that line of propriety. Darrin just chuckled softly—after he filed away the Linotype information in the back of his mind. The gentleness that first attracted her emanated through him like the painting of a haloed saint at the Metropolitan Museum of Art, at once alien and yet noble.

"I'm not sure they'd have me," he said, referring to her comment about conversion. "But I will tell you that I am passionate about God's miraculous hand on His chosen people, throughout history and today. And I will also tell you that I hate anti-Semitism, and I'm not quiet about it."

Naomi was taken aback by that comment. She'd never heard a Christian, let alone a Gentile, talk like that. And she didn't quite know how to respond. For his part, he knew he'd missed his chance to bring up Marc Silver. He had long since left his professional approach behind. And yet something inside him said that was okay—for now.

Naomi stood up.

"Well, I've got to get back to work."

He stood up as well.

"I guess we both have to go. That was very helpful. Thank you for telling me about your father. I hope to meet him sometime, and to see you again as well. Well…as I said, I've got an appointment I've got to get to."

Naomi reached out and shook his not-kosher-for-passover hand in a very business-like manner, just as she had greeted him earlier from behind the register. And then just like that, they parted ways.

Darrin had to get over to the criminal courts on Centre Street, then back to the *New York Times* to check some archives not available online or at police headquarters. As he walked toward the subway station, he resolved in his mind that he would call on Naomi again in the near future—and he would definitely bring up Marc Silver. That was settled. But he knew that something else *wasn't* settled. And he also knew what it was.

Thus far, he hadn't been willing to admit to himself just how much he enjoyed spending time with this sweet forty-something Orthodox Jewish woman from Brooklyn. But now his feelings were too obvious to ignore. Of course, he was keenly aware that he could never pursue any real relationship with her even if he wanted to. He had his own deep spiritual commitment. Almost since he was able to talk, his mother periodically taught him about unequal yoking, from 2 Corinthians 6:14. He would grow up to meet and marry a committed Jesus-loving believer. That made total sense to him. After all, as another Bible verse from Ecclesiastes asks, *How can two walk together unless they are agreed?* Yet, in spite of Lester and Velma's hopeful expectations, the wedding never took place. As he navigated the streets of Manhattan on his way to the subway station, Darrin mused about the reasons for this.

As a charming and cute—yet gangly—teenager, Darrin had his pick of church girls to spend time with. In time, he even dated a few of them. But those dates were always painful, and ended awkwardly. He was too shy to bring up anything more than the pastor's sermon, about which his date always had better things to say than he did. And when he would finally drop the girl off at her house, he could never even bring himself to kiss her on the cheek. He would just shake her hand like he was closing the deal—except that the deal was never closed. He never dated any girl more than once during those years.

In college, he was too busy studying criminal justice to date frequently. And when he did end up taking a woman out, he found he had very little in common with her—besides a penchant for police work. All of those dates ended up falling flat as well. By his last year of graduate school, he put dating on the shelf. The truth was, he had hoped to find a *high school sweetheart* in his church that he could stay close to through college, graduate school, and eventual matrimony—like his friend Edward Stiles. He and his wife did indeed find each other in high school, attended the same church, and were still happily married in their late forties—with three children and two grandchildren. But such was not the fate of Darrin Brock.

Even during his early professional years working under the Rudy Giuliani administration, Darrin found no romantic success. He believed his job incurred the kind of dangers he would not want a wife to endure, especially while the mafia bosses—or their free surrogates—still threatened the welfare of the city. So he avoided serious relationships. He was well aware that ten years earlier, before he worked for the department, Mafia boss John Gotti had tried to put out a contract on then District Attorney Giuliani. That's when all five heads of the key families ended up with hundreds of years of jail time. Things were somewhat safer in the early nineties, but never safe.

Then, after those threats finally diminished, he found himself helping his father nurse his mother though her several years-long illness. Now he was forty-eight, and had just about given up all hope of finding *the right one.*

By the time Darrin arrived at the subway entrance, he made a conscious choice to bury these unproductive thoughts. His trained eyes scanned the crowd around him as he headed down the steps and through the turnstiles, ticket in hand. As he entered the train, the eyes of a man entering through the next set of doors caught his. Instinctively, he recognized him as one of the many Russians he'd run across in the course of his business, one of those who made a serious effort to look more Cossack than Jewish—with his hair cut and combed to look like a cross between a rug and a hairbrush, and stereotypical sun glasses. He always thought it was ridiculous that these Russian gangsters stuck out so, like Mormon missionaries. But he also realized that they probably wanted it that way, like they owned the world and had nothing to hide.

He felt something oddly strange about this chance encounter. Could it be that he was being followed? Why would they follow him, someone dealing with small time extortion rackets run by yesterday's left-over Italians? The Russians weren't his responsibility, and therefore he never considered them his business. He walked through various cars just to see what would happen. The man seemed to follow him for a short distance, and then disappeared. He wondered what violent crimes this man may have been guilty of. After all, the Russians had no scruples, and not much of a code. They all seemed to have a violent side, although for some reason they also always seemed to evade justice—certainly not like the Giuliani days. And there were no "families," like the five from the eighties. Of course, he figured there had to be *some* kind of organization, or it wouldn't be *organized* crime—different from the Italians but still something. Yet, as brutal as they were and as much as they had their plants in the government, they generally stayed away from the police department—as far as he knew.

He got off the train. That episode was over. It was time to get on with his day. He had some research ahead of him.

CHAPTER TWENTY-TWO

Marvin knew how to get around New York using public transportation. He was actually a pretty bright fellow in his own way. He just never did anything much with it. His mother used to bemoan the fact that as a young child he never applied himself in school. He was too busy watching the *Three Stooges* on TV while eating Keebler crackers with a *schmear* of peanut butter on each one. He got to be pretty good with a butter knife, so good in fact that he became too heavy to qualify for sports activities. Consequently, he ended up spending a lot of time home alone, which made for more TV watching and snacking. Only on Shabbat did he refrain from the Stooges and the *schmearing*, until adulthood brought a wider diet and variety of television shows.

No one realized that Marvin had an almost photographic memory. In fact, he barely realized it himself. Therefore, he never used it to his advantage in school, which meant he never received a formal education beyond high school. Although it was never investigated, some of his peculiar tendencies may have been attributable to the mild end of the autistic spectrum. But it didn't cross his mother's mind to have him tested, nor the faculty at the small Orthodox school he attended.

However, as an adult, Marvin did at times use his unusual powers to his own advantage. His navigation of the New York City Transit System proved to be a perfect example. He never had to look at the maps on the subways or buses. He stored the whole tangled mess in his head, laid out in pictures that looked like a bundle of geometric neurons. He knew every stop on every line, and all the connections between the lines. So when he wanted to visit David Kaplan, he could hop on the subway anywhere in New York and, like a human GPS, end up there. Not that he actually had to travel the length of the Island on this day. He lived in Brooklyn, so he only had to travel on one subway line for ten minutes.

Marvin never made a habit of visiting David unless he was also visiting Naomi. He didn't feel comfortable carrying on a one-on-one conversation with him. There was no way he could put his best foot forward in that environment, and end up recommending himself as Naomi's future husband—that is, without stumbling over *both* feet. So he always tried to make sure Naomi was in the room when he visited.

However, this overcast spring day would be an exception. The ride to Teaneck and back with his Aunt Ida had driven him to desperate measures. Naomi had claimed that her father didn't think they were a perfect match, which Marvin figured was another way of saying they were no match at all. Although he was by no means accustomed to talking man-to-man with *any* adult male—let alone David Kaplan—he saw no other choice in this case. In fact, he began to feel strangely proud of himself for actually having the backbone to travel ten minutes on the subway and knock on the door of his possible future father-in-law. But he still almost backed out as he approached the station. And as he moved forward, he half hoped that David Kaplan wouldn't be home when he got there.

In spite of his hesitancy, he made it to the block of the Kaplan house, then to the house itself, and then to the front door. He took a deep breath and knocked, giving himself about thirty seconds before he left. David was in the front hallway and opened the door almost immediately. He was surprised to see Marvin standing there in his black Macy's Yankees t-shirt and the ball cap which Naomi had given him, as well as his cheap Wrangler husky jeans.

"Marvin. Is everything okay? Is Naomi okay?"

"She works days."

"Yes, I know that Marvin. So she's alright?"

"She's at Macy's."

"I know. So she's okay."

"The problem is, I haven't talked to her for a while."

Marvin didn't know what came next. He had memorized what he *should* do, but all that disappeared in the awkwardness of the moment. This wasn't like remembering the Subway stops. Those don't carry on conversations. He just stood there slightly weaving from side to side with his eyes averting David Kaplan's until David made the next move.

"Okay. Come in, Marvin."

Marvin followed him in and grabbed a seat for himself at the dining room table. He glanced at the brass menorah, now up on the mantle next to other items of Judaica. It had been cleaned and polished, waiting for the next Chanukah season. David walked over and stood over him.

"Can I get you something?"

"A cookie."

"I think we have some of those. So you want me to get you a cookie?"

Marvin desperately wanted a cookie, but he wanted to tell David some very important things even more. And he didn't want to wait.

"No...no cookie. Could you not stand there...I mean, could you sit down? I feel like you're Aunt Ida."

David took the chair next to Marvin.

"Well, I don't want to be her...especially if that makes you so uncomfortable. How can I help you, Marvin?"

That was Marvin's cue. His eyes got closer to looking directly at David Kaplan's.

"Um...did you tell Naomi we weren't a good match?"

"I didn't exactly say that. I...I leave those decisions up to her."

"Well...I want to get married, and she won't say yes. I'm a good man, a good Jew. We would have a kosher home. I would make sure. We would be *frum*, totally religious in every way, just like you...like you raised her. I...I...I...have always...always been...I don't know...I'm not good at words...I like...I like her a lot. My mother likes her too. My mother wants me to marry her...and...and I do too, Mr. Kaplan. I'm trying to get a job. Can I have a cookie now?"

David nodded.

"Why not."

He went into the kitchen and brought out three kosher Mi-del oatmeal cookies and a glass of milk. Marvin continued as he ate.

"I can be a hard worker. I can be. I'll take good care of her...very good...*tov m'ode*. Very good, Mr. Kaplan. I...I love...her...please..."

David realized that it was time to speak straight with Marvin. If there ever was a time and a place, this was it. He pulled his chair a bit closer and placed his hand on Marvin's t-shirt sleeve.

"Yes...yes, Marvin, you are observant. I'm very happy about that and so is Naomi. But...I know Naomi and..."

"I know her too, Mr. Kaplan."

"Let me finish. I know that observance is important to her, but so is a little common sense. And I also know she will want a man to think about what all those observances actually mean...things the sages pondered. Are you that man, Marvin?"

Marvin didn't know exactly what David was talking about, but he knew he had to keep recommending himself."

"I am. *I am.*"

David continued.

"I know you want to care for her, but Naomi will want a man who will take care of her even more than she takes care of him. I know her. She doesn't want to be a mother to the man she chooses. She wants a man she can depend on...a take charge kind of man. Are you that man, Marvin?"

Marvin knew he wasn't that kind of man. Still, he had to say something.

"I am...*Im yir-tzeh Ha Shem.* If God is willing. And He *is* willing. I can be that man. I...I mean I will be...that man."

"Well...Naomi is like Abigail, the wife of the fool Nabel, in the Writings. She's no fool. And she wants the same in a husband. Can you say that about yourself, Marvin?"

David knew he was practically accusing Marvin of being a fool. But Marvin didn't catch it.

"That's why I like her. All those Chabad girls are fools, and all the other frum girls in Brooklyn. *I* want *Naomi.* Please Mr. Kaplan, *I want Naomi.*"

Marvin was starting to sound like a spoiled child demanding a shiny new bike, and David Kaplan wasn't even his father. Besides, David couldn't deliver Naomi like she was a plaything Marvin had seen in Macy's toy department.

"Look Marvin. If Naomi wants you for a husband, I won't stand in her way. If that's what you came to find out, then you know that now."

Marvin smiled the smile of a toddler. David continued.

"But...

Marvin tried to sit still.

"If she doesn't want you as a husband, I will do everything I can to discourage you from pursuing a relationship with her."

Marvin knew he had one weapon left. It was a weapon that appealed to one of the deepest and richest Jewish traditions—one that went back thousands of years to the very books of the Bible—one he had seen in the movie "Fiddler on the Roof"—one that put the responsibility for the decision squarely on the father's shoulders. It was a decision that David's daughter would have to submit to, and be glad sooner or later that she did.

"Mr. Kaplan...you are a religious Jew. Don't our sages...of blessed memory...teach us that if a man is truly a man...a father...is really a father...then *he* makes the decision...who his daughter would marry? I think you should tell Naomi who to marry...and I'm a good man...a very good man. I'd be very good to her. I promise. And if we should have a daughter, I will choose a husband for her."

A barely imperceptible ripple of anger crossed David Kaplan's eyes, like a pebble disturbing a placid pond.

"First of all, she's too old to have a daughter..."

"We could adopt."

"Don't interrupt me. Second, you have dishonored my favorite rabbi and sage, the great Chofetz Chaim. We're no longer in nineteenth-century Kiev. We're in twenty-first century New York...for better or for worse. But even if we *were* in nineteenth century Kiev, the Chofetz Chaim would oppose all the other rabbis in the city and leave the decision *to the daughter!* He is my rabbinic counsel in this matter, not you! I have spoken. Now I have things to attend to."

Marvin didn't know quite what he had said that upset David Kaplan. But under no circumstances did he intend to lose hope, no matter *what* David was upset about. His visit to the Kaplan house wasn't totally wasted. He had discovered that David Kaplan would respect his daughter's decision. So he could still try to convince her that she should marry him. He got up, stretched his arms, and headed for the front door. He reached out his hand and David Kaplan took it, firmly shook it, and then quickly let it go.

"Goodbye Marvin."

"I love Naomi, Mr. Kaplan."

"I heard you, Marvin. Goodbye."

"Goodbye."

Without another word, Marvin left and David shut the front door behind him.

CHAPTER TWENTY-THREE

Lisa Silver had observed Marc's strange behavior for over two weeks, after the night he refused her. Under different circumstances, she might have suspected another woman. But considering his many approaches during the few prior weeks, that didn't seem to add up. Still, she concluded, anything was possible.

She weighed her options as she sat on the patio deck in a wrought iron chair, which was covered with a black-and-white checkered pillow-pad. The robins were flying from tree to tree in the spacious backyard, gossiping with each other about something or other. But she hadn't followed suit that morning. Her iPhone sat inactive on the table. She decided to just clear her mind with an espresso and consider a plan of action.

Direct communication was out of the question. Marc's style was almost all transactional and very little relational. The word that came to mind when describing him was *opaque*, which actually worked quite well for Lisa most of the time. She certainly had her relational side, but it was always about *her* world, which she had no great interest in sharing with Marc. She had her buddies with which she shared a common suburban

New Jersey sensibility. They were all Reform Jewish women pretty much exactly like her.

However, she did crave one kind of shared time with Marc, the kind that took place during long luxurious vacations. There they could find agreement over expensive cuisine and seashore sunsets on top-of-the-line cruise ships or five star resorts, dancing and drinking exotic drinks, and making lots of love—or at least having lots of sex. Things worked a lot better in that area on four-star Hyatt Hotel and Princess Cruise balcony room beds.

As Lisa drank her espresso and strategized, it dawned on her that they hadn't had a real vacation since Noah was born. In fact, Noah was the result of that last vacation. Lindsay was maybe two and a half years old, and Marc's mother took her for all ten days. It was hard being away from her daughter for that long, but the soft white beach in St. Martin made it easier.

Now both children were old enough to be without her for the length of a genuine break. Perhaps she could take the opportunity of a long vacation to light a fire in Marc, or at least find out why his fire was almost out. An excursion of that sort would be expensive. But then again, having the old Marc back would be worth any amount of money.

She began to search vacation websites. Where had she always wanted to go, or at least get away to? There were so many choices. First, she eliminated the places they'd already been to, or *she'd* been to when she was single and part of the college party set. The south Caribbean was out, as was the east and west. They'd also been to Alaska, and the whales didn't even show up. So that was out too.

The next search was all about Europe. They'd never done that. Naturally, it was more expensive, but who cared about the money? Certainly Marc wouldn't care. They both had plenty of that, thanks to his ridiculously successful job. She clicked on one exotic destination after another. She knew that if Marc agreed to go on a vacation, he'd say yes to anywhere. The truth was that she always made those choices anyway, once the overall decision to go was made.

Florence, Paris, Venice, Vienna, they all looked luscious. She was just about to click on one of those when she happened to glance at a cruise that she guessed none of her friends knew about, let alone had ever been on. "A Baltic Sea Cruise is the best way to experience the historic beauty of Northern Europe!...Sweden, Finland, Russia, Latvia." It went on to mention other lands Lisa had never visited. They included ports like

St. Petersburg, Copenhagen, Helsinki. It seemed like one couldn't get much farther away from New Jersey than that. And if they were a bit cold even in the spring or summer, that might make for better snuggling. She might even be willing to forego a few beaches for that, especially in this emergency situation.

It turned out most of the cruise lines went on the Baltic Sea cruise. And there were so many options to choose from, so many ports of call, so many excursions. The more Lisa clicked her mouse and browsed the pages, the more interested she became. The full color photographs of Copenhagen alone seduced her, with row-like homes lined up on the river's edge like a multi-colored set of children's blocks. And that statue of the Little Mermaid was particularly inviting. It was like jumping recklessly into a Disney cartoon. Places like St. Petersburg in Russia looked just as striking, if not a little dangerous and full of intrigue—in an amusement park sort of way. After all, she was a tourist from Englewood, New Jersey.

Lisa wasn't the kind of person to research long or stress greatly over things like vacation destinations. Certainly, she could have checked out other places, like the Mediterranean Sea, or Japan. She'd never been to either of those ports of call. But the Baltic Sea sounded perfect, as long as the accommodations were luxurious and the food was gourmet.

That night, she dressed in her sexiest negligee, the one he loved and that was more less than more, and wore her sweetest perfume. Marc was brushing his teeth when he saw her in the mirror. He continued brushing, and when he was finished he turned the light out, got into bed, and turned over. The perfume, far from stirring any interest, just temporarily kept him from dozing off. He was beginning to finally fall asleep when Lisa spoke softly.

"Marc."

He heard her but said nothing.

"Marc."

He pretended to be fully asleep.

"Marc, I've chosen a vacation for us. You'll see the deposit in the Amex statement next month."

She hadn't really put down a deposit, but she wanted to get his attention. He sat up in bed.

"What?"

She sat up too.

"We're taking a Baltic Sea cruise."

"Who is, and where the hell is the Baltic Sea?"

"*We* are. We're going next month when the kids get out of school and your mother can take them.

"Right. Baltic Sea. Is that in Russia somewhere, or near Baltimore? Anyway, cancel the deposit. We're not going. The only place I'm going is to sleep."

"We *are* going. Talk to your boss. I know he'll agree with me. He knows you need it. *We* need it."

"What do you know about him? You've hardly met him. What are you, prying into his life or something?"

"What would I do that for?"

"You tell me. You tell me!"

"Tell you what? What's the matter with you?"

"Nothing. What's the matter with you? That's what I want to know."

"See? That's why we're going. I want to see my husband again. I miss him. And I want to share expensive champagne and dance in Helsinki and...and Copenhagen."

"You can see me right here and take a drink downstairs from the kitchen cabinet...and dance by yourself with Pandora on the TV. And by the way, I don't want to dance with you anyway. I want to sleep and go to work and be left alone."

She threw off the sheets and jumped off the bed, standing near where he sat, with her tucked tummy an inch from the bed's edge.

"What's with you?," he asked as he stared at her negligee.

"We're going! I don't care how many times I've met what's-his-name that sends you to the restaurants...I know, Prima. You're telling him we're going, and we are. Period!"

That was at 11:00 p.m. By 1:00 a.m., he'd given into temptation, made the kind of passionate love with Mata Hari that resulted from three weeks of male sexual tension, and the Baltic Sea cruise was in the works.

The next day, Marc was in Prima's office, unexpected and uninvited. Prima was pre-occupied with something and obviously irritated that Marc was there. This was clearly not his suit-wearing moment. Instead, he was dressed in his casual Steve Jobs work outfit—tight jeans, and a black tee shirt. Marc wondered if he should just leave. But it was too late. Prima shrugged.

"What are you doing here, eh? What's this about?"

"Um...my wife thinks I need a vacation."

Prima's facial expression changed.

"Hey, my Jewish *pizon*. I told you, didn't I? I'll make a few calls. Italy is magnifico this time of year. I can even get you an audience with the Pope…I think. What do you think about *that?* We'll cover the whole thing."

Prima gently punched him in the shoulder. Marc winced and spoke in a half whisper.

"She wants to go on a Baltic Sea cruise. She says it's also beautiful this time of year."

Prima came to within inches of Marc's ear, and whispered low.

"What? What the hell does she want to go see those lousy Russians for…excuse the expression between you and me. I see too much of them here."

"I…I don't know. She found it on the Internet."

"That rotten Internet…it could send a person to the grave, excuse the expression."

"Well…she says it's not just Russia…it's Denmark, Sweden, Finland…I don't know."

"Okay. Okay. Baltic Sea it is. *Sheesh.* Tell her we'll get her a better deal than your Jewish family in…in…whatever business they're in…excuse the expression. I've got better family in the business. *Capiche?*"

Prima was more energetic and lively than usual. Marc liked that. He was glad that he showed up when he did.

"Now get the hell out of here. I've got work to do…and congratulations. A vacation…I told you, you needed one, didn't I? Didn't I tell you? Get her to send me what she has. We'll cut the cost in half. Tell her *that.*"

He shook his head and waved Marc off, which was the signal for him to leave immediately. As he turned to face the door, his eye just caught a strange man walking into the room from an opposite door. The man spoke with a thick Russian accent. But even if he hadn't said a word, Marc would have known he was Russian by his square haircut and his too tight black jacket.

"I was under impression we were alone," he spoke in somewhat broken English.

"Go!" Prima pointed to the door. Marc quickly left as if he hadn't seen the Russian. His mind returned to the prior discussion.

Well, she may stab me in the back later…but not until after the vacation, I guess.

CHAPTER TWENTY-FOUR

Darrin Brock sat on the subway train, rehearsing for the surprise meeting with his boss that he'd been considering for more than a week. He kept going over the concept of three in his mind.

1. *No interest in dealing with the old mob.*
2. *Possible interest in dealing with the Russians.*
3. *Possibly quitting altogether to help kids caught up in gang violence, sex trafficking, drugs.*

He finally arrived at the Midtown South Precinct NYPD police station, located at 35th Street and Ninth Avenue. The Midtown South precinct serves the top tourist sites, including a number of midtown restaurants. It's one of dozens of precinct stations dotted throughout Manhattan.

The New York Police department was established in 1845, just under forty years before the menorah sat on the dining room table in faraway Kiev.

At that time, there was just one precinct station and 51 officers. Needless to say, the NYPD had grown since then.

Darrin Brock entered the four story light tan structure and climbed the stairs to the second floor. Whenever he got a chance, he chose stair-climbing over taking the elevator. It presented one of the few opportunities to exercise during his busy week, that would be impractical inside tall structures like the *New York Times* building. But it worked perfectly here. He entered door number 208 and strolled right into Inspector Ralph Lewis' private office, greeting no one on the way in—like the seventy two disciples Jesus sent out in Luke 10. He knew he had to remain serious and resolute. There could be no small talk. He swung the door open, ready to do business, only to find the room itself clean and neat and yet unoccupied—like the man out of whom Jesus had cast out seven spirits. The desktop was another story. He walked back to the outer office and ended up finally greeting one of the staff.

"Where in the world is he, Margaret? I thought he'd be here."

At one time, Margaret had been very interested in Darrin. But that was a few years ago. He hadn't reciprocated, or even noticed her attractive smooth complexion, neatly pulled back chestnut brown hair, and well-pressed Manhattan police uniform. Since then, she had been merely cordial. Being about Naomi's age, she had no time to waste. She was now living with a man five years her junior and $20,000 beneath her salary.

"He'll be back soon. He went out for one of those huge roast beef sandwiches of his. You know him. He never takes a break for lunch. About now, he starts to get claustrophobic and famished. So as you know, a few times a week he ends up with a huge Dagwood at four, which tees the Mrs. off whenever he goes home for dinner…which is like never. It's the same old story."

"Right. Of course."

He went back into the office and shut the door. He'd never been in there alone, and Lewis could walk in at any moment. But he didn't care. He was ready to walk out on the job anyway. So what difference did it make? He reviewed the three points over and over, as he nervously circled the small room again and again—eyeing the file cabinets and wall certificates as he passed them.

"No Italian work…maybe Russian work…possibly leave work altogether for youth work if something doesn't change. Again, no Italian work…maybe Russian work…possibly leave work altogether for youth work if something doesn't change."

After about fifteen minutes of repeated recitation, Inspector Ralph Lewis came in with his roast beef sandwich in his right hand and a can of Dr. Brown's cream soda in his left. He was over six feet tall, with an intimidating beer belly. To top it all off, he always wore his cap when he went out. He took it off now and put it on his desk.

"Can I help you, Brock?"

Lewis acted totally unsurprised about Darrin's presence in his office, as if he was there every time the Inspector opened the door. Darrin was surprised, but not deterred.

"Inspector Lewis…"

"*Sit down.*"

Darrin stood in front of the desk. Lewis sat down behind it and put his sandwich and drink down.

"Inspector Lewis…"

"Sit down, damn it."

Darrin didn't want to sit down, as the chair on his side of the desk was slightly lower, and therefore would take the wind out of the sails on his side of the stormy conversation. But Inspector Lewis insisted.

"Sit down!"

Darrin plopped down, shooting up a silent prayer as he did.

Help me Jesus.

"Well, Darrin. Glad to have you here. Anything on your mind?"

"I…I've been thinking."

Lewis unwrapped the aluminum foil around his sandwich, and popped his Dr. Brown's soda open.

"You want some?"

"No. I'm not hungry."

Lewis took a huge bite, amounting to one third of one side of the sandwich, which distracted Darrin from his mission. But he would not be deterred, even as the sandwich dripped cole slaw and Thousand Island dressing onto the aluminum foil.

"Inspector Lewis…"

"Go on," Lewis said with his mouth full.

"You know I used to work for Rudy…"

"Didn't we *all.*"

"Yes, well, some of us did, like…you for instance. But…to get to the point…I helped clean up the left-over mess with the five families during the nineties…that is, from the eighties, and…"

"Didn't we *all.*"

"Yes, we did…and that's why…I don't really…that is, I'm not interested in Prima and his small-town hoods. I mean, this is a big town, and..."

The two-thirds eaten sandwich in one hand, Lewis slapped the other on his desk, rustling piles of paper in the process.

"Damn it, Brock...pardon my French with a church goer like you... but, damn it, you're providing an important service. We've been through this before."

"Yes, I know, and..."

"You can't deal with the Russians. I've told you, you help with them when you deal with Prima...with *any* cheap crook in the city. I've got a department for them, and another with the people from the Secret Service for dealing with the anti-counterfeit trade, and so forth. I've told you all this before, damn it. Everyone does their part."

He waved at the flat computer screen on his desk like they were all in there agreeing with him.

"Like I said, everybody's doing their part. Isn't that in the Bible somewhere, Brock?"

Having finished the last bite of the sandwich and washed it down with Dr. Brown's, he got up and crossed over to the other side of the table, laying his large hands on the still seated Darrin Brock like a pastor overseeing his congregant.

"Look, you've got that demented mother of yours, don't you? And your sick old father. You don't need a change now. It's the worst thing for you."

Lewis had stolen Darrin's second point, like the proverbial thief in the night.

So there was nothing to do but move to the third point.

"Well, okay...so, I was thinking..."

"More of that? You think too much, Brock. Did anyone ever tell you that?"

He went to the other side of the desk and took his seat again. Darrin took a deep breath. The next sentence could change the rest of his life, possibly for the worse. But He felt compelled to open his mouth and speak it. He'd been praying about it for months. He believed his life was in a transition of some sort, and he had concluded that it was now or never. He had to say *something* or he'd never say anything.

"Yes, well..."

He wanted to stand up, but didn't dare.

"Well, I'm grateful for everything...I truly am. But...maybe I need to look at another career, sir. I've been thinking of children...young people in crises."

"The minister side of you, Brock. I understand. There's lots of hurting people in this city. No question about that. But, big mistake just walking away, Darrin...*big* mistake. You don't know what you bring to this department...to New York...the importance of the work you do. Actually, it's *my* mistake. I should have given you an "A plus" evaluation a long time ago. I get so caught up in all the..."

He threw some papers around on his desk.

"...papers. What a mess. Listen, I'm putting you in for a raise right now. Where's the damn form?"

He knew where the form was, but considering the circumstances, he felt the need to be dramatic. Darrin held his hand out.

"No, that's not it."

"All right. You want to help kids out. Okay. So do you *really* want to help them?"

"Yes sir. Yes, I do."

Inspector Ralph Lewis took a paper from the top of the pile and slapped it in front of Darrin.

"All right. Some jerk killed this family's father...a Chassidic Jew from Brooklyn who was in the wrong place at the wrong time. As far as you're concerned, it doesn't matter who did it. A good man got caught up in someone else's crooked business. He was from Brooklyn, of course. You know where that is? You're damn right you do. Well?"

"Well what, sir?"

"Well, they have five frickin' kids and they're going frickin' crazy losing him. I happen to know that. See, I've got a heart too. Pay them a visit and let them know we care. Can you do that? There's your kids in crises...right *there*."

He emphasized the point by slapping a pile of papers twice.

"You take a week off and get over there. That's the address."

"This is the one I read about in the paper."

"You're damn right it is, pardon my French again. Take the week, be the friendly investigative cop. And you can visit as many times as you want after that. And guess what? There's plenty more where that came from. And you can still stick it to Prima too, while you're at it. What do you think?"

"Well, it's not exactly what I had in mind, but..."

"That's okay. I didn't have it in mind till you walked through that door...or had walked through it already, as the case may be. So is it a deal?"

Within the next few minutes, they had shaken hands over the new *assignment*. After Lewis told Darrin that a positive evaluation and raise came with the deal, he scribbled the name and address of the widow onto a post-it note and handed it to him. Within a few minutes, Darrin was back on the street. It all made him a bit dizzy, especially mixed with the sweet exhaust-tinged midtown Manhattan spring air.

CHAPTER TWENTY-FIVE

Darrin didn't know what to do with a whole week of paid vacation, which in this case happened to include a surprise visit with total strangers in the Crown Heights neighborhood of Brooklyn. He had visited Chassidic families there before, including once to record a lady's testimony concerning a vandalized wall. The crime consisted of some swastika graffiti marks. They never caught the kids that perpetrated it. At least he *concluded* that they were kids.

But this was different. What would he say, what *could* he say to a widow and her children who had lost someone so dear to them? He decided to visit the family right away, just to get it over with. Then he would decide what to do with the rest of the week. Maybe he would take his parents to the shore, even all the way to Atlantic City in South Jersey. After all, it was spring and a great time to be outdoors. And the salt air might do his mother some good.

He rode the dimly lit subway tunnel out of Manhattan toward Northwest Brooklyn. The commuter train rose above street level as he headed in the Crown Heights direction. He accessed the street address on his iPhone. He was familiar with the neighborhood, with its rows of brownstone duplexes in various shades, ranging from burnt dark brown to reddish to pale pink. Beyond the rails' rhythm, he spoke out the names of the widow and her five children.

"Chaya, thirty-five years."

He tried to pronounce it with that guttural sound. He practiced it a few times, although he knew he would be addressing her by her last name, Mrs. Mendel.

"Leah, 15 years, Shimon, 12 years, Rhena, 10 years, Shmuel, 7 years old, Natan, 4 years old."

Five children...five fatherless children.

Well, at least these people live in a tight-knit community, he thought to himself. *There will be plenty of other Chassids to support the widow in every way possible...plenty of aunts and uncles, or whatever they call them here, to be second parents to the children.*

He was pretty well convinced his visit would be useless and unnecessary. He felt ridiculous even attempting it. Obviously, Inspector Lewis was telling him what he wanted to hear so he would just shut up and get back to work after one week.

This is just a convenient group of children for me to help. I should have declined the offer as soon as Lewis brought it up. That's what I should have done.

But he knew why he didn't decline the offer. He couldn't think straight when the offer was made. He could never think straight when Inspector Lewis was responding to some request or complaint of his. And he said yes far too often. But it didn't matter now. He had agreed to visit the... what were their names? Oh yes, the Mendels.

It turned out the house was somewhere between reddish brown and purple—like Mandy Mendel's blood that was spilt in the streets of Manhattan. He passed the point of no return—the ornamented black forged-iron fence just beyond the sidewalk—and walked up the massive concrete stairs. He knocked on the wood-framed glass door and then pressed the door bell. He waited for maybe thirty seconds. A very attractive brunette, in a stylish black thin sweater jacket and a sparkling white shirt above an ankle length black well pressed skirt, answered the door just a crack. Darrin didn't expect Mrs. Chaya Mendel to look like this, and wondered if it was someone else—perhaps one of the helpful neighbors. She looked younger than thirty-five, and far too pretty to be a widow.

"Yes, what is it you want?"

She kept her eyes locked on his. He looked down and up at her again.

"Um...is this Mrs. Chaya Mendel's home?"

"And who should I say you are?"

"Um…my name is Darrin…Darrin Brock."

"And you're here for…?"

There was a very short but awkward pause. He suddenly realized that his detective badge might be helpful at this point. He took it out and flipped it open for her to see. She nodded slightly.

"This is about my late husband, yes?"

So it *was* her. It was Chaya Mendel. Just then he noticed that her well-groomed pulled back brunette hair was actually a wig, but obviously an expensive wig, a stylish wig.

"Well, yes. Sort of."

"Sort of or *yes?*"

"Sort of yes. May I come in?"

"That depends. Are you really from the police department?"

"Yes…yes I am that…the Manhattan police department…one of the districts, that is…I mean, I do represent the New York Police Department…in Manhattan."

"It sounds to me like you don't know exactly *who* you represent…but yes, you may come in."

He entered to find a most charming house interior. The two sofas in the living room were off-white but spotless. He took note of that, considering that there were young children living there. The theme was modern with a dash of Victorian thrown in, expressed in items like a few polished wood chairs graced with brilliant red fabric, and the heavy majestic dining room set in the adjacent room. He quickly eyed the Judaica, tastefully and judiciously placed on various walls, glass enclosed hutches, and mantles throughout the room. He recognized the portrait of Rabbi Menachem Schneerson, called by many The Rebbe. He had seen the portrait when he visited a few homes in the 1990's, not long after Schneerson's death in 1994—a year after Giuliani had visited during his mayoral campaign. At that time, Darrin read all about his contributions to the Jewish and wider world. And he knew that some Chassidic Jews believed he was the long awaited Messiah, who might at any time rise from his Queens, New York grave like a ghostly figure in a Marc Chagall painting. He didn't know whether the Mendels believed that, and he didn't want to know. He wasn't there to satisfy his curiosity about the Jewish people, Chassidic or otherwise. He had a job to do, and he needed to focus on that.

Chaya Mendel stayed several feet from him and waved her hand, inviting him to sit on one sofa while she proceeded to sit down on the other. A low glass table sat between them. Normally, she wouldn't have had any business with an NYPD policeman, let alone a police detective. The Chassidic community took care of itself. It had its *own* police force. But this case had gone way beyond the local community. The NYPD was involved in solving her husband's murder, and needed to be.

"Well, Mr. Brock. How can I help you?"

She seemed so poised, like Jackie Kennedy in the old black-and-white broadcast, showing off the JFK White House in the early sixties. And yet, she was also a good percent Brooklyn brash.

"Well, my department sent me here to see if there was anything we could do to be supportive of you…and the children."

"For starters, find my husband's murderer, Mr. Brock."

He wasn't surprised by her blunt response.

"Well…I assure you, Mrs. Mendel, our department is doing all they can on that score."

"And?"

"Well…"

"Aren't you here to give me some news about that? That *is* why you're here? And by the way, I *am* glad they were thoughtful enough to send you and you were thoughtful enough to come all this way."

He knew he had to tell her the truth before things went any further.

"Well actually, that's not my department…the department that's investigating your husbands…murder. To tell you the truth, I don't know exactly how that's going. But I'm confident, as I said, that they're doing…all they can."

She leaned forward, her eyes betraying a slightly confused look.

"I'm sure they are. So how else can I help you today, Mr. Brock?"

"Well, I'm…I'm a detective, but I also help children who might have any…questions."

"What kind of questions?"

"Well…just any questions that I can answer to let them know that the police care, that someone like myself…that I care."

Now he felt completely foolish. What questions about the fact that they would never see their father again could he possibly answer? And even if he could, he was pretty sure he wouldn't be the one Chaya Mendel would refer them to with questions about the next world.

"That's very nice of you, Mr. Brock. But we do have a number of neighbors who care for them…answer questions…and our rabbi…he has, of course, spent time with them as well. But I thank you just the same."

"Well, if you…or they…ever need anything, I just want you to know that the police department is ready to help you."

"I appreciate that, Mr. Brock. That's very thoughtful of the department…and you."

That gracious comment seemed to herald the end of his visit. Now it was time to leave and get on with his vacation. Inspector Lewis' mission trip idea to comfort her grieving children fell far short. But then again, it wasn't *Darrin's* idea, And anyway, there were many other children in crises that he could and would reach out to at some point. This was obviously not the time, the place, or the people to help. At least he could tell Inspector Lewis he had paid a visit.

Before he got up to leave, he noticed once again how composed and poised Mrs. Mendel seemed to be, for one who had just lost her young husband. It was, however, impossible for him to see all that she was struggling to conceal.

He wouldn't know—he couldn't know—how she had wept into her husband's ritual bowl and cup just before Darrin arrived at the door. The ritual bowl was the bowl next to her husband's side of the bed that he used to rinse his hands upon waking each morning, a Chassidic Jewish tradition called *Netilat Yadaim, The Washing of the Hands*. It's done to acknowledge the kindness of God in returning the soul that has been entrusted to Him the night before. But on that one fateful day in February, her husband's soul left when he went to work and never came back. This day, the day Darrin visited, was the first day she had wept into her husband's bowl and cup—and she hadn't been able to stop until just before Darrin arrived. She had quickly dried her eyes as he knocked on her door. And when he entered, he had been too uncomfortable to look into them and notice.

As Darrin rose, Mrs. Mendel rose also to show him the door. Just in that second four-year-old Natan—his round black velvet yarmulke firmly planted in the midst of his brown curly hair and his long Orthodox side locks bouncing—skipped into the room. Darrin's eyes followed him as he jumped up on the off-white sofa about three feet from him. He noticed that the child was in his socks so he wouldn't soil the fabric. Chaya Mendel realized introductions were in order, even if they needed to be short introductions.

"Mr. Brock, this is my son Natan. Natan, this is Mr. Brock."

Darrin naturally bent down to address Natan.

"Natan, I'm Darrin."

Unexpectedly, Natan grabbed ahold of Darrin, putting both of his arms around his neck and squeezing. Darrin didn't know what to do except stand up, taking Natan with him as the little boy dangled like an ornament. Then Darrin fell back on the sofa and Natan stayed attached.

"Abba. Abba."

Chaya stepped in and tried to pull the child away without touching Darrin, which is forbidden among Chassids. In fact, all physical contact with men beyond one's spouse is forbidden. But Natan would not give in to her attempt.

"Natan, you know better than that! You let Mr. Brock go right now!"

"Ima, I love Abba."

"I know you do, Natan. He was a special daddy. Do you want to let go of Mr. Brock now?"

She began to tear up for the first time during Darrin Brock's visit. The tears were running down her face as she fell back onto the sofa. Darrin saw her out of the corner of his eye. He directed his attention to Natan.

"Do you miss Abba? I bet you miss Daddy."

"Abba's away. You can be Abba until he comes back."

Darrin kissed him on the cheek that was now pressed against his face. Then Natan let go, only to crawl down and scamper out of the room. Chaya didn't know quite what to say.

"I apologize for my son's behavior. He doesn't quite understand...but still he somehow knows. Please..."

"It's fine. Really..."

As Darrin was about to get up to leave, Natan scampered back in the room holding a child's Bible story puzzle in both hands. He tossed it on the floor in front of Darrin.

"Will you play with me?"

Now Chaya started openly crying, intermittently drying her tears with a tissue she'd taken from her dress pocket.

"He used to play puzzles with my husband."

She half giggled and half wept.

"You look absolutely nothing like him...believe me, absolutely nothing like him."

"I believe you. But I'm a man nonetheless, with the heart of a daddy, even if I'm not one."

"I suppose so. But his behavior surprises me. He spends time with other fathers in the neighborhood. But nothing like this."

She laughed through her tears.

"Are you sure you're not a Jew in disguise?"

"Someone recently told me I'd make a good one...but, no. I'm just a

Gentile, and a Christian one at that."

Chaya didn't know quite how to respond to that. But she didn't have to. Natan had had enough of all the talking. He waved a large puzzle piece in front of Darrin, one that was shaped something like the state of Texas. Darrin took it from his little hands and asked, "Where does this go, Natan?"

For the next hour and a half, the two of them built at least ten children's puzzles and read at least five children's books, including one about the *Rebbe* himself. When the older children came home from school, Darrin was introduced to them one by one. By the time he got up to leave, he sensed a bond with Natan that he knew would draw him back for other visits. From the intentional few feet away, Chaya Mendel spoke from her heart.

"I thank you for coming, Mr. Brock, and for staying as late as you did. Please come visit Natan whenever you like."

"I will do that, Mrs. Mendel. I will definitely do that."

He gave Natan a huge hug, and then finally left. On the subway ride home, he thought about Inspector Ralph Lewis' orders. It turned out he was right. This *was* a worthwhile visit. Something else also rose up in his heart—a newfound desire to see justice occur for this grieving mother. He was part of this family now, and their business was his business.

CHAPTER TWENTY-SIX

Darrin Brock arrived back at the house in Teaneck late in the day. He reached up and pressed on the garage door opener clipped to his car's visor. The traffic had been thick from the moment he had pulled out of the NYPD parking lot in lower Manhattan. That was not unusual. Neither was the fact that in just a few minutes he would begin the nightly ritual of helping his father take care of his mother, from helping feed her to putting her to bed. And neither was it a burden. In fact, he considered it to be much more than his duty. His detective work was his duty. The assistance he provided his parents in the home where he was born was an honor of fifth-commandment proportions.

And yet, after he turned the car off and pulled the key out of the ignition, he closed the garage door behind him and sat in complete darkness. *That* was unusual. He could just hear the distant thud of a basketball bouncing on the garage door of a neighbor's house, along with the high-pitched chatter of children playing in the golden-hours glow of an approaching spring dusk. He sighed and then just took in the near-silence. He felt the need for a pause, a decompression. He had just visited an ultra-Orthodox Jewish widow in Brooklyn, and comforted her fatherless four-year-old boy. He had been surrounded by Jewish stars, Passover plates, menorahs, and a portrait of Rabbi Menachem Schneerson, not to mention the intimate surroundings of a tight-knit black garment-wearing one-hundred-percent Jewish world.

Just beyond the darkened car where he now sat, through the inner garage door, was an unassuming suburban American kitchen with a small marble island, upon which sat a green glazed pottery jar full of Oreo cookies and a small white plate stacked with bananas—among other kitchen related objects. Beyond that room were pictures on the dining room wall of his parent's younger days, posing with him as a small child of six. There was also a simple mass reproduced painting of a straight-haired Jesus playing with three children approximately the same age of six, one of which looked somewhat like the portrait of him on the adjacent wall.

He knew his father would be in the living room sitting on one easy chair, while his mother would be sitting on the other, her wheelchair close at hand. He was almost ready to leave the car and walk through the garage door, but not quite yet. He was decompressing from that other world.

His next thoughts were partly work related, partly motivated by his on-again off-again fascination with and study of Jewish history and culture, and partly...well, partly personal. He had to admit that he was intrigued by this forty-something religious woman named Naomi, with her charming curly hair, remarkable dark brown eyes, and an undying devotion to her aged father.

Even in the dark, he knew just where the basic button was on his iPhone, and when he pressed it, the glow pierced the car interior. He had two choices. He could use the extensive police database, or he could just try whitepages.com. The bars from his house's wireless signal shone on the upper left side of the phone. He decided to try the public website first. He typed David Kaplan's name into the search engine and Brooklyn into the address space. Up came two David Kaplans. The age of one seemed like it fit the age of Naomi's father. After all, the other one was only thirty-four years old. When he clicked for more information, up popped Naomi's name. But there was a charge to access more information, such as the address and phone number. So he finished his search on the closed NYPD site. Suddenly, there was the phone number, staring right at him. He looked at the time on the top of the phone screen—6:20 p.m. There was no way she would be home, even if she got off at 6:00 p.m. He would have to wait at least an hour to call her. The phone faded to black, and he sat in darkness once again.

He grabbed the handle with his left hand and opened the car door. The dome light brightened the interior. He stared at his pensive face in the mirror. Then he watched his own mouth as he prayed out loud.

"Please help me, God. You know me better than I know myself. You know my sitting down and my rising up. I just need You to help me know how to interview Naomi…please."

He was asking for wisdom about his business connection with her, the connection that gave him information on her brother-in-law. But in his deepest heart of hearts he knew he *really* needed wisdom for much more than that. And he was well aware that God knew it too. Still, he was in no mood to pray openly about all of his tangled feelings. Perhaps he was just too tired. Or maybe he couldn't quite bring himself to pray with a neutral heart, ready to hear.

He got out of the car and walked through the door, into the kitchen with the marble island. The lights were dimmed, as usual. He grabbed a banana off the plate, and walked through the dining room and into the living room. There were his father and mother, sitting as usual on the two lounge chairs. The wheel chair was in its usual place. The local evening news was just about over. The weather was being repeated just before sign off. *Sunny and mild tomorrow.* A perfect spring day.

Lester Brock looked toward Darrin and smiled, as his wife Velma stared straight forward.

"You're a little late tonight. Everything okay?"

"Yes, I'm okay. I…I just got held up. You need help with dinner?"

"It's ready. It looks like a nice day tomorrow. I'll walk her outside again…like today."

"Did she like that?"

"She did."

Lester Brock rose slowly and deliberately, taking his position at one side of Velma's chair. Darrin rolled the wheelchair to the other side of the chair and locked the wheels. With no need for words, they both lifted Velma and swung her around to the wheelchair and into it. She had been expecting that as a matter of habit and cooperated with them, if somewhat passively. They rolled her into the dining room, where the table was already set for three. Darrin went into the kitchen and took the pot off the stove, turning the knob for the gas burner from low heat to off. He knew there would be one of three things in the pot—roast beef, thick lentil soup, or roast chicken. It was always one of those three. He brought out the roast beef, and then went back for the green beans, basket of white and whole grain bread, and butter. Lastly, he got the pitcher and poured water in the three glasses. Meanwhile, Lester got Velma's red and white checkered bib, designed to look like it came from an appetizing Italian kitchen—thereby hopefully creating a corresponding appetite in her.

Everything was ready. Now Lester and Darrin each took turns feeding Velma for at least five minutes each before taking anything themselves, just as they did every night. When she had eaten her full, they wiped her face and began to talk as they both ate. They never talked about her condition. They fully believed she could hear them, so they kept all communication positive.

"I'm off for a week, Dad. Inspector Lewis wants me to just take it easy, other than visiting a widow whose husband was murdered in February...and to reach out to her children. And I did that today."

"Well, that doesn't seem like the Inspector Lewis I know, Son. You sure you'll have a job when you get back?"

"Yes, I will. I told him I wanted to quit and do outreach with kids, and this was his alternative...one week's paid vacation and a few kids who need a police detective to let them know he cares."

"Did you pray about that decision to quit, Son?"

Darrin knew that question was coming. It always did in situations like this. And he took the question seriously.

"Yes Dad, I did."

"And what did He say?"

"Not much. But I told Inspector Lewis I had to have some kind of change. And God knows I do. You know how I feel about chasing small time hoods at this time in my life, and how much I care about kids in crises. I thought if he had some other division for me to work in...but he didn't. I told him about my heart for the sex-trafficked girls, and the cracked-out boys, but..."

"Yes, I know. And He didn't give you an answer?"

Darrin knew his father meant God and not Inspector Lewis.

"No Dad."

They both instinctively looked toward Velma at the same time. A subtle smile appeared on her lips. Darrin thought it was probably gas. But Lester was convinced it was in response to Darrin's heart of compassion for children—other people's children. Lester turned back to Darrin.

"Your mother always loved your heart for Jesus...and the little ones He spoke about. What about the children of that widow you visited today? How did that work out?"

"They're Chassidic Jews, with the side locks, head coverings...

everything. I fell in love with a four-year-old boy, and he fell in love with me. I must admit, Inspector Lewis' suggestion was right. And now I also have the week to spend with you and Mother. We can even go all the way to Atlantic City, all the way in South Jersey, just like Mom likes. We can take in the spring air. It's so good for her."

"The little boy is a close relative." Lester didn't ask it as a question. He spoke it as a fact.

"Well yes, of course, Dad…that is, of his mother Chaya…and his brothers and sisters."

"I didn't mean that."

"What did you mean?"

"I meant of Jesus."

About an hour after dinner, Darrin Brock finally got up the courage to call the Kaplan household. He went into the bathroom and used his cell phone. He wasn't ready to tell his father anything about Naomi. Not that he was doing anything wrong—or was he?

The phone rang three times before David Kaplan picked it up. Darrin could have just hung up, but he didn't.

"Um…is Naomi there?"

A surprised David Kaplan responded.

"Who is this, please?"

"Um…my name is Darrin…Darrin Brock. Is she there?"

He could hear David speak into the air.

"Naomi…a Darrin…a Darrin Brock is on the phone."

Darrin could hear a muffled sound and then more muffled sounds. He knew David Kaplan's hand was covering the phone transmitter. Meanwhile, Naomi blushed beet red in front of her father and told him she'd get it in the other room. Darrin heard the click and then the hollow room-tone associated with the use of another phone extension.

"Um…your father has a nice voice."

Naomi was part surprised, part pleased, and part suspicious.

"How did you get my phone number? I can't believe you called my father's house. He's not at all used to…to…strange men calling me out of the blue…right in his house."

Darrin tried to think of something clever to say. But all he could say was, "It's your house too, isn't it? That's what whitepages.com says."

He didn't want her to know that he went on the NYPD database, like a detective would.

"Well, what is it you want?," she responded much too coldly. He was a bit taken aback.

"I don't know. I just want to talk about you...and your father...and your community. I'm helping out the little four-year-old son of a young Chassidic Jewish widow...and I just want to understand."

"Understand what?," she asked with a now softening heart.

"Understand you...and the boy...that's all. I was sent there by the police department to help...and I thought maybe you could help me with that...help me understand."

"Well...how do you propose for me to do that?," she inquired, hoping he would ask to see her again.

"Maybe we could meet at Ben's Deli sometime soon and talk about it. After all, it's not Passover."

By this time, she was floating on a cloud of romantic ecstasy.

"That's true. It isn't," she whispered. When she spoke those words, the *way* she spoke those words, he could tell she would probably be willing to meet with him. It was just a matter of setting up the day and time. But this was not a conducive time for that, not with her father in the room.

"I can't talk more right now," she continued to whisper. "I have to go. Maybe I'll see you in the Housewares department."

She hung up. She hoped he would get the message and visit her at work. The farthest thing from her mind had been how she would answer her father when he asked about Darrin Brock. But now she knew she had to say something. She loved her father with all her heart, and would never countenance deceiving him. But she couldn't very well reveal her feelings about Darrin. So she told him it was a work-related call, and hoped he didn't notice her red face. His response was short and unassuming.

"He couldn't talk to you tomorrow at work?"

But of course, he observed more than he let on. This was, after all, his beloved daughter.

CHAPTER TWENTY-SEVEN

David Kaplan hadn't visited his friends at the Dewitt Wallace Periodical Room, in the New York Public Library, in over a month. He figured they missed him, but had probably adjusted to his absence by this time. He was convinced he had made the right decision to be so scarce. The time would be better served engaging in volunteer activity, especially visiting sick children, as he had on December 25th.

However, David's good intentions didn't add up to the good work of a blessed mitzvah. He had never actually followed up with regular visits to the Maimonides Medical Center, or any other institution. And it was already spring. He wanted to start before summer, but he decided that today wasn't the right day. Instead, it wouldn't hurt to visit Stanley and Mahmoud. That would be a mitzvah too, the kindness of visiting old friends.

He prepared his sliced egg sandwich and carefully placed it in a brown paper bag, along with a spring peach. He left the house at 10:00 a.m., swinging the bag gently from his right hand as he walked toward the subway.

When David arrived at the Dewitt Wallace Periodical room, there were Stanley and Mahmoud, sitting in their usual places—as if they'd remained there since the last time he saw them. Each responded differently to his surprise visit. Mahmoud gave him a big overwhelming hug and kissed him on both cheeks.

"My brother…my friend…David!," he whispered loudly.

More than a few people looked up from their newspapers and laptops, and then turned back to them. Stanley looked up from his New York Post.

"Where the hell have *you* been? Too busy studying Torah to spend time with us?"

"Oh, come on Stanley. I'm here, aren't I?"

Stanley rose and pushed back his chair in his usual way. David extended his hand. Stanley let him wait for a few seconds before grabbing it with his larger, fatter hand and squeezing tight.

"All right, you big *macher*…you big shot. I guess you have a little time for us little people. Where've you been anyway?"

"I've been…I don't know.…"

Where had David been? He hadn't been anywhere much, but he suddenly realized that he *had* been to Midwood Press to see the Linotype machine.

"Well for one thing, I made my semi-annual trip to Midwood Press to smell and touch the old Linotype Machine there. They demonstrate it for school groups."

Stanley scoffed.

"That's a museum. What are you going to a stupid museum for? That's for *Alta Cockers,* old men."

"I *am* an old man. Stanley. What, did you get up on the wrong side of the bed this morning?"

"Maybe *you* did."

"Anyway, it's not a museum. It's a genuine company where they do real typesetting for customers that have real taste…not these computer printer ignoramuses."

"You should be such an ignoramus. Computers are ten times better than that noisy smelly old contraption."

Stanley's irritability may have been infectious, but Mahmoud wasn't taking the bait.

"That sounds very interesting, my friend. The printers in Ramallah have that kind of…of hand-crafted taste, so to speak…nothing cheap when it comes to our printers."

Of course, he was only guessing. Stanley challenged him.

"That's crap. Your printers are the same as ours…*worse.*"

David changed the subject.

"I want to do something with my time…if you get my drift. I would love to operate one of those machines again. I used to be the best Linotype operator at The *New York Times*. But alas…"

He finally sat down next to his friends.

"To tell you the truth, I don't like not doing anything. Actually, I planned to visit children at Maimonides on Tuesdays and Thursdays. I just haven't gotten around to it. Maybe I've been a little tired. I got sick after I was here that cold winter day, you know?"

Stanley waved his hand and spoke as loudly as he could while still keeping his voice down.

"More mitzvahs!"

"Yes, mitzvahs. What's wrong with that?"

"Doing nothing is a mitzvah too. Look at us. We're full of mitzvahs… like Shabbas every day. Why can't you be like us…happily retired?"

"Because I'm bored."

Mahmoud approached the conversation from a completely different direction. He had become somewhat of a problem solver since he had come to the United States. That's one of the things he loved best about America. In fact, he was fond of saying that his Palestinian friends back home could use a little more innovation and a little less agitation. However, he would never actually say that to anyone back home. He more or less just said it to himself and people like Stanley and David. But he liked saying it nonetheless.

When he was younger, he had wanted to start an Arab cab company, one that offered faster service at competitive prices. He imagined a fleet of inexpensive compact cars zipping around New York, weaving in and out of traffic. However, Mahmoud was old now, and the fleet of compact cars never materialized. Still, he liked the idea. Indeed, every so often he was still capable of coming up with a truly brilliant thought. Today was one of those times. He turned to David right in the middle of the conversation, which was going nowhere.

"David, my dear Jewish brother…why don't you apply for a job with Midwood Press? You say you were the best Linotype Operator at the *New York Times*. You could put that right on your resume´. You say you love to help children. You could show off the machine and teach them how it prints. And that could go on your resume´ too."

He was orating now, giving a speech worthy of the Palestinian Prime Minister.

"You say you're bored. Well, get to work! There are many verses in the Koran about that. Now *that* would cure you...a good job...in your field. What do you think of *that,* my friend?"

There was silence as David absorbed Mahmoud's wisdom. Stanley broke in.

"They better pay you well. Don't let them take advantage. I had an uncle once, who went for a job interview, and the *gonafs,* the thieves..."

"I don't care about the money, Stanley. I'd do it for free,"

There was more silence, which Stanley broke again.

"I guess you *are* a mensch. Nevertheless, I'd ask for something... anything...just for your self-respect. You deserve, David, you deserve."

Mahmoud realized things were getting off-track.

"What do you think?"

David nodded.

"It's good, Mahmoud. It's worth a try, whether they'll have me or not. I'm glad I came here today."

Stanley changed the subject.

"How's your son-in-law, by the way?"

"I guess he's doing well...I suppose he is."

Stanley couldn't resist probing David.

"You know, I happen to have met him. I know him."

"Oh. That's not surprising, you being in somewhat the same line of work...at least you *were.* I don't think I've ever introduced him to you. Why didn't you tell me you knew him."

"We didn't know you were related," Mahmoud chimed in. "He came here, and it just so happened we met him."

"Yes, he used to come into the deli...with his wholesale service. Do you know about his food service job?"

"Yes, of course I know about the job. What's there to know? He's my son-in-law."

"Oh, so you know what he does...in the job?"

"Like I said, what's there to know? He has a good job, with the restaurants."

Stanley realized that David knew nothing about Marc Silver's employer, so he dropped the topic. But he couldn't help throwing out a hint just for the sake of doing it.

"You remember that Chassid who was murdered in the diamond district?"

"Of course I remember. I don't forget things like that easily. I...I...I even remember one from my Linotype days...a very sad story I had to edit and typeset. Of course I remember. Why do you bring it up?"

"Nothing. It's only that…"

Stanley tried to think fast.

"The wife…I understand the wife has a lot of children. They *all* do. I'm sure it would be a mitzvah to visit them too, just like you visit the sick children at Maimonides. There are many kinds of pain, you know."

"I know that, Stanley. Well, thank you for that. It's a good idea too. Now I'm *really* glad I visited you two today."

"Well, we're keeping you busy today. That's for sure."

David didn't want to stay until the usual time. He hadn't planned on that, and wasn't up for it. He chose a simple exit strategy by telling them he was a bit tired and needed to go home and rest—which was true. With a hug from Mahmoud and a handshake and a "don't make yourself so scarce" from Stanley, David left the Dewitt Wallace Periodical Room and headed for the subway. After he left, Stanley turned to Mahmoud.

"Poor *schmo*. He doesn't know about Marc Silver and the mob."

Mahmoud put his arm on Stanley's shoulder.

"I'm very glad you didn't tell him."

CHAPTER TWENTY-EIGHT

Firmly ensconced in late spring, the first part of June was Lisa Silver's favorite time of the year. She could sit on the patio and drink martinis in her bikini. Noah and Lindsey would be finishing up the school year in about a week or so. But for now, Lisa wouldn't have to pick up after them or watch over them. She could just sit and talk endlessly on the phone, and watch the pool reflect the sun like a sea of polished blue glass. There truly was nowhere she could be more relaxed.

However, this year she sacrificed those few precious weeks for a few weeks' vacation on the other side of the world. Instead of drinking and sun-bathing poolside, Lisa stood among various pieces of matching light green metal luggage that sat in the front hall, with a pink silk scarf presenting an adorable appearance around her well groomed, short, dyed, jet-black hair. Marc was in the second floor bathroom. The children were still at school. Marc's mother was planning to be at the house an hour or so before they arrived home, and after Marc and Lisa left for the airport.

By the time the taxi arrived at their door, Marc was out of the bathroom and dictating to the cab driver.

"There's a thirty percent tip for you if you get us to Kennedy fast,"

The driver, who looked like a young Mahmoud, nodded.

"I will do what I can, sir. No guarantees, sir."

He took three bags, putting one under his arm, and walked out the front door. Marc, dressed in a Steve Jobs jeans and black tee shirt outfit similar to Prima's, slipped an ultra-thin black jacket on. He spoke more to himself than to Lisa.

"He'd speed if he was in Pakistan, or wherever in the hell he's from. All right, let's get this thing over with."

"You sound like you're going to an execution," Lisa shot back.

"Do I? Maybe I am," Mark responded cryptically.

The taxi ride to the airport was a study in silence, except for the driver's attempt at small talk while he weaved from one lane to the other.

"It's a good day to fly…good weather. It won't be too crowded. The vacation season is not here yet…just around the corner."

Marc responded with a series of "yeahs."

The first class flight to Copenhagen was uneventful, save for the drinks. Lisa ordered seven glasses of wine. Marc had never seen her drink like that. She began to slur her words at approximately glass number four.

"You…you should…it's very…furry…it's good stuff. Join me. Cheers."

Her volume was slightly inappropriate, which caused more than one person to stare. *What's Mata Hari up to,* he thought to himself? He wasn't sure. But *Lisa* was. Being with Marc was becoming more and more painful, and she was doing everything she could to loosen up and just have a good time, either with him or without him.

Marc decided on one glass and overall sobriety, so he could stay alert and on guard. Lisa dozed off after the last glass and slept the rest of the flight. Marc watched a mindless action movie. The vacation hadn't started very well. And this was just the beginning. He made a preliminary decision that he knew he couldn't realistically act on, but which nevertheless reflected his mental state.

Things better improve, or I'm taking a flight home from the nearest port and filing for divorce. She can marry that damn Darrin Brock…especially after she's filled his head with lies about me, or visa versa.

Neither Marc nor Lisa had ever seen anything like the cities their Princess cruise ship was destined to dock in. A first look at Copenhagen had the odd effect of softening Marc's hardened heart at least a few degrees, and in fact had a similar effect on Lisa. As the taxi drove the last mile toward the port, the small red-roofed pastel houses created a cinematic experience. Lisa's hangover headache even decreased in intensity. She grabbed Marc's arm instinctively.

"Oh honey! It's so beautiful, like doll houses when I was a little girl, like stories by Hans Christian Anderson. Aren't they cute? I think this will be our *best* cruise yet."

She let go of his arm and squeezed his hand. He almost blurted out, "I didn't know you *were* an innocent little girl." But he restrained himself and managed a more positive response.

"It *is* very nice."

From that moment forward, Marc gradually became less and less obsessed with Lisa's plot against him and more and more interested in each port of call. That included the emerald-green full-orbed trees among red slate roofs and spires in Tallin, Estonia, the silver and white never-ending palatial structures in St. Petersburg, the indescribable and overwhelming Hermitage museum, the evenings cruising the bright blue Baltic Sea, and the slot machines in the ship's casino.

Marc endeavored to forget his suspicions, relax, and share with Lisa the sites and sounds of his first real vacation in years—except the casino. He reserved that for himself. But the things he *did* share, candlelight dinners, walking tours, the intimacy of their cabin room bed, almost made him feel young again. His marriage began to feel almost brand new, as in before the Englewood house, Noah and Lindsay, and this whole present mess—whatever in the world that was all about.

He reserved a few late nights for the casino, spending until two or three in the morning, trying his hand at the relentlessly stingy electronic one-armed bandit. He didn't care how much money the thief consumed. He was there to have a good time, the cost be damned.

On the fifth night of the cruise, he left the casino for his cabin at one thirty in the morning. After losing a considerable amount of cash, he had ordered a few stingers, which left him a bit woozy. He decided he needed to get outdoors, beyond the claustrophobic blinking bright lights of the gambling area. He walked out on the starboard deck and breathed the fresh Baltic Sea air. He watched the ship's powerful propellers hypnotically churn the sea waters. He tried to empty his mind of everything except the rhythm of the engine and the sky full of stars, ones that were never visible back in New Jersey even on dark moonless nights. He enjoyed being totally alone, unconnected to any other human being, responsible to no one—not even Lisa, or Prima.

This solitude lasted for only five or ten minutes before a man in a tight-knit black sock cap, black wind-breaker, and tight jeans, came and stood next to him. He didn't want the man to be there in the worst way. After all, this was *his* rare and precious alone time. But he realized that this gentleman, whoever he was, was on his vacation too. He figured if he said a few nice words to him, the man would probably end up eventually going away, leaving Marc to meditate a few more minutes before he turned in.

"Nice night, isn't it?"

"Not nice."

The man was Russian. Well, after all, this was *their* turf. The ship had recently departed St. Petersburg. "Might as well be nice," Marc concluded.

"I think your part of the world is beautiful. I'm glad we came."

"Not nice," the man repeated. "Not nice at all…for you!"

Without warning, the Russian grabbed Marc by the arm with his left hand and put his other muscular arm around Marc's neck, squeezing it hard and closing Marc's vocal cords, making it impossible for him to cry out. Instantly Marc perceived that this man knew what he was doing. He kept a lock on Marc while he forced him across the boards. Marc tried to stop the forceful dragging with his sandal-clad feet, but it was useless. The Russian pushed Marc up against the ship's railing. Then he forced his head over the railing, knowing that this was the heaviest part of Marc's body. Marc's eyes bulged as he saw the converging foaming wake a few decks below. A few seconds earlier, Marc was taking in a quiet Baltic Sea evening. Now he realized in an instant that his short life was at an end. His heart was speeding uncontrollably, driven by pure adrenaline. He felt the Russian's hand, the one that had pulled his arm back, reach in and pull his wallet out of his back pocket and then grab him by the pants belt, preparing to heave him overboard. In that exact instant, Marc heard a shout over the incessant roar of the sea and hum of the engine.

"See here! What are you doing?"

He felt the man's grip loosen as he fell backwards onto the boards, hitting the back of his head hard. He saw a quick flash and then blacked out for what seemed like a second or two. When he came to, two young ship's mates were standing over him, dressed in sailor white. They spoke with some kind of European accent.

"Are you alright, sir?" one of them said.

Marc lifted his head and felt it ache. He staggered as he struggled to stand up, now totally sober but greatly shaken.

"I don't know. I think so. Yes, I think I'm okay."

"Do you know this man who assaulted you?," the other mate asked.

"I don't… no, I don't know him."

"He's a thief. We found this on the deck."

He showed Marc his wallet.

"Is this yours?"

"Yes, it's mine."

"Check and see if everything is in there."

Marc had no desire to check the wallet. He had just escaped certain death. Besides, there was only cash in it, no credit cards. And as far as the cash was concerned, he didn't even know how much was left after gambling.

"That's okay. I'll just take it."

Marc took the wallet and slipped it into his pants pocket.

"You're sure you're okay?," the other mate asked.

"Yes, I'm okay."

"We encounter this very infrequently, and we truly regret it. The thief is in custody and will be taken away at the next port. We will provide a free cruise of similar length for you and one other party as compensation. You do not have to involve yourself further. The cruise company will press charges. We truly appreciate your business."

Marc was still too much in shock to want to prolong the discussion any further.

"No problem."

He staggered away and toward his cabin, falling asleep almost instantly when he got there. It wasn't until he woke up the next morning that he felt the size of the lump in the back of his head. Lisa's side of the bed was empty.

For the first time since the incident, he began to remember the details. As he went over them in his mind, he couldn't help but conclude that he was definitely in the process of being pushed overboard when the process was interrupted. Yes, his wallet was pulled out of his pants back pocket. But what kind of cheap Russian small-change thief would be so brutal as to throw his victim into the wake of the whirling propellers just to steal his wallet? This was no simple robbery. But what was it all about? Why would this stranger try to kill him? It didn't make sense—at first.

And then all at once it came to him. Lisa must have planned the whole thing. Sure. She set it all up—the cruise, the itinerary, the murder. It was all so clear. Perhaps this is why she hadn't complained about his late night gambling. The later the better, when no one would be looking. But her plans had failed. Someone *was* looking, and he was saved.

Marc figured Lisa and Naomi must have received information about his work from this Brock operator. And then Lisa planned with Brock to have him taken out. Of course, Marc had no concrete evidence. But Prima's suspicions were evidence enough. He knew something was going on, and now whatever it was had turned out to be true. Marc vowed not to turn his back again during the cruise. He would tell Lisa nothing of what had happened, and watch her for any sign of surprise when she saw he was still alive and in one piece.

Marc was convinced that the sign occurred when Lisa returned to the cabin and said with eyes that seemed to be a little wider than usual, "When did *you* get in last night?"

"Why? Are you surprised?"

"Of course not. You've been getting in late every night for the last few nights. I was just curious."

She must be covering her tracks, he thought to himself.

"I'm sure you *are* curious."

He grabbed a shirt and pants out of the drawer.

"I'm going to breakfast. I don't think I'll be going ashore today. You can go without me."

"Why? This is a good one. Helsinki. It's supposed to be fabulous. I was looking forward to seeing it with you."

"You go. I'm not feeling too well. I'm sure you understand."

"I *don't* understand. You felt fine yesterday. I think it's too much gambling, and too much drinking."

"Like you didn't drink too much on the plane."

"I'm not talking about that. I'm not feeling sick. You are."

"I'll be okay. At least I'm alive."

He looked deep into her eyes for any response. If there was a response, she seemed to be hiding it well.

"Whatever. It's your choice," she said with an edge of irritation in her voice.

For Marc, the rest of the cruise was ruined. He couldn't wait till it was over. Until then, he would keep a close eye on his mutinous wife.

SUMMER

CHAPTER TWENTY-NINE

Darrin Brock lay on his bed on a sultry summer afternoon. He had returned to his regular schedule. But his work week now looked and felt different. Inspector Lewis had cleared a weekly visit to the Mendel home, usually on a Tuesday afternoon. Natan would stand at the front door of the brownstone Brooklyn home, waiting for Darrin as he walked up the sidewalk. His side curls would bounce up and down as Darrin walked up the few front steps and into the house. The same familiar books and puzzles would be strewn on the floor in front of the immaculately white sofa. Chaya would bring two glasses of milk and two big cookies—big round spongy ones that Darrin knew were certified kosher, whatever it took for that to occur. He would eat one and Natan would eat the other, and they would play on the floor for about an hour. It had become the high point of Darrin's week.

Darrin thought about the undeserved and unusual bond that had formed between him and the precocious little boy. He knew that *natan* means given or gift. And he considered his visits with Natan to be gifts from God. As a result of them, he saw everything in a bit of a different light. That included his deep and abiding relationship with another Son of Abraham, Jesus of Nazareth—or *Yeshua HaNotzri,* as it is pronounced in the same language as Natan's name. In fact, he almost saw the greater Son reflected in this youngest son of Chaya Mendel more than he did in anyone else, except perhaps his parents.

On the night table beside Darrin's bed was a small stack of books, some thicker and some thinner. Two of the thicker ones sat on top, Metaxas' *Bonhoeffer* and Paul Johnson's *A History of the Jews.* He picked up the latter and opened it to the bookmark, about half way through, in the midst of the Crusades and the Inquisition.

The air-conditioning in the room struggled to overwhelm the warm sticky air that hung over all of Teaneck. The atmosphere was pregnant with water, but had not borne actual rain in several days. Though the bedroom was slightly cooler than the outdoors, Darrin decided to take a short walk. He put the book back down on the night table and walked downstairs, past his parents as they sat in their usual chairs.

"I'm going out for a short walk. I'll be back in a few."

Lester looked up from his Sunday *New York Times* and nodded. Velma was dozing. As Darrin left the house, the warm air below thick low-hanging clouds assaulted his senses and stuck to his skin like gray cotton candy. He walked down the suburban street, eyeing the waving sprinklers as they labored to keep the baking grass green. His thoughts shifted to Naomi Kaplan. Indeed, he very much wanted to focus his thoughts on her. She was in her late forties like him, strangely exotic and attractive in her own way—and with a wealth of Jewish sensibility and heritage.

However, instead of Naomi Kaplan, he found himself thinking about his ongoing and probably too slow-moving investigation of her brother-in-law Marc Silver. He knew Silver wouldn't be good so much for detailed information, as he would be for evidence. And Naomi would be one of the keys to obtaining access to that evidence. He hadn't communicated with her since the call to her house some weeks earlier, when he suggested going to Ben's. But he hadn't followed up yet with a visit to Macy's, as she suggested. It seemed to him that this quiet summer Sunday would be a perfect time to connect with her. She hadn't been totally comfortable with that last call, but this was the only number he had, and he didn't want to wait until he saw her in the housewares department. He wanted to give her a heads up on the phone. He figured she'd be home. He would take his chances and call her there. He headed back to the house. As he walked through the front door, his father blurted out, "That was fast."

"It's hot out there!"

Darrin walked directly into the kitchen and shut the door. He picked up the phone and dialed the number, which he had committed to memory—as any good detective would. After several rings, Naomi answered. Her heart immediately began to pound so hard, she was sure both her father and Darrin could hear it as loudly as the thumping bass drum in a love song. In the absence of any recent contact with Darrin, her daydreaming had once again gotten totally out of control, exacerbated by Lisa and Marc's Baltic cruise.

Naomi had, since her teen years, longed for a love-boat cruise with her *own* beloved. She had also spent hours during the last few weeks regretting how curt and cold she had been during the last call, when her father was in the room. She had firmly decided not to let that happen again. That superseded the fact that her other beloved, her father, was once again in the room. She impulsively blurted out Darrin's name, this time wanting her father to hear it.

"Darrin! Darrin!"

David Kaplan looked up from the dining room table, where he had been tinkering with an old wind-up clock that vaguely reminded him of a Linotype machine. Naomi rushed into the kitchen just in time to hear Darrin ask her if she would meet him during her lunch break the next day at Ben's Deli.

"Yes, yes," she gushed like Jeanne Crain to Dana Andrews at the conclusion of the old romantic movie, *State Fair*.

Darrin was somewhat taken aback by this response, and wasn't sure why she said yes twice. He knew—as he figured she also knew—that they were not compatible. After all, they were from two different cultures, had two different beliefs, and had *no business* being more than just friends. On the other hand, he did have *another* kind of business, business as a detective who had something to discuss with her. After she said yes those two times, they agreed on an exact time. Then he said goodbye and hung up as any detective who has just set up an appointment would.

CHAPTER THIRTY

Manhattan summers rise from the grates and manhole covers that dot the steaming streets of the steel and asphalt island. Sweet spring exhaust gives way to oppressive waves of bitter-sweet sweat and humidity. The sun bakes the upper windows of the tall skyscrapers, its beams never reaching down to the bottom floors. And everyone who is able to wears short sleeves. Those who can't, including businessmen and Chassids—as well as professionally dressed women—would be advised to slather on plenty of deodorant.

Naomi wasn't able to eat anything all Monday morning. Her stomach rumbled and churned through the morning break. She spent most of that in the bathroom. By the time the lunch break approached, her hands began to shake. She had to hold one hand down with the other while serving the last customer. She sold a very nice Cuisinart food processor. And she couldn't wait for the nice gentleman to leave with it, exclaiming as he went how much his wife will love it.

She visited the bathroom once more as her lunch break began, risking the possibility that Darrin would arrive while she was gone. When she got back, there he was, with a movie star summer tan gracing the perfect structure of his rugged yet gentle Anglo-Saxon face. His yellow hair was bleached a shade lighter, and was straighter than ever. And his off-white knit short sleeve shirt exposed strong secure arms, the kind that are good at enfolding. Next to him, she felt plain bordering on ugly. But he saw something else, a completely different Naomi—exotic deep dark-eyed olive-toned Middle-Eastern, by way of mysterious Kiev, and in her flowery summer dress strangely sultry.

The two left Macy's for Ben's Deli. The period of separation, along with the tension of the earlier phone call, created an awkward silence between them as they walked. Darrin knew that he had to somehow break through to accomplish his professional objective. But that would have to wait until they stepped out of the heat and into the air-conditioned comfort of Ben's.

When the formality of ordering matching corned beef sandwiches was over, Naomi was the first one to break the ice over a cool Dr. Brown's cream soda. She leaned over the booth table and spoke in a hushed voice as if others could hear her—which due to the typical deli noise around them, they couldn't.

"Mr. Brock, may I ask you a question?"

She leaned even closer, almost threatening to knock over his matching Dr. Browns by the straw.

"If I may ask, why are you so fascinated with my religion?"

She had wanted to ask this question ever since he had first mentioned his interest in Judaism months earlier. And she had imagined his answer many times. It would go something like this.

I have wanted to be Jewish ever since I could remember. Maybe I'll convert someday, but now I just want to learn more.

She waited while he nervously grabbed a Kosher pickle and stuffed it into his mouth. He had not wanted the conversation to start this way. He had committed himself to a more professional approach, beginning with a discussion about his visits with the Mendels, and then shifting to questions about her family, which included her father, sister, and then her *brother-in-law*. Now he had to answer her perfectly legitimate question before getting to Marc. He would still start with the Mendels. He knew that was nowhere near where his interest in Israel and the Jewish people started. But he couldn't very well share about his and his parents' deep Christian faith. If he did, it would have represented unprofessional behavior for a detective on the job. He swallowed the pickle and began, hoping to be interrupted by the arrival of the corned beef on rye. He leaned over the table and spoke low to match her actions. He began with the Mendels.

"Um...see...I'm visiting a little Chassidic boy whose father was murdered. I met him a few months ago. I need to understand him in order to help him."

"That's very nice of you to visit the boy. You're so much like my father."

There it was! The entrance to talk about her family. But then she ruined it by asking, "But didn't you tell me you were interested in Judaism before that? You're not telling me everything."

Now he was stuck. So he resorted to the old philosophy that a good investigator must be honest when he himself is investigated. He concluded that a little truth couldn't hurt.

"Well, you're right. There *is* more. See, it has to do with my parents. You met them, remember? Lester and Velma."

"Yes, I remember. In the restaurant parking lot in Teaneck."

"Yes, that's right. Well...you see...their faith is very strong."

"Faith in what?," Naomi whispered, waiting for an answer that would give her hope.

"Their faith in God...and..."

He knew he had to explain their faith in more detail in order to make his point. Usually, he was thrilled to speak of his beloved parents' spiritual life, as well as his own. But this was one of the few times in his life that he hesitated.

"And...and Jesus...their faith in Jesus. You see...you see...Naomi..."

He leaned slightly closer just as she leaned slightly back.

"They...my parents...feel indebted...grateful...to the Jewish people for their deep faith in God...the God of Israel...and so do I."

Naomi sat completely back in her seat and spoke up. The God of Israel was music to her ears, but Jesus ended that with a thud.

"The God of Israel? But...but..."

The word hardly escaped from her mouth.

"J...J...Je...sus?"

"Yes...It's because of Him that I have this gratefulness, and love...for Jewish people and Jewish heritage."

"My father said...Christians..."

She had to swallow hard before saying that word too.

"...want to convert us, God forbid."

This was the very direction Darrin Brock was trying to avoid.

"I'm talking about...about something else. My faith would not be possible without...without...well, for instance, He said, 'Salvation comes through the Jewish people.'"

"Who said?," she responded, hoping against hope that he wasn't talking about Jesus. His answer, of course, disappointed her, and she responded emphatically.

"I'm sure the sages said that first. Everyone's always copying the sages."

"Anything that's true is worth repeating, don't you think?"

She let out a slight giggle, the first time in the conversation a bit of tension was released.

"Now you're sounding like my father again."

"Maybe he's sounding like me," he joked.

He could see a slight sparkle in her eyes. She felt a sudden warming of her heart that led to an unexpected familiarity.

"Oh, Darrin. You're teasing me. He's so much older than you. But I have to admit, sometimes you do seem like you're quoting the sages."

"I don't mean to. But I *do* agree with them that God will never forsake Israel. And that agrees with the Bible."

"And just who said that?"

"Well, Jeremiah, for one thing...and others."

He thought it unwise to tell her that one of the others was Paul, in the book of Romans. Finally, he said, "Look, I just want to learn for the sake of learning. Is it okay if I just want to learn? There's *so much* to learn."

Naomi paused and thought for a few seconds. She detected in Darrin's eyes some of the same voracious curiosity about the world that she always admired in her father. David Kaplan wasn't at all like the Chassids. They were closed minded. Her father had always wanted to understand other cultures and religions. After all, wasn't he even willing to wear a Santa hat so he could identify with the faith and longing of a little dying boy?

As she reminded herself about her father's Christmas mitzvah, she considered bringing it up. But she decided against it. After all, what point would there be in discussing it? It was obvious by now that her dreams had turned into a nightmare. Darrin Brock had turned out to be nothing more than a committed Christian, one of the millions of zealous fanatics that constantly roamed the streets of New York, like beasts looking for prey of one kind or another.

On the other hand, there might still be hope for him. If he learned more about her Judaism, he might see through his Christianity. After all, there was something different about him, something unusual. Perhaps there *was* a Jewish soul under there somewhere. And perhaps she could uncover it. So Naomi changed her mind about bringing up the mitzvah, hoping to show Darrin how tolerant her father was.

"Um…my father visits sick children on Christmas day. He respects other religions. And so do I."

Then she capped off her comments with a message she hoped would not be lost on him.

"We know who we are as Jews. So we can appreciate other religions."

She was sure that came out just sounding defensive. Darrin, however, responded instantly.

"I can totally identify with that. I'd love to get to know your father. He sounds wonderful…and a little like my father."

Normally, Naomi would crave that kind of talk about her father, But not in this case. Something about Darrin's words seemed like a comeback to her words. She tried to follow up, but nothing would come out. She just wanted to kick herself hard under the table for ever having given him a second look. She decided right then and there that whatever it was, it was over, and she wanted to just leave and get back to work before her lunch break was over.

"I have to go. I'm sorry about the corned beef sandwich. Perhaps your parents who love Jewish things would like to have it as a take-out."

That *more* than came out wrong. It was insulting and sarcastic. She saw pain pass over his face, as if she had slapped him, and she knew she had to apologize immediately or she would never forgive herself.

"I'm so sorry. I…I didn't mean anything by that. I just…wouldn't want the sandwich to go to waste, and I've got to get back."

He looked directly at her. He realized that at this point he probably wouldn't be able to talk to her about Marc, or anything else.

"I see. I'll take care of the sandwich."

She got up and tried to take his hand and shake it while he sat in the booth.

"You're very kind. Thank you for your time. Perhaps we'll meet again sometime."

She walked out of Ben's Deli without looking back. All the way back to Macy's, she tried to hold back the tears that blended with the Manhattan humidity. She began to run so she would pass onlookers quickly. She hoped against hope that her eyes would return to normal before she got back to the store.

CHAPTER THIRTY-ONE

David couldn't get Mahmoud and Stanley's idea out of his head, especially after he had one of those Linotype dreams that he often took as a sign to visit Midwood Press. Only this time, he wasn't planning to come as an observer. He was looking for a voluntary—if not modestly paying—position. He hadn't actually operated a Linotype keyboard in forty years. But as he sat at the dining room table of his Brooklyn home, he could almost see every key reflected on the walnut finish before him—ninety keys representing ninety channels that the matrices steadily flowed down, released from the distributer bar. Yes, they were like snow in the winter, but they were equally like a soaking rain shower in the summer. There they were, lower case letters on the left, upper case letters on the right, and pretty much all the rest in the middle—and with a few important symbols like "&" and "@" on the extreme right. How he loved that configuration!

He could hear the ratchets, gears, and cams orchestrating the text as it was neatly carried into place on the tray, and could smell the molten lead, antimony, and tin mixture that formed the neatly trimmed slugs. It had been a long time, but not long enough to forget. Still, actually operating the machine was different from imagining it. After all, a concert pianist couldn't imagine a concerto he hadn't played in years, and then step out cold onto the Carnegie Hall stage. Was he still lightening fast? He had been the fastest Linotype Operator in the room. They didn't dare question his weekly Shabbat observance at the *New York Times* when they saw that *speed,* and that pinpoint accuracy, which was just as important—more important. He still remembered the speed test that had startled them all. But that was so many years ago, and he was an old man now. He was old and way out of practice.

He quickly put together his egg sandwich and apple bag lunch and left the house at the usual 10:00 a.m. There was a slight breeze on his tree lined street that made the eighty-seven degree temperature seem almost pleasant. He headed for the much cooler subway ride to the Midwood section of Brooklyn.

When he arrived at Midwood Press, he realized that if he wanted to back out he could just go in as an observer, as he had done many times before. True, this wasn't a Thursday. There would be no group of elementary school students visiting today. But he could still say he was there to observe. This gave him the courage to actually approach the door to the shop and enter.

As usual, the shop was full of Victorian era printing equipment that was always a feast to his observant eyes.

He thought of the 1882 menorah, and something not quite conscious in him saw in this equipment a shared holiness with that precious religious object. He would have considered that a silly thought if it was a fully conscious one.

Off to one side of the shop was the prized Linotype machine. There were so few of them these days. Most had been junked a long time ago. And yet, there it was in all its "Rube Goldberg" steel and iron glory—not a museum piece, but a truly working model.

A shop owner he recognized was working at the keyboard. David could hear all the familiar sounds and smell all the familiar smells. And there right in front of him was the assembling elevator carrying the matrices back in place on the distributer bar as the man continued to smoothly press the keys, being careful not to rest his fingers on any of them lest matrices be released by mistake into one of the ninety channels taking them down to create the slug mold. As dozens of matrices were being released, they created that familiar sound, like a thousand keys clinking, like a Mozart symphony to his ears.

The man was fast, but not as fast as the fastest operators at the Old Grey Lady, the *New York Times*, where *all the news was fit to print*. The sentences continued to fall into place, each letter and sentence perfectly justified by the space bands in an ingenious mechanical process that no modern computer geek even deserved to understand.

Just then, the man turned for a second and saw David. He was a young man in his thirties, with a slim build and a thin shock of blonde hair protruding from his grey ball-style cap. He wasn't yet born when David last pressed the keys of a *New York Times* Linotype machine. But the man was the operator of one of the few working machines left, and that made him worthy of respect. He had turned back to work, but then turned around again.

"Good morning. It's good to see you again. Um…the school tours are the first and third Thursdays of the month."

"Yes sir. I know."

The man turned back to the machine. Another young printer came from across the room.

"Can we help you?"

"Well…"

"Is there something you want printed? We can show you the different options. Traditional letterpress printing looks very different from more modern methods. We love it. For instance, this is where hot-metal typography takes place."

"Yes, I know."

Just then, the man also recognized David as the Orthodox Jew that sometimes visited.

"You come here when the children come, don't you?"

It was now or never. David had always stood in the corner and watched the school groups as they were taught about how the Linotype machine worked. He took it for granted that the shop workers saw him as just a curious old rabbi or religious teacher of some sort, with his black yarmulka and fringes, or *tsit tsit,* protruding from under his white shirt.

"Um…I'm not here to watch the machine. I'm here to operate it."

"Operate it?"

The man at the machine responded.

"I see. You know how to operate one of these?"

"I did…once."

"Once? These aren't very easy to operate. For one thing, the keyboards are different."

"Yes, I know. Ninety keys. Yours has ninety-one."

The four workers in the shop stopped and stared at one another. The man who approached him earlier asked a question as the entire shop fell silent.

"So where'd you operate one of these things?"

David Kaplan confirmed everyone's silent suspicions.

"The *New York Times*."

The silence was broken by the man at the keyboard, whose name was Ben, as he enthusiastically stamped a foot repeatedly on the hard concrete floor.

"Dang! Dang! Dang!"

The other man asked another question.

"By any chance, are you Kaplan?"

There was a pause. Everyone in the shop knew the names of all the legendary *New York Times* operators, just as cartoonists know the name of every Disney animator from the golden era, men like Ward Kimball and Ollie Johnson.

"Yes, I am. How did you know?"

From the moment David Kaplan's words hit the eardrums of the closest man in the room, spontaneous applause began to ring off the cast-iron and steel machinery scattered throughout the shop. The four workers came and surrounded David, proceeding to howl and shriek as they clapped. David didn't know quite what to make of it. But he knew that their response couldn't be a bad thing, considering the fact that he was there to ask for a job—even if it *was* a voluntary one. Before he knew it all the workers, as one man, escorted him to the machine and seated him in front of the familiar keyboard. Ben extended his hand.

"You were one of the great editors behind the editors, printers behind the printers, layout artists behind the layout artists...at the greatest newspaper in the whole world. We salute you. Type...*anything!*"

David looked up at each of them, speechless. He gently put his hands on all the keys without pressing them. No matrices were released. That was a feat in itself.

"It's been so long."

"We understand. It would be an honor...please."

David looked over and spied the bucket hanging off the left side of the machine. There in that bucket was the true test of speed he had so often aspired to pass, and *had* passed only a few times. A meager handful of people in the industry could type so rapidly that the molten lead that had been collected in the hanging bucket as used slugs—and then melted down—would be sucked completely out of that same bucket. He took a deep breath. What would he type? He knew the English translation of Genesis 1, from the Jewish Publication Society. Why not just type that?

With authority familiar only to Moses, David began. He started slow. *In the beginning, G-d created the Heavens and the Earth.*

He even made sure to put a dash between the "G" and "D" of God, a tradition Orthodox Jews practice when writing in less than permanent records, out of respect for His name.

As he typed, the matrices flew like little messengers of silver light down the ninety-one channels, activating the caster and plunger. As the slugs were formed at five hundred degrees Fahrenheit, David began to speed up. Everyone's eyes shifted to the bucket. It was all coming back, at a pace that shocked even him. *It was good* repeated itself flawlessly as he typed verse two, then nine, ten, twenty-five.

The molten lead mixture in the bucket kept diminishing as he typed faster and faster. Everyone held their breath. By the time he had completed the last verse in the chapter, it was gone. They all cheered so loud that it sounded more like a stadium full of people than a shop of a half-dozen or so. Then they began to chant, using the slogan that was rarely fulfilled in the *real* world.

"He hung the bucket! He hung the bucket! He hung the bucket!"

The rest of the morning was spent answering questions and telling stories about the Grey Lady's golden years. For the first time since 1978, David felt like a true and appreciated artisan, a professional at a craft that someone still cared about. His cup overflowed with thankfulness to the God who had given Stanley and Mahmoud such a wonderful idea.

Before his visit was over, he was given a job on the third Thursday of each month—showing off his considerable skills before wide-eyed school children, telling them stories of his years as a Linotype operator. And even though the job didn't pay anything, at least he had an agreement that his train fare would be covered.

He ate his apple and egg sandwich as he rode the subway home. And he thought, *This is what it feels like to be alive! This, and visiting children in the hospitals. I can't wait to tell Naomi about this day. And Lisa too.*

Chapter Thirty-Two

Marc Silver hadn't said anything to anyone about the incident on the ship. He *had* considered purchasing a gun, primarily so he could protect himself from Lisa—as well as anyone else who might push him into oncoming traffic, out of a window, or anything else possible on land. But he hadn't been able to bring himself to apply for a permit. He had always left that kind of thing to Prima and his friends. He did, however, make one firm decision. He told himself he would definitely not make love with the enemy. That decision lasted exactly two weeks.

While Marc was traveling his usual Manhattan route—coming out of the heat and into air conditioned stores and back out into the heat—he made another decision. He decided he would visit Prima for the express purpose of telling him about the attack. He hadn't been able to bring it up in the course of normal business. The body guards were always hovering nearby. Finally, he decided that the attempt on his life was an important enough reason to break the normal rule and arrive unannounced. He also realized that he shouldn't be afraid to see the one man who could protect him from those he should *really* be afraid of, starting with Lisa. With each floor of the elevator, his heart rate rose.

"Stop it!," he mouthed to no one, as if he could direct his heart like a mystic of some sort. When he got to the office and buzzed in, he tried rudimentary breathing exercises that amounted to no more than a minor panic attack. But at this point he couldn't afford to concern himself with his body's involuntary actions.

The summer sun had its special way of reflecting off the glass table and throughout the room. It was clear and intense, the result of bouncing off the upper floors of the other glass and steel buildings, way above the street level it barely reached.

He sat nervously at the table, watching his well-shined black oxfords through the glass. He always hated this part, and he also always thought about how much he hated it. It took about fifteen minutes for Prima to show up. By that time, Marc's nervousness was exacerbated by a need to go to the bathroom. But he never used the bathroom at the office. He was never told he was allowed to. Prima arrived with a mixture of irritation and curiosity on his face. He was dressed in his summer jeans and black polo shirt outfit.

"*Nu?*"

Prima had a vocabulary of about ten Yiddish words, reserved for his Jewish associates. He sprinkled them sparingly throughout conversations with them, especially when a little lightness was warranted to temper his dark mood.

"And?"

Marc tripped over himself as he stood up and then reached his hand toward Prima.

"Put your hand down, Marc. Do we have an appointment?"

"Um…no. Look, I know this is unexpected."

He glanced around the room.

"Can anyone hear us? I mean…"

"Why should you be concerned, Marc?"

"I'm not…I mean, not really. But I meant to…to tell you about my vacation a month or so ago."

Prima's mood suddenly lightened.

"Oh…a friendly call. I'm a little busy, but…how was it?"

"Well…that's what I came here to talk to you about. See…"

Prima took a seat around the table and started swiveling.

"You're welcome. I'm glad I suggested it. I hope my people in the travel industry treated you well."

Marc stood there feeling utterly vulnerable.

"Well…I meant to tell you…

"Thank you is enough."

"Thank you…but, I forgot to mention that…that…"

"That what?"

"That…some Russian guy tried to kill me…um…throw me overboard."

Prima tried to rise from the chair slowly, as if he wasn't surprised or worried. He looked around the room quickly and then back toward Marc.

"Really? Interesting."

"I…I think it's Lisa. I'm sure it is. She chose the cruise. She must be working with that Brock guy, whoever he is. I guess she knows something…not that I told her. You must know who he's working for… your competition, or whatever. I'm sure you could deal with him. But what do I do about Lisa, Prima? What do I do? Please…."

Prima tried to suppress any and all emotion. His heart rate was rising, just as Marc's had, but he was much better at hiding those things. He totally changed his approach, and put his arm around Marc.

"You just be a good husband to Lisa, and let us take care of sending a gentle message to her. Everything will work out. Just do your job, and do it well and wisely. The businesses we're protecting are depending on you. All of these other things will work out. Now you get back to work. We'll keep an eye out for this Brock fellow. We're good at those things. And if Lisa tried something on the boat, she wouldn't dare try anything now. Let Prima take care of it. That's what I'm here for."

"But…"

"It'll be all right. You go along now."

Marc was a bit puzzled, but also oddly comforted. He left and resumed his route, feeling something he'd never felt before—fatherly affection from Prima. He was never able to feel that from his own father, who had been too busy as a pharmaceutical salesman—and too closed emotionally—to show affection. At the very least, Prima's Italian extroversion seemed to allow for the kind of affection Marc craved. He longed for that kind of relationship with David Kaplan, but David seemed to reserve all of his fatherly affection for Naomi. And anyway, Marc could never live up to his father-in-law's religious expectations.

Marc hadn't been gone for twenty seconds when the Russian Igor stepped out of a side door and into the office. He marched right up to Prima, who had already concluded that something more was going on than just Lisa talking to some low level police detective.

"Please don't hurt him. He's…sort of a son to me."

Igor, quickly and mechanically put Prima into a head lock.

"You listen to Igor, Prima. We don't have sons. You understand? I don't care about this Jew Silver."

Even as Igor tightened his grip, it crossed Prima's mind how silly that last comment sounded, since Igor himself was a Russian Jew.

"And I don't care about you, you dead relic. Eliminating Silver lowers risk…risk for dock business…fruit, vegetables, and everything else… *everything else.*"

Prima knew what *everything* meant—drugs, prostitution, and future control of the diamond trade—once resistant Chassids like Mandy Mendel were eliminated. Igor continued.

"Police detectives mean nothing. Wives mean nothing. You understand…you loser fool wop with *big heart?* Your father was good at murder, but you…you've lost art of killing."

As he squeezed even harder, Prima gasped for air, and Igor let him have not quite enough.

"Better not turn your back. Your body guards obey me, and they know when to cease being body guards and be killers."

He released Prima, who groaned as he collapsed to the floor.

"Be careful, do your job, and you'll live. I can't promise the same for your little Jew friend."

Igor left the room as Prima's two body guards walked in. One looked down at him and spoke flatly.

"Hey boss…you alright?

Prima got up and straightened out his polo shirt.

"I'm fine…just fine…just fine."

CHAPTER THIRTY-THREE

Darrin Brock was not happy about his last meeting with Naomi, to say the least. As a police detective, he felt a professional responsibility to call and restore his connection with her—for professional purposes. He hadn't reported to Inspector Lewis about the Ben's Deli meeting, and he had no intention of doing so. It was a minor glitch in an ongoing association that would hopefully yield something the department could use to unravel the underworld restaurant food service connection. There were other leads, of course, and other detectives. But this was *his* lead and *his* alone, and it was time to close the deal.

It was 7:00 p.m., and he had just left the Midtown South precinct station. As he headed down 35th Street, he pulled out his cell phone. He knew that if the Kaplan home had caller ID, his call would appear as *unknown*. So perhaps no one would answer. If Naomi *did* answer, she might be surprised and even upset to hear his voice. But he had to try to reconnect. It was his duty to do so. He decided he would take the direct approach, which he realized he should have taken as soon as he found out that Marc Silver was her brother-in-law. All of this interest in Judaism—and dare he say it, interest in her—was just a distraction. It had hindered his work. Now it was time, really past time, to get busy and make some headway on this particular case.

He dialed Naomi's home number, pausing only to breathe a quick prayer for favor. The phone rang…one, two, three times. Naomi picked it up.

"Yes? Who is this?"

"It's me…Darrin."

There was a very long pause. He slowed down his walk, held his breath, and tried to shield the phone from the sound of passing cars. Finally, she spoke again.

"What do you want?"

David Kaplan, seated in the stuffed chair in the corner of the living room, looked up from his Jewish Daily Forward and then back at the paper. Darrin spoke as directly as he could.

"I need to talk to you about a business matter."

"Business? Who's business, Darrin?"

Her father listened while he stared at the Forward.

"*My* business…detective business. I just have a few questions to ask you."

Naomi raised her voice.

"What, am I in trouble for something I've done? Were my answers about my religion not satisfactory, or what?"

David didn't even pretend to stare at the paper. He lowered it and looked at Naomi, who was now anxiously biting her little finger like she did when she was a little girl. Darrin stopped and then stepped into the first floor hall of a small office building.

"No. No. This is about something else…something else entirely… something we've never talked about."

"I see. Well…I'm sure I couldn't be of any help. You're…"

She began to tear, and then sighed before continuing.

"…a very kind person. You've been very kind to me…helpful at times. But…I don't think we should…."

Now David was staring right at her, and she glanced back at him.

"…should meet to discuss that matter…or any other matter. I appreciate all you've done, but…"

Now she avoided her father's eyes.

"…I don't think we should meet about that business matter. I don't think I could help you."

"But you don't even know what it's about…or *do you?*"

"I need to go. My father needs me. I'm…I'm sorry. I need to go now."
She hung up the phone. Her father got up from his chair.

"Naomi…"

"Not now, Abba. Please, not now."

She went up the stairs and into the bedroom, shutting the door. At the same time, Darrin headed for the subway, a dozen questions filling his head.

Does she know about Marc Silver? Is she shielding him? Or is she just pushing me away? Perhaps she just doesn't want a detective to ask her questions about anything, like the Chassids…that is, except Chaya Mendel. But she had no choice.

Naomi fell down on her bed and grabbed the box of tissues on the night table. She lay on her stomach and wept as quietly as she could. Then she curled up in a fetal position. Loneliness pierced her like a sharp blade. Darrin was more like her father than anyone she'd ever met. Perhaps he was even, in some strange way, more like a Jew than most Jews she'd ever met—despite the off-putting Christianity he believed in and Gentile ways he practiced.

"After all, he didn't even know when Ben's Deli closed for Passover," she whispered to herself. "But still…"

New tears welled up. She felt like she was on the precipice of the rest of her life, a long way down a tunnel of empty solitary existence, punctuated by moments of fleeting joy with her father—at least while he was still on this Earth. A sudden swelling emotion swept like a tsunami from the top of her head all the way to the tips of her toes. She involuntarily admitted to herself, for the first time, something she had never spoken out loud or silently.

I love him. I love him. What am I going to do? What am I going to do? I love him.

Her crying became more audible. David could hear the heaves of jagged weeping from downstairs. But he didn't dare disturb her. He respected her too much to interrupt her when she'd asked him not to. All he could do was to try to piece together what was happening and ask her about it later, when she was ready to talk. This was his dear daughter, heart of his Jewish heart, soul—*nashamah* in Hebrew—of his Jewish soul. And something was terribly wrong—something he had suspected for a while, but now *more* than suspected.

Chapter Thirty-Four

Marvin was the last person on David Kaplan's mind. The only thing that occupied it in the morning was the night before. Naomi tried to keep to herself during the hour or so between the time she got up and the time she left for work at Macy's. David passed her once in the hall and quietly said "good morning", *boker tov* in Hebrew. But she didn't respond. She made every effort to avoid him after that. She wasn't angry at him. She was embarrassed and ashamed, and didn't want him to ask her any questions.

For his part, David knew that if he started asking questions, he wouldn't be satisfied with short answers. And it seemed to him that short answers were about all she was in the mood to give, or had time for. Then he remembered again that she'd said "no" when he'd reached out the night before. He would have to wait until she was ready to talk.

After Naomi left, David began his morning prayers, looking down at his small frayed black prayer book as he swayed back and forth, periodically bending his knees to the *Blessed are You, Lord our God* parts.

The phone rang. Normally, he would let it ring while he continued praying. But he wondered whether it might be Naomi, perhaps just to tell him she loved him. That was something she told him almost every other morning before she left for work, but hadn't told him that morning. He couldn't know who it was, because he had never gotten caller ID, contrary to what Darrin Brock had supposed earlier. So he did something he had rarely, if ever, done before during his morning *Shacharit* prayers. He answered his phone—and immediately, he regretted it.

"Marvin, what do you want? You shouldn't be calling. You should be working at this hour, or at least looking for a job. So what is it?"

"A man yesterday said to call back next week. My mother says I'm a hard worker."

"What did you call me for, Marvin?"

David knew he was being unkind. But the call seemed like such a curse, occurring as it had during his morning prayers. He stood there in his black jacket and dark blue yarmulke, impatient to return to his prayer book. Marvin, however, was still in his green striped pajamas.

"Mr. Kaplan, I'm thinking that you're a father to me."

David knew these probably weren't words of appreciation. Marvin wanted something.

"You're the most righteous man I know...the wisest man."

"Okay Marvin. Thank you for that, but you've interrupted my *Shacharis* prayers. I need to get back to them."

"But...HaShem wants me to ask you something."

David was tempted to ask Marvin why he didn't just get his answer from HaShem Himself. But he held his tongue.

"So what, if I may ask, has He touched your heart to ask me?"

"Well...I believe He would have me ask you, Mr. Kaplan...why Naomi and I should know each other from when we were little children if He didn't want us...married. She won't talk to me...not for a month. She always has something else on her mind, I don't even know what it is. Isn't that a sin for two Jews not to be able to even speak to each other, when HaShem practically raised them together Himself?"

David had heard enough.

"You're not thinking about Naomi, Marvin. You're only thinking about yourself. We've been through this before. You're interrupting my prayer time."

Marvin's voice rose persuasively.

"I'm ready to perform any mitzvah...any kind at all. Just ask me... any mitzvah. This is what kind of Jew I am. Then you'll *beg* me to marry your daughter instead of her becoming an old maid."

Marvin was too oblivious to realize he'd stepped over the line.

"I mean…what's she waiting for, for God's sake?"

David wanted to just protect the honor of his oldest daughter. But he couldn't resist challenging Marvin's claim for himself.

"Any mitzvah, Marvin? Really? I don't think I've ever seen you perform even one mitzvah for anyone…*ever.*"

David didn't even know why he was having this conversation, but he had now so invested himself in convincing Marvin that he was not a good Jew, that he had to prove it. On top of that, communicating that message in itself seemed like a mitzvah. So he decided the prayers could wait ten minutes.

"So what mitzvah have you ever performed? Tell me! Tell me!"

Marvin paused for several seconds, as if he had lost the train of thought. Finally, he answered.

"Well…I take care of my mother…my dear *Yiddeshe* mama."

"No. No Marvin! She takes care of you! *Everyone* takes care of you. If you ever get married, your wife will take care of you too."

"Ask my mother, She'll tell you."

"She already has."

What was David Kaplan doing? He was arguing with Marvin like they were both schoolboys. He was finished with this conversation and was just about ready to hang up and get back to his prayer book, when the well worn Talmudic edict suddenly crossed his mind.

Instead of giving a man a fish, teach him to fish.

Perhaps he should teach Marvin what a mitzvah truly was. The rabbis were emphatic that this was the right thing to do. And with that came another idea that had first occurred to him months before, after hearing about the death of the Chassid in Manhattan.

The idea proceeded from David's ongoing problem. He still suffered infrequent pangs of guilt over his passivity after the death of the young Jewish truck driver who had gone to the police in the nineteen-seventies, when David was still a Linotype operator. During a bout of recent pangs, after one of his DeWitt Wallace Periodical Room discussions with Stanley and Mahmoud, he had used the library computers to look up the name of the young Chassid's widow in the *New York Times* Internet archives. He discovered that her name was Chaya Mendel. From there, it didn't take much effort to call an insider he knew at the Times to get her street address. Apparently, she lived in Brooklyn—in Crown Heights, not that far from him. The prompting to perform a mitzvah and visit her had been increasingly gnawing at him, but so far he hadn't had the courage to act on it. Perhaps the opportunity to *kill two birds* presented itself now—although he realized that was not the most appropriate turn of phrase, considering the circumstances. Marvin could come along and learn about doing something thoughtful for someone else. And he, David, could comfort the widow of a man who suffered the same fate as the truck driver. He would *do* it. He would take Marvin to visit Mrs. Chaya Mendel.

All the while these ideas were taking shape in David Kaplan's mind, Marvin blathered on in disjointed sentences about all the things he did for his mother, and how proud she was of him. David broke in mid-sentence.

"Marvin...enough about your mother. You're going to accompany me on a genuine mitzvah."

"Can Naomi come?"

"No," David instantly shot back. "Get dressed" were his next words, based on his correct instinct that Marvin was still in his pajamas. "Meet me here in an hour. We're going to pay someone a visit, someone who I'm sure could use some loving care. And bring some of your mother's parve cookies," he threw in, referring to kosher baked goods that could be eaten with milk or meat dishes. "Why not let her get in on the mitzvah too?"

"Last night it was chocolate chip. My mother makes the best kosher cookies. Ask anyone, anyone."

"Okay, okay. Enough about your mother. Chocolate chip it is. One hour."

David hung up before Marvin had a chance to make excuses and back out, which he sometimes did. Then he went back to his Shacharit prayers, putting a special emphasis on the prayers that speak of the loving-kindness of God. Two and a half hours late, Marvin showed up in a bright red tee shirt, matching bright red silk Yarmulke, and stained tan dockers. He carried an aluminum foil covered paper plate.

"My mother says hi," he said matter-of-factly.

"Tell her thank you for the cookies."

"How did you know they were cookies?"

"How did you think I knew?"

"Because...you asked for them? You know, I have a good memory, Mr. Kaplan."

"I'm sure you do, Marvin."

"Okay, but she said I should tell her how surprised you were."

"Well I wasn't."

"I can't tell her that, Mr. Kaplan."

"Oh come on, Marvin. Bring the cookies, and let's go."

"Where are we going?"

"To a Chassidic Jewish widow's house."

"But I don't want to marry a widow. Is that the mitzvah?"

"Believe me, she doesn't want to marry you either. Let's go."

David tried to fill him in on the bus. But it was noisy, and Marvin was distracted. It wasn't until they got to the house that Marvin got nervous.

"Her husband was murdered?"

"Yes, Marvin. Keep your voice down, and don't say that inside the house."

"Why couldn't Naomi come? She'd know what to say. I don't know what to say. Naomi would know."

"Be quiet."

David rang the bell. Within a half a minute or so, Chaya Mendel answered.

"Shalom. We gave to the mentally handicapped at synagogue. But thank you very much."

Marvin was too anxious to understand what she was saying. She began to shut the door.

"No, please," David spoke in a particularly kind compassionate voice, even for him.

"Would you do me the favor of letting an old man perform a mitzvah? One the Rebbe himself would approve of?"

David had gotten her attention. She couldn't quite bring herself to shut the door on a man who invoked the name of Menachem Schneerson, the great Chabad rabbi of the last century and the sage on her living room wall that just could be the Messiah. She opened the door wider.

"And what is this mitzvah, Mr...?"

"Mr. Kaplan...David Kaplan...with my...well, you understand...my *friend* Marvin. You see, I was a Linotype operator at the *New York Times* during the 1970's, and I ran across a case..."

David went on to tell the whole story, right there as he stood at her door. He also threw in the fact that Marvin needed to perform his first real mitzvah. He was almost finished when Marvin—who was tired of carrying the cookies—began to hold them sideways, like a schoolboy holds his books. David grabbed them before they could slide out of the aluminum foil covering and fall to the ground. He interrupted the tail end of his own explanation.

"These are fresh…and parve. They're from his mother…chocolate chip."

Just then Natan, who had been listening from the white couch without understanding a word that was being said, got up and ran toward his mother.

"Cookies, Ima!"

"We'll see, Natan. Are these really kosher, Mr. Kaplan."

"As kosher as Moishe's manna," he responded, using her specific dialect for the Hebrew name of Moses."

The story had softened her heart, and she was convinced David Kaplan was genuine. There was no one who ever met him who thought otherwise, and Chaya Mendel was no exception.

"Please, come in."

The two visitors came in and were invited to the dining room table.

"Would you like some tea?"

"Coke," Marvin demanded.

David betrayed embarrassment.

"Marvin."

"We have that," Chaya interjected, with all the sympathy and pity appropriate for the mentally handicapped. David wanted to pinch Marvin into behaving, but he wasn't close enough to him.

"I don't need anything. Please don't put yourself out."

"It's no problem. Tea?"

"No tea, please. Thank you."

She went to get the coke while Marvin ate his first cookie. David gave him a look, which he ignored. When she got back, she addressed David's earlier comments while Marvin drank the glass of coke in three swallows.

"I'm so sorry about your friend. But I'm sure you did what you could, Mr. Kaplan. You seem like a very good man. I would have expected no different from a similar employee of the *New York Times* after *our* tragedy."

"It's very kind of you, Mrs. Mendel. That makes me feel so much better, although I know I could have done more at the time."

"They're thugs, Mr. Kaplan. What can you do about thugs?"

Natan was acting like a puppy in begging position. He had been trained not to interrupt adults like he was trained to not wear his shoes

166

on the white sofa. But he knew how to get his mother's attention. She responded.

"I'll take the plate of cookies over to the floor, and you can each eat two of them…just two."

Marvin was delighted.

"My name is Marvin."

"Yes, Marvin. He'll show you his puzzles."

Marvin instantly went over to perform his mitzvah…eating most of the cookies as he played with little Natan.

David realized that this was not becoming any kind of lesson for Marvin. But all was not lost. He had confessed his guilt to possibly the most appropriate person in New York City, and he was feeling very thankful to God for providing this wonderful gift—more wonderful than he ever could have imagined. As far as his own mitzvah was concerned, he realized that the most important thing he could do would be to listen to Chaya Mendel while she shared the challenges of raising her children as a single mother, and the blessing of the support from her family, her late husband's family, and the whole Chassidic family around her. He was in the process of listening intently, when he happened to overhear Natan saying something in the animated tone of an excited four-year-old.

"You're not as much fun as Darrin Brock, but I like you too. He's like Abba. You're like my brother."

Chaya overheard him too.

"Don't compare, Natan? They're both nice."

"Marvin eats a lot more cookies than Darrin, Ima."

David couldn't help himself.

"Darrin Brock?"

"Yes, he's a very nice man from the police department who visits Natan. He's a Gentile…a very nice man."

"I see."

Anything Chaya Mendel said after that was a blur. David nodded, but his thoughts were elsewhere. This couldn't be a coincidence, not with so many people in the city of New York. Just who was this man? Something was not right. He wasn't sure what it was, but something definitely felt wrong.

Marvin slept like a baby during the bus ride back to the Kaplan house. But David couldn't sleep all that night. He felt followed, haunted, intruded upon, and deeply concerned for his oldest daughter.

CHAPTER THIRTY-FIVE

Darrin Brock had solidified his conviction that he would speak to Naomi about Marc Silver. And not only Naomi, but he would also speak to her father, as well as Marc's wife Lisa, if possible. Then he would go for Marc himself, after he gathered enough information from the others. He had always known that this case had to proceed in stages, so he wouldn't tip off Prima too early in the game. And the time for stage two was long past due.

He walked past the pedestrians on the comparatively small but still well traveled 35th street, from Eighth Avenue towards the precinct building, just shy of Ninth Avenue. The hot humid August city air clung to his skin like dirty motor oil. He passed through the few wooden barricades and entered the building, taking the stairs to the second floor. He knocked on Inspector Ralph Lewis' office. Lewis opened the door after a few seconds. Darrin could see over his shoulder that his desk was messier than usual.

"Is it important, Brock? 'Cause I'm busy with all this community relations stuff. They've got me overwhelmed here."

Darrin looked back toward the desk.

"I can see that."

"Yeah, well…what do you need?"

"It's about the Prima thing, and Silver."

"Oh yeah, that. Hey, by the way, how's the widow?"

"She's doing very well…and her children. Natan, that's the one I've spent time with, he's something else."

"I'm sure he is."

"Thank you for sending me there, Inspector. It's really been a high point."

"You're welcome I'm sure."

Inspector Lewis grabbed Darrin by the shoulder and moved him toward the door.

"Listen, maybe we can set up a meeting about the Italian mob thing. You can see I'm swamped. They've been around a long time. I'm sure whatever you have to tell me can wait a week or two. Know what I mean?"

"Sure. I just wanted you to know I'm going in for the kill with Silver's relatives. That's all."

Inspector Lewis was both genuinely thankful that Darrin had agreed to continue pursuing the leads, and too busy with a dozen more important things to hear the details. He went back and sat at his overwhelming desk, leaning forward in his chair while simultaneously slapping both hands on top of the various documents connected with the police relations agenda.

"That's good, Brock. You do that, and give me a full report. We've got to wrap that up. I see it as operation Giuliani Mop Up Drive. You know what I mean? It's been long enough. *Case closed*…that's what I want to hear. And we'll connect after you go in for that kill of yours. Hey, could you do me a favor and close the door on the way out?"

Darrin got the message, and left the office. As he headed past the few wooden barriers and out into the street, he felt an odd combination of professional loneliness and professional obligation. Italian organized crime still needed to be addressed, and he was one of the few who were responsible for addressing it. That made his job that much more essential. Someone, actually a whole department, would take care of the Russians. And a whole other department would take care of the Asians. But he was practically the only God-appointed yet reluctant super hero who was taking care of the classic Mafia. And although he didn't feel anything like a super hero, he did feel the need—by some sort of step of faith—to act like one. This was his plan for the Kaplan house surprise visit he was just about to embark on.

Darrin waited until about 6:00 p.m. to leave for Brooklyn. He had never actually visited the Kaplan house. He'd often imagined what it looked like, and had once or twice been tempted to check out the Google image. But he realized that the appearance of the house was irrelevant to his work, so he never did. When he finally turned the corner and saw the house sandwiched between two other Brooklyn brownstones, he wasn't surprised that it looked somewhat similar to Chaya Mendel's house. And he was relieved. This was a routine house, part of a routine visit by a routine New York City Police Department detective.

He knew the family wouldn't insist on the neighborhood Chabad police that were active in places like Crown Heights. Not only wasn't this neighborhood dead center in that unusual jurisdiction, as the Mendel house was, but he also had the benefit of knowing at least Naomi. He was sure she wouldn't demand that force's involvement. However, he did realize that he had never come in his detective capacity. That would be new. And he was sure it would seem strange to her.

As he neared the house, he grasped his flip wallet detective's badge in his right hand. And he prayed while silently moving his lips.

"Lord, I think I've gotten myself into some kind of a mess here. You know that. And I admit it was totally my fault. *Totally*. It's true, You gave me a heart for this people You call by Your name…I mean a love, a genuine love. You *have*. But…but…I…I think I…went beyond Your will…and most of all, beyond the responsibility of this job you gave me. I don't know what to say. You know my heart. You know I'm not neutral about this…this…this…Naomi…this Naomi person. I let my emotions get in the way, and threw my professional responsibility pretty much under the bus, so to speak. And You know that's true…even though You also know I hate this case I'm on and this whole part of my job. I know You know that too. I should be thankful I *have* a job. I *should* be. So I really ask Your forgiveness for that. Plus, if that weren't enough, she doesn't believe in You, Jesus. And that's *so* unfair, really to her, to…to… put that on her. So okay, okay…I think I've flirted with her. I admit it. A few times. I admit it…and purposely taken at least one item back to her department just so I could see her…even though it was in the basement level. I admit it. I admit it. I do."

At that point, he shifted from entreating God to berating himself.

"I can't believe I got in this deep. What am I going to do? What's the matter with me? What in the world is the matter with me. What is it with this stupid foolish heart of mine? Foolish is what it is. I'm such a stupid fool…an absolute idiot. That's it! It's over!"

He clenched his left hand into a fist and raised it into the air.

"I'll tell you what I'm gonna do. I'm gonna go in there, flash this badge, and do my job. That's what I'm gonna do. And then, when I've said my peace and asked my questions, I'll leave…and I won't see her again until she's a witness in a court of law. End of story. Done. Period!"

After he boldly pronounced that proclamation, a still small voice seemed to whisper somewhere just beyond his inner ear.

It won't be done…not today.

Intentionally ignoring those few words, he marched right up to the door and knocked on it hard several times with his left hand. In his right hand, he clutched the badge.

David Kaplan rose from the dining room table, where he had been tinkering with a broken old turntable Stanley had given him. He went over to the door and called out.

"Who is it?"

The loud thumping against the door had alarmed David, and he wasn't about to just open it.

"NYPD Police…Detective Department," came the strong confident response. David was unconvinced.

"Is that so? You'll have to produce evidence."

"I have evidence, Sir. Please open the door. I just have a few questions."

"About what?"

"About your son-in-law, Marc Silver."

"What about him?"

"May I come in?"

David slowly opened the door. As soon as it had been opened wide enough for him to clearly see who was there, Darrin flashed the badge, flicking the cover over like a switchblade.

"NYPD Detective Division, Sir. May I come in?"

David stepped aside just as Naomi was coming down the stairs.

"Who is it, Abba? What's all the commotion about?"

As soon as Darrin came into her line of sight, she stopped cold.

"What are *you* doing here?"

The fold-out portion that held the badge was still displayed. David could just see Darrin Brock's name and picture on the laminated card that had been inserted into it. A foreboding sense of horror swept over him.

"It's *you!*"

"I need to ask a few questions, Sir. May I step into your dining room there, or should I stand here?"

Naomi walked up and stood by her father's side.

"Darrin, what's this about? Why are you here?"

"Hello, Miss Kaplan. I just need to ask a few questions about Marc Silver."

His eyes averted hers.

"Miss Kaplan, Were you aware that your brother-in-law may have connections with an underground ring of extortionists...and worse?"

Clearly agitated, David turned toward his daughter.

"Naomi, is this the Darrin Brock who's been calling you at all odd hours of the night?"

He wanted to add that Brock made her cry, but he thought the better of it and left that out.

"Yes, Abba. He has called here a few times."

"Naomi...just who is this...this..."

He wanted to say goy, the Yiddish and Hebrew term for Gentile, usually spoken derisively. But he thought the better of that too. He had enough presence of mind not to call even an enemy who was created in God's image names—and in a shaming tone yet. The sages taught him that much. But he could still speak his mind about the man's evil actions, at least evil as far as he could tell.

"Get out of my house," he thundered to the best of his ability, considering that he was a gentle man. "Leave these premises immediately, or I'll call the...the police. I don't care *what* kind of supposed detective big shot you are."

His black yarmulke almost flew off his head as he jerked it back.

"You have stalked and harassed my oldest daughter, intruded on a poor grieving widow...and now *this!* How dare you accuse my only son-in-law, and smear his name...faithful husband to my youngest daughter and loving father to their children. You leave immediately, you...you... you troublemaker!"

Naomi stopped him short.

"Wait, Abba."

She looked directly at Darrin, who could not look back at her, lest she detect his feelings for her and his whole mission collapse like a chair with two legs. Naomi, however, took the direct approach.

"Darrin Brock, you look at me right now and tell me to my face that my own brother-in-law is a crook!"

Darrin tried as hard as he could to look at her, but could only make it as far as her nose. It occurred to him right then and there that he'd fallen in love with her and that he needed to fall out of it fast. Looking into her eyes would be like looking into a deep well and then falling into it. Her eyes were impossibly dark, and full of tender sweet pain—something he had noticed way back in the spring at the Channel Gardens, but hadn't wanted to admit. And they were just the most beautiful part of this extraordinarily beautiful woman. Naomi, dissatisfied with Darrin's response, grabbed her father's hand.

"It's not true. You can't speak of my family that way. Go please."

Desperate, Darrin took the "objective" Joe Friday approach.

"I just need to ask you some questions, Ma'am. I'm not saying he's guilty."

"What's with the Ma'am, Darrin? Are you crazy, or what? Just *go*. My father and I want to be left alone."

Darrin didn't know what to say. He knew what he *wanted* to say, but he knew he couldn't say it. Nevertheless, he let down his professional guard and just spoke her name, "Naomi," in such a way that she thought she could for the first time sense some kind of feelings for her—but perhaps not. His gentle goodness, which she had detected from the start, also bled through—like the bleeding out of the Yom Kippur offering from Holy Scripture. But that just made it more urgent that he leave.

"Please, could you go now? I need you to leave, like my father is asking."

Darrin had no choice. He folded his badge into his pocket and walked out of the house. The slowly cooling dusk of the warm summer evening met him as he walked down the street, head bowed. Naomi shut the door and turned to David Kaplan, who was clearly ashen and exhausted.

"Abba…"

He began to walk toward the living room couch, collapsing onto it with a sigh. From a sitting position, he peered at the menorah in the dining room. He could just make it out in the low light of the setting sun.

Naomi came over and sat down next to him. She put her arm around him, not knowing what to say. She wanted to say, "He's actually a very good man, like you, Abba." But when she finally could speak, all she could say was. "I really don't know what he's talking about when he speaks about Marc. It couldn't be true or Lisa would tell us. But…maybe the police are mixed up about Marc. Maybe it's not this person Darrin

Brock's fault."

David turned to her, sensing guilt and shame in her eyes. He chose his words as carefully as he could. But he knew he had to say something to teach his daughter about the ways of the world she seemed so ignorant about.

"You know, Naomi, Linotype operators typed out many evil things about this world to print in the daily newspaper. They could sense evil's presence a long way off…sometimes before hardly anyone at the newspaper, or in the city. I believe there was genuine evil in this house this evening, dressed up as a handsome blonde-haired police detective. You know, sometimes even handsome movie stars play evil roles. And sometimes even seemingly good Christians are really evil. Not always, but sometimes. As Samuel said, 'Man looks on the outside. God looks on the heart.' Do you understand, Naomi?"

For the first time in her whole life, which stretched from her first conscious moments in her infancy all the way to her late forties, Naomi realized that her father was wrong about something. But she didn't dare confront him about it. Waiting for her response, he repeated himself.

"Do you understand?"

"Yes, Abba, I understand."

"Good."

He gave her an affectionate hug. She hugged him back with all the love and affection with which she always hugged him. The depth of that love could never change. Still, something *did* change that evening. She couldn't put her finger on exactly what it was, but she knew something changed. Something would never be the same.

CHAPTER THIRTY-SIX

Naomi went to bed early that night. She lay under the covers with so many competing thoughts flying around in her head that she knew she was headed for a sleepless night. She threw off the covers, sat up in bed, and grabbed a book about the Sabbath off her night stand. It was written by scholar and rabbi Abraham Joshua Heschel. Although he wasn't an Orthodox rabbi, she recognized the same wisdom in him that she saw in her father. She figured she could use some of that wisdom just now. Maybe if she read a chapter or two, she would be comforted by the words of this modern day sage and then doze off after a while. But as she tried to read, she couldn't concentrate. She put the book down face open on her lap and closed her eyes. She had to find something else to take her mind off the disturbing events of the evening.

She hadn't looked at her phone since before Darrin came to the house. She grabbed it off of the same night stand next to her bed. There, in his usual text style, was a message from Marvin.

How are you? I have money for lunch at Ben's tomorrow. Will you meet me at noon?

Maybe, in those short but spelled-out words so typical of Marvin's texts, was the wisdom she was seeking. Perhaps the Almighty was directing her toward the treasure in her own back yard. *Okay,* she thought, *That may be taking it a bit far. And my father thinks I deserve better. But he was wrong about Darrin. Maybe he's wrong about Marvin too.*

She quickly typed *okay* back to him. Something in her felt regret as soon as she pressed *send.* Still, she pushed the open book aside, threw off the covers, and got out of bed, walking straight into the bathroom. She turned on the light and stood in front of the mirror. "Ugly woman," she whispered. "I hate my hair, I hate my eyes, I hate my nose, I hate my mouth. Just a plain ugly middle-aged invisible woman. I *hate* myself!"

She took her long curly black hair and pulled it up with her right hand, as if it was a rope she was hanging by. She cocked her head to the side and stuck her tongue out of the corner of her mouth. Then she tightly squeezed her neck with her left hand. Her face began to redden. She stood there like that for perhaps thirty to forty seconds. Then she released her neck, and then her hair, which fell into a bushy tangled mess.

"I wish I was dead, God forbid."

She slapped her own face hard with her right hand, making her cheek even redder, and releasing tears from both eyes like liquid spilling out from a freshly broken bottle. Then she opened the medicine chest and took out some rouge and bright red lipstick. She wiped her tears with a tissue, and began to paint her face with the rouge. Tears fell again over the freshly applied make-up as she applied the lipstick, outlining her lips grotesquely. She began to weep as softly as she could, so as not to disturb her father, whispering between the weeping.

"I'm a clown, I'm a virgin prostitute who loves a gentile Christian who worships other gods, I'm a miserable alta moid, an ugly old prune. Look at me. I'm perfectly hideous. Now Marvin *really* deserves me. I'm just perfect for him. I don't have *one* friend, not even *one* girlfriend…just my father. I don't even have a sister. Not really. So I might as well have a schlemiel for a boyfriend. That's all I deserve. I should be grateful for what God gives me. Isn't that what Abba always taught me?"

She turned on the faucet and stuck her head in the sink, washing off all of the make-up along with the tears. The water turned blood red and then pink. Then she dried her face with a towel. She took out the bottle of Advil and took twice the recommended dose—not enough to end her life, but just enough to numb her pain with sleep as quickly as possible. It worked. When she woke up the next morning, the summer sun was higher than usual for a workday. She looked at the clock radio on the night table. It was indeed late, but not too late to make work, if she rushed.

She ran into the bathroom. Her eyes weren't as puffy as she thought they'd be. But they were still a bit swelled. She usually wore very little make-up, the night before being a rare exception. But today was an emergency. So she put on a little eyeliner and some light pink lipstick and quickly dressed in her summer flowery dress. She left her room and quickly passed her father in the hall, obscuring her face.

"I'm late. I'll grab a banana and leave for work. I'm seeing Marvin for lunch."

"Marvin. That's good. He really misses you."

She detected an unusual sense of relief in her father's voice. She looked back at him from the bottom of the steps.

"I miss him like I miss the flu. But I guess you have to have the flu once in a while."

"He's not *that* bad. Maybe you should give him a chance, Naomi."

"I've never heard you say *that* before. Gotta go!"

Naomi flew out the door. Even as she ran toward the subway, she thought about why her father had said that about Marvin. Indeed, she *knew* why he said it. He was concerned about Darrin. His few words to her the night before betrayed that. He wanted her to find a man with whom she would build an Orthodox Jewish home, even if that man ended up being Marvin. She actually loved her father for feeling that way. She knew deep down inside that he still felt she was too good for Marvin. But he also wanted the best possible husband for her as his precious *Jewish* daughter. And if God chose Marvin for her as His best, then that would satisfy him. It was a matter of priorities, and she loved her father's priorities.

Morning in the housewares department went slowly. There were two suspiciously cracked dish customers and a happy wedding registry couple, perfectly timed to put her in the mood for the pressure she was expecting from Marvin over lunch.

The walk from Macy's to Ben's Deli felt like a walk to the gallows that Naomi had already rehearsed for in front of her bathroom mirror. She marched in step with the traffic as it acted like a drum processional—the retail operations on either side of Broadway serving as escorts to her execution.

When she arrived at Ben's on 38th Street, she looked through the front window, and there was Marvin. He was dressed in his bright orange shorts, which matched the orange booth seat, and a slightly off-yellow tee shirt. And he was already drinking a coke. Naomi went in and sat across from him. He didn't miss a beat.

"Where've *you* been?"

"Let's not get into that."

"You look nice. I like your dress."

Naomi was too irritated with Marvin's opening remarks to receive his compliment graciously.

"That's what I work in. I see *you're* dressed appropriately...for a day off. Did you find a job yet?"

"You look very nice. I like the flowers on your dress."

"Thank you, Marvin. Thank you very much. What about your job? Did you find one?"

"I have some irons in the fire. Mother says she sees me trying. You're wearing nice lipstick."

"My father told me to wear it."

"Really?"

"No, not really. So you're treating? I'm hungry."

"Well...I have money."

"Right. So what should I get? How much do you have?"

"Um...I have money...for myself. My mother gave me some money from savings. You don't have to pay for me. It's not enough for..."

"For me? Marvin, when a man says he has money, it usually means... never mind. I'll cover both of us. Keep your mother's money."

"I'll save my part and pay for both of us the next time, when my mother gives me money again...or probably I'll have a job by then."

Naomi slapped her hand down on the table and looked him straight in the eyes.

"Who says there will be a next time, Marvin?"

Marvin grabbed her hand with both hands, trying to be the man he knew she wanted.

"There *has* to be. The Holy One Himself has created us for each other. Please Naomi. Aunt Ida knows it. She told us. Everybody knows it. Please. Be my wife."

"*I* don't know it, Marvin. And your crazy Aunt Ida doesn't know it either. She doesn't know what she's talking about."

She pulled her hand out from under his and sat back in her seat. She closed her eyes and then opened them, noticing a tear escaping his left eye and trickling down his cheek. She was struck by just how desperately lonely he was. A barely detectable dose of compassion rose up from somewhere within her Jewish soul.

"Look, Marvin. Um…you're a good upright observant Jew and a…a good man. You have something to give for the right woman."

Marvin's eyes fully welled with tears.

"But I've been…waiting my whole life. I *need* you. Please Naomi… before we order lunch, just say yes."

Naomi suddenly stood up.

"I can't do that, Marvin. I need to go. I was going to ask you all about your job search…and about your mother, just like usual. That's all we talk about anyway. But I can't now. Marvin, I'll say a prayer for HaShem to help you. But I'm sorry…I'm so, so sorry…I can't. I just can't. I just can't."

Naomi walked out, too upset to look back at Marvin, who was drowning his tears in his Coke, and about to order another one—with a corned beef on rye. The truth was, he didn't quite know how to process emotions connected to the death of the only thing in life he had been looking forward to for as long as he could remember. He just sat there, paralyzed. But that didn't last long. By the time he took the first big bite out of his corned beef sandwich, he was planning his next appeal to Naomi.

Meanwhile, she walked down 38th Street, with its old worn out garment shops, feeling emotionally assaulted. But she couldn't take her anger out on poor old Marvin, not after she saw him crying like that. There was only one person she could take it out on. And that was the person who had showed up at her house uninvited, and had coldly called her "Ma'am." She still had a half hour of lunch break time left, so she decided to at least locate the precinct station where he worked.

Naomi didn't have one of those phones that accessed the Internet. Hers flipped open, received and sent calls and texts, and told her the time. That was about it. Sometimes she wished she had one of those phones that told where things were in the city, so she didn't have to use her computer before she left home. She knew that some phones could do that kind of thing, just like Aunt Ida's car GPS could tell how to get to places by car.

As she was trying to figure out how to find out where Darrin worked, she suddenly realized that she didn't need a fancy phone. She could just dial zero and ask for the closest police station. She stopped and stood in the baking summer sun, her flowered dress gently waving in the urban 38th Street breeze. In her left hand she held access to all she needed to know. She took a deep breath, and flipped her phone open like a Star-Trek communicator.

"Yes, um…I'd like to speak to the police at the nearest station to my…present location. I'm on 38th Street in Manhattan, near I think 7th Avenue…thank you."

It took only a matter of seconds before she was connected to the NYPD Midtown South Precinct station. She was amazed to hear that it was only blocks away, on 35th street near Ninth Avenue. And she was doubly pleased when she found out that Darrin Brock did indeed work there. Considering the size of New York City—and even of Midtown Manhattan—Naomi took this as a sign, a miracle. She had already decided not to get angry at Darrin on the phone. She wanted to show up in person, totally unexpected, as he had when he visited her house. She also decided what she'd tell him—that he was wrong about her brother-in-law Marc, and that he had no business showing up at her house unannounced. The close proximity of Ben's Deli to the precinct station meant it might be possible to do that right now, in the next fifteen minutes!

She headed toward 35th Street near Ninth Ave. When she got to the precinct station, she noticed the short white wooden barriers that seemed inadequate to protect anything from anyone. She was in the process of walking through them, like an army on the march, when she was stopped by a middle aged dirty-blonde female officer.

"Can I help you, Ma'am?"

She wondered if they *all* used that term.

"I'm here to visit Darrin Brock," she proclaimed boldly.

The officer seemed unimpressed.

"You'll have to wait here. Who should I say wants to see him?"

"Naomi…Naomi Kaplan. And you can tell him it's a surprise visit."

"We don't like surprises around here," the officer responded with a deadpan tone. She left, and was gone for at least five minutes. When she returned, she said, "He's out, but Inspector Lewis wants to see you."

"Inspector who? Who's he?"

"You'll find out. Come with me."

All of a sudden, bold Naomi wanted to retreat back to work, mission unaccomplished.

"I don't think so. I don't even know who this Inspector Lewis is. Why would he want to see me?"

"He knows who *you* are. And when Inspector Lewis wants to see you, you'd better see him, Ma'am. Case closed."

A wave of Orwellian fear swept over Naomi, just as the officer's deadpan tone became insistent.

"This way."

She took Naomi by the arm and brought her past the barriers and into the building. Naomi felt sucked in, apprehended, arrested, all as a result of something that had originally been a whim, and her own stupid idea. They took the elevator to the second floor. The officer escorted her past a room of desks, to an office door with *Inspector Ralph Lewis* written on it. She knocked on it and he responded from the inside.

"Yeah?"

"Naomi Kaplan, sir."

"Open the door and let her in, for God's sake."

They entered the office. There was Inspector Lewis, sitting at his messy desk.

"Thanks Lois. I'll take it from here."

He got up, fully intending to sit back down. He gestured to Naomi to be seated in the chair in front of the desk and then took his own seat. Then he waved his hand over the full folders, piles of documents, and his computer.

"Damn. Between the terror threats and community police relations with all of Midtown Manhattan, for God's sake, you can see I got my hands full. So *you're* Naomi Kaplan."

"Um...is there a problem with that? I mean, you couldn't have been expecting me. I didn't make an appointment, or anything like that."

He let out a short howl...more like a blast. Then he looked straight at her.

"No, I guess you didn't. But you asked for Detective Brock. Is that right?"

"Yes sir. I just wanted to speak with him, and I don't have his phone number or anything. But...how do you know me?"

"Oh, believe me, I know who you are. Let's put it this way. Any friend of Darrin's is a friend of mine."

"I don't understand...Inspector."

"That's because he's not doing his job. He keeps telling me he's doing his job, but he never seems to quite get around to it. He's supposed to ask you some questions..."

Naomi became visibly agitated.

"Look, Inspector…I met him where I work, at the housewares department at Macy's. He was returning something…not even a housewares item…a sweater, as a matter of fact. Maybe he had some other reason for coming that day. Maybe he was spying on me, which is unconstitutional, if I'm not mistaken. But I haven't done anything wrong…not one thing. And my family…may God bless them and keep them…hasn't done anything wrong either."

"You sure about that?"

"Yes, I'm sure. And I don't appreciate the insinuation, with all due respect…Sir. And I don't appreciate Darrin's either…that is, Detective Brock's. I just want to give him a piece…a…piece of my mind! Please forgive me, but…before I go *out* of my mind!"

Inspector Lewis leaned way back in his chair.

"If you haven't done anything wrong, Ms. Kaplan, then you have nothing to worry about, do you?"

"What do you mean by that?"

"I mean, Detective Brock isn't going to hurt you. He's a very nice man. In fact, he's too damn nice. All he wants to do is help kids out. Can you believe it? You know, the same kids we're always arresting? Did you ever hear of such a thing? A hard boiled detective with a soft spot for troubled kids. Well *that's* Darrin Brock. A little too religious, if you ask me. But at least he's an honest detective, if such a thing is possible. Anyway, you want to talk to him. That's why you're here. And *frankly,* Ms. Kaplan, he wants to talk to you too. So that works out real well. This department is doing a little…shall we say, inquiry…and he just has a few questions to ask."

"He's already tried that. My brother-in-law is a good man, Inspector Lewis. My whole family are good people. And *frankly,* to use your word, I don't know what you or he want with us. I must tell you, this is all very disturbing to me. I met him at work, I saw him a few times since, and now I find out he's been investigating my family all this time. I should get a lawyer…is what I should do."

He leaned forward.

"Don't get excited. Don't get excited. He hasn't been tailing you all this time. What do you think, you're the damn Russian ambassador or something? We don't pay him enough to tail you. Besides, he's got better things to do. You want to talk to him? Go out there and they'll connect you."

"What?"

"Go on. Go on. Go out there."

He pointed to the office door.

"Out there, right beyond that door. Just give us a chance to connect with him. They'll hand you a phone. Just stand out there and they'll get to you."

"But Inspector Lewis…"

"Goodbye, Ms. Kaplan. It's been a pleasure meeting you."

He waved his hand, indicating she should leave. She stood up while he stayed seated, and left the office. Inspector Lewis picked up his phone and speed dialed Darrin Brock.

"Brock, call the precinct office…now, damn it. Your Kaplan contact is here waiting for a call. How do I know? Just call."

He looked at all the papers on his desk. He picked a few up with his left hand while the phone was still in his right, and then dropped them, turning to his desktop computer.

"What a waste of time. Let's see. Administrational paperwork and databases of Russian mobsters. That's all I live for. God, I miss the streets."

Naomi stood outside Lewis' office door and considered leaving. She was about to, when a policeman who was seated at the desk closest to her picked up a phone that had just rung and then turned to her.

"Yes, sir. She's right here. Ma'am, phone for you."

She took the phone. Darrin was on the other end.

"Naomi?"

"Yes, it's me. I need to talk with you, and I can't do it right here."

Darrin was at the *New York Times* building, on the seventh floor, waiting for a meeting with a staff writer.

"Look, I've got an appointment in a few minutes. Can I meet you tomorrow at Ben's?"

Somehow, Naomi didn't want to go anywhere near the place where she had just had such an unpleasant conversation with Marvin.

"No, not there. I'll meet you at the Channel Gardens…where that flower thing was."

"You mean the Easter bunny?"

"Yes, that…thing…yes. Where we sat when we were there… tomorrow, noon."

"I'll see you then. Are you bringing lunch?"

"No…no lunch…just talk…business."

"Okay. No lunch. All business."

"All business. Goodbye."

Naomi felt a great sense of relief. Tomorrow she would be finished with this whole strange relationship once and for all. She would get some questions answered, erect some boundaries to protect her family, and move on. Tomorrow couldn't come soon enough.

CHAPTER THIRTY-SEVEN

It turned out tomorrow didn't come as quickly as Naomi desired. She couldn't sleep. She tossed around in her bed, went down to the kitchen to eat some gefilte fish, and tried to read the Abraham Joshua Heschel that she kept on her night table. But her mind kept rehearsing what she would say. And with each recitation, she became angrier, more incensed.

How dare he accuse my family! He's a sick man. Probably all Christians are like this underneath...real nice, real friendly on the surface, but down inside...nosing into the affairs of Jews and accusing them of who knows what! Maybe Abba is right...of course he's right. He's always right! How stupid of me. Why didn't I believe him! Darrin Brock is an evil man, and I must protect my family from him.

By the morning, several nighttime hours of *straw dogging*, constant anxiety, and minimal restless sleep had taken its toll. Naomi had a headache and a racing heart, and felt somewhat nauseated. She left the house for work without saying goodbye to her father. She didn't even realize she hadn't. She walked like an automaton down to the subway, and dozed off on a crowded bench seat like a transient. Near her destination, she almost missed the 34th Street stop, but woke up just in time to escape the subway door before it closed.

She barely functioned all morning. Fortunately, there wasn't even one customer. That sometimes occurred during the hottest days in August. Usually, the boredom of a quiet basement level was difficult to take. Today it was a good thing. Her concentration was so bad, she didn't know if she could focus on a customer's needs if there *was* one. She knew her demeanor was unprofessional, but that's how she felt.

When the lunch break finally arrived, she wasn't even hungry. She decided to just go to the Channel Gardens on an empty stomach. She would fast for her family, like Esther, with the exception of a small mint to freshen her breath during the fast. When she got there, Darrin was already sitting on the same bench where they sat together in the spring. She stood over him. The rehearsals paid off. The words flowed out like hot lava.

"This won't take long. Mr. Brock, you stay away from my family. I don't know what your game is, but it won't work. Leave me alone. Leave my father alone. Leave my sister alone, and by all means, leave my brother-in-law alone."

"Please sit down, Naomi."

"No. Will you do what I'm asking? That's all I want to know. Then we can go our separate ways."

"No, I can't."

Exasperated, she sat down, making sure to keep her distance.

"What do you *mean*, you can't? You've been using me to get at my family all this time. I just want to know…why do you hate us?"

Darrin turned and looked at her with his penetrating electric blue eyes. She backed up even more. He spoke as softly as the midtown Manhattan traffic would allow.

"Naomi…"

She fought against melting when he gently spoke her name. She had to be strong for herself and her family. He spoke it again.

"Naomi…I don't hate you, and I don't hate your family. I was given a case before I met you. And…I didn't know when I met you that the case involved someone in your family. I had no idea. I'm so sorry that I haven't told you sooner. I've tried, but we never seem to get to it. Do you remember when you first mentioned your sister's husband?"

Naomi sat there stoic, trying as hard as she could to end this agony and walk away. But she knew she wasn't finished. She had to convince him to leave her and her family alone for good.

"No, I don't remember. Well, maybe I do. The point is this. I'm a religious observant Jew. Some of my family back in Kiev died at the hands of Christians like you…well, maybe not exactly like you…but…Christians of some sort…and now here you are, investigating my family…and… and to…to…make matters worse, you've bewitched me with your wise sayings that sound suspiciously like my father's…and your good looks… and I admit to my shame…my terrible, horrible *shame*…as a Shabbas keeping Kosher keeping, God worshipping Jew…I admit to my shame that…that I day dream about you…even at night…and it's a curse from the evil one and *must* stop. And it *will* stop!"

He reached his hand out for hers, and she pulled hers away. He took a deep breath and tried to gather his thoughts.

"Okay. Okay. First of all…first of all…I am *so* sorry for all of the hatred Christians…*some* Christians…*many* Christians have harbored… more than harbored…acted on…what can I say?"

"There is nothing to say. We have nothing to say to each other. And after this, we *won't!*"

"Wait a minute, Naomi."

"Stop calling me Naomi like that!"

"I'm sorry. Please, let me explain. First of all, even Jesus…*especially Jesus*…didn't teach hate. He said in the Bible that salvation comes through the Jewish people."

That came out so inane. He wanted to say other things about Jesus that expressed stirrings so deep inside his heart that words could only outline the shadow of them—elusive yet genuine things like, *He's everything that's honest in a world of dishonesty, everything that's right in a world gone wrong. He's the only one who knows me better than I know myself—and He lets me know it.* But he shared none of them.

"I've heard that one already. Don't you have anything better than that to tell me?"

"Naomi, I don't hate you. On the contrary, I'm very grateful for you."

"That's completely ridiculous. Please! Don't do me any favors! And please, don't you ever say that…that name to me…*ever!* It's a sin for me to say it, and I don't want to hear it from you, or anyone!"

As soon as those words came out of her mouth, words she had heard from some teachers in Hebrew school—or *Cheder*—as a child, she immediately regretted saying them. In her mind's eye she could see her father, in his Santa hat, holding a dying child's hand. And with that, she recalled the respect he always demanded of her for all religions. Her heart became full of guilt, conflict, and complete confusion. She knew she had to apologize.

"No, wait…I'm sorry. My father told me to respect others' faiths, and I just insulted yours. That's *so* wrong. I'm sorry. It's just that I'm…well, to tell you the truth, I'm afraid. I'm afraid of you…and how you make me feel…and your questions about my family…and…I don't know… everything. I shouldn't be here with you. I just shouldn't be here. I need to leave now."

Tears began to trickle down Naomi's cheeks. She was glad she hadn't had the time to put on eyeliner that morning. Nevertheless, this was the last way she wanted to be seen by anyone. Darrin reached out his hand again, and this time she didn't withdraw hers. She knew she should, but she could sense some sort of unexplainable warmth in his touch that felt a lot like tenderness—and love—the kind of love she grew up with. And she just couldn't seem to withdraw from that. Darrin spoke her name again.

"Naomi, Naomi…I have to tell you now…I have so much to say… but…first of all…"

He tried desperately to return to his professional self, even though he knew it was hopeless.

"I regret to inform you that…"

Small tears formed in his eyes as well. He tried to wipe them off with his free hand, as grown men often do.

"…that indeed…I hate to tell you this, but…"

"But what? Just tell me. I'm on my lunch break. And I really need to leave."

"That your brother-in-law works for…has ended up getting mixed up with…unfortunately…with an Italian man named…Prima…an old school mobster who…who…kind of controls the food services to some…a lot of…a number of…small New York restaurants. Marc probably didn't want to get involved…but he ended up getting involved…with the money end of it at least. I'm so sorry."

As soon as Darrin was finished speaking, she knew deep down in her heart that what he was saying was true. And she instantly put two and two together, realizing that this finally explained the high lifestyle Marc and Lisa lived. She also knew instinctively that Lisa didn't understand what was going on. The few things Lisa had said about Marc's financial success more or less confirmed that. She waited for Darrin's next words.

"I hate that part of my job, Naomi. I wish I didn't have to do these things. But that's what I do for a living. And I trained for this job so I could help the people who live in our city. Yet I know that no matter how hard I work to do what's right, people like your brother-in-law will get hurt. That's what I don't like. But…"

"Go on. I'm listening. But I have to get back to work. So please tell me quickly."

"I can't. You see…there's something else I must tell you. But it's harder. It's so hard for me…because I know that I have a commitment… spiritually, that is…a certain commitment…about relationships, that I've always believed in…and I still do now. But I must tell you, and then you can go back to work and we'll never see each other…because it's not fair. It's not fair, Naomi…first of all to you or your wonderful big-hearted father…because I saw that heart when I met him…but, I must tell you that…of all the millions of women in New York…of all those women… out there…all the women in New York and beyond, Naomi…"

As soon as he said the last few words, Naomi knew something incredible was coming. And she instinctively knew what it must be—even though she was convinced it *couldn't* be. She had imagined it for months, but she never believed it was true or could *ever* be true. It was always just her imagination, and her sinful dream. And much of her didn't even want to hear it now. It was too dangerous. So she considered just pulling her hand off of his like she had Marvin's, and then running back to work like a little girl on the school playground running away from some little boy who has a crush on her. But another part of her couldn't wait for his next words.

"Of the millions of women…I've…and it's so unprofessional of me… but…I must say…that…here goes…I've fallen in love with you, Naomi Kaplan. There, I've said it. I've fallen totally head over heels in love with you. It's crazy. But…I love you. I love your stunning sturdy Eastern European Jewish face. It's so magnificent, so stunning…and those eyes… as deep and wise as all eternity with your father's wisdom…and your sweet perfect natural lips that I've wanted to kiss ever since I returned the sweater, even though I've never kissed a woman's lips before…*ever.* And…your…adventurous thick curly jet-black hair that I've spent hours in my parents' house wanting to run my hands through…and feeling so so guilty about it."

Naomi was sitting there trying to drink all this in—and yet with great difficulty. She suddenly remembered her rouged up grotesque face in the bathroom mirror. Could he be talking this way about *her?* He must be lying to get something from her. Perhaps he could say this about her sister. But her?

"Please stop, Darrin. I can't…I can't hear it. You…must be lying…or talking about someone else. How can you lie like that and…"

"No Naomi. I'm telling the truth. There is no one who has your beauty…inside and out. *No one!* How is it you can't see that?"

He held her hand up to the wrist. He could feel her heart pounding, and she could feel his too. She knew she had to say something.

"I'm Jewish, Darrin. I'll always be Jewish. Don't you understand that?"

"I know, Naomi. That's what I love about you most. I've saved myself for the right woman all my life…all my life…but…."

Their faces drew close as he said that. She knew they would kiss any second, even though she felt it was wrong, terribly wrong. And what about the bacon he had probably eaten for breakfast? And yet, it was unbelievable that Darrin Brock truly loved her, and that she knew she loved him. The last thought that crossed her mind was that it was her first kiss too, and it wouldn't be a very good kiss because her lips were chapped the way lips can get chapped in the summer. But when he drew close and their lips finally met, all she could think of was how soft and warm and perfect *his* lips were—perfect enough for both of them. And she was also very thankful that she had included a breath mint in her Esther's fast.

They kissed for a good thirty seconds, as he ran his right hand through her soft curly hair and over her left ear, while people walked all around them. It seemed like the sweetest thirty seconds she had ever experienced. She realized she would be condemning herself by evening, especially in her father's presence. But that could wait. She had to admit, there was something of Heaven in this moment.

When they finally finished kissing, Her face was sunburn red.

"I have to leave now, and get back to work. Maybe we can meet again just…just once more to finish discussing this…because I've…I've also fallen in love with you, and I don't know what to do about it. So I think we have to discuss it in a businesslike way, and try to resolve it…so to speak…with one more meeting."

Intoxicated, Darrin just stared into her eyes and said, "Whatever you say, Naomi. Whatever you say."

Naomi got up and walked away, looking back just once to see Darrin still sitting on the bench. She passed by a Russian man in a black knit hat, sunglasses, and black t-shirt and pants. She didn't notice him. But Darrin would have, if he wasn't still trying to regain his composure.

CHAPTER THIRTY-EIGHT

On the subway ride home from work, Naomi determined to hide the strange intoxication she was experiencing. But having never experienced this kind of imbibing and to this extent, she wasn't sure how to accomplish that. Her mouth kept forming itself into a contented smile, the result of the continual taste and feel of Darrin's lips. And her heart kept skipping beats—or at least she felt like it did.

When she entered the house, she crept like a cat toward her room. She was sure that one look in her eyes by her father would expose everything. She had to get upstairs, and fast. Once she got there, she would be safe, for the time being. But she hadn't gone twenty feet when David Kaplan called from the dining room.

"Marc and Lisa and the kids are coming over for dinner. I picked up some cold cuts from Meyers' Deli, and I even set the table. They'll be here any minute. How'd I do? Doesn't it look nice?"

Naomi was afraid to even say a word, lest he detect some sort of change in her voice. She had to suppress the joy that was, at least for now, surpassing her guilt. She caught a glimpse of the fancy kosher meat *fleischic* dishes on the dining room table. She could even smell the vinegar in the kosher pickles. But she said nothing as she headed to her room. Her father popped his head into the hall.

"Naomi...did you hear what I said?"

She stopped in her tracks. but didn't turn around.

"Yes, Abba. It's lovely. Can I rest until they get here? I've had a big day."

"Of course."

Naomi scampered upstairs, now more like a puppy dog than a cat. She fell into her room and onto her bed, rolling over from her stomach onto her back, sighing like a teenage girl in the musical "Bye Bye Birdie." She mouthed words she would never before allow herself to speak out loud at home.

"I wish I had a picture of him to kiss...and a recording of his voice speaking words of wisdom like our sages...or maybe a nice short video would be nice."

She was once again conveniently forgetting that Darrin was a Christian, and not a Jew—and that whatever wisdom he had learned, it definitely wasn't the wisdom of words by Rashi or Maimonides, sages of old who would more than frown at her now.

In fact, Naomi had come to the place where she wasn't even daydreaming that he had converted and had become a better Jew than Marc, or even Marvin—a Jew worthy of her father's approval. Now that at least part of her daydreams had become reality, she skipped that step and just thought of him as someone who was as wise and gentle as her father. She had no room for other realities in her present ecstatic state.

As she reveled in the miracle of Darrin's declaration of love for her, she could hear the front door open. Lindsay and Noah's high voices penetrated her room first.

"Zaida! Zaida!," one child after the other exclaimed, using the Yiddish word for grandfather. She could hear the timbre of Lisa's voice, and then Marc's. Her father's unmistakable voice came next, and she could tell that he was responding to the children with the laughter and banter typical of grandfathers. She sat up in bed.

"Oh no. They're here. What am I going to do?"

Before long, her father called her down to dinner. She loved informal foods like corned beef and pastrami, piled high on New York Jewish rye and garnished with cole slaw that had no dairy products in it. Normally, she would run down and dive right in, starting with the pickles she had smelled earlier. But she had no appetite this night. She had feasted on love that day like Solomon's lover in the *Song of Songs,* and she was satiated. Still, she knew she had to go downstairs and "face the music" sooner or later, so it might as well be sooner. She left her room and walked downstairs.

Lindsay and Noah had already retired to David's upstairs bedroom to play with their portable video devices, accompanied by their earbuds. Lisa let them occupy themselves this way until dinner, which they were told would begin in a few minutes. During that few minutes before the meal, everything important that would occur that evening took place.

Lisa was the first one to notice something different about Naomi.

"What's with you? Did you take dancing lessons or something?"

"No I didn't" Naomi said with the irremovable smile still on her face. This gave the impression that she was hiding a luscious secret that she wanted to share but couldn't. In fact, she didn't want to share any secret with anyone. Marc chimed in next as he sat down on the living room couch.

"You *do* seem different. What's going on, Naomi?"

"Nothing."

"You're blushing."

David came to her rescue.

"You're embarrassing her. The sages say that joy is a mitzvah in that it stems from loving others. She loves her family. Let her alone to rejoice with us."

Naomi was relieved and once again grateful for her wise father. The thought did occur to her, however, that she must have always seemed pretty miserable before if everyone saw such a change this night. And as for his part, David also noticed something was different, but had the wisdom not to ask about it—at least not in front of Lisa. He chose instead to change the subject.

"Marc, some guy came here asking about you."

"Really?"

"Yes, he said he had some questions. But we threw him out before he could ask them."

Naomi instantly lost the smile and tensed up. Marc also clearly showed signs of agitation.

"I wonder who that might be. Do you happen to remember his name?"

David shot a glance at Naomi.

"Do you remember his name Naomi? I know you've met him before."

Naomi began to feel sick to her stomach. She wanted to leave, but knew she couldn't.

"I don't know. I think his name is…if I'm not mistaken…"

David was surprised she was putting on such a front. She knew Darrin's name so well when he visited, and those times he called on the phone. Marc was becoming impatient, bordering on anger.

"You know his name. Spit it out!"

Lisa was taken aback by his outburst.

"Marc…"

He wheeled around to her.

"You know it too! It's Darrin Brock, isn't it? Isn't it?"

Lisa had a vague recollection of the name, but nothing more, and she didn't know where Marc was coming from or where he was going.

"I don't know. I really don't know who that is, Marc."

Then a very small light bulb lit in her memory.

"Wait a minute…Naomi, isn't that the handsome man you introduced me to in the Macy's housewares department before I took the kids to the Cinderella musical?"

"Um…I think so."

Marc had had enough.

"You both know him, you liars! He set you up, didn't he? Admit it!"

Naomi stepped in.

"Darrin didn't set *anybody* up. I think I know him well enough to know he wouldn't do that."

David felt it was time for some fatherly wisdom.

"Naomi, the sages inform us that it is not wise to defend a man until you know him thoroughly. And Solomon has something to say about that also. I told you before that I sense something dangerous about this man."

Marc jumped up and poked his finger in Lisa's face.

"What'd I tell you!"

"About what, honey?"

"Don't give me that *honey* business!"

Lisa became agitated too.

"What is going on here, Marc?"

Naomi had bigger concerns at the moment than to just explain to her father who the real Darrin Brock was. She stood inches from Marc's face, and looked him straight in the eye.

"Let me ask *you* some questions, brother-in-law of mine. Just what is it you do in all those restaurants?"

"If you want to know, *sister-in-law of mine*, I work hard, *very* hard to take care of my family, which is far more than you do at that dead-end Macy's job of yours."

Naomi was undeterred.

"I'll take that as a compliment, Marc. I am a credit to my Jewish people where I work. And observing the Torah decrees on morality is my first responsibility. Which leads me to another question. Just who is *Prima?*"

Marc clenched his fist and just held himself back from taking a swing at her. Lisa was shocked by her sister's accusatory attitude. She'd never seen her act this way with anyone but her. She stepped in to defend her husband. She could sense that her pulse was elevated, as was her voice. She was just glad that Noah and Lindsay were wearing their earphones, and she hoped they hadn't taken them off.

"Naomi, that's just his boss…and don't you talk to my husband with that tone of voice!"

David raised his hands.

"My daughters, please don't argue. Remember the Psalm…*Hinei ma tov…how good and pleasant it is for brothers to dwell together in unity.*"

That comment by his father-in-law gave Marc just enough time to prepare his attack on the *conspirators*. He waved his finger at both sisters simultaneously.

"You two!"

He turned to David.

"They tried to murder me. I can prove it. It's a plot. and this Darrin planned the whole thing. I saw pictures of him with them. And she…."

He pointed at Lisa.

"She took me on a cruise to God knows where in the Balkans, and when I was alone, she sent some Russian idiot to kill me. And he *would* have, if someone hadn't shown up. He would have! I'd be food for the fish right now! What are you gonna try next, Lisa? Killing the father of your children? Murderer!"

Lisa was overwhelmed.

"You're crazy, Marc! You're absolutely insane!"

He turned to Naomi.

"And you don't get off the hook so easy, big religious fanatic Orthodox Jew with a holier-than-thou look and ugly hair…Miss spinster goody two shoes! It says *don't kill*, doesn't it? And you're just as guilty as she is!

And that Brock! All he wants to do is destroy me, and my job with me! He's evil, and he's got you both in his clutches. You're all guilty of trying to murder me!"

Whatever the truth was, David decided the conversation was way out of control.

"Enough Marc! *Shecket!* Be quiet! We have to discuss this reasonably… as a family, in the proper Jewish way."

Naomi decided she'd had enough too.

"I don't know what in the world you're taking about, Marc Silver! But I *do* know that Darrin Brock is a good man…a very good man. He has a heart to do what's right. He doesn't want to do any harm to you or anyone else. As a matter of fact, he wants to help you. But he does have a job to do as a police detective. Now I must tell you all that…the truth is that Darrin Brock is…"

Tears began to stream down her face, but she tried to ignore them.

"He's the most…the most…"

Everyone froze, waiting for her next words. After a long pause, she tried to start again.

"Next to you, Abba, next to you…he's the most wonderful…the most wonderful…."

She looked at Lisa, then Marc, and then her father. They just stared at her. Then without finishing, she left the room and went into the kitchen. At that exact moment, Lindsay and Noah came bouncing down from David's room.

"We're hungry," Lindsay declared. Noah chimed in.

"Yeah. Doesn't anyone eat around here?"

Lisa took a deep breath and let out a short giggle.

"All right kids. Sandwiches coming right up."

The children cheered and found their usual seats around their grandfather's dining room table. Lisa took the opportunity to approach Marc and whisper in his ear.

"What was all of that nonsense about? I should get a lawyer tomorrow. You and I are going to a therapist next week or I *will* get one."

It was beginning to dawn on Marc that he might not have gotten everything just right. For one thing, Prima had never told him that Darrin Brock was a police detective. Marc had taken for granted that he was some sort of competition.

Naomi came back into the room and took her seat. The evening continued with discussions about the quality of the pastrami and the beautiful late August weather. Lindsay and Noah protested their impending school year, insisting that school in late summer was torture for children, and everyone laughed.

Chapter Thirty-Nine

Naomi and her father hadn't said two words to each other since the night the Silvers visited, until the next Shabbat. She knew that the restful summer day's walk to synagogue, garnished with a gentle rain shower, would change that. She wore a clear rain bonnet and an off-orange raincoat over her black dress. There was no wind, only high humidity. And yet she loved every minute of it. David wore his black hat and coat. The walk was short enough and the summer shower light enough to keep him from being soaked through. As they walked, he spoke sparingly.

"At our lunch meal together we'll talk, as usual."

"Yes, Abba, like usual…the sages."

"Yes, the sages."

They didn't say another word, even as they entered the synagogue and headed to their separate men's and women's sections. Naomi looked down from the balcony at her father, watching him sway back and forth and to and fro to the silent standing prayer. As she waited for him to turn and make eye contact with her, she noticed that the side of his face was more easily distinguishable in the light of the blue and red stained glass during summer than it had been in winter. In fact, this was her favorite time of year to watch her father from the balcony, and to wait longingly for him to periodically turn upwards and back toward her with a loving smile on his face, the smile of a proud father. But as the service proceeded he looked straight ahead or down, but not back—with one exception.

When the Torah was chanted in Hebrew, Naomi recognized familiar words from *Devarim*, or Deuteronomy—words she heard every year at this time.

If your brother, the son of your mother, your son or daughter, the wife of your bosom, or your friend who is as your own soul, secretly entices you, saying, "Let us go and serve other gods which you have not known, neither you or your fathers..."

David Kaplan quickly turned around just as the words *son* or *daughter* were chanted, and then just as quickly turned back. She didn't see the usual smile on his face. Something akin to a minor panic attack began to grip her, hindering her breathing. But she resisted it. She chose instead to ask herself some relevant questions, strictly Jewish questions. And she would find the right answers, if it was the last thing she did. This was a safe environment. Here in this holy place, the Holy One of Israel would give her the wisdom she needed, perhaps even before the lunch discussion!

Naomi had the rest of the morning service to meditate on those few verses. She had heard and obeyed them since she was a little girl. But now for the first time, things were not so simple. She wanted to know how it was that a Gentile like Darrin Brock worshipped another god, and yet was so gentle and loving. She decided right then and there that his god may indeed have taught him something about love, but nevertheless it wasn't *her* God. It couldn't be her God. And therefore his god wasn't God at all, because she knew hers was the only God. It all seemed so confusing. But it had to be the truth. And the worst thing about all of it was that she was being enticed, exactly as the Torah had predicted. Now if she could only become un-enticed, that would solve everything.

By the time Naomi and David walked home, the misty summer shower had ended and the sun had appeared. Hopefully, she would fully emerge from her own mist by the time the afternoon meal was over. They entered the house, and David washed his hands and took out the sandwiches he had prepared beforehand. The tea was warming on a hot plate.

These were the few minutes Naomi looked forward to every week. She hoped this week would be no different. The service was inspiring, as usual. But she hadn't received the wisdom she was looking for. Now maybe her father would say just the right thing to free her, like a gazelle being loosed from a net. And she would be really happy, with no regrets.

David took out his *Ethics of the Fathers* and a few other books, including the *Tanach*, or what Christians call the Old Testament, and sat down across from her at the dining room table. He prayed the simple prayer before the meal. The longer comprehensive one, the *Birkat Ha-mazon*, would come later, after the meal. He looked directly at her for the first time that morning, or even the last few days. Then he opened the *Ethics of the Fathers*, the Perkei Avot.

"You heard about idolatry from today's Parshe, the Torah portion *Re'eh*."

"Yes, Abba, I heard it…when you looked up at me."

"Just so, my precious Naomi."

Naomi braced herself for the wisdom that would liberate her from bondage, although like a child waiting for an inoculation, the love-infected part of her dreaded it. He continued.

"Rabbi Shimon, of blessed memory, said, 'Three who eat at one table and do not speak words of Torah, it is as if they have eaten idolatrous sacrifices. But if they eat at one table and speak words of Torah, it is as if they have eaten at God's table.' Well, we are two, but His presence makes three. And we are speaking words of Torah. So there you are."

That was it? She was sure her father was onto her. And that was all he had to say? Perhaps not. He took out his Jewish Bible from under the Perkai Avot, and turned the pages until he reached the *Song of Songs*, or *Song of Solomon*, near the end of the book.

"Let's see what I would compare the words of Torah to…or contrast it with…including prohibitions about idolatry, as we heard today. You know when I touch the Torah with my *tallis*, my prayer shawl, before kissing it?"

"Yes. I love watching you do that, Abba."

"Yes, well listen to this verse. 'Let him kiss me with the kisses of his mouth. For your love is better than wine.' That is what it means to love the Torah."

He looked directly at Naomi again. She tried her best not to blush. But she was sure she was doing a poor job. Was he testing her, like the ancient test for an adulteress in the Torah? Or was this just a coincidence? She knew she had to say something.

"Well Abba…that's interesting."

"You will know more about that comparison when you kiss the man who truly loves you."

Her eyes averted his for a split second. He continued.

"But it's enough to know now that Torah is sweet, and comes to Israel from HaShem Himself. He loves us as a husband, who is jealous for all of his wife's affection. This is why we kiss the Torah. So stay close to it, Naomi. It will keep you, if you keep it."

"Yes, Abba. I will."

"Do you have any questions? You always have questions. I don't think our Shabbas together is complete without them."

Naomi had never held back any question from her father. She always learned so much from his answers. Why should this day be any different? She had been thinking about what the verses she had heard in the synagogue meant—and meant for her. Those were the questions that were on her mind. And here was her father before her, ready to answer them with wisdom. Where else could she go for help, even if she couldn't quite tell him *everything*?

"Okay, Abba. I do have a question. Um…you know how you visit the Christian children on Christmas?"

"Yes, of course I do."

"Well, I don't think I've ever told you this, but…it's one of the things I love so much about you. That's why I get so upset when Marc makes fun of you about it. I'm…I'm so proud of my father for seeing God's image in the *other*…as you say. You're the wisest Jew in Brooklyn, Abba…in the whole world."

"Well, it's true I raised you to see God in *all* others, Naomi, as Ben Zoma said."

"Yes, Ben Zoma. But…I was thinking, listening to the Torah portion today. So, are those children you visit worshipping other gods…or our God?"

David sat back in his seat. He knew Naomi was asking some really big questions, bigger than the ones she used to ask when she was a small child—big like the big world she now lived in, like the big city of New York. A more grown up question deserved a grown up answer, provided in this case by a man who asked those same questions in the early twentieth century, and came up with what might be called *new* answers—the answers of a man who lived in that big world. David had never before told Naomi what this Jewish scholar taught, or even mentioned his name. Perhaps now was the time.

It had been many years since David Kaplan had thought about the thick academic writings of Franz Rosenzweig. David didn't understand much of Rosenzweig's work then, when he was in his twenties, and a curious reader of Jewish philosophy. But what little he did understand seemed particularly relevant now.

Rosenzweig was born in Kassel, Germany, in 1886, four years after the Kiev menorah first sat on the table of the Kaplan ancestors' home.

He died 43 years later, in 1929, of Amyotrophic Lateral Sclerosis, commonly known as Lou Gehrig's Disease. David's challenge was to sum up a few of the key conclusions Rosenzweig came to during his short life. He kept Naomi waiting as he tried to put his thoughts together. He knew that this might be the most important talk he would ever have with her.

"Abba, did you hear what I said?"

"Yes, I did. And I was thinking…thinking about a man named Franz."

"Franz?"

"Yes, Franz, a Jew who lived in Germany many years ago…Franz Rosenzweig, of blessed memory."

David leaned forward and spoke softly as he focused his deep wise eyes on hers.

"Franz was born in Germany in 1886, not long after our precious menorah over there began shedding light on Chanukah."

He pointed toward the mantle.

"He studied philosophy, and became friends with a Christian named Eugen…a good and sincere man. He actually considered converting, God forbid. But first, he decided to live as an observant Jew…like us. Well, the long and short of it is that he went to an Orthodox synagogue on Yom Kippur…and something happened. No one knows exactly what, but…I can tell you that he never converted, thank God. He ended up becoming a great writer of books on Judaism. I admit, they are difficult books to read, but they are important books. Do you understand?"

"I guess. What's not to understand, Abba?"

Naomi tried to strike a relaxed pose. After all, she wasn't about to convert to anything. At least she wasn't guilty of *that*. David came closer.

"Well now, I'm not finished. I want to answer your question. Franz Rosenzweig will help me do that, if you'll be patient."

"I'm always patient when you teach me, Abba."

"All right then. Where was I? Oh, yes. Franz became a good Jew, a thinking Jew…the best kind, you know…and an important scholar. But he had a problem. You see, many of the sages, of blessed memory, were of the opinion that the Christians who believed in *that name,* as they called him, were idolaters. *That name,* of course, is Jesus. You know that."

Naomi had never heard him say Jesus' name before, even as a swear word, and it sounded strange when he said it.

"Yes, Daddy. I know."

"Well, being a philosopher and a deep Jewish thinker, Franz had a problem. Do you know what that problem was?"

"No, Abba. I don't."

Naomi didn't know what was coming, but she knew she enjoyed her father's slow deliberate explanations. It reminded her of the way he explained things to her when she was little. And it made her feel safe and protected. David leaned back again.

"Well, Naomi, the problem was…he knew that Eugen, who was still his close friend, was no idolater. He was in fact, a godly man in his own way…as a Gentile. You see, Franz lived at a time when a Jew could have a good Christian friend, like you are with…what's his name?"

He knew the name, but he wanted her to say it.

"Um…Darrin?"

"Yes, that's him."

Naomi *couldn't* blush now. She took a breath and tried the best she could to look relaxed…and innocent. David continued.

"In the old days, before the *Haskalah*—as the Jewish enlightenment in early nineteenth century Germany was called—Jews didn't have Christian friends. So they could see them as idolaters, and go on with their lives. But after the Haskalah, things were different, kind of like they are now in New York. So Franz studied, something he was good at, and prayed. And he discovered a word. That word was a Hebrew word called *Shtuff.* Do you know what that word means?"

"No, Abba. I don't."

"Well, it means *partnership.* You see, he came to the conclusion that Christians believe in a kind of partnership between Jesus and what they call the Father…the Father and the Son, as they say."

"I don't understand that at all, Abba. It sounds silly."

"Yes, well, they don't understand it either, but they *believe* it. Anyway, that's not the point, Naomi. The point is this. Franz came to understand that Jesus was used by God to help Gentiles believe in the one true God, our God, the God of Israel. Rosenzweig began to see Jesus as the back door, so to speak, to God…for Gentiles…a way for them to connect to Him as His children, as those created in His image. So then they were not idolaters. They still believed in our God, you see."

"I guess so, Abba."

She began to get up, but David gently motioned for her to sit down again.

"One more thing, and this is a very important thing. Rosenzweig taught that for Gentiles, belief in that name pointed them to God…but *not* for Jews. For Jews to believe in him would be counted as idolatry, because we have our direct connection through Torah. So you see, the passage about idolatry we heard today in synagogue does *not* apply to our Christian friends. But if we believed what they believe, it *would* apply to us. Do you understand now?"

This was different than all the other words of wisdom Naomi had ever heard from her father. They were easy to understand, and they made sense right away. Today's lesson seemed complicated—confusing. It seemed to raise more questions than it answered. But she tried to settle for the answers it *did* give to her question. So Darrin wasn't an idolater, although what he believed would be sinful if she believed it.

Although Naomi wasn't fully satisfied with the answer, she kept that to herself. After all, *she* didn't have to study Franz Rosenzweig, or even hear his name again. He had served his purpose, Now she could be safe in the presence of her father, and hopefully in Darrin's presence too. She arose and kissed David on the forehead.

"You are so wise, Abba. Thank you."

"You understand?"

"I understand."

"I know you don't. But no matter. This is the way God intended for us."

He poured a cup of tea for himself and offered to pour for Naomi.

"No thank you, Abba. All that thinking tired me out. I know we are permitted to study on Shabbas. But still, my brain has worked awfully hard today. I think I'll take a nap."

She left the dining room and headed for her bedroom.

CHAPTER FORTY

Armed with the new information he had learned at the Kaplan house, Marc Silver drove his just polished black Mercedes through the August streets of Manhattan, toward Prima's office. The extreme air conditioning blasted onto his face and under his sun glasses, as a few-years-old hit by singer Usher blasted out of the audio system. All that blasting just helped him clear his head. He realized that Prima hadn't been exactly up front with him. It was time to ask some tough questions, and get some real answers. He would not be intimidated. There was nothing to be afraid of. What could Prima do to him? The fact was, he knew that Prima liked him, even with all that bluster. Being direct would be the best approach.

He parked in his usual space and walked through a few feet of broiling heat into the air conditioned office building, and up to Prima's office. He found himself once again staring at his shoes through the smoked glass table that reflected the beaming summer sun. He waited for Prima longer than usual. Finally, he arrived with his two body guards. This time he was dressed in a sharp expensive silver grey suit, a black dress shirt, and a black tie.

"Marc. This is a very busy day for me…very busy. Like I always tell you, I wish you would call first."

Somehow, Marc knew he had to stand up right away and face Prima if he was going to get his questions answered. He rose, and reached his hand out to shake Prima's. Hesitant at first, Prima eventually took Marc's hand. He whisked the body guards out of the office and turned to Marc.

"All right. All right. Make it quick, will you? What is it?"

"Well, I just wanted to ask you…"

"Go on. Go on."

"Well…"

"Look, I'm leaving. Make an appointment or talk to me later when you bring the money in."

Marc knew he had to just plunge in.

"Why didn't you tell me Darrin Brock is a police detective? I mean, I thought he was the competition. I mean…well, you know what I mean…like, *serious* competition. After all, *someone* tried to kill me on that cruise. I thought it was him. But who the hell was it, if it wasn't him? I mean, like, what's going on here, Prima? I'm in the dark. Help me out. My life is hanging out there, for God's sake. And now, I find out this guy who's snooping around my wife and sister-in-law is nothing but a two-bit police detective. You could have told me, so I could've evaded the guy. You could have done at least *that* for me."

Marc could see, even as he was giving his passionate soliloquy, that Prima was not his usual loose cocky self. He seemed tense, anxious, nervous. Still, he put his arm on Marc's shoulder in his usual way.

"Look kid. It doesn't matter who Darrin Brock is. He doesn't matter. I just wanted to see if you knew who he was. It's of no importance."

"It didn't seem like it was of no importance when you showed me all those pictures."

A flash of anger crossed Prima's eyes.

"I *said*, it's of no importance. Now will you get out of here? I'm busy."

"Yeah. But if Brock and Lisa aren't trying to kill me, who is? Look, I'm just trying to do my job, deliver the food, collect the money. You always told me everything would be okay. I've got two kids, Prima…two beautiful children to feed, and raise, if you know what I mean. I'm a nice Jewish guy from North Jersey. I don't need this stress. You've always told me it would be okay, that you would take care of me. And you have, like a father. You know, my father didn't do *bubkis* for me. So please, tell me what's going on."

Prima usually hid his fond affection for Marc when others were anywhere nearby, and even when they weren't. But when he heard Marc's words, his feelings got the best of him. He pinched Marc's cheeks lightly then gently shook his finger in his face.

"Listen to me, my young Jewish son. I will never...I said *never*...let anyone hurt you...and I said *never*...do you understand that?"

He slapped Marc hard on the shoulder and then gave him a tight Italian hug.

"It'll be okay. Now get out of here and do your job. *Capiche?*"

"Yeah, sure. I trust you Prima. I do."

As soon as Marc left the room and got into the elevator, Igor stepped in from the opposite door.

"What was *that* about? *You* know he's dead man. *I* know he's dead man. What's with promises? What's with the hugs?"

Prima tensed up even more.

"Look, Igor. Kill the detective. But not him. He's a low level piece of..."

"Low level and about to blow...everything. This is more than fruit and vegetables. This is *everything, everybody*...and he's being followed by NYPD, for God's sake. Your father had useless stupid code, and he killed...just like I kill. You have code and you don't kill. That is not good for no one. I have no code and I kill! He dies, this Silver...or you do. You...you just stay in the office and keep your mouth shut. We take care of everything."

He walked out, leaving Prima to collapse into the chair that Marc always sat in.

CHAPTER FORTY-ONE

The follow-up Channel Gardens luncheon appointment between Darrin and Naomi took place two weeks after their last one. Naomi had asked for the meeting so that the dilemma of their feelings for each other could be resolved. Therefore, a business-like approach was essential. She spent the morning selling a fifteen piece cookware set, a rice cooker, and several assorted spatulas and soup ladles. These sales and a few others almost made the time go by quickly. By the time her lunch break came, a drenching rain had begun. Fortunately, she had checked the weather before she left for work and had worn a tan full length L.L. Bean raincoat and an umbrella.

The Channel Gardens' summer selection of lush green plants and flowers glistened in the rain. The usual crowd were passing through the gardens, but no one was sitting on the benches. Naomi stood in the downpour, protected by the coat and her large matching tan umbrella. After a few minutes, she went over and sat down on *their* bench. He was late. Perhaps he wouldn't even show up. She began to berate herself for never asking for his cell phone. It would have been so helpful to have it for just such a time as this. She lowered the umbrella over herself like a tortoise shell. She just wanted to disappear, taking all of her confusing feelings with her. Ten minutes went by, then fifteen. She tried to remember her father's admonition about kissing the Torah with the love of a dutiful wife. How could she return to *that* lover?

She closed her eyes as tears escaped and ran down her face, mixing with the unavoidable raindrops on her cheeks. She didn't know how much time she had left before she had to return to work. A darkness crept over her, even darker than the dark day. It seemed so real, like the shadow of a great eclipse. She instinctively looked up at the inside of her umbrella and then moved it aside to wash away her tears with rain. But there was no rain. Instead, there was another umbrella, a big black one—*his* umbrella. And there under that umbrella was Darrin, in a black raincoat. He took a seat by her. The rain pelted his umbrella as she closed hers. Their faces came unbearably close, and he put his arm around her.

"No Darrin. Please."

His gentle voice spoke just millimeters from her ear.

"I'm sorry I'm late. Inspector Lewis says there's some chatter about me out there somewhere. He gave me a thousand things to do to stay safe. I couldn't get away."

She looked into his rain-moistened eyes. He could see fear in hers.

"I'll be fine, Naomi. What do they want with me? I follow the has-beens to nowhere…the small time hoods. They haven't assaulted anyone in years."

She had resolved to be standoffish and focussed on closure. But that fell apart as soon as he shared those words with her. She grabbed the hand of his free arm and squeezed it. He continued. She could feel his breath on her ear.

"I've been thinking. We have to do the right thing. I will never give Jesus up. It's because of Him…His sacrifice…His atonement…that I have your Bible…that I love your God."

There it was, the back door to God. Her father was right. Franz Rosensweig was right. Now she and Darrin could agree on something. She had to take the front door, and he had to take the back door. There was no way to meet in the middle. But she realized that there was one more thing she needed to say. She returned the favor he extended during their last meeting, when he told her he wanted her to remain Jewish.

"I wouldn't want you to give him up. I would never expect that. But I can't…of course, you wouldn't expect me to…"

"Right. So I was thinking…we must part ways. As Amos so wisely said, *How can two walk together, unless they have agreed?* But you must promise me something."

She nodded, even as she marveled at his knowledge of a verse from the Jewish prophet Amos. He continued.

"You must not tell your father about our...our feelings...and I won't tell my parents. This will be our last time seeing each other. It's only right. You will find a good Jewish man...someone to take care of you and cherish you as you deserve."

Naomi's heart sank. She knew that meant Marvin, or no one. Still, she tried her best to face reality, and accept it. At least Marvin wanted her, and they could keep a kosher home together. *Kiss the Torah. Kiss the Torah.*

Darrin whispered into her ear, "Promise me that our love for each other will be a secret we will take to our graves with us. Please. God will give us strength. Promise me."

"I will...I do," she said, realizing she would never speak those words to him in any other context. He whispered in her ear again.

"Well, I think I should leave now."

Naomi lifted her head slightly and turned her face toward his. Impulsivity suddenly took over her beating heart.

"Wait. Once more."

She kissed his lips more passionately than the last time. Having used chapstick that morning didn't hurt. She'd learned a little something during their last kiss, as had he. It came more easily, and stayed longer. This time, they kissed for about two minutes or more, hidden under his big black umbrella, serenaded by the falling rain. And like Sleeping Beauty suddenly waking up after a decades long dream, her body began to awaken in response to Darrin's loving affectionate kiss. Her heart was racing so fast, she felt like it would explode out of sheer joy. This was not like the first kiss. The possibility of feeling this way didn't even occur to her then. This time, years of modest self-control were quickly evaporating, replaced by seismic desires she hardly knew she had. Where would it end? Fear and guilt shot through her like a snake bite antidote. Out of sheer will power, she forced herself to pull back.

"Wait. No! No! I'm sorry. We have to stop! I've never...never had those feelings with a man before. What have I done? What have I done? I...I..."

He held her gently now, carefully.

"It's okay, Naomi. It's all new for me too. But it's over now."

He endeavored to slow down his own breathing, which had become labored. He had to think of Naomi. He didn't want to leave with her feeling overwhelming guilt.

"I know God will forgive...both of us. He is full of compassion."

She looked deeply into his eyes.

"Yes, He is...full of loving kindness and compassion...*rachameem*. You're right."

He spoke softly.

"Remember, tell no one anything about us...our feelings for each other. It will be easier that way."

He let go of her hand.

"I wish you well, Naomi...a very long healthy life. Well, you'd better get back to work. Goodbye Naomi."

Naomi folded her umbrella, got up, and left without looking back. It was over. Things would be so much easier now—except for the hopefully temporary condition of a broken heart. She knew the time would come when Marvin would again ask her to marry him. And she would say yes. But until then, she would hopefully have some time to finish crying, get over this, and move on with her life.

Darrin sat on the bench for at least another half hour, crying quietly to himself under the protective cover of his umbrella. When he had regained sufficient composure, he left for the short subway ride toward the Midtown South Precinct. He headed down the subway stairs, paid his fare, and stood on the platform, lost in thought.

He knew he had done the right thing by ending things, by putting Naomi on the altar and walking away. In the long run, his romantic feelings for Naomi didn't matter. Not in the long run, anyway. All that mattered was his faithfulness to his call, the call to make a difference in the lives of children created in the image of God. Someday perhaps Naomi would understand the faith that resided so deep in his heart, and gave him the capacity to love the people she held so close to *her* heart— even if he wouldn't be around to witness her understanding. But if the at risk children of New York could only know a fraction of the love that was available to them—love from the One who created them and provided endless forgiveness and hope for them—then his life on earth would have been worth living. As a police detective, his ability to reach those kids was limited. But it wouldn't always be that way. God had something more for him. He knew it. It was only a matter of time until he had more time for the children. He would talk to Inspector Lewis again. They would work something out.

Even as he considered his future, Darrin could still feel his heart ache. He opened his mouth and spoke silent words to the passing trains.

"Still, I'll never find such a kind, sweet, beautiful woman again. Such is life."

As his lips formed the word "life," he felt a sharp pain in his chest.

That's funny, he thought, just before he collapsed on the platform. At first, no one noticed him. Everyone was pressing to enter a train that was just slowing to a stop. But after the doors opened and passengers were exchanged, he became more noticeable. Someone yelled, "Hey!," and someone else called 911 on their cell phone. Darrin had lost consciousness by that time. He didn't notice the people who were now surrounding him, the blood that was soaking through his shirt, jacket, and raincoat—or the deep bleeding cut in the back of his head.

CHAPTER FORTY-TWO

It had been almost a month since David Kaplan interviewed for his voluntary job at Midwood Press. He wondered whether they had forgotten him. But that seemed improbable. They were so impressed with his *New York Times* experience, and they cheered so loud when he hung the bucket. Still, he told himself, they were in a serious printing business, and he was just an old retired Linotype operator. He wondered if he should call and ask which Thursday he should start, but he hesitated. *Solomon the wise told us not to be too forward,* he reminded himself.

The third Thursday morning of the month arrived, and he still hadn't heard anything. He got up too late to see Naomi off—a habit he always tried to avoid. He stared at his face in the bathroom mirror, and asked himself why it was so important to him to teach children about his Linotype craft. Was it because no one else was interested in the old machines? Or perhaps it was pride. Was hanging the bucket just about showing off? Maybe the God of Israel was telling him there were more children at the hospital who needed him than in classes of kids at Midwood Press. Or perhaps it was too early in the school year, which had barely begun, for such tours.

Regardless, it was already late for his morning Shacharit prayers. Perhaps after that, he would surprise Stanley and Mahmoud at the DeWitt Wallace Periodical Room. It looked like a beautiful sunny day, and the three of them could eat their bag lunches outside. He finished in the bathroom and was headed for the living room when the phone rang. He considered not picking it up, and just beginning his prayers. But then he decided to get the phone first. What if something happened to Naomi on her way to work? Or one of the grandchildren? He picked it up on the fourth ring.

"Kaplan residence."

"Mr. Kaplan?"

From the tone of the caller, he realized it probably wasn't an emergency. But God would forgive him for that.

"Yes, it's me."

"Yes, well this is Ben. Remember me?"

Ben…Ben…who was Ben?

"From Midwood Press."

He sat down on the closest chair.

"Right. Ben. The Linotype operator."

"That's right. But not as good a Linotype operator as you are."

"Well I…"

There was that pride. Ben continued.

"Listen…I know it's short notice, but we've got a great group of grade schoolers coming here in about an hour and a half, an end of summer program. You'd be just the ticket to show them the machine…and hang the old bucket, if you know what I mean."

"Well, it's a little…"

He looked at his prayer book, then back at the phone. What greater sign did HaShem have to show him? He had just been thinking about this very thing.

"I'll be there."

"Great. I'll let the teacher know. Ten o'clock. They eat lunch at eleven thirty and then leave."

"Right."

David hung up the phone and then looked back at the prayer book.

"Well, we have ten minutes, prayer book. Can you help me *daven* the morning prayers in ten minutes? *Mr. Siddur*? Of course you can. And I'll mean every word of them, especially today. Thank you, God, for giving me this gift."

By nine o'clock, David called the Macy's housewares department, and left a message for Naomi when she arrived, letting her know where he'd be. That was the least he could do, considering that he hadn't seen her off with a fatherly hug. Then he left the house. However, Naomi had heard the whole conversation. She hadn't gone in at all, and hadn't yet called in. She was in her bedroom, with the door left open a crack, lying in bed under the covers.

When David arrived at Midwood Press, he was welcomed like a war hero. The whole staff gave him another standing ovation. Within a few minutes, a fresh-faced young Jewish teacher by the name of Ms. Cohen escorted twenty-eight black and latino third graders like a mama duck her ducklings. They all had box lunches and back-packs. After they lined up for the two restrooms and then all came out of them, Ben directed them to a spot on the concrete floor near the Linotype machine. He introduced David, and David introduced the Linotype Machine.

"My precious children...my wonderful friends...all of you...I will show you something today that very few New Yorkers have ever seen...a special magical machine that I used to sit at every day, many years ago... before you were all born."

David continued by showing the children every aspect of the Linotype Machine. Poetic imagery flowed from his lips as he described how the letters, the matrices, flowed down the channels like rain. And then, after the slugs were molded from hot lead, the letters automatically rose again and returned to the magazine above, like the rain returning as moisture back into the clouds again. He knew he had their attention when he noticed that several children's mouths were wide open, and their eyes were almost as wide. He hung the bucket as they cheered him on, and gave them all small pieces of paper with the printed end product on them. He would have given them all lead slugs, but the city had determined the material might be too dangerous to handle—especially if it was inadvertently sucked on or chewed. The first question came from a boy named Deshan. He wanted to know what David's little hat was for. Was it one of those Jewish hats? Ms. Cohen tried to intervene, but David stopped her.

"Yes...yes Deshan. You see, God used something like a Linotype machine when he gave the ten commandments. You know about them."

Various children shouted commandments out. Most chose murder and adultery.

"Yes, well, he gave Moses a hat to wear as all those letters fell into place. The hat said these were special words…and that was a special Linotype machine."

A number of children at once told him he wasn't telling the truth.

"Well, I sort of am. It's a special kind of story that teaches something more than just all of the facts. No, it wasn't a Linotype machine…but it just as well could have been."

He had every child's attention. And then, after that first question was out of the way, other questions began to flow like melted lead, like silver matrices in their channels. When he finally asked what the children liked best about the machine, most said the sound. He couldn't have agreed with them more. He had missed that sound all of these years. It spoke of a job well done, and pleasing to the Almighty. But he didn't share that thought with them. That was just for him.

As might be expected, lunch was the noisiest time. But he loved that noise too. It was the music of little lives created in the image of a thunderous, mighty, and glorious God. And he felt very alive just being around it. Certainly, the Lord had given him this day.

After the children left, he sat at the machine and ate his kosher cheese sandwich lunch—something he used to sometimes do at the *New York Times* when things were tight. The staff was pleased with his morning's work, and he was given a schedule, the third Thursday of every month whenever there were school tours. He gladly accepted the schedule, and then went to the now vacant bathroom. When he got back, there was a phone call waiting for him. It was Naomi.

"Abba…I just thought you should know…that…"

He could hear the sadness emanating from the receiver.

"That…Darrin…Darrin…"

She began whimpering. David prepared for the worst. It was that kind of phone call, and Naomi was speaking with that kind of voice.

"Darrin Brock was shot in the subway yesterday…yesterday…it was on the news…and newspapers."

The word *newspaper* shot through him. Who had to lay that page out, he wondered? Naomi was breathing heavy. David didn't know everything about Naomi's relationship with Darrin—but he knew she cared about him. And why not? He had raised her to care about people. This was the compassionate Naomi he loved, coming to him in a time of need. *This Darrin fellow must have died, and she needs solace,* he thought. She caught her breath and continued.

"And…he's at Mt. Sinai…in critical condition…I just wanted you to

know. They don't know if he'll live. But…I'm okay…I'll be okay. But…
Abba…I know he's not Jewish…and he's…you know…just a friend…
acquaintance…sort of…but…could you say a Mi-shebeirach prayer for
him? I just thought if you…"

David sat down at the Linotype machine again and stared at the
keyboard.

"Of course. I will start on my way home. I'll see you after work,
Naomi. I love you."

Naomi didn't think it was necessary to tell him she hadn't even gone
to work—or that she'd be there when he got home.

CHAPTER FORTY-THREE

"Everything will be okay," Naomi said out loud as she walked into the kitchen. "I'm sure he'll live a long life, just as he wished for me… but even if he doesn't…if he dies…God's will be done. He knows what's best."

She tried to comfort herself that things would be simpler now. "I could use a little Torah simplicity," she again spoke aloud to herself. "I like that…Torah simplicity…Abba would like that. It's not too hard to keep, as *Moshe Rabeynu* said. I just need to remember that. Maybe I'll go to the movies tonight. That would be fun…maybe a war movie… anything but romance. I'll have to see what's playing."

She walked into the bathroom, for no other reason than that she couldn't stop herself from nervously walking around. She looked into the mirror, and peered into her own eyes. What did he see in those plain-looking eyes? *Perhaps I can see what he saw…or maybe not,* she thought. *Oh well, you deserve a break, Naomi…a nice movie to escape into. It's over. You can relax.*

She breathed in and out, and then breathed in and out again. It would be okay, she told herself. Then she breathed in again. This time she felt like she couldn't get enough air. At the same time, she could feel an ascending pulse in her wrists and in her chest. Her face began to flush in a matter of a few seconds, while she was still looking at it. Then the room began to spin, first slowly and then faster and faster. A ringing began in her ears, and try as hard as she could to stop it by cupping her hands over them, it just got louder and louder, as her heart rate got faster and faster. She had to get to the living room before she fainted and her head hit the hard tile bathroom floor. Quick! Quick!

She spun out of the bathroom, through the dining room, and onto the living room couch, the same one her father lay on months ago when she found him sick with a fever. Now she had a different kind of fever. And she had no one she could go to for help. Suddenly, tears began to spill out uncontrollably. The pain in her chest was excruciating. She had to cry out! She had to scream!

"DARRIN. NO. I CAN'T EVEN SEE YOU…EVER AGAIN! BUT… YOU CAN'T DIE! NO! NO! NOT WHILE I STILL LOVE YOU! NO! NO! NOOOO!"

She fell off the sofa and began to crawl around on the floor. Who could she call? Who would understand? There was no one, absolutely no one. Or was there?

She stopped crawling and sat on the floor, leaning against the sofa. Yes, maybe there *was* someone who would understand. Of course! Marvin's Aunt Ida! She was the only Jew Naomi knew outside her own community, besides her sister—and talking to *her* would be unthinkable.

Aunt Ida wouldn't answer with the wisdom of the sages. But maybe that would be okay, for now. Naomi *knew* what the sages would say. She didn't have to ask them. But Aunt Ida would at least be a listening ear. As much as she irritated Naomi with her worldly Reform ways and incessant talk, at least she wouldn't get angry with her or judge her. This could be the start of the true end of this whole—affair. Okay, maybe that wasn't such a great word for it. But how to reach her, that was the question.

The only one who knew Aunt Ida's number was, of course, Marvin. And he vied with Lisa for being just about the last person Naomi wanted to talk to. But then again, why talk to him? Why not just text him? She went into the bedroom, grabbed her phone, and quickly texted.

Marvin just need aunt ida's number. Can U Text

If there was one good thing about Marvin, it was his fast return texts, spelled out in his kosher way—meticulously. This one took a bit longer than usual, due to its length.

I can give it to you. But why do you need it? Why can't I see you in person and give it to you then? And we can see her together, and talk about marriage. She is very good at those things, and she knows how much we belong together. I've never seen a Reform Jew with such an Orthodox heart. I can give you the number when I see you, and we can call her together. Okay?

She texted back furiously.

Not ok! give it now or wont ever speak to u again!

He got the message and just responded with the number, and no other comment. That was done. Now she just had to text Aunt Ida. But how would she catch her attention?

Aunt ida...must see you immediately. love a man i shouldn't. please help! keep private

Aunt Ida wasn't as quick to respond as Marvin. Ten agonizing minutes went by. Fifteen. Soon, her father would come through the front door and see her like this. What would she say to him? She decided she would go to her bedroom and hide from him. But that couldn't last forever.

Just then the text alert sounded.

Aunt Ida to the rescue. around corner with super religious Chassidic friends. walk outside

Naomi got up and ran into the bathroom. She had to take care of the usual business and at least wash her face and dry it. She looked terrible, but no matter. She threw her shoes and shawl on, grabbed her keys, and ran outside, just in time for Aunt Ida's silver Lexus to pull up, like a luxury ambulance responding to a 911 call. She opened the passenger window.

"Get in, honey. Hurry. I see your father down the street, walking home from God knows where. I take it you don't want to see him."

Naomi nodded.

"Come on. I'll take you to a late lunch far away, where *no one* will know you."

Naomi got in and they drove off before David Kaplan noticed them. Naomi slid over on the leather seat and then slumped to the side. Aunt Ida glanced over at her. She was still flushed, and slightly shaking.

"The flu?"

Naomi shook her head.

"Fast pulse?"

Naomi nodded yes.

"Dizzy?

She nodded yes again.

"Chest Pain?"

Yes again.

"Panic attack, for God's sake. You just rest. It'll be a while before we get there. Here. I'll put on some music."

The music was anything but relaxing. In fact, it was somewhat counter-productive, between the loves lost and cheating men in the lives of everyone from Taylor Swift to Megan Trainor, covering two to three years of shattered romance top forty hits. But somehow, between the breaking up and making up, Naomi fell asleep for the rest of the trip. Maybe it was the excellent suspension system. When she finally woke up, they were pulling into a parking lot. She recognized a restaurant sign that she'd seen in Manhattan.

"Applebee's. It's not Kosher."

"You got it. No one will find us here. We're in Newark, New Jersey at an Applebee's. That's about as far away from Brooklyn as you can get, don't you think? Come on. Let's go and see how most of the world eats."

"But Aunt Ida…"

"Come on."

Ida got out of the Lexus, and Naomi followed her. They entered the restaurant.

"Two for the corner over there," Aunt Ida pointed out to the hostess. She went over and sat down at a booth in the far corner of the dining area. Naomi stood next to her.

"I've got to go to the bathroom."

"We'll both go. Don't worry. They clean them, and you can put toilet paper on the seat. Come on."

When they got back from the bathroom, there was silverware wrapped in napkins at their places and a waiter handing them menus. Aunt Ida handed both menus back to him.

"I'll make it easy. I'll have a cheeseburger, fries, and a mango iced tea. She'll have nothing."

Naomi was startled.

"Cheese and meat! And un-kosher meat at that! I shouldn't even be here. I can't eat…I can't even touch the silverware, Aunt Ida."

"You think I don't know that? Relax. There's nothing to panic about. About the other issue…I don't know. But this is nothing."

"So I'm supposed to sit here and watch you eat meat and cheese?"

"You knew I didn't eat kosher. But *you're* another story. Here."

She took a large folded linen napkin and a bottle of water out of her pocket book, and handed them both to Naomi, who unfolded the napkin. Inside, there was a sweet warm Jewish noodle kugel. Aunt Ida smiled.

"See. Aunt Ida takes care of everything. I just grabbed this from the Chassid's house last minute. See, it doesn't even have to touch the table. Sorry it's a little sloppy, but you'll live. Now what's going on?"

Naomi let out a sigh and began to relax in Aunt Ida's presence. She realized that if nothing else, Aunt Ida was resourceful. Perhaps she would be a good resource about Darrin as well. Naomi took a bite out of the kugel, along with a sip of the bottled water. Then she closed her eyes, and a few tears escaped. Aunt Ida took a sip of the mango iced tea that had arrived by that time.

"Okay, we have all the time in the world. Here's a tissue out of my pocket book. I guarantee it hasn't touched any *traif*…no bacon in this pocket book. Take your time."

When Naomi opened her eyes, the cheeseburger and fries arrived.

"It's got blood, Aunt Ida. It's a sin."

"It's called pink, Naomi. Pink. Could we forget the food for a minute, and get down to business?"

Naomi took her eyes off the burger and focussed on Aunt Ida's iced tea, just to have something else to look at.

"Where should I start?"

"Why don't you start with the *love a man I shouldn't?*"

"Right. Well, I met this handsome man named Darrin Brock at the housewares department…on the 26th of December…"

"You remember the date…interesting."

"Did I say he was a Gentile?"

"No, you didn't."

"Well he is. But there's something about him, Aunt Ida. I know it's ridiculous, but he reminds me of my father. The gentleness, the wisdom… the sweetness…and we happened to see each other a few other times…I don't know, by chance at first…like luck…besheirt…no, that's not right. He's a Christian…maybe it was the evil one. Oh, I'm so mixed up."

"Uh huh. I agree with you there."

"He's like…like a movie star…Brad Pitt…and his lips…"

"What! Tell me you haven't kissed him."

Naomi's face turned beet red.

"God is punishing him, I'm sure. And it was my fault. I'm the one who kissed him, and he's being punished for it, I'm positive. Oh, what have I done!"

"What in the world are you talking about?"

"I didn't tell you something. He…was shot…yesterday…at a subway station…after we kissed in the rain under his big black umbrella…and we said goodbye for good."

She began to cry until it came on hard, in heaving waves.

"He's…crit…crit…Mt. Sinai…he may not…"

A light bulb went off in Aunt Ida's head.

"He's the detective…in the news…the subway shooting…"

Naomi nodded as she tried to compose herself. Aunt Ida's face took on a stern and serious look that Naomi had never seen before.

"Don't you *ever* in my hearing…*ever* talk that way! God is *not* punishing him. Were the six million punished?"

Naomi was surprised by her tone.

"Answer me. Were they slaughtered because God was punishing them…every last one of them?"

Naomi hung her head down.

"No."

"You're damn right! No. A good man is a good man. Is this Darrin a good man?"

Naomi lifted her head with confidence.

"Aunt Ida, he's the best man I've ever met, Jew or Gentile…the best…"

As she spoke those words, Ida thought she detected a familiar sparkle in Naomi's eyes.

"All right then. No talk like that. So this is the *rest* of the story behind that good looking Gentile man I drove you all the way to Teaneck for."

Naomi's face turned a shade redder. Aunt Ida put down her burger.

"Well, he *is* handsome. That's for sure. Of course, you understand he's probably a ham-eating card-carrying, white-bread church-going Christian. And you're a good little very observant Orthodox Jewish virgin…"

Naomi interjected as she swallowed another small bit of kugel.

"So is he."

"That's what they all say."

"No! He absolutely *is.*"

"You've discussed that?"

"And he never kissed a girl before me…ever. He's very religious, like his parents. And he's a very conscientious police detective. And he loves children in crises, and I couldn't stop daydreaming about him for months. I tried not to. I really did. I knew it was wrong. But I couldn't stop. It kept coming back, even when I didn't know how to get in touch with him and I didn't think we'd ever meet again. And then...all of a sudden...it happened."

"Hold it right there! Wait a minute. What happened?"

"My dreams became reality, of course...and he loves me...and wants me to be a good observant Jew. Anyway, he said we can't see each other ever again, or tell our families. And it's over, and we should move on. So I'll never see him again. I promised. I gave him my promise."

"So?"

"So..."

"So does Marvin know about him?"

"Oh no! And I'll probably marry Marvin and settle down, and we'll have a nice kosher home."

Aunt Ida slapped her hand on the table so hard her fries jumped.

"Problem solved!"

"You're right...problem solved."

Naomi began to feel the tightness in her chest again, and the shallowness of breathing.

"No...no...not right...I can't...breathe. Not right."

"Not right?"

"Not..."

"Okay. Okay. Take it easy."

Naomi began to cry so hard, everyone around them turned to see what was going on. Aunt Ida reached out and took her hand.

"Shhh. Take it easy. It's okay."

She gave Naomi three more tissues. Naomi tried to catch her breath.

"What...what do I do? It's over. It *should* be over. everything's... as it...should be. But...he...can't die! I...I...I admit it...I love him so much...I love him *so* much, Aunt Ida! It hurts...It hurts so much...I...I can't breathe...I can't...it'd break my father's heart...it'd kill him...he'd... what do I do?"

Aunt Ida sat back and surveyed the situation. She took her time answering the question, even though she already knew the answer. As she looked at Naomi's teary eyes, she noticed for the first time how lovely they were. She had never thought of Naomi as the least bit beautiful. Lisa was the beautiful one. Naomi was plain. But in the light of the Applebee's restaurant, she could see that wasn't true. There was a spark of beauty in Naomi that had lain dormant, and it was clear that this Darrin fellow had awakened that in her. Finally, Ida spoke in an uncharacteristically low even tone.

"I'll tell you what I'd do. I'd get over to that damn Mount Sinai Hospital right away, and run over to this Darrin's room if it's the last thing I'd do. And I'd tell him I love him and I'll never leave his side."

Naomi's crying began to slow down. She took a deep breath, and then answered Aunt Ida without a pause, as if the answer was the only possible and logical one.

"Oh no, Aunt Ida. I couldn't do *that*. I promised him I wouldn't let his parents know. It's out of the question. We're not to see each other again…ever. I promised."

"Right. But…isn't there some kind of vow breaking mechanism in Judaism…like a *Kol Nidre* for occasions just like this?"

"I gave him my word. I *can't*. Besides, he's not Jewish. It would never work. He goes through the back door and I go through the front door."

"What the hell does that mean?"

"I don't know. It's too complicated. I just can't."

The waiter brought the check and Aunt Ida handed him her credit card.

"Well, I guess I'm just a hopeless romantic first, and a good Jew second. But if you can't, you can't. Case closed. Just do me a favor, and keep in touch with me. And finish your kugel. You've only taken a few bites. You'll need the strength to get through this."

"I'm not hungry."

"You're not taking my advice about this Darrin *or* the kugel. It looks like I'm batting a thousand."

Naomi put her hand on Aunt Ida's.

"No!! You just don't know what it means to me that you're here, and that I can tell you everything. There's no one else…*no one* else. I love you, Aunt Ida. I really do."

That did it. Aunt Ida's heart burst like a dam. She moved over to Naomi's side of the booth and held her in her arms, hugging her for several minutes. People were peering over their booths to watch, but she didn't care. She wouldn't let her go. And she purposed that she wouldn't let her go in the days and weeks to come, either.

Chapter Forty-Four

David Kaplan hated electronic devices, especially computers. He knew he was being irrational. After all, they performed many very important functions. They saved lives in hospitals, gave knowledge to millions, and kept the country safe, among other things. Still, he hated them. He preferred machines with moving parts he could see up close, like Linotype machines.

As a consequence of David's disdain for computers, there were also many other computerized devices that he purposely avoided. Topping the list were cell phones. And the smarter they were, the more he loathed them. But even the simple kind irked him. That's why he chose not to own one, in spite of the inconvenience. And that's also why, when a text from Marvin appeared on Naomi's phone, he didn't know what to do. If this was just a regular text, he wouldn't have paid any attention to it. But when he saw the word *emergency* staring at him from the little window, he felt he should probably do something. That, in addition to the fact that Naomi almost never left her phone at home, caused him to at least pick it up and hold it in his hand.

"Stupid device. I don't even know how to open it up."

He shook it several times, and was about to give up when it flipped open.

"What do you know."

He pressed the button in the middle, and then pressed on four others. He was again ready to give up when Marvin's text popped up.

Emergency. We need to talk about a date. You've made me wait too long...

David figured there must be more, but from what he read so far it didn't sound like an emergency. It just sounded like Marvin. Still, he pressed the same button again. Up came more words.

I don't know why you asked for my Aunt Ida's number, but she knows we should be married. Ask her. And your father knows I'm a mensch and that we should get married too.

"No I don't."

David was about to toss the phone on the dining room table, when curiosity caused him to press the button once more. Aunt Ida's name replaced Marvin's.

"Hmm. Tricky little thing for a stupid phone. So this is what texts are. Nothing really but foolish talk and a waste of time."

He pressed the button again.

Aunt ida...must see you immediately. love a man i shouldn't. please help! keep private

His face grew ashen.

"Oy vey."

He closed the phone and threw it on the table. He sat down on the nearest chair and buried his head in his hands.

"Naomi...my beautiful *shayna* Naomi. What are you *doing?*"

As he sat there, stunned, he couldn't help wondering why Naomi went to Marvin's crazy *meshugena* Aunt Ida, and not to him. But deep inside, he knew why. She wasn't ready to hear what he would say. She wanted another opinion. She wanted Reform Jewish worldly Aunt Ida's opinion. Terror swept over him from head to toe. He was losing his only observant daughter. It was like having his beating heart ripped out of his chest and stepped on. She was slipping away. And he strongly suspected it was with that slimy Gentile Darrin fellow.

"I hope he dies."

He put his hand over his mouth as soon as he said those words.

"Forgive me, God. It's a sin to wish that on *anyone*. Forgive me. But God, what do I do?"

David spent the rest of the afternoon crying out to God. His mind wondered back over the years, to when Lillian was alive and the girls were little. What could he have done differently all these years? Maybe he should have insisted on Marvin years ago. This was all his fault. He should have encouraged a marriage when they were younger, even with the schlemiel that Marvin was.

He went up to his bedroom and reached up into the clothes closet. There it was—the old box of pictures. He took it out and placed it on his bed. He gingerly opened it, making sure not to let the dust go everywhere.

He spent the rest of the afternoon looking at the old pictures. He was particularly struck by the pictures of the family in Atlantic City, and the cities of Ventnor and Margate to the immediate south. Normally more of a Philadelphia summer destination because it was only about an hour away from there, it was too far away for many New Yorkers. It was much farther than Rockaway Beach, or even Beach Haven. But that made it more of a getaway, a real vacation. and the perfect place to connect with his struggling daughter—and his whole family. The kids would love it. It would be good for Lisa and Marc. And Naomi would be miles away from *that man* at Mount Sinai Hospital.

He smiled as he handled the piles of beach and boardwalk snapshots of young Naomi and even younger Lisa, as they scooped sand and caught waves, and walked tanned on the boardwalk in their bright and colorful dresses.

There *he* was, shortly after his career as a *New York Times* Linotype operator ended—younger and thinner, and sporting the same yarmulka he still wore, And there was Lillian in the prime of her life, yet with a loving husband and two beautiful daughters. He sighed.

By the time Naomi came home late in the afternoon, he had made up his mind. As soon as she came through the door, closing it quickly so he wouldn't see Aunt Ida's Lexus driving away, he met her. She looked more relaxed than he expected.

"Shalom,"

"Shalom, Abba."

"You left your phone. It's not like you to…"

"Yes, Abba. I rushed out this morning."

"Marvin…he texted you, I think."

"I'm sure he did. That can wait. I'm tired."

"Um…would you like me to make some dinner?"

"I'm not hungry now. I can make you some."

She headed for the kitchen. He stopped her.

"No. I'm not hungry either. How is he?"

"Who?"

"You know. Your friend…in the hospital."

"Oh, him. I don't know. I guess we'll hear something sometime on the news…either way."

"I said a Mi-shebeirach prayer."

"Thank you, Abba."

"I hope he lives."

"It's in God's hands whether he lives or dies. I'm tired. It's been a long day. Maybe I'll lie down for a few minutes. Then I'll cook something up. How does that sound?"

"Naomi…"

"Yes, Abba?"

"I've been thinking…and I've decided to take the whole family to Atlantic City. Do you remember Atlantic City?"

"Of course, Abba."

"They were good times…your mother was alive. You were my precious little…"

He sighed again.

"Abba? Are you okay?":

"Nothing. I was just looking at our old pictures."

"I remember those old things. I don't know if I can get off work."

David put his hand on her arm as she was about to leave.

"We need it, Naomi. *You* need it. Tell them that. You have some days. I'll talk to Marc and Lisa. We can go in style…in his Mercedes… or maybe in Lisa's Escalade. That would be nice. Lindsay and Noah have never seen Atlantic City. They'd love it."

"For how long?

"I don't know…maybe four or five days during the week. We'd be back before Shabbas. Remember pizza at Bubbie's Bistro in Ventnor? Middle-Eastern and steaks at Jerusalem Glatt Kosher?"

"Yes, I remember, Abba. I remember."

"You don't mind…leaving when your friend is…not doing well?"

Naomi shook her head and smiled.

"No, Abba. What will be will be."

"You don't want to visit him? Maybe that would be a nice thing to do."

"I have no plans to, Abba. Now that I think of it, I would like to take that vacation with the whole family. I can ask off for next week…while it's still summer. You'd better call Marc and Lisa."

She gave him a quick hug and went to her room. He had no way of knowing whether she ended up talking to Marvin's Aunt Ida. But if she had, maybe she got the right advice after all. Perhaps the worst was over, and Naomi was her old self again. Still, the vacation could only help her turn the corner.

Within the next twenty-four hours, all arrangements had been made. David insisted on renting a few rooms in a cottage house on a charming little street he remembered from the old days. Marc would cover everything else. They would take the Escalade, and travel in class. Lisa insisted that Marc get the time off from Prima. And as with the cruise, she usually got her way with things like that.

On a beaming cloudless late August day, the Silver family drove all the way up to Brooklyn and picked up Naomi and David. And then they were off. Naomi opened her window half way on the Garden State Parkway and let the wind run through her hair. It was safer than Darrin's fingers. The wind was a comfort to her, and a good way to start the family vacation.

Lindsay and Noah took turns counting mile signs and calling out various states' licenses. And sometimes they fought, and asked Lisa how long it would be until they got there.

"Wait until you see *The Elephant*," Lisa told them.

"I don't like circuses. I don't like elephants" Noah shot back. "I thought we were going to swim, and build sand castles."

"You'll like *this* one," she said.

Naomi wasn't thinking so much about the old memories. She only wanted to rest, and prepare to move on with her life. She was almost forty-nine years old. It was about time she stopped dreaming and started living. She decided she would be the one to call Marvin when they got back. That would definitely surprise him. She would propose and set the date, just like she would do everything else for Marvin after they were married. And she would be thankful. She'd learned her lesson. She would be very thankful to the Almighty.

When they arrived on the Ventnor street and looked at the house, it seemed like a different street, not at all what David remembered. Marc was the first to comment.

"You reserved this dump? Figures."

"I don't remember it this way."

"Right. Your memory is right up there with your taste."

Naomi came to her father's defense.

"Shut up, Marc. Maybe your friends in New York spent all their dirty capital on those sleazy casinos, and didn't have any money left for this neighborhood."

"Keep your trap shut, you old maid!"

Lisa giggled. Naomi shot her a look that could kill Wonder Woman. Noah was inquisitive.

"Is Aunt Naomi a maid, Mommy? I thought she sells pots and pans at Macy's."

David stepped in.

"Enough! Such words are Lashan Hara…the evil tongue…and I won't have it on this vacation! Let's go in and register."

It was obvious that the property values had gone downhill. And Hurricane Sandy a few years earlier didn't help. But the house was a block from the beach, and that was still as magnificent as ever. Marc looked around the foyer of the old house and rolled his eyes.

"I've got some friends uptown at the Tropicana. They can get us in there right now, two suites for a song."

"I bet they can," Naomi said under her breath.

David had made his mind up.

"We're staying here. No uptown. No casinos. The kosher restaurants we like are here. The beach we like is here. We're staying right here."

"Whatever you say, chief."

Marc sulked off to the car to bring luggage in. David turned to Lisa.

"Lisa, this vacation is not about luxury. It's about family."

Lisa kissed him on the cheek.

"I agree, Dad. You're as wise as Naomi always says you are…wiser. I'll take care of Marc."

The first day was cloudy in the Atlantic City area. But the second day ended up being a perfect beach day. Everyone was satisfied with that. Lisa sun bathed next to Noah and Lindsay, who built sand castles with cups and popsicle sticks when they weren't burying each other. Marc spent a lot of time in the water working off his endless stress. And Naomi and David were on beach chairs supplied by the rental property, which were situated several yards away from the rest of the family. David lay on his chair and tried to totally relax, with eyes closed. Naomi knew he was resting, but she also realized that she might not get another opportunity to be alone with him. The ocean air seemed to open up her heart, and she spoke softly but clearly.

"Abba…Abba…are you awake, Abba?"

"Hmmm."

"No secrets, Abba. No secrets when it comes to you."

She waited for him to say something, while he kept his eyes closed and waited for her to continue. She was actually hoping he'd keep them closed. It was easier that way.

"No secrets, Daddy…none. Yes…yes, I confess that I love him. I love him deeply. I love him more than any man I ever met…except you. But he knows it would never work. He put an end to any hope I might… that I might…foolishly have. That's the kind of man he is, Abba. He's wise like you. And somewhere inside him beats a…believe it or not…a Jewish heart…somewhere…not that he would ever give up his…his… his Jesus. I don't think he would ever do that. I think that's what moves him in some strange way…sad to say, but true."

She paused for a few seconds.

"So I've decided I will marry Marvin, Abba. I will love and obey him. He will be my husband and I will be faithful to him. But…but I can't fall out of love with Darrin just like that. Right now he's the love of my life. I can't help it. I need time, Abba. Please give me time. Please."

David turned and looked at her, putting his suntan lotioned hand on her suntan lotioned arm.

"You have it if you need it, Naomi. But Naomi, how did you get mixed up with this whole thing in the first place? Our ancestors in Kiev never looked outside. *None* of our ancestors looked outside. God provides among us. You know that, Naomi. You've always known that."

The shame she had been trying to resist since her talk with Aunt Ida shown plainly on her face.

"I know Abba. I'm sorry. I'm so sorry."

"You're still my daughter, and I love you. I will always love you."

They both lay on their chairs and closed their eyes, as the sun beat down on them. After a while, Naomi rented an umbrella on the beach, and they both lay under that. She felt some relief, more because of her honesty than the shade. At least she had told her father the truth. David, on the other hand, had a myriad of feelings all competing for his heart at the same time. The overriding one concerned his daughter's continuing vulnerability. He knew she wasn't in the clear yet.

On the third day, they all drove down Atlantic Avenue through Margate. At the appropriate time, the children were asked to close their eyes and then open them again. In front of them was the strangest building they'd ever seen.

Lucy the Margate elephant was built in 1881 and occupied in 1882, the same year the menorah first occupied the Kaplan house in Kiev.

It was built by inventor James Laferty, who took out a seventeen year patent on animal-shaped buildings. He constructed the six story pachyderm to attract land buyers to what was at that time called South Atlantic City, now called Margate.

Lafferty built two more elephants, a smaller one called the Light of Asia, in Cape May, New Jersey, and one three times the size of Lucy in Coney Island, called the Elephantine Colossus. That one ended up as a brothel before it burnt down in 1896.

By the early 1960's, Lucy was rotten through and through and was slated to be torn down. But a committee was formed, money was raised, and she was restored to her original condition, becoming a registered national landmark during the early 1970's. By the time the family vacationed there in the late 1970's, she looked brand new.

Noah was half scared and half fascinated by Lucy. She was certainly more interesting than a circus elephant, especially because you could climb her stairs and look out of the howdah that rested on her back. He learned the word *Howdah* that day. Lindsay wasn't as interested, but nevertheless she accepted the time spent at the Elephant as a day's outing. She climbed Lucy's stairs with Noah, and waved at Lisa and Naomi from the Howdah at the top of the structure. Naomi and Lisa stood next to the building and remembered the last time they were there, when they were perhaps eleven and six years old respectively. Marc caught up with Noah and Lindsay, paying the small fee and climbing the spiral stairs through the hind leg as well. He figured it was as good a bonding time as any.

David sat on a small bench across the parking lot and stared at the victorian building. Deep emotions, stirred by his beach conversation with his oldest daughter, were still swirling around his heart and mind. Then, as he watched his grandchildren and son-in-law waving and shouting six stories above his head, his thoughts zeroed in on the architectural novelty before him. He began to mutter to himself, moving his lips ever so slightly.

"So this is America...this useless...grotesque...thing. This idol. This is what my people came all the way from Kiev for, on that ocean over there. So they could climb up that hind leg...that...back door to her insides...and enter the belly of the beast...commit adultery with an unclean world that treats Torah like an old broken down carnival ride...like this elephant when she was rotting from her insides out... and her guts were sagging with corruption. This is what the city of New York...this whole country...did to my oldest daughter. *It violated her!* It's not enough that I care about all the *other* people, that I have compassion, accept them as children created in God's image...that I try to understand them, with their Christmases and their Easters, and their New Testament...and their Son of God. No! They have to suck us in like this ridiculous elephant, and then spit us out and leave us without a Jewish soul. Look at her grotesque eyes...round, hollow, and vacant. Look at her mouth. It's laughing at me with that sick smile. Look at her red tongue. It's sticking out at me. I can just hear her saying, 'I'll take your daughter. I'll make a good Gentile Sabbath-breaking American out of her.'"

His face began to redden. He took a deep breath, and tried to calm himself.

No, it's not that man's fault. I believe Naomi. I'm sure he's not the trouble-maker I thought he was. I trust her judgment. If she says he's a good man, he's a good man. After all, she knows a good man when she sees one. I've taught her that much. No, it's not him. It's this...this wicked elephant...this six story...thing...this idol...this great big cheap carnival attraction. It's America! This is what the United States of America, may she be forgiven, has done to my Jewish children!

In the middle of his inner rant, he heard a voice.

"Abba, it's time to go."

He turned from Lucy the Elephant to his daughter.

"Yes, of course, Naomi. Of course."

As the family drove back up Atlantic Avenue, David watched the Elephant's cream and brown striped howdah slowly disappear behind three-story shops and houses. And as it disappeared, he tried to view the day in a more objective light. Things weren't *that* dire. There were rays of light. After all, Naomi had trusted him as her loving father, and had opened her heart to him. And most important, she was trying to get over this disturbing and terribly wrong relationship. That was definitely a step in the right direction.

CHAPTER FORTY-FIVE

Lisa Silver's black Cadillac Escalade pulled up in front of the Kaplan house about 11:30 p.m. on Thursday night. It had been a long hot beach day, followed by a large meal at one of the nicer Kosher restaurants in Atlantic City, and everyone was exhausted. The children were sleeping in the back seat. David and Naomi quietly said good night to Marc and Lisa, and took their luggage into the house. Naomi went up to her room and fell asleep in five minutes.

The next morning, knowing she had the day off as one of her vacation days, she slept later than her father. When she finally came downstairs, he was already cooking scrambled eggs for her. Two glasses of orange juice were on the dining room table. And two pieces of Challah bread had just popped up from the toaster. She knew that this was her father's way of expressing his love for her, without any need for words. She went over and kissed him on the cheek, and then sat down. He dished out the eggs and buttered the bread.

As her father was about to pray the blessing before the meal, Naomi's phone, which was on the mantle next to the menorah, made the usual sound of an incoming text. She looked at her father and then over at the phone.

"Well, it's probably Marvin. I told myself that when he contacted me, I'd invite him over and then…with your blessing I'd…."

"It can at least wait until after the blessing before the meal."

He spoke slowly and deliberately.

"*Baruch Atah Adonai, Eloheynu Melech HaOlam, hamotzi lechem meen ha-aretz.* Blessed are You, Lord our God, King of the Universe, who brings forth bread from the Earth."

He detected an anxious look in Naomi's eyes.

"Well, I guess you might as well just look at it."

She got up, went over to the mantle, and opened the phone. Then she stood there, silent. David broke in.

"Well, is it him? Our eggs are getting cold, Naomi, and I want you to sit with me."

"No Abba…it isn't him."

"Well, okay. Whoever it is, I'm sure it can wait."

Naomi stood there for several more seconds, frozen. Then she spoke softly and hauntingly, as if from another world.

"It's his Aunt Ida, Abba."

"I suppose she can wait too. Why don't you contact her later and have some breakfast?"

"She says, 'Did u see the news? still touch and go just woke up out of coma u should get over there…now!'"

They locked eyes. Naomi's began to fill with tears. She sat down next to David and gulped down her orange juice. David gently put his hand on her shoulder.

"God did not create oranges to be eaten so quickly…in any form. Eat your eggs, Naomi. If the Holy One wanted you to eat cold eggs, He would have had me make you egg salad."

Naomi picked up her fork and then put it down.

"I'm not hungry. Should I go to the hospital?"

"I think maybe you should take a deep breath and then eat your breakfast."

She picked up her fork again, and started picking at her eggs with one hand while she wiped her eyes with the other.

"Is there anything else you want to say to me, Abba?"

He sighed deeply.

"Well, as a matter of fact, yes. I know you're very upset right now. Anyone would be upset if their friend was in critical condition in

Intensive Care. But I want you to remember who you are...and who he is. I know you told me in Ventnor that he's got some kind of Jewish heart. But the truth is, Naomi, he's not Jewish."

She nervously took a tiny bite of her eggs and her buttered Challah.

"Yes Abba, I know that."

"So what does that mean about the future? You *must* think about that."

"I understand, Abba."

"I want you to understand that I'm very sorry that this happened to him, Naomi. It shouldn't happen to anyone, especially an innocent man."

She put down her fork again.

"Well...maybe...maybe it would be best then if he died. Don't you think so, Abba? I mean, he's a righteous Gentile. He's a true defender of Israel. You should see him talk about it. So...he will have a place in the world to come with other righteous Gentiles. And then I'll be the daughter you want me to be. Isn't that what you want, Abba?"

After she spoke, a hardly noticeable tremor rippled through her upper body.

"Maybe we should ask God to take him. Wouldn't the sages want that?"

David's expression changed. He pounded the table.

"God forbid, Naomi. Don't say such things!"

Naomi flinched, and shivers ran through her body. David spoke the next words carefully, one by one.

"The preservation of human life takes precedence over all other commandments in Judaism. That's *pikuach nefesh*, the saving of a life."

He saw Naomi's nervous response and took on a more gentle, teacherly tone.

"You see, Naomi, we're not to wish the death of any man, especially an innocent victim...for any reason whatsoever. The sages are very clear about this."

The tremor was now a trembling, and was increasing.

"Then what do I...what do I...oh...Abba...I don't feel well. Abba..."

She leaned over sideways in what appeared to be a faint.

David moved closer and held her tight.

"Oh Naomi...my Naomi..."

He turned his eyes towards heaven.

"God, please help my daughter. Please...help...please. You see how she's suffering."

Naomi tried her best to get control of the shaking. But somewhere deep inside her, she knew that if her shaking was to stop, she had to tell her father all that she was feeling.

"Daddy...Daddy...I care about him...I can't just let him die."

Large tears began falling from her eyes and running down her face. She tried to speak, even as the shaking continued.

"I know...I know this hurts you deeply...Abba. I know that. And I also know that Darrin...Darrin didn't want me to ever...ever see him again. And he didn't ever want to...want to...tell his parents about our feelings...for each other. But I must...I must go to him...I must...I must go, Abba. I'm sorry. I must..."

The shaking began to abate. She put her head on her father's chest.

"I must, Abba. I must...before he dies. I could never live with myself if I didn't. I *must*."

David kissed her on the top of her head.

"If you must go, you must go. After all, it is a mitzvah to visit the sick in their distress. Go. I promise you, I will be praying the Mi-shebeirach prayer. Just remember who you are."

He carefully let go of her. She sat upright and looked at him. Then a thin smile appeared on her face. She leaned over and kissed him on the cheek.

"Thank you Abba. Thank you."

She left his side and went up to the bathroom to freshen up before getting dressed. She looked at herself in the mirror, particularly at her eyes. They were bloodshot and swollen. But even in their present condition, she detected a sparkle in them—the same spark Darrin had probably seen. This was not the face she had grotesquely piled make up on weeks earlier. Like it or not, this was the face that was loved by the man of her dreams.

She finished dressing and grabbed her pocket book, running out of the house and down the block toward the subway. When the train finally came, she sat on an inside seat and repeated the Mi-shebeirach prayer to herself over and over, at least ten times. Then she spent the rest of the ride slowly breathing in and out, trying to calm herself down. It wouldn't be helpful for Darrin to see her like she was just an hour before.

She ended up on the number 6 subway, taking it to 96th Street and Lexington Avenue station, then walking up 96th Street to Madison Avenue. There before her was the massive Mount Sinai Hospital. The attractive blue Jewish Star logo above the main entrance was a comforting sign that she was doing the right thing. Once inside, she stepped up to the information desk and asked where Darrin Brock was. The woman seemed to know the information without looking it up, and gave it to her on a small slip of paper—along with a few verbal directions. Naomi clutched the paper tightly as she proceeded to the Intensive Care section of the hospital.

She asked no questions of anyone else as she followed the directions, and then slipped into the Intensive Care area behind a man in a white coat that seemed to have access she didn't have. There, in the distance, was *his* room—room number 7. Her heart began to pound with a combination of fear and excitement. She saw a policeman who was obviously holding some sort of sentry to the right of the room. Perhaps he would ignore her, just as everyone else had. As she was about to step beyond the door and into the room itself—beyond a glass wall that was cloaked on the inside with a beige curtain—a nurse at the station opposite the room called out to her.

"Excuse me. Are you immediate family?"

She turned to see an obese middle-aged grey-haired RN staring at her.

"Well, no…"

"I'm sorry. Visitation to this room is restricted. Only immediate family can visit."

She closed her eyes and took a deep breath, trying to slow her heart down. Then she began pleading her case.

"But I *must* see him. It's…an emergency. Please."

"I'm sorry. You may return to the waiting room and speak to family members there."

"I…I don't even know where that is. But I need to see him. I need to…"

"I'm sorry…"

Suddenly a familiar voice interrupted the nurse.

"Let her in."

"Inspector Lewis!"

"Nurse, she needs to see Darrin Brock. She's his girlfriend."

Naomi had never heard that word applied to her. She blushed slightly. The nurse acquiesced immediately.

"Certainly, Inspector Lewis."

Ralph Lewis escorted her beyond the curtain. She whispered to him as she entered.

"Um...I don't think...I can't say that I'm exactly his...girlfriend, Inspector Lewis."

He whispered back.

"You could have fooled him, as of a conversation we had a few weeks ago...not without a broken heart, I might add. Let's see if your visit will help. They just removed the respirator, but he's by no means out of the woods yet. Go get 'em, tiger. You're our secret weapon."

She looked back at him as he gave her a quick pat on the back and a slight shove into the room. A few seconds earlier, she was trying to figure out how to get into the room. Now she was resisting Inspector Lewis, overwhelmed by his marching orders. He rolled his eyes.

"You came here to see Darrin, didn't you? Now get in there!"

She entered the room, as Ralph Lewis watched from the door. There was Darrin, lying immobile, with his eyes closed. His breathing was somewhat labored, and his face was paler than she'd ever seen it. But his features were still striking and flawless, and every strand of his blonde hair was in place. Someone was obviously keeping it well combed. Lester was sitting at his bedside, with a Bible on his lap. He was reading some sort of Bible verse. His left hand was holding Darrin's right hand, just below a taped intravenous portal. Velma was sitting on a wheelchair in the corner of the room. She seemed to be staring right at Darrin, so Naomi figured she must be cognizant of the situation. At first no one noticed that Naomi was there. But then Lester stopped reading and turned toward her. He seemed confused as to exactly who she was and what she was doing there.

"Yes?"

"I'm...a friend...a good friend."

"Yes. Don't I know you from somewhere? Didn't we meet you at that restaurant, in the parking lot? I never forget a face, you see."

Naomi betrayed a slight smile.

"Yes, that's right. I'm Naomi."

"Well Naomi, I'm not sure he's ready for visitors, other than family. But it was so nice of you to come. I'm sure you understand. He just needs rest now."

Naomi got the message.

"I...I...understand. I'll leave now."

She was trying to hold back tears.

"Just...just one thing...is he...can he...I mean, does he know you're here? I'm sorry to ask, but..."

"You're crying, my dear."

"I'm sorry."

"No need to be sorry. Well, we've all been in much prayer, and just today we think he said something. But we're not sure. You see, he lost a lot of blood, and…but he's no longer in a coma, or on the ventilator, as you can see. We've been rejoicing for that, Velma and I."

Out of the corner of Naomi's eye, she could see that Velma's expression was unchanged.

"Well, when…when he wakes up, will you just tell him that I was here to visit him? You can say I came. Please tell him I came *anyway*. He'll understand what that means. Naomi…Naomi Kaplan."

"Naomi Kaplan. I'll do that. I never forget a name, either. I guess that's where he gets his detective skills from."

Suddenly, a thin barely audible breathy voice spoke from the direction of the bed.

"N…N…Na…Na…Naomi. N…N…Naomi."

She put her hand to her mouth and gasped. Lester's head swung over to Darrin. Then he turned back to Naomi.

"I don't understand."

Naomi didn't know what to say. But words of thanksgiving flowed involuntarily.

"Oh my God…*Baruch HaShem*. Blessed is His name. Oh my God!"

Her hand was still over her mouth as tears started flowing again. Then Darrin turned toward her voice and opened up his eyes a crack. Lester leaned forward.

"Oh, praise the Lord!," he muttered.

Darrin began to appear agitated. Naomi came closer to him as Lester sat there in his chair, mouth open in shock and wonderment. Inspector Lewis just watched raptly from the doorway. Darrin was now clearly doing everything he could do to reach toward Naomi, considering that he was strapped down and plugged in. This time, his voice was clearer and more insistent.

"Naomi…my…my Naomi…my…my love…"

She completely broke down in sobs and went over to the other side of the bed, coming close to his face.

"I'm here. I'm right here, my love. I'm right here."

She reached out and tussled his hair. Then she reached over with her eyes wide open and gently kissed him on the mouth. Lester was stunned. Velma's eyes focused intensely. At least it seemed that way. Darrin became more excited, wanting desperately to get his words out.

"I...I...I P...P...Pr...Prayed...Naomi. I...I said..."

His voice began to get clearer, stronger.

"I said...I said...God...Jesus...Lord...I said...she'll never come. I told her...I told her not to...you know, I said it...in...in...in...my...heart..."

Naomi picked up his left hand and began kissing it over and over, wetting it with her tears.

"Yes, my love...my precious Darrin. I hear you. I hear you."

"So I said, she'll...never come."

Lester stood up.

"Maybe I should tell the nurse that he's started speaking."

Naomi spoke to him with her cheek still glued to Darrin's hand.

"No, Mr. Brock. Please. Not yet."

He sat down. Darrin struggled, trying to finish his thought.

"So, Naomi...my Naomi...do...do...do you know...what He said?"

"Who said, Darrin?"

"The Lord, Naomi...the Lord...Do...you...do you know what the Lord said?"

Now Darrin had really gotten Lester's attention. He leaned completely forward. Naomi held Darrin's hand tightly.

"Tell me, Darrin. You can tell me."

"Well, He said...He said, 'Who do you think this daughter of Abraham will listen to...you...or...Me?' You or Me? That's what...what He said."

Darrin tried to laugh, getting a few quiet chuckles out. Naomi laughed along with him. Then he opened his eyes fully and looked right at her, while she held his hand to her cheek.

"And you came. You're here. You're here."

"I'm here, Darrin. I'm right here."

"Please stay. Don't leave."

"Never never never never never...ever again. never. I'm right here."

Lewis shook his head.

"I'll be damned."

Naomi looked over to Lester, who still had an extremely puzzled look on his face. She went over to him and placed her hand on the Bible.

"May I read this to him? Where were you reading from?"

Still stunned, Lester showed her the first verse of the chapter he was reading from in the Tree of Life Version Bible translation. As he handed her the Bible, he said, "He never told us about you."

"He didn't think we'd ever see each other again, Mr. Brock. Then… then this happened. Thank you for the Bible."

She took it, went back to Darrin's bedside, and sat on its edge. She looked at the strange book. She could see the word *Matthew* at the top of the page. She was fully aware that she had crossed the uncrossable gulf between the *Tanach*, the Jewish Bible, and the strictly forbidden New Testament. But this was obviously a lifeline for Darrin, and she obviously was, too. So she didn't have to believe what was in it. She only had to comfort him with it, at a time he desperately needed comfort— like her father wearing the Santa hat on Christmas day for the children at Maimonides Medical Center. She looked for the first verse of the chapter, Chapter Five. When she found it, she held Darrin's hand and began to read as slowly and lovingly as possible. He didn't take his eyes off her the whole time.

"Matthew 5. Look at that, Darrin. Just like *Matisyahu*, the Orthodox reggae singer. What do you know about that? Have you ever heard of him?"

He subtly nodded.

"Well, okay. This is another Matisyahu. But I don't think he sings. Verse One. 'Now when Yeshua'…that's Hebrew for *salvation*, like we say every Shabbas…'saw the crowds, He went up on the mountain. And after he sat down, His disciples came to Him. And He opened His mouth and began to teach them, saying,

Blessed are the poor in spirit. for theirs is the kingdom of heaven.
Blessed are those who mourn, for they will be comforted.
Blessed are the meek, for they shall inherit the earth
Blessed are those who hunger and thirst for righteousness, for they will be satisfied.
Blessed are the merciful, for they will be shown mercy.
Blessed are the pure in heart, for they shall see God.'
Blessed are the peacemakers, for they shall be called the sons of God.'"

She looked up from the book, surprised.

"Oh my, Darrin. This is beautiful. This is *very* beautiful."

The thought instantly occurred to her that this didn't seem *at all* like back door language for Gentiles, designed to connect them with the God of Israel. It seemed more like *front door* language for Gentiles—the same door that she, a daughter of Israel, was told about all her life. Darrin interrupted her mid-thought.

"It is, Naomi," he spoke just above a whisper. "It's very beautiful… like you are."

Naomi responded like there was no one else in the room but the two of them.

"I love you, Darrin Brock. I love you with all my heart. I can't help it. I love you like…like you love *Him*."

She held the Bible up and then put it down. Inspector Lewis just stood there by the door and shook his head again.

"I'll be damned. I'll be damned."

CHAPTER FORTY-SIX

Naomi was home before the sun went down and Shabbat began. David got the candlesticks off the cupboard and put them on the dining room table. He wanted to ask her how things went at Mount Sinai Hospital, but he knew she'd bring it up when she was ready. From the look on her face, he was pretty sure her friend hadn't died—unless he had, and she was relieved that her conflicts were at an end. She came down from her room, went over to him, and kissed him on the cheek.

"I'm hungry, Abba. I'm sorry I wasn't home in time to prepare something for dinner, especially on Friday night."

"Can't you smell the chicken in the slow cooker?"

"I guess my nose is stuffed up from crying so much."

"Well, at least you have your appetite tonight."

He waited for her to give a report, but all she did was go into the kitchen to put the chicken on a plate and prepare two small salads. She brought them out, and then kept going back in the kitchen for plates and silverware, wine glasses, wine, challah bread, and margarine.

When the blessings over the candles, wine, and bread were finished, they both sat down to eat. She knew she had to say something then. But she couldn't look directly at him.

"He's doing better, Abba. I believe he will live, *Baruch HaShem*. You were right. It's good that his life is preserved."

"Did he speak?"

"He did."

"Did he speak to you?"

"He did. Could we speak about this tomorrow night, after the Shabbas is over?"

"If you wish. But…we wouldn't be breaking the Shabbas if we spoke about it. In fact, the sages might have something to teach us about your experience today."

"I'm sure they might, Abba. But I'm also sure there's a rabbinic source somewhere that says resting one's voice on Shabbas is a mitzvah…"

She looked her father in the eyes for the first time since she got home.

"…and I don't want to talk about it tonight."

"Then we won't. We'll talk about something else. For instance, your sister Lisa has the flu."

Naomi's face contorted at the mention of Lisa. She was the last one she wanted to talk about at the end of this day.

"Well…I'm so sorry to hear that. It's probably too much bacon in the morning and ham at night."

"Naomi, you don't have to eat traif to get the flu."

"But I'm sure it doesn't hurt."

"I detect that old anger that I've told you about many times, Naomi. Remember the *Hinei ma tov* verse from *Teheelim*…Psalms, chapter 133. 'How good and pleasant it is for brothers to dwell together in unity.' And that includes sisters too."

"I know that, Abba."

"Knowing it is one thing."

"Then why do you approve of the way she eats…and does everything else?"

"I don't approve of it. But she's my daughter and she'll always be my daughter."

Naomi looked down again. He put his hand on her arm.

"What is it?"

"Would…would I still be your daughter if I married Darrin?"

He was ready for this question, and he answered without hesitating.

"Yes. I don't approve of this *you're buried in my sight* nonsense. You'll always be my daughter, and I'll always love you. But I wouldn't approve of the marriage. I couldn't bless it. And this thing would hurt me deeply, no matter how nice a fellow he is."

"Well, what do you know. Here we are discussing it, when I said I didn't want to…and it's my fault. No more until tomorrow night… please."

David wanted to ask more questions, but he bit his tongue. The meal continued without a further word. When it was over, after they had finished reciting the special Shabbat blessings after the meal, David left to go to the bathroom. Naomi sat and stared at the two Shabbat candles. Was she burning down their whole way of life, like those candles were burning down? She was sure that God was angry at her—except that Darrin said that He was the one who made her go to visit him. And if that were true, God didn't seem angry with her about that. Were Darrin and Aunt Ida of the evil one? Her head hurt from all the conflicting thoughts that were invading her consciousness. It was time to stop and go to bed early. She called to her father while he was still in the bathroom, and told him she was going to bed. When she went upstairs, he left the bathroom, with tears in his eyes.

The next day was a typical Shabbat. David and Naomi walked to synagogue together. Summer was almost at an end, but its weather pattern was still in full force. It was hot and humid out. Still, at least it was overcast. David felt his wet shirt under his black wool suit. Perspiration dripped from under his black hat. Naomi tried to catch whatever slight wind there was by holding her arms out to ventilate her beige summer dress.

The service proceeded as normal. They were both thankful for the central air conditioning, which had been left on sixty-nine degrees Fahrenheit before Shabbat. David was again looking back at Naomi in the balcony, and smiling. And she smiled back.

The walk home was pleasant enough, although hotter. And the meal and discussion time didn't include anything controversial. David honored his daughter's wishes. Finally, evening came, and with it the traditional short in-home end of Shabbat *Havdalah* service. Then Naomi went up to her room and brought down a blanket and an overnight bag, while David watched her from the dining room table. She disappeared into the kitchen for at least five minutes. She finally came out with a supermarket bag which obviously contained some kind of food. Then she sat across from her father and spoke to him clearly and directly.

"Abba, I don't claim to understand all things. I know I'm an observant middle-aged Jewish woman from Brooklyn, and I'll always be observant. I also know that Darrin wasn't talking before I came to his room yesterday. He had been in a coma and came out of that. But he wasn't very responsive. When he heard my voice, everything changed. He called my name out, and a lot of other things. I just called the hospital, and he's in a regular room now, upgraded to stable condition. I'm going to see him tomorrow morning, Abba, and I'm not leaving his side until I go to work on Monday."

David took a deep breath and shook his head.

"Naomi, you can't sleep in the same room with an unmarried man. I don't care *who* he is. I've taught you *that* much."

"We won't be in the same bed, Abba. I'll be on a lounge chair, fully clothed. And there'll be nurses constantly coming in and out. He could still take a turn for the worse."

"Naomi…"

"I've made up my mind, Abba. If he could convert and still believe what he believes, he would. He would choose a kosher home. I know that for a fact."

David shook his head again.

"That's like the Messianics, Naomi. That's not acceptable with any Jewish authority, even Reform. You know that."

"I know, Abba. I know. He won't give up his belief, and he can't convert. But I also know I need to be with him right now."

She came close to her father.

"Listen to me, Abba. I did some thinking of my own late last night… actually very early on Shabbas morning. You've taught me all that the Bible and the rabbis teach on right and wrong better than any father ever taught his daughter. And now after all these years, in my late-forties, the time has come for the next chapter of my life. I'm ready to apply what you've taught me in new situations. It's right for me to be by Darrin's side tomorrow, *and* tomorrow night. God will take care of the future. Anything could happen, and that's okay with me. I must do this now."

David held both of her hands in his.

"Naomi, he's a Gentile and a Christian…albeit obviously a Zionist Christian. And God knows the country of Israel needs those people in these terrible days. But, can you honestly tell me that you love this man? I mean, are you really in love with him?"

Naomi answered without hesitating.

"Yes, Abba. I'm in love with a true mensch…one Chaya Mendel

trusts to be a father figure to her four-year-old son Natan. Inspector Lewis sent him there to help the family, and Natan took to him. What child wouldn't? Like you on Christmas, Abba."

That resolved an unanswered question David had had since he overheard Natan mentioning Darrin's name. Naomi wasn't finished.

"I wouldn't trust Marvin with a puppy, let alone a child like Natan. Yes, I love Darrin Brock. He has my heart, and I don't want it back. I chose...*chose* to read those beautiful *Blessed are the poor in spirit* verses to him the other day. His father had been reading them to him. And I took the Bible and read them. He needed to hear those magnificent verses. And he needs me."

David pressed his finger to the table several times as he spoke.

"Of course the Sermon on the Mount contains many very beautiful verses...some like the sages. But are they *our* verses?"

She tried not to be astounded that he knew not only the verses, but what they were called.

"Okay, maybe not. But right now I can say that they're his, and he's mine. I can't think beyond that now. Maybe I sound like a foolish unthinking teenager who's in love for the first time, but Abba..."

She began to weep gently, and then put her head on his chest.

"For the first time in my life, I'm truly in love. And he feels the same way. He's saved himself. He never kissed a woman before in his life, before..."

She stood up.

"...before he kissed me, Abba...in the Channel Gardens at Rockefeller Center. Yes, he kissed me, right there on a bench. He's as handsome as a movie star, Abba, and in his forties. And that was the first time he ever kissed a woman. I feel like a princess when I'm with him, Abba, like Queen Esther...exactly like her. I've never been so happy in my whole life. Please let me be happy. *Please*."

He sat there and looked at her for what seemed like an eternity.

"I understand that he's an extraordinary man. I believe you. But promise me one thing."

"Yes, Abba?"

"Promise me you will always talk to me like this. As you said on the beach, no more secrets."

"I promise you...no secrets. I need to get some sleep tonight. I may not get much tomorrow night. Good night. I love you."

"I love you too. Good night."

CHAPTER FORTY-SEVEN

Naomi rarely, if ever, took the subway on Sundays. She had never traveled on Shabbat, so the only days she had taken public transportation were weekdays. On this Sunday in late August, there was a quiet spareness in the train that contrasted with the weekday travel Naomi was used to, and she liked it.

Her overnight bag and bedding triggered an even stranger feeling that she couldn't quite put her finger on. What was it? Finally, she realized that her luggage reminded her of the mail order brides she had read about in novels—brides who left the comfort of their places of origin to enter an unfamiliar new world beyond their culture and history.

By the time Naomi got to the Mount Sinai Hospital information desk, those feelings had dissipated. And when she entered Darrin's private room, all she could think about was being with him. In contrast to the last time she saw him, there was no one else in the room. His bed was cranked up to a sitting position, and he looked more like himself, although she could see that he still had intravenous tubes. And he was still catheterized. The bag hung on the side of the bed. He was surprised to see her.

"Naomi! What are you doing here?"

She threw her bags and bedding on one chair and pulled another up to his bed.

"You look so much better, honey."

She had never used that word before, and it felt good. Darrin, however, looked somewhat confused.

"Have I seen you recently? It feels like I saw you. But that couldn't be right...could it?"

Naomi hadn't counted on Darrin forgetting her last visit. That threw her off. She felt awkward, vulnerable.

"Yes, it's right. Darrin. I saw you a few days ago in Intensive Care. You spoke for the first time when you saw me. Don't you remember? You must remember. I read the Bible to you. I...I...told you I...I..."

There was a long pause. Finally, a glimmer of recognition crossed Darrin's eyes.

"You told me you loved me. Now I remember."

Relieved, Naomi sighed.

"Yes."

Then he continued.

"Yes, I remember. And I vaguely remember you reading the New Testament to me. How did that happen? I hope you didn't feel under pressure to do that. Did I ask you to do that? I don't remember...."

"It's okay, Darrin. It was an honor for me to read Matthew 5 to you."

"But...Jesus...Yeshua...means so much to me...everything...it's not a small thing, Naomi. It would be an issue...for both of us. That's why I told you we shouldn't see each other anymore."

"I understand. But there's one problem. You prayed that I would come to you. Do you remember that? And I came."

His eyes widened.

"Yes, yes! I remember...when I was asleep. I remember that now. Strange."

He shook his head *no*.

"But...it wouldn't work."

Naomi felt the clear confidence she had with her father rise up in her. To Darrin's surprise, she reached out and gave him a tender kiss on the mouth. Then she sat down again and leaned forward.

"Now you listen to me, Darrin Brock! I'm not giving you up just because we haven't figured everything out yet. I found you, the love of my life, and I'm not letting you go...not for my beloved father, not for *anyone.* I told him that, and I'm telling *you* the same thing. I couldn't wait for the Shabbas to be over to get back here. And I was thinking the whole time. I know I should marry an observant Jew, and you should marry a committed Christian. It's the right thing. My father is right. Your father is right. But we're mature adults in our late forties, and both of us love truth. So I have an idea."

"Yes, but…"

"Just let me finish. Here's what I've decided. I'll read the Gospels with you, and you'll read the Gemara commentary with me. You'll read Maimonides with me, and I'll read…Matisyahu…Matthew…with you. I'll read the Sayings of the Fathers, the Pirkei Avot, with you, and you'll read…what book starts with a "P?"

"Peter?"

"There's a book called Peter?"

"There's two of them."

"Well, there's only one Perkei Avot."

He grinned and then reached over and kissed her twice on her nose. "Then we'll read it twice."

"Right. You've got it. And we'll ask God for His wisdom. And He'll give it to us. I have the courage to see where that takes us if you do. But I'm not leaving your side. You woke up when you heard my name the last time I came, and I'm waking up right here in this room tomorrow morning before I go to work."

She emphasized the point by throwing her blanket over the lounge chair in the corner. Tears came to his eyes. She took a tissue and began tenderly wiping them just as Chaya and Natan came in the room. Natan couldn't contain his excitement. He came over and jumped on the side of the bed before his mother could stop him.

"Darrin…Darrin…Mommy and I have been praying the Mi-shebeirach prayer for you."

Chaya rushed forward, as Naomi got up. Darrin reached out with his intravenous hand and stroked Natan's hair.

"It's okay, Chaya. It's okay."

Natan tried to give Darrin a big hug, reaching his little arms around his leg.

"I've missed you *so* much, Darrin. Mommy and I were so worried about you. But the nurse said you'll get all better. And you *have* to. You have to, so we can play and read books."

"I am getting better every day, Natan. And this lady is helping me.

This is my...my girlfriend Naomi. She's going to pray a *Mish*...Mi-shebeirach prayer right now with you and your mommy. And I'll get all better. I promise."

Naomi smiled and reached her hand out to Chaya's, and Chaya took Natan's hand. They all stood around the bed and prayed the prayer together. Darrin repeated the prayer as it was spoken.

"Mi-shebeirach...May the One who blessed our ancestors—Patriarchs Abraham, Isaac, and Jacob, bless and heal the one who is ill...."

After the prayer Naomi looked in Darrin's eyes, and detected exhaustion in them.

"I think you need to get some rest, my beloved."

Darrin nodded his head.

"I think you're probably right, Naomi."

Chaya reached out and took Natan's hand. She told him they needed to leave, but they would come back soon—and before he knew it Darrin would come back to the house and they would play with puzzles and read books together. She said a warm goodbye to Darrin. Natan gave him one last hug. Then Chaya and Natan walked out of the room. Naomi followed them out.

"I want to thank you for bringing Natan to see Darrin. You don't know what it means to him to see little Natan."

"You're welcome...Naomi, is it?"

"Yes, Naomi. I live in Brooklyn."

"You're Orthodox, aren't you?"

"Yes, I'm very observant. I brought my own food today. It's better than their regular fare, I'm sure," she joked.

"I see," Chaya responded. "So...I suppose he's going to undergo an Orthodox conversion."

Naomi realized that this wouldn't be the last time she would hear that. And she hadn't yet figured out how she would respond."

"Well...I..."

Chaya interrupted her.

"Well listen. If you got him to do that, you got an incredible catch. Not only is he gorgeous, but he's an absolutely amazing man with a heart of gold. But I'm sure you know that. Well, *mazal tov* is all I can say."

"Um...thank you."

Chaya and Natan left, and Naomi went back into the room and spent a few more minutes with Darrin before they both went to sleep. She had brought a small volume from her father's library. Between that and

Matthew, they read a few verses. Then she gave him a gentle kiss before retreating to her easy chair.

FALL

CHAPTER FORTY-EIGHT

Prima swiveled back and forth in his executive chair. Even though he couldn't see any foliage from his massive office window, he could tell the season from the tiny figures walking on the street below. The light jackets and sweaters told the story. It was early October, and carried with it the promise of darker days and colder nights to come. And that's just how Prima felt—dark with sadness and cold with despair.

How could he stop the machinery of the Russian Mafia and extract Marc Silver from its clutches? Without a code, the possibility of mutual favors, and at least the sliver of an open crack in the door of decency, Marc Silver was a dead man. And Prima knew it. If they had tried to knock off a police detective—and he knew they would try again—there was no hope for Marc.

Perhaps Igor was right about his father. Maybe he wasn't the fair-minded person Prima pictured in his mind when he thought of him. The truth was, he had to think hard to remember what he was like, because he was usually gone when Prima was growing up. But when he *was* there, he brought candy, toys, and other special treats. The father who brought those things didn't seem like he was capable of bumping anyone off, or rubbing them out. If he was, Prima's mother hid that part of his father's life from Prima very well. Whatever the truth was, one thing was certain. Prima's underworld was a kinder gentler underworld than the prior generation's underworld was, the generation Giuliani went after. And that's the way he wanted it to stay—kinder and gentler, and still financially lucrative. If Prima had anything to do with it, Marc Silver would not die under his watch.

The only solution was to do the unthinkable. It might bring the whole enterprise crashing down to the ground, where those people in light fall sweaters and jackets were walking so many floors below him. And he'd also be out on the street, at best. Or it might free him from the Russian Mafia for good. But either way, he knew he had to do it. He would never be able to live with himself if someone he secretly thought of as his second son was killed or severely injured. That would be unacceptable. Maybe he should have never taken over the enterprise from his father years ago. But the fact was, it wasn't an organization worth leading now—not with the Russian Mafia calling the shots.

He called his two body guards into the room. They took their time, but they finally showed up.

"I'm going out. I've got some very important business to attend to. If I don't come back in two hours, contact one of the lawyers…probably Garfield. Tell him I've been arrested, and to make arrangements to bail me out."

The body guards looked at one another, and then back at him.

"Boss, what's happening?", one of them asked.

"Well, to be honest with you, we'll either be on top of the world by tomorrow, in full control of this outfit and doing better than ever, or completely finished…kaput."

"That sounds like not such great odds, boss," the other one said.

"Well, let's just say I'm a gambling man who loves a good bet. Sometimes you have to bet everything in your hand."

He went over to the closet and put an expensive black fall jacket on, like those worn on the street below, but nicer.

"Remember, call Garfield if I'm not back in two hours."

He left the office. One body guard turned to the other.

"Hurry up and call the Russian. Tell him they need to tail him."

"I think he's going to the cops to cut some sort of deal. That's what I think."

"Of course he's going to the cops, stupid. Just get them on the phone."

CHAPTER FORTY-NINE

David Kaplan arose much earlier than usual that fall Thursday morning, two hours before the sun rose. He held his breath and went into the hallway. Naomi's bedroom door was closed. He couldn't remember whether she shut it when she came home from the hospital after work the evening before, to prepare some food and pick out a change of clothes. Every morning starting Monday, he had checked the room. The bed had been empty each time. He was afraid to open the door a crack, lest he be deeply disappointed again. Monday through Wednesday were a total loss. He could hardly bring himself to say the morning prayers, let alone do anything else. And to top it all off, today was a day he had been looking forward to for weeks—his Midwood Press teaching day. The children were back in school now, and there would be a full house of precious little faces to fascinate. But if Naomi's bed was empty again, he didn't see how he could even leave the house, let alone travel to Midwood Press.

Very cautiously, he opened the door just a crack. He could just see the covers in the dark. They were performing their intended function, covering his daughter. His heart jumped and he smiled broadly. Then he closed the door.

"Thank God! Thank God! At least she's home."

He went back to bed. Perhaps he could get a few more hours of sleep, better sleep than he'd had in three days.

When he woke up, he could tell that Naomi was in the bathroom. He went into his own bathroom, which was attached to the master bedroom. After he quickly brushed his teeth, he hurried out into the hall to meet her. She was already downstairs preparing breakfast. He went down into the kitchen. She was at the sink with her back to him. He sat at the small kitchen table.

"It's good to see you home this morning."

She turned the sink off and came to sit next to him.

"Abba. I have wonderful news."

He was hoping she would say the relationship was over, but inside he knew that wasn't the wonderful news.

"I could use some good news about now."

"Well, you know you told me about the importance of preserving life…you know, Pikuach Nefesh? Well, Darrin is out of the woods. You should see him, Abba. He's walking…with a cane I admit, like Jacob in the Torah…limping, but walking! And he's getting stronger every day."

"I see. So will you be coming home tonight?"

"That's the good news, Abba. He'll be going home soon…probably late today or tomorrow. I won't be visiting him tonight."

"That *is* good, Naomi. Then you and I can both get a good night's sleep. That's important, especially because I'll be going to Midwood Press today, and that makes a big day for me."

"I'm so sorry you haven't slept well, Abba. I've probably slept better than you. Yes, I'll be home tonight."

She went over to finish at the sink. Her back was to him.

"Abba…did you know that Isaiah is quoted in the book of Matisyahu? I didn't know that kind of thing was in there."

His heart skipped a beat. His greatest fears were coming to pass— the greatest fear of *any* Jewish father, and especially an Orthodox Jewish father. He knew he had to be careful how he answered.

"The book is called Matthew, Naomi, not Matisyahu."

"But that's his name in Hebrew."

"That's beside the point. The book is written in Greek. Will you come here and sit down next to me so we can talk?"

"Let me just get my cereal. If I don't eat now, I'll be late."

"Of course."

She prepared a quick bowl of cereal and sat down next to him. They usually ate in the dining room, so it seemed strange to eat in the kitchen. The light was so strong, so yellow, like an interrogation room Inspector Lewis might use with criminals—or perhaps Darrin. She began to eat between speaking, trying not to be nervous.

"So did you know Isaiah is in Matthew, Abba?"

"Yes, of course I knew that. There are a lot of quotes from the Jewish Tanach in the New Testament, Naomi, usually from an earlier Greek translation."

"I see. Well, there are some quotes there that say surprising things, things I've never heard before. I checked my Bible, and they're in there just like they are in Matthew."

David knew the verses she was talking about, and responded more firmly than he wanted to.

"They're taken out of context, Naomi. The Christians took them out of context."

If his answer didn't quite satisfy her, she didn't show it.

"Oh. I see."

She averted her eyes from him and then faced her cereal. He continued.

"He's trying to convert you."

Naomi raised her head, put her spoon in her bowl, and answered emphatically, pounding the table just as she'd seen him do.

"No, Abba. That's not true! It wasn't his idea to read Matthew. It was my idea. The whole thing was *my* idea. We're reading Perkei Avot too."

"Yes, I saw it was missing from my shelf."

"I'm sorry. I should have told you. But Abba, he didn't even say *anything* when we read those Isaiah verses in Matthew. *I* noticed them, and I asked him where those verses were from. He hesitated, but then he told me. He's so sensitive, Abba…like you. You don't know him."

"No, Naomi. I don't."

As Naomi took a few large spoonfuls so she could finish on time, David's voice took on a more serious tone.

"You know, Naomi, if you go on like this, you'll want to marry this man. And no Jew will marry you, except the Messianics. You know that…no rabbi, even Reform. Just the Messianics…and they're not even rabbis…maybe not even Jews, according to some authorities."

"Abba, I've never met one of these Messianics. I don't even know who they are. I mean, I've seen Jews for Jesus people in Manhattan, with those T-shirts. But I don't think they marry people. They just hand out things and get screamed at. I…I suppose Messianics must be observant Jews who believe like Darrin…but Abba, I can't think about that right now."

"But you *must* think about it!"

"But I *can't*, Abba. Not now. If that time comes, God will provide a way."

"The God of Israel?"

"Yes Abba. Our God…and Isaiah's God…and isn't He Darrin's God too? I don't know about Rosenzweig's back door, but front door or back…isn't He Darrin's God too, Abba? Isn't He his God too?"

A smile brightened David's face for the first time since they began their conversation.

"I can see you're asking very difficult yet important questions, Naomi. I can't say I didn't raise you to ask such questions."

"Then may I ask one more difficult question?"

"I don't think I could stop you if I wanted to."

"If…If I married Darrin…I mean, just if…would you come, no matter where it was and who married us?"

He looked straight into her eyes, and detected a daughter's pleading heart in them. It had come to this. He had always feared he might someday hear this question. But if he ever did hear it, he thought it would be from Lisa and not from Naomi. Still, he had to admit it was a valid question. And he *had* told his daughter to be open with him about everything. He paused, and then gave her the only answer he could give.

"Yes, I would be there if you marry this man…excuse me, but God forbid. It would be hard for me, very hard. But I would be there. You are my oldest daughter, and I love you. I would not abandon my oldest daughter, no matter what other people would think or say."

They both stood up at the same time. They gave each other the longest strongest hug in their entire history as father and daughter, as tears came to both of their eyes. Naomi kissed him on the cheek.

"You are still the wisest Jew in the whole world."

She looked past her father and glanced at the kitchen clock, realizing how late it was.

"Oh, I've got to go, Abba. I'm late."

She wiped her tears, grabbed her pocketbook, and ran out of the house. David Kaplan took a bowl of cereal himself, and quickly scooped it down. Then he went to get dressed for his day at Midwood Press.

An hour and a half later, David visited the only Linotype machine in Brooklyn, and probably in all of New York. It sat in its stately corner, in all of its victorian splendor. He had missed seeing it, and running his fingers over its unusual keyboard, being careful not to depress a key lest the process that ended with a freshly molded lead slug was initiated.

After the children came into the room, and Ben introduced him as one of the greatest Linotype operators that ever worked at the *New York Times*, he began his colorful and illustrative class. As usual, the children sat open mouthed as they watched the machine swing into action, creating lines of text with clinks, clicks, and whirs. But this time, as he faced the channels and watched the matrices pouring down, he saw them not as individual snowflakes, or as rain, but as individual people created in God's image—each special like the children sitting on the floor at Midwood Press. And he knew full well that Darrin Brock represented one of those individual people. Of course, he had always held this view about human beings. That's why he made a habit of visiting suffering little ones on Christmas day. But now he realized that if he could visit them, he could visit Darrin Brock, whether he was still at the hospital or at home.

Along with that thought came a sudden awareness that if Naomi's words about Darrin were true—and in his heart he knew that they were—then this man would never hurt his oldest daughter, but would always care for her deeply and protect her from anything that would harm her. The fact was, this man loved Naomi in a way that Marvin never would or could. So David decided that, although he still couldn't approve of a marriage between Darrin and Naomi, he would at least care about him, and love him as the good man he was. When he turned to answer the children's questions, that was settled. He would visit Darrin Brock later that day, even before Naomi got home from work.

CHAPTER FIFTY

Late Thursday afternoon, New Yorkers in light fall jackets and sweaters walked by the two bodyguards as they stood at street level, twenty stories below Prima's office. They leaned against the glass wall next to the entrance. One looked at his watch.

"That Igor and his friends are never on time when they go to kill people. It's a wonder anyone ever dies around them."

"Don't let them hear you talk like that, or they'll kill you while they're at it, like two birds with one stone."

"They'd kill you before they'd kill me. I'm the one who tracks Prima for them. Without me, they'd be blind…like he is."

"Shut up. Here they come."

Igor walked up to them, accompanied by another Russian. He was dressed in a light black sweater, tight black pants, and sun glasses. The other Russian was dressed in a black jogging outfit. Igor betrayed irritated impatience.

"Get inside, stupid hooligans. Silver comes with Prima. If they see you standing here and suspect something, I have bullet with your names instead of theirs."

The bodyguards tried to beat one another through the revolving door. The Russians followed them into the lobby and then into the elevator. Igor turned to his friend and castigated the bodyguards.

"Stupid morons. Anyway, we do this fast, then to Teaneck to finish off Brock when he's home. All we ever do is unfinished business. They should have finished Silver on the boat, but Sasha's an idiot. We don't do this ourselves, doesn't get done."

They exited the elevator and entered Prima's office. Igor directed the bodyguards.

"Disappear in other room."

Igor sat at the glass table and swiveled in his chair.

"I hate this table. I shoot it after we shoot them."

He spoke in English deliberately, as he did during all of his hit jobs. He was a New York gangster, and he made a point to never speak Russian on these occasions.

"They're in elevator. Draw your gun."

Then unexpectedly, his phone text alert went off. He quickly rose and looked at it.

"Cops in lobby. We work fast, get out. Let them get bodyguards. Don't make mistake."

"I don't make mistake like Sasha."

"We see."

The door lock turned. Prima entered the room with Marc Silver just behind him. They immediately saw the Russians with their guns drawn.

"You stupid Prima. You go to same precinct Brock works at. And you come back with no gun. Stupid *wop*...dead man."

Prima quickly shielded Marc.

"You give the New York Mafia a really bad name. But you don't get my son. Run Marc, run!"

Marc backed out of the room and ran down the hall. Halfway to the elevator, he heard two shots. Then five policemen poured out of the stairwell and ran past Marc. They gathered by the door to Prima's office. Marc screamed out, "They're in there and I think they shot Prima!"

One policeman pushed in the door with a swift kick and stood to the side. There was silence for a few seconds. Then all five cops stormed the room, eyed Prima lying lifeless on the floor, and then started shooting up the whole place and the door to the next room. One bullet came at them through the door. They unloaded round after round at the door and then kicked it in. Igor was wounded and bleeding, but still held onto his gun. His friend put up his hands, as the bodyguards were trying to beat each other through the door to the next room. Igor lifted his gun to shoot, and an officer shot him directly between the eyes, splitting his sun glasses in two. He was propelled backwards onto the floor. Blood splattered all over the perfectly shampooed off-white carpet. Three other policemen handcuffed the second Russian and the bodyguards. Another officer had already gone into the hall and cuffed Marc Silver. One of the officers in Prima's office stood over Igor's body.

"What a bloody mess. I guess Inspector Lewis will be glad we got Igor. But poor Prima. That's another story. At least he died doing the right thing. May his mobster soul rest in peace."

WINTER

CHAPTER FIFTY-ONE

The weather outside the Kaplan home was definitely wintery, although the calendar said winter was still a week away. A few days before, New York had been hit by an early nor'easter, and was still digging itself out. Traffic was just becoming unsnarled by the eighth night of Chanukah, and Naomi decided to ask family and a few friends over for a little last night of Chanukah party. She managed to get off work a few hours early, notwithstanding the fact that this was the busiest time of the year. She needed the time to clean the house and cook the potato latkes. By late afternoon, David was taking a short nap in his bedroom.

Naomi pulled the old Kiev Chanukah menorah off the mantle, and placed it in front of her on the dining room table.

Just then, the front door opened and Lisa came in, bundled in a warm light green coat, wrapped in a tan cashmere scarf, and topped off with a dark red wool pullover hat. Even covered in warm practical clothes, she was the personification of class. And when she shed them, she was wearing a violet wool designer dress worthy of any cocktail party. She removed her designer boots and walked into the hallway. Naomi was beginning to remove the old wax from the seventh night with a knife, when her sister entered the living room.

"I guess it wouldn't be Chanukah unless you made your traditional mess on the dining room table."

Naomi continued to work without looking up.

"No, it wouldn't be. It's traditional."

"Look who's talking traditional?"

Naomi had determined to be pleasant with Lisa, no matter what. And now the first test had already occurred. In contrast to past arguments, in which Naomi generally responded to Lisa's sarcastic remarks with a comeback quip, she just stopped working on the menorah and closed her eyes. Perhaps it was for this reason that Lisa's heart experienced an unusual softening. She sat down next to Naomi and gently touched her on the shoulder.

"I've hurt you."

Naomi nodded.

There was silence between them for several seconds. Then Lisa hesitantly spoke words that Naomi never thought she would hear.

"Please...please...forgive me, Naomi."

Naomi nodded her head again. Lisa could see tears through her closed eyes.

"It's...it's just that it takes a little while to get used to. You know what I mean? I know you told me you would still be an observant Jew. But still it's a bit of a shock."

Naomi kept her head down and her eyes shut. Then Lisa did something she hadn't done since they were small children. She reached out, put her arms around Naomi, and hugged her.

"Listen, big sister. I'm *so* happy for you. First of all, you look terrific. Second, I'm proud of you for finding Darrin. He's a truly wonderful man. I'll tell you, he's wonderful with my kids. And he's really cute too, which doesn't hurt."

Naomi began to hug her back. She couldn't believe this was happening. It was truly a Yom Kippur moment and a last night of Chanukah miracle. And the miracles didn't stop, because while they were hugging, Naomi said something she'd never said to Lisa.

"I love you, Lisa. I've always loved you. But I haven't always treated you with love. I've been jealous of your extreme beauty. And frankly, sometimes I've been plain old mean. But I love you. I really do. I'm *so* sorry I've never told you that until now."

They hugged some more. Then, when they had both dried their tears,

Lisa spoke quietly so her father wouldn't hear her.

"What am I going to do, Naomi? Now that Marc is on probation, he's not making what he was. They let him keep his job, which was Inspector Lewis' work, and I appreciate it. But of course, he doesn't get what he did working for Prima. It's not anything near that. I know I probably have to go to work, but I'm not like you. I've never done anything like that. And we have to arrange something for the kids if I *do* go to work. I'm feeling so overwhelmed. And on top of that, I have to encourage a very depressed man. He won't even…not since Prima, back in October. Oh, I'm sorry. I shouldn't talk about those things in front of you."

Naomi put her hand on Lisa's chin and lifted her head.

"Then you make love to *him*, Lisa, and don't stop until he gives in. Do you understand?"

"Naomi!"

"Relax, Lisa. I'm still a virgin. But I understand more than you think I do about those things. And you and I are getting together next week about these other things. I'll help you sort all of this out. Believe me, it will work out. Now let me get back to my table mess."

Lisa gave her another heartfelt hug.

"Thank you! Thank you! Thank you!"

About 6:00 p.m., David came downstairs.

"Good evening, Lisa. Happy Chanukah. I see the menorah's ready, Naomi, and I can smell the latkes. Well, it's six o'clock. The others should be here soon."

Just after he said that, the door opened. And it kept opening over the next fifteen minutes. Marc came first. As soon as he saw Naomi, he noticed that her hair had been styled in attractive curls, and her dress was a stylish light blue. It clung to her like no dress she'd ever worn.

"Naomi, you look…nice. Dressing up for Mr. Christian?"

Naomi responded without a beat.

"Yes, As a matter of fact. I want to look nice for Darrin, if you want to know the truth. I have nothing to hide, Marc."

"Well, maybe *he* does. Did you check to see if he's…"

Lisa grabbed Marc's arm.

"Come on Marc. Let's go into the kitchen. You can test Naomi's Latkes."

She dragged him through the dining room and into the kitchen. He pulled his arm away.

"Ouch! That hurts. What was that for?"

"Like I said, I'm taking you into the kitchen to try the Latkes. Taste this first."

She planted a passionate kiss on him, fully ten seconds long.

"What...what are you doing?," he said, trying to catch his breath.

"That's an appetizer for when we get home tonight. And I'm not taking no for an answer. Do you understand?"

"Okay...okay. If you say so."

"I say so. And you listen to me. I just had the best talk I've ever had with my big sister. No smart talk with her. Understand?"

"I understand. I understand."

"All right. Let's get out there."

A few minutes later, Darrin Brock came in, limping and walking with a cane, with Lindsay and Noah at his side. He eyed Naomi as he took his black winter coat off.

"Wow!"

He went over and gave her a quick kiss.

"You take my breath away. You're so beautiful, I can't take my eyes off of you."

No one in the room could miss the glow on Naomi's face—and the sparkle in her eyes—in response to Darrin's comment. Then Noah spotted his mother and ran to her.

"Darrin bought us Chanukah toys, Mommy. They're in his car. You should see how big the boxes are! But we can't open them until we light the candles. Can we light them right now?"

"Soon, Noah. Not everyone's here."

At that moment the door opened again, and Aunt Ida came in, followed closely by Marvin. She didn't even wait to take her faux fur coat off before she saw Naomi.

"The new Naomi. What do you know?"

"Same Naomi, different clothes and hair, Aunt Ida."

"You could've fooled me. Anyway, Happy Chanukah, everyone."

Marvin tried not to look at Naomi...or Darrin. He walked up to David.

"Happy Chanukah, Mr. Kaplan. Thanks for inviting me."

"It was Naomi, Marvin."

"Well, I'm glad we're celebrating Chanukah, and for once we don't have to hear about the Goyim and their stupid Christmas."

"Shut up and behave yourself, Marvin," Aunt Ida shouted from across the room.

The door opened again. Mahmoud and Stanley entered the house. They were the last guests. Inspector Lewis had been invited, but he was on the job at the Midtown South Precinct. Mahmoud made it his business to go over and shake everyone's hand personally, just to put them all at their ease. He learned this as a taxi driver after 9/11. Aunt Ida got a kick out of it. Marvin, however, looked like he had eaten five lemons at once.

When everyone had arrived, Naomi turned out the lights. Then they lit all eight Chanukah candles with the ninth servant candle.

As the Jewish members among them sang the Chanukah blessings, David watched the nine flames on the menorah. Each cast a golden glow on the two well-worn lions that adorned it. They seemed to awaken in the nine dancing flickers of light, as if from a hundred-and-thirty-three year sleep. David could almost hear them roar to one another, heralding that the people of Israel—against all odds—were alive and well in the Kaplan home in Brooklyn, New York. He couldn't help thinking that—each in their own way—this little menorah and the massive Linotype machine that was born in the same decade both preserved ancient tradition. And by God's grace that tradition would live on, whether in few or many.

Then they all distributed gifts. Everyone got at least one. David and Naomi took care of that. Darrin's gifts for Noah and Lindsay were brought in from his car. The boxes were indeed large, and so were the toys. Naomi gave Darrin David Stern's *Messianic Jewish Commentary of the New Testament*. She'd found it on amazon.com. Everything quieted down when that gift was unwrapped. But she didn't care. She had decided she would hide nothing from anyone. Darrin gave her Telushkin's book *Jewish Literacy*. The tension broke as the guests laughed about that. It struck everyone funny that they'd exchanged those particular gifts.

After the latkes were served, David told an abbreviated account of the Chanukah story. Mahmoud was very polite as he listened to the history of the Second Temple's defilement and rededication. Stanley looked over to him, as if to say, *See, I told you there was a Jewish temple on the site of your mosque.*

Then the small talk began. The topper of the evening was Stanley's story about the time one of the New York delis went for the Guinness world record for the largest latke in the world.

"They could never get it off the griddle in one piece. They lost the contest, but the customers got free latkes for a month, until the oil went rancid."

272

As everyone laughed, David scanned the darkened room full of Chanukah party guests. He suddenly realized that family and friends who might never come together at any other time of the year were there with him that night, and enjoying themselves—except for Marvin. And he thought to himself, *This is a true mitzvah, a true Chanukah mitzvah.*

CHAPTER FIFTY-TWO

The weather in Brooklyn on the twenty-fifth of December was sub-freezing and dry, with a windchill of between five and ten degrees at noon. Naomi had convinced her father to wear one of her thick red scarves, which, along with his usual black coat and his hat over his black cloth yarmulka, gave him the appearance of a rare and exotic Arctic bird. He carried his usual sack of toys for the children at the Maimonides Medical Center.

Maimonides began as the New Utrecht Dispensary in 1911, about thirty years after the menorah first sat on the Kaplan ancestors' Kiev table.

In 1919, several dispensaries, including Utrecht, formed the Israel Hospital of Brooklyn. Another merger resulted in United Israel Zion Hospital in 1920. It wasn't until 1947 that United Israel Hospital merged with Beth Moses Hospital to form the Maimonides Medical Center.

David knew the way to the pediatric cancer wing by heart. He prayed a quick prayer for God to give him the strength to comfort the children and then got off the elevator. He saw redheaded Anna in the distance. As he approached her, a huge smile appeared on her face.

"Mr. Kaplan! Mr. Kaplan! I've been waiting for you! I have some good news for you."

"Anna. Faithful Anna. What would I do without you to greet me before I go in to see the children on Christmas day? So what's this news?"

"It's about Sammy. Do you remember Sammy? The little African-American boy in room 451?"

"Certainly I remember Sammy. I've thought of him often over the last year."

"Well…he's doing wonderful! He's all better. See, Mr. Kaplan, your visits do make a difference."

"Well, don't give me so much credit, Anna. I think God had *something* to do with it. He had *everything* to do with it. Please greet him from the Santa who says *oy oy,* will you?"

"I will do that, Mr. Kaplan."

"Well, let me just change hats here for a minute."

He took off the black hat.

"Could you keep this for me? It wasn't this cold last year. And here are my other things."

"Sure."

She put the hat, coat, and red scarf under her desk.

"Okay, here comes the transformation."

He took his red Santa hat out of the sack and pulled it over his head.

"How do I look?"

"Perfect, Mr. Kaplan."

"Very good. Okay, who do we have today?"

"Well, let's start with six-year-old Sarah, in the same room Sammy was in, bed one…inoperable cancer. She has a mother who'll be in later. She's working. There's no father in her life. She's adorable, Mr. Kaplan, and bright as a shiny penny…the sweetest thing you can imagine. She had hair as red as mine…*had.* Here's the information."

"Very good. Thank you Anna."

He traveled down the hall toward room 451. When he got to the door, he took a deep breath and looked back at Anna, sitting at her station. Just then, a recognizable figure exited the elevator and began to walk toward him, limping and using a cane. As he came closer, David could see that it was Darrin Brock.

"Darrin, what in the world are you doing here at Maimonides on Christmas day?"

"I'm here to visit the children."

"Shouldn't you be home with Lester and Velma, Darrin, celebrating Christmas and maybe going to church to honor the birth of your Savior?"

"I think this is where He'd be if He were here in the flesh celebrating His birthday with us, Mr. Kaplan."

"But won't your parents miss you on this special day?"

"I guess they would if they weren't special parents. Could I possibly join you?"

David hesitated for a few seconds before he answered.

"Well, I don't see why not. Six-year-old Sarah is in there…bed one."

Then he came close to Darrin and whispered.

"Inoperable brain cancer. What's in your bag there?"

Darrin pulled a bright green pointy felt hat out of a small brown lunch bag he was holding in his left hand.

"Here, hold my cane."

David took the cane while Darrin pulled the hat over his head.

"Well?"

"Let me guess. Santa's elf's hat."

"You guessed it."

"Well, I've got the sack of toys."

"I made those toys in the North Pole, that is, the ones that weren't made in China."

"Which is probably all of them. Are you ready?"

"Well, 'Lord, please strengthen me'. Okay, I'm ready."

They walked into the room. There was Sarah, with the biggest brightest emerald green eyes one can possibly imagine, a little button nose, and no hair. She was lying in her bed, holding a small plush horse.

"Hi Santa, are you here to see me?," she said in a matter of fact tone.

"I am. Oy Oy Oy. I'm here for you, Sarah."

She sat up.

"You're a Jewish Santa. That's so funny. I love it."

Both David and Darrin recognized instantly how precocious this child was. She turned to Darrin.

"And you're Santa's elf?"

"Well, that's absolutely right."

"They're not supposed to be as tall as you are. And they don't have canes."

Darrin laughed.

"They're not all short, you know. And I happen to know a few other elves who have canes. They just usually leave them at home."

David reached into his bag and pulled out a large rectangular package. It was the nicest gift he had, and he quickly decided it was Sarah's. If Sarah sounded grown up a few seconds earlier, that all went by the wayside after she tore the wrapping off the gift. In a large attractive box was a doll worth at least fifty dollars. He had purchased it for just such a little girl. Nothing in the sack had cost anything near that amount. After he removed the doll from the box, the perfect blonde curls were released, and her blue plaid dress revealed little patent leather shoes under it. She was truly a beautiful doll. Sarah grabbed her and hugged her tight.

"This is…this is the best doll I've ever owned. And she's all mine! Thank you! Thank you Santa and Mr. Elf!"

David and Darrin spent much more time with Sarah than they expected. She told them about her other dolls, and the bike she couldn't ride anymore. She talked about her bedroom at home, and her favorite flavor of ice cream. And she asked about *their* bedrooms and *their* favorite ice cream. Then, she turned to Darrin.

"Is there a girl elf, Mr. Elf?"

"Well, yes there is someone."

She shrugged.

"Well, you're too old for me anyway. What's her name?"

Darrin looked over at David and back at Sarah.

"Well, her name is Naomi. She's kind of like my girlfriend."

"That's a pretty name."

"It's in the Bible, Sarah."

"Oh. Like my name. My name means *princess*. Does Naomi mean anything?"

"Well Sarah, it means *pleasant*. But at one point Naomi wanted to be called *Mara*, or *bitter*, when sad things happened to her."

"That's *terrible*," she exclaimed as she shook her head.

"Well, Sarah, Naomi eventually found out that even when you're sad, you're still totally loved in every way."

She thought for a few seconds.

"Oh. Like Jesus, the Birthday boy, loves me."

"Yes, that's exactly right."

"And like you love me, Santa, even though you're not the real Santa. And you, Mr. Elf, even though you're not a real elf."

David responded.

"That's right, Sarah. That's how much we love you. And I have to say, you're just about the brightest little girl I've ever met."

"That's what my Mom says. She says she doesn't know where I get it from. She'll be here later. She's working."

Darrin spoke up so he wouldn't begin crying.

"So what are you going to call your doll?"

"That's easy. Naomi. Her name is Naomi."

David and Darrin spent another half hour with Sarah. They had a hard time leaving her. But after a group hug and a goodbye, they walked out of the room and into the hallway. Darrin spoke quietly to David.

"I've got to wait a minute before the next one, Mr. Kaplan. It's too intense."

"Please, call me David."

"Okay…David. Well, I certainly do love kids with all my heart…that child, Natan, really all children. But of course I'll never have one myself. Oh well. That's life."

David put his arm on Darrin's shoulder.

"That's not true, Darrin. You do have children. You had *that* child. You had her heart, and her love. And you have my daughter's heart too, and her love."

He came closer, keeping his hand on Darrin's shoulder.

"I want to tell you something, Darrin. I admit to you that the possibility of a marriage between the two of you is very difficult for me. I find it very hard to imagine, and I don't know how I would deal with it. After all, I'm just an old Linotype operator who loves his Jewish people and his God."

David looked directly into Darrin's eyes as his free hand grabbed Darrin's right hand.

"But there is one thing I am thankful for, Darrin, in spite of everything. And that one thing is you…knowing you, seeing the mensch you are. I'm thankful for you, Darrin. I'm very thankful for you."

Darrin smiled and put his left hand on top of David's.

"Well, are you ready for the next child?"

"I'm ready if you are," David responded.

They walked a few feet down the hall and disappeared into room 455.

*T*he *Linotype Operator* is Michael Robert Wolf's second novel. His first novel, *The Upper Zoo,* was released to high acclaim in 2012, and rose to number three across all genres on Amazon.com. He also wrote and directed an independent motion picture, *The Sound of the Spirit,* which was released the same year. The film consistently hovers around eight out of ten stars on the Internet Movie Database (IMDB.com). Wolf is also active in ministry related work, and regularly writes blogs and articles. He lives in Landen, Ohio with his wife, fine artist and author Rachel Rubin Wolf.

CPSIA information can be obtained
at www.ICGtesting.com
Printed in the USA
FFOW02n0501160517
35569FF